W9-AVK-351

Justine Napier

Praise for the "outstanding"* anthology
Living Large
**Featuring stories by Donna Hill, Brenda Jackson,
Francis Ray, and Rochelle Alers**

"Four touching stories about curvaceous African-American women at pivotal points in their lives. . . . Full of humorous encounters, sweetly charming heroines, and the message that living large and loving one's self are good things, this gem of a book is sure to leave readers happy."　　　　　　　　　　　　　　　　*—Booklist*

"A real winner. . . . Readers of all shapes and sizes, especially those tired of waiflike heroines, will find this anthology the perfect diversion."　　*—Library Journal*

"This anthology could easily have doubled in size, as each tale screams out for its own book! . . . Four outstanding stories from four outstanding authors!"
　　　　　　　　　　　　—*Romantic Times (Top Pick)

"All four tales in this delightful collection star strong protagonists who make for an entertaining anthology. Fans of contemporary romances . . . will enjoy each contribution in which the road to love is filled with detours."
　　　　　　　　　　　　　　　　—Under the Covers

"A nice treat. . . . It was a pleasure to read about strong, likable, plus-sized heroines who have much more to focus on than their waist measurements."　*—The Best Reviews*

"A fantastic book about love and the healthier-sized sisters that it ensnares in its trap. I loved each story. . . . [They] have proven that true love is blind to size, but seeks only what's in the hearts of the people in the relationship to be happy."　　　　　　　　*—The Romance Reader's Connection*

"Four wonderful African-American authors bring readers four fabulous stories. . . . Each story is unique. . . . A fun book, great for those quickie reads while soaking in a bubble bath."　　　　　　　*—The Word on Romance*

A Whole Lotta Love

Donna Hill

Brenda Jackson

Monica Jackson

Francis Ray

A SIGNET BOOK

SIGNET
Published by New American Library, a division of
Penguin Group (USA) Inc., 375 Hudson Street,
New York, New York 10014, U.S.A.
Penguin Books Ltd, 80 Strand,
London WC2R 0RL, England
Penguin Books Australia Ltd, 250 Camberwell Road,
Camberwell, Victoria 3124, Australia
Penguin Books Canada Ltd, 10 Alcorn Avenue,
Toronto, Ontario, Canada M4V 3B2
Penguin Books (N.Z.) Ltd, Cnr Rosedale and Airborne Roads,
Albany, Auckland 1310, New Zealand

Penguin Books Ltd, Registered Offices:
80 Strand, London WC2R 0RL, England

First published by Signet, an imprint of New American Library,
a division of Penguin Group (USA) Inc.

First Printing, January 2004

Copyright © New American Library, a division of
Penguin Group (USA) Inc., 2004
"Over the Rainbow" copyright © Donna Hill, 2004
"Tempting Fate" copyright © Brenda Streater Jackson, 2004
"When Wishes Come True" copyright © Monica Jackson, 2004
"The Wright Woman" copyright © Francis Ray, 2004
All rights reserved

 REGISTERED TRADEMARK—MARCA REGISTRADA

Printed in the United States of America

Without limiting the rights under copyright reserved above, no part of this
publication may be reproduced, stored in or introduced into a retrieval system, or transmitted, in any form, or by any means (electronic, mechanical,
photocopying, recording, or otherwise), without the prior written permission
of both the copyright owner and the above publisher of this book.

PUBLISHER'S NOTE
These are works of fiction. Names, characters, places, and incidents either
are the product of the authors' imagination or are used fictitiously, and any
resemblance to actual persons, living or dead, business establishments, events,
or locales is entirely coincidental.

ISBN 0-7394-4157-4

Contents

Over the Rainbow

 Donna Hill

Acknowledgments

I want to thank all the wonderful readers who have been so supportive of my work over the years and challenge me to do better with each story, each novel. To my family who keeps me grounded, and especially to all the voluptuous sisters who inspired this delightful collection! I hope that you will enjoy the love story of Jessica and Russell as much as I enjoyed creating it, and always believe that dreams do come true.

Peace and blessings
Donna Hill

Chapter 1

Jessica Morgan strolled down Amsterdam Avenue en route to work, waving and smiling at familiar faces in the neighborhood: Mr. Wilson, who religiously sat in the same chair on the corner of 135th Street, rain or shine; Ms. Millie, who owned one of the last beauty salons in Harlem that only specialized in press and curl; old Mr. and Mrs. James, who held hands every morning on their way to a one-time storefront that was now the Truly Saved and Delivered Baptist Church for early devotion.

As she headed for her restaurant, wrapped in the light spring breeze, Jessica thought about how blessed she was. She had a viable business, good friends, and a wonderful relationship with her two sisters, Bernadette and Marcelle. Her biggest bone of contention with them was that they constantly nagged her about finding a man, getting a new wardrobe, doing her nails, and getting out from behind the restaurant counter and into the world. She knew their concerns were genuine, but to be honest, it got on her last nerve.

"A new wardrobe is just the thing you need, girl," Bernadette would say. "It will make you feel like a new person."

"But I feel fine just the way I am," Jessica would counter.

"You should get out more. Come with me to the gym," Marcelle, the youngest of the trio, would offer. "The exercise will do you a world of good."

Obviously, both her sisters thought her size eighteen was intolerable, but she was happy with her size, her clothes, and her hair—at least most of the time.

The truth of the matter was, it felt safe where she was. It was clear, at least to her, that men weren't all that interested in big women. The magazines, television, and movies were filled with razor-thin women and the men who loved them.

So she made herself content with working in the restaurant and serving folks who came in for her home-cooked meals. She may not be a cover model, but she was a damned good cook.

Jessica turned the key in the lock and opened the door of Lip Smacking Good. She turned on the radio to her favorite gospel station to keep her company until her staff of three arrived, and began whipping the batter for her mouthwatering pancakes. "It's almost like tasting a piece of heaven," Russell McDaniels, one of her regulars, always said. She chuckled as she plopped the dough for her biscuits on the baking tray and turned on the coffee. That's what Russell said about all her food, even the glasses of iced tea.

Russell had stopped by the restaurant almost every day for about a year and they'd become great friends. Jessica looked forward to the times when he would drop in, especially if it wasn't too crowded so that they could have a chance to talk. Russell was funny, intelligent, sexy as hell, and single. Everything a woman could want in a man. She only wished he felt the same way about her. But no man as fine and as available as Russell McDaniels would be interested in her.

So she resigned herself to her late-night fantasies, where he'd ravish every inch of her body with hungry kisses and expert fingers that explored all her secret places. She knew deep in her soul that if she ever got a hot minute she would whip something on that man he wouldn't soon forget. She had a whole lotta love to give, and all she needed was opportunity. She had plenty of motive.

Some nights she'd wake up, her entire body throbbing with desire; nipples taut, the dampness between her thighs slick and hot. She could almost see Russell looking down into her eyes seconds before telling her how beautiful she was, and how long he'd waited—

"Mornin', Jess."

She jumped at the sound of the voice and almost cussed.

Russell smiled and Jessica's heart did a little two-step in her chest.

"Didn't mean to scare you, doll. The door was open, so I came on in." He straddled a stool at the counter and her blood pressure shot into the danger zone. "You looked like you were in another world. Sure wish I could get into that head of yours."

I wish you could get into something else. She smiled, put down the bowl of batter that had been whipped into an almost unusable watery liquid, and wiped her hands on her apron.

"Hey, Russell. You're early."

"Busy day ahead. I need my jump start."

She reached for a mug and filled it with piping hot coffee.

He nodded his head in thanks, reached for the cup, and brought it to his lips, taking a short sip. He briefly closed his eyes as if in the throes of ecstasy. "Woman, you sure know how to treat a man first thing in the morning."

You ain't seen nothing. "Oh, go 'head," Jessica said with a grin. "So how are you today?" *Other than fine.*

"Better now. Enough about me." He took another sip of coffee. "How are you doing? Last time I was here you were telling me you'd planned to take your two-year-old niece up to the Bronx Zoo. How'd it go?"

Jessica slapped her palm on the countertop and chuckled. "Russell, let's just say that I survived. That child nearly ran me into the ground. There should be some kind of law against that much energy and asking that many questions!"

"They can be a handful, that's for sure."

"But I loved it." She smiled wistfully.

"Ever think of having some of your own?" He took another sip of coffee and watched her over the rim of his cup.

Jessica glanced away and began wiping down the counter. "I guess I'm still an old-fashioned girl at heart. I want the husband *before* the babies." She inhaled deeply and blew out a breath as she reached overhead for a juice glass, placing it on the counter in front of Russell. "At the moment, I have no plans or prospects for either." She poured him a glass of fresh-squeezed orange juice.

Russell watched her graceful movements as she went

about the business of preparing for the morning arrivals: the way her hands moved from one task to the next; the thoughtful expression in her flawlessly beautiful face; how she moved as lithely as a dancer, even for someone of her size. Most men went after those long-legged model types, but he was always one who loved a woman with some meat on her bones, a real woman. If he didn't think he'd be crossing the line of propriety, he'd sure make a play for Jessica. But she never gave him the impression that she was interested in him that way. So he kept his desires to himself. He would pacify himself with being in her presence as much as he could. He truly had no real reason to be up and out of his house at six thirty every morning other than to see Jessica. But as far as she knew, he just had "very busy days."

"Hey, Jess . . ."

"Hmmm?"

"If you had the chance to travel anywhere in the world and do something outrageous where would it be and what would you do?"

Jessica laid out a pound of bacon on the grill, lining the strips up like soldiers, opened the oven and pulled out the first tray of biscuits, then turned to him. She put her hand on her hip and tugged on her bottom lip. Russell loved when she did that.

"Well now . . . let me see." Her eyes began to sparkle with mischief. "Outrageous? Anywhere?"

He nodded.

"I'd be stretched out on the beaches of Tahiti in a two-piece bathing suit and send the pictures home to my sisters." She tossed her head back and laughed. "I can almost see their faces now."

"That's not so crazy. I think you'd look great in a two-piece."

Jessica felt her whole body flood with heat—from embarrassment or pleasure, she couldn't be sure.

The bell over the door chimed as old Mr. Johnson stepped in. The spell was broken.

"You don't know my sisters," Jessica said with a half smile before turning to Mr. Johnson. "Morning, Mr. J. What can I get for you?"

Russell plucked out some money from his pants pocket and placed it on the counter before getting up. "Guess I better get going. You have a good day. You, too, Mr. Johnson."

Jessica watched him leave and kept her eye on him until he was out of sight.

"You ought to tell that man how you feel," old man Johnson murmured into his coffee cup, but loud enough for Jessica to hear.

She cut her eyes in his direction and sucked her teeth long and hard. "I told you about that, Mr. J, coming in here with that mess every morning."

"I call 'em like I see 'em."

"Then you need to have your glasses checked. I told you a million times, I'm not thinking about Russell McDaniels."

"Humph." He rubbed his stubbled chin. "If you say so."

"Mr. J, stop meddling in my business. I'm a big girl. I can take care of myself."

"If you say so," he repeated. "But I know what I know."

Jessica waved her hand in dismissal and turned back to the grill. She sure hoped Russell's vision wasn't as clear as Mr. Johnson's, she worried as she flipped the flapjacks and slid another tray of biscuits into the oven. She would die from embarrassment if she thought for a minute that Russell had any inkling about her true feelings for him.

The bell over the door rang six times in a row as the morning crowd filtered in. Her thoughts about Russell McDaniels would have to take a backseat, at least for the time being.

"Hey, Jess," Melonie greeted. "Sorry I'm late." She hurried behind the counter and put on her apron. "Ran into Russell on my way in," she said, snatching her order pad from the overhead counter. "That is one fine man." She shook her head as she wiggled her way over to the nearest table with its waiting customers.

Jessica pursed her lips in dismay as she looked at the slender waist, perfect round hips and pert breasts of Melonie Davis. She was the kind of woman that men salivated over, dreamed about, and walked proudly down the street with on their arm. The kind of woman that women like her wished they were.

Jessica brushed a hand across her brow. Hey, we are who we are, she consoled herself. She was in good health, financially stable, and for the most part pleased with her life. She was at a point where she thought she was ready for Mr. Right. That would be the icing on the cake. But until then, she could always dream— of Russell.

Chapter 2

Russell arrived at the SoHo studio with just enough time to unpack his gear and get on the set. He was shooting ten models for an upcoming fall fashion catalogue.

As he adjusted his lens and the lighting umbrellas he thought about how incredibly lucky he was. How many men not only had jobs they loved, but had the added perk of being around beautiful women all day long?

"Hey, man, whatsup?" Brandon, his assistant and staging manager, asked as he sauntered in and adjusted the screen backdrop of a mountain setting.

"Hanging in. We have a long day ahead of us. Just looked at the shot sheet. They want the world for this catalogue."

"Yeah, I know. Checked it out over coffee. I have all my props lined up. So long as the ladies don't get temperamental on us we should be outta here by nine tonight."

Russell chuckled. "Man, when was the last time we had this many women, egos, and hormones together for this many hours and "temperamental" didn't join us?"

Brandon laughed. "You got me there, brotha."

"Hey, sugar," Stacy greeted as she strutted onto the set, all 205 pounds of her.

"Humph, humph, humph," Russell murmured in appreciation. "Looking good, Stacy, looking good."

"Thanks." She smiled, flashing perfect teeth. "Where do you want me?"

Brandon chuckled mischievously. "I know you don't want me to answer that."

"Mr. B, you need to stop," Stacy said with a giggle and an extra *umph* in her hips.

Russell watched the two murmur and laugh together as Brandon worked with her to set up the first shot. Russell knew for months that Brandon and Stacy had a thing going on. Every time they were in a room together you could feel their energy, as much as they tried to hide it from the other models and the crew and especially from the boss. Getting involved with the models was a big no-no and reason to get your walking papers. Even though Brandon was treading a real thin line, Russell envied him in a way. He'd found someone who made him happy, had him smiling all the time and looking forward to the next day. Russell, on the other hand, had a thing for a woman who treated him like her brother.

"You all set, Russ?" Brandon called out, stirring him from his musings.

"All set."

Other than several breaks to change lighting, reload film, and lunch, the day progressed without a hitch. The models were cooperative, even though he knew they were exhausted. They gave their best.

As Russell framed each face, each pose, and each outfit to the best shot he could, he imagined Jessica on the other side of his camera lens. Although she hid herself behind a shapeless smock and was unadorned by makeup and flash, she was an incredible-looking woman. Her warm, brandy-toned skin was as smooth and flawless as a newborn's. Her eyes were perfectly set in an oval face, with a slight tilt at the edges that gave them an almost exotic appearance.

That aside, in his mind what made her glow was the warmth that radiated from inside. *What he could get his camera to do with that face* . . .

"All done, man," Brandon called out, coming toward him. "That was the last one." He exhaled. "I don't know about you, but I'm beat."

"I hear ya. But my day isn't over yet. I want to start working on developing the contact sheets. Ms. Lady wants them like yesterday."

"Rumor has it that this is a big push to find *the* face to launch a new publication."

Russell nodded as he disassembled his equipment.

"Do you think Stacy has a chance?"

Russell looked up. "Just as good as anyone else. From what I could see on my end she looked great— always does."

"Hmmm. Well, work your magic, bro. It would really make her happy. And when Stacy is happy"— he grinned—"I'm a happy man, if you get my drift."

"I'll do what I can."

"Cool." He looked around. "You need any help or can I cut out?"

"Naw, I'm just about done. I'll lock up."

"Thanks. Don't want to keep my lady waiting too long."

Russell laughed. "Don't hurt yourself, now."

Brandon was already heading for the door. "Then what would be the point?" he called out over his shoulder. "Later!"

Russell shook his head, put the last of his equipment in his bag and was just about to leave when Eleanor

Turner, the head honcho for the studio and the signature on his checks walked in.

Now, in anyone's estimation Eleanor Turner was a big girl, but she had so much style and grace and impeccable taste in clothing that her size took a backseat to the striking woman she was.

"Good evening, Russell. How did it go today?" She walked gingerly toward him, careful of the wires and cables that ran like snakes across the floor.

"I think it went well. I'll know for sure once I get the film developed."

"That's what I wanted to talk with you about. When you're done would you come up to my office? I know it's late, but this is important."

"Sure. I'm finished here."

"Great."

They walked out together and Russell wondered as they rode the elevator in silence what was so pressing that couldn't wait.

Chapter 3

Jessica checked all the locks and windows, tucked the day's bank deposit deep into her purse, and shut off the lights. Her feet ached and her back was killing her. What she wanted to do was go home, sit in a hot tub, and then zone out on television with a bowl of buttered popcorn. But she'd promised her sisters that she would meet them at their Aunt Marie's house in Brooklyn for their weekly visit. It was a solid one-hour ride on the A train and probably longer getting back. But family duty was family duty. Aunt Marie stepped in and raised her and her sisters since their mother passed when they were in grade school. Their dad, who had since passed as well, had been in no emotional shape to take care of three little girls. So Aunt Marie took in the three heartbroken sisters and raised them like her own. It was their turn to take care of "Auntie Mama" as they lovingly called her, now that she was getting up in age.

Just as the sun was sure to rise, every Wednesday night and Sunday afternoon, Jessica, Bernadette, and Marcelle turned up on Marie's doorstep ready to cook, clean, and have a good time. The only downside was that invariably the trio would launch into a conversation about the state of Jessica's love life, her life in general, and what they knew would fix everything.

Jessica shoved her deposit into the lockbox of the bank on her way to the train station and headed toward Brooklyn.

Always the perfect hostess, Auntie Mama greeted Jessica at the door with one of her famous bear hugs.

"We were waiting for you, chile." She kissed both of Jessica's cheeks.

"Looking good as always, Auntie Mama," Jessica said, noting that she was all dolled up as if she were ready to hit the town.

"This old thing," she said, grinning like a schoolgirl.

"That's what you always say," Jessica teased. Aunt Marie was from the old school, Jessica thought fondly, a time when folks dressed for dinner when they had company, even if that company was family.

Marie put her arm around Jessica's shoulder and

ushered her inside. "Your sisters are up front running their mouths. Go join them, while I finish turning these pots."

"I'll help you."

"No you won't. You've been on your feet all day. I've been on my rusty dusty watching the soaps!" She laughed in that hearty laugh of hers. "So you just go on and relax yourself."

"All right," Jessica agreed with reluctance and handed her a bag. "I brought dessert. Peach cobbler."

Marie rolled her eyes to the heavens. "Can't wait," she said and rushed off to the kitchen.

Jessica heard the animated voices of her sisters and headed in the direction of the living room. She halted briefly at the entrance and gazed upon her sisters who looked as if they'd just stepped off the pages of *Essence* magazine. Self-consciously, she smoothed her rumpled but practical cotton dress, patted her short Afro and hoped that the tug she just felt at her heel wasn't a run ready to race up her leg. Taking a deep breath, she walked in.

"Hey everybody," she singsonged and was greeted with bright smiles and loving hugs.

Being the oldest of the trio, Jessica always felt responsible for her sisters and believed that she must set an example that they would be proud to follow. And with the help of Auntie Mama, Jessica was able to do just that. She finished school with solid grades, stayed out of the usual teenage trouble and went on to study restaurant management. Landing a job at one of the major hotel chains, she'd saved enough money working in the kitchen to help put her sisters through college, and finally after years of working for someone else, she purchased the little storefront on Amsterdam

Avenue and transformed it into Lip Smacking Good eight years earlier. Her sisters married successful businessmen who provided a more-than-comfortable life for their wives.

Now it seemed that the tables were turned. Her two baby sisters believed it was Jessica who needed looking after and they were determined to do just that, even if it drove her crazy in the process.

"How was your day, Jess? You look a little tired," Bernadette commented, stroking Jessica's hand.

"Yeah, Sis," Marcelle agreed. "Everything okay?"

"Everything is fine. Both of you worry too much."

"With good reason," Bernadette said, removing her Donna Karan suit jacket and draping it on the back of the armchair. "You work from sunup to sundown in the hot-ass restaurant, on your feet serving folks all day long."

"Not saying that owning your own restaurant is a bad thing, Sis," Marcelle chimed in. "But you never have the time or energy for yourself. When was the last time you went to a movie or on a real date?"

"Or bought yourself some new clothes or had your hair and nails done?" Bernadette interjected.

Jessica had a good mind to turn around and leave, but the truth was she was too damned tired. Instead she took her favorite seat by the window, plopped down, and pretended to listen to her sisters alternately run their mouths. She'd learned long ago that the more she interrupted, the longer their diatribes would last. By her guesstimation they should run out of steam in about seven to eight minutes. In the meantime, she nodded in all the right places while mentally preparing the lunch menu for the next day and wondering if Russell would prefer grilled salmon or crab cakes. She just loved the look on his face when he sank his pretty white teeth into her crab cakes.

"Why don't you two leave that chile alone?" Aunt Marie said upon entering the room. "Maybe she likes her life just the way it is."

"We're just trying to help," Jessica's sisters chorused in unison.

"If you really wanted to help you'd kick off those fancy shoes and get this dinner together," she scolded good-naturedly.

Duly chastised, Bernadette and Marcelle headed toward the kitchen.

Aunt Marie took a seat next to Jessica and lovingly patted her thigh. "They mean well, sugah," she offered.

"I know. I really don't let it bother me. They think it's their turn to look out for me, that's all."

Aunt Marie studied Jessica for a moment. "You deserve looking-after, Jess. You need someone in your life that's going to put you first for a change. You're a beautiful woman, inside and out. A good man would be lucky to have you."

Jessica lowered her gaze. There was a good man out there, she thought. A man who made her toes curl just by walking in the door. The only problem was she was the last thing on Russell McDaniels's mind.

Chapter 4

"Make yourself comfortable, Russell," Eleanor said, waving her hand toward a side chair.

Russell looked around. It had been a while since he'd visited the inner sanctum. The walls were tastefully done in a soft sandstone color and adorned with the framed faces of the plus-sized models. The furnishings were sparse but essential and in the same color as the walls. Eleanor's office was a reflection of her: basic, up-front, and all business.

Russell rested his right ankle on his left thigh and set his traveling equipment bag on the floor next to him.

"I'll get right to the point, Russell," Eleanor began as she sat down behind her desk. "I know you've all heard the rumors, some true, some not so true about a new magazine."

Russell nodded and wondered where this was leading and what it had to do with him.

Eleanor leaned to the side as she opened her desk drawer, extracting a leather portfolio. "I pay attention to things around here, and I pay attention to my staff." She opened the portfolio and slid her half-frame glasses onto the tip of her nose. She glanced at him above the frames. "And I've been paying attention to you . . . and your work." She turned several pages, then spun the book toward him, pointing her index finger at one of the images. "This is what I'm talking about. Perfection. An eye for perfection. You have it. Of all the photographers who've worked for me, you stand out as one of the best. More of your shots have made the covers than anyone else's."

Russell wasn't quite sure what to say. He was so taken aback by the effusive compliments coming from the head honcho, all he could do was mumble a thank you.

"My point is," Eleanor continued, snapping the portfolio shut and removing her glasses. "I am launching a new magazine. I want the premiere issue on the stands for the fall. My writing team has been working behind the scenes with the articles, interviews, etc. But what we don't have is a cover model."

"There are plenty of great faces on our roster. I'm sure any one of them would be thrilled."

"I'm sure they would. But I want a new face. A face that will not only grace the cover of *Living Large,* but become the model to rep the line of clothing that will accompany the launch of the magazine." Eleanor beamed with delight when she saw the stunned expression on Russell's face. "So folks around here can keep a secret." She laughed. "Yes, this is major. Never been done before and I want it done right. That's why I want you to find me that new face, the new plus-size woman."

"Wow." It was all he could find to say. He slowly shook his head. "I really appreciate the confidence you're putting in me."

"Well deserved. I know this is a job generally reserved for the talent scouts at the agency. But I feel in my gut that you're the one for this job. There is a catch."

He leaned forward.

"I need her in no less than two weeks. And I don't want a size fourteen cutie. As quiet as it's kept, a size fourteen is average for women, although our competitors would have us believe zero to six is normal. What I'm looking for is a real plus-size woman, at least an eighteen, good bones, great smile, and willing to step into the spotlight and become an international star."

"International?"

Eleanor grinned slyly. "Oh, did I forget to mention that the mag will be launched here in the States and in Europe simultaneously?"

Russell tossed his head back and laughed. Only Eleanor Turner could pull off a coup like that. He stood up and grabbed his bag. "Then I guess I'd better find your star—and fast."

Chapter 5

Since Bernadette and Marcelle both had cars out front and husbands at home, shortly after dinner and cleaning up the kitchen they said their good-byes and prepared to head out to Hempstead, Long Island, where they lived.

Jessica saw them to the door, as Auntie Mama had earlier bid her adieus and was getting ready for bed.

"Drive safe," Jessica warned, kissing Bernadette on the cheek. "I know how you like to challenge every yellow light."

"I'll be fine. Besides, I'm sure Larry is waiting up in bed for me. And I don't want to keep him waiting too long." She gave Jessica a wicked wink. "I'm telling you, Sis, nothing beats having a good man to come home to after a hard day."

"You got that right," Marcelle chimed in, pecking Jessica's cheek. "Just the thing you need," she said, tossing her newly installed weave over her shoulder. "I'm sure Kenneth has some friends—"

Jessica threw up her hand like a shield, halting Marcelle's impending monologue in its tracks.

"Enough! Both of you." She looked hard from one startled face to the other. "Don't you think I'm old enough and wise enough to know what I want for myself? I helped raise the two of you and ya'll didn't turn out too bad. Now let me live my life the way I want to and if it's in a housedress and orthopedic shoes serving food to hungry folks or dressed to the nines, sitting in some upscale restaurant being served, then so be it. And whatever man I get is gonna want me for who I am inside, not what addition I put on the outside."

Bernadette subtly closed her jacket over the implants that took her from a 34AA to a C. Meanwhile, Marcelle slid on her shades to mask hazel contacts and tucked her weave beneath a designer cap.

"Now, go home to your husbands."

"Night, Sis," they murmured with lowered eyes and turned to leave.

As Jessica watched them saunter down the driveway to their respective cars, she couldn't help but shake her head and laugh. The two little girls whose bottoms she had to clean were all grown up and telling her how to run her life. What next? She closed the door and went upstairs to sleep in the spare bedroom.

*   *   *

Jessica was up, dressed, reading the newspaper and halfway to work on the A train by five A.M. Baring any delays, she estimated she'd walk through the doors of the restaurant in another ten minutes, ready to start her day.

As the train screeched to a halt at her stop, her thoughts immediately segued to Russell and if she would see him today or not.

She caught sight of her reflection in a murky shop window and her spirits sank down to her thick-soled shoes. Her sisters were right. Who in their correct mind would be interested in a size eighteen who was pushing thirty-eight years old, and in desperate need of a perm, a manicure, and a new wardrobe?

Russell tossed and turned most of the night, his thoughts running in a million directions at once. Eleanor had handed him the assignment of a lifetime. If he found the right face, his future would be secure. She was depending on him and he had no intention of letting her down. There was one catch: Who was the face that would launch *Living Large International* and its clothing line? The candidate would have to be not only beautiful, but photogenic, self-assured, ready for a challenge, and have no real ties to hold her down, like a husband and kids. And someone who was prepared for all the good and bad that stardom could offer.

After packing his equipment bag with everything needed for his afternoon location shoot in Central Park, he headed to the restaurant for what he knew would be a hearty breakfast and good conversation. The truth was, his day was never quite right if it didn't start out with seeing Jessica.

By the time he arrived, most of the tables were full and the counter was lined from end to end with the early risers. Melonie and the newest waitress, Iris, were busy filling orders and catching up on the latest news in the neighborhood.

He eased around two of the round tables and squeezed into an empty chair when he looked up and caught a glimpse of Jessica in the kitchen. The muscles in his belly tightened and he could feel his entire body getting lighter as if a weight had suddenly been lifted.

As if sensing his presence, Jessica turned and warmed him with the most beautiful smile. It was at that instant that he knew he'd found the cover model for *Living Large.* Even hot and sweaty with nothing on more fabulous than a hair net and a pale blue and white uniform, there was no doubt, to his trained eyes, that Jessica Morgan was a stunning woman. With the right makeup, hairstyle, and clothes she'd be even more incredible.

He signaled her over and watched as she gracefully moved in between the tables, pausing briefly to chat with everyone.

She stopped in front of him and placed one hand on her hip. She cocked her head to the side. "You're late today. Didn't get your usual seat." She pulled out her pad, ready to take his order. "So what will it be? I made some fresh blueberry muffins." *Just for you.*

"Sounds good with some coffee."

"Be right back." She turned to leave, when Russell grabbed her wrist. Jessica thought she would faint. She looked quizzically at him from over her shoulder.

"I, uh, need to talk to you. In private."

Jessica's heart started beating so fast she could barely breathe.

"I'll come back at closing . . . around eight?"

She nodded numbly, imagining all kinds of scenarios. "Sure," she finally said as if Russell McDaniels's asking to meet her in private after work was an everyday occurrence.

"If it's not too much trouble, could I get the coffee and muffin to go?"

"Sure," she muttered again and headed to the counter on spaghetti legs.

Moments later she returned with a container of coffee and a toasted blueberry muffin wrapped neatly in foil and tucked in a brown paper bag.

"Here you go," Jessica said, placing the bag in front of him.

Russell looked at her for a long moment as if suddenly seeing her for the first time. Jessica felt her entire body flush with heat.

Russell cleared his throat and stood. "So I'll see you later this evening." He picked up his package, pressed two dollars into her hand, and slung his duffel bag on his shoulders.

"Sure," she uttered inanely for the third time, squeezing the bills between her fingers. She watched him leave and the balance of her day moved at the pace of a slow drip.

Jessica finally ushered out the last customer and saw to it that both Melonie and Iris got safely into cabs and on their way. Herman—her dishwasher, busboy, handyman, and waiter, when she needed him—came from the back.

"Everything's all tidy in the kitchen, Jess." He wiped a hand across his brow. "Busy day."

"Hmmm. Hmmm," Jessica muttered, watching the front door.

"I'll wait until you lock up—"

"No!" she almost shouted. "I mean, it's okay, Herman. You go on home to Ellen. I'll be fine."

Herman, who was at least seventy if he was a day, raised a gray brow of curiosity. "Sure everything's all right? You've been jumpy as a jackrabbit all day."

Jessica tried to avoid his searching gaze by busying herself with register receipts. Herman had been with her almost since the day she opened her doors. He was the first one to respond to her handwritten HELP WANTED sign in the window. She'd been skeptical to hire him, certain that he was entirely too old and frail to withstand the demands of a full-time job. But Herman Winslow had proved her wrong every day since.

"I'm fine, Herman, honestly. Now, go on home before Ellen calls here looking for you."

He gave her another once-over and rubbed his pointy chin as if he was still thinking about it, before snatching his Mets baseball cap from the hook and setting it, just right, on his bald head.

He pointed a warning finger at her. "Don't you stay here too long, now. You need to get yourself a husband to go home to—nice girl like yourself."

"Good night, Herman. If you stand around running your mouth any longer you won't have to go home—it will be tomorrow."

"Humph! Good night, then. See you in the morning."

Jessica blew out a breath of relief when she saw Herman ambling down the street. She locked the door and darted to the bathroom to freshen up and pat down her short afro, which was now a mass of tight ringlets. She sighed at her reflection and for a New York minute wished that she was one of her sisters: slim and trim, decked out in the latest fashion, nails and hair done and her makeup applied to perfection.

The knocking on the glass front door jarred her from her doldrums. Almost with reluctance she headed for the door. But the instant she set eyes on Russell's face, her heart lifted in her chest and a smile like sunshine after a storm streamed across her mouth.

I wonder what he would do if I tossed him down on one of these tables and just used him up until he fainted? "Hey, Russell, come on in."

Chapter 6

Man oh man, that smile. "Sorry I'm late. Traffic was pretty bad tonight." He set his equipment bag down on the floor.

"I put a plate aside for you. I wasn't sure if you'd be hungry or not. But it's here if you want it."

Russell grinned. This was the kind of woman a man ran home to, he thought. Pretty, sexy, smart, funny, and could cook. Lethal combination. "Ms. Lady, you must be reading my mind."

"All right, then. Pick a seat and your food will be coming right up."

Relaxed in front of a plate of smothered pork chops, seasoned string beans, potato salad, and to-die-for cornbread, Russell launched into his spiel.

"I know I probably sounded like some kind of

undercover agent this morning. I didn't mean to be vague." He took a long swallow of his sweet tea.

Jessica folded her hands in her lap and tried to imagine what Russell could want.

"You know I work as a photographer."

She nodded.

"And my boss is in the process of launching a new magazine, *Living Large International*."

Jessica nodded again and wondered what it had to do with her.

"Well, they are looking for a new face. I've been assigned to find it . . . her."

Now she was really confused. Her forehead knitted into intricate lines.

"That face is you, Jessica."

Jessica sat there and stared at him for several seconds waiting for the punch line. It didn't come. She burst out laughing anyway.

"Russell, you need to stop. What did you really want to talk to me about?"

He leaned forward and held her in place with his gaze. "This is for real, Jessica. All I do every day is take pictures of beautiful women. But none of them compares to you. You're a natural beauty, the face that my boss is looking for."

"Russell—"

He held up his hand. "Just listen before you tell me I'm crazy. Let me explain everything that's involved and the opportunities. After that, if your answer is no, I'll leave it at that and never bring it up again. Deal?"

"All right."

Jessica listened to what sounded like something out of the *National Enquirer*—too fantastic to be real. But beneath all her skepticism was the light of possibility that made her heart and mind race with excitement.

After about twenty minutes of outlining all that was entailed, Russell sat back and waited for her reply. So much hinged on her answer—an incredible opportunity for her and he would be able to see her every day for hours instead of a few stolen moments.

Jessica tried to process what Russell was saying: magazine launch, her face on the cover, fashion shoots, world travel, a clothing line! Her head was spinning. Surely he must have her confused with someone else. But if he didn't . . . Lawd have mercy!

"Well, what do you say, Jessica? I know it's a lot to digest."

"You really are serious?"

"Yes, woman! Do you think I've been running my mouth for nearly a half hour for fun?"

"Look, I'm just trying to make sure I have all this straight," she replied, then jumped up and began pacing the floor. Her forehead creased in concentration. Suddenly she whirled toward him. "What about my restaurant?"

He hadn't really thought about that. "Well . . . you have a solid staff. They should be able to handle it."

"Hmmmm. How soon do you need to know?"

"By the end of the week. They want to get started as soon as possible." He paused and leaned forward. "This is a lot to take in all at once. Think about it. But this is a great opportunity, and if I didn't feel in my gut that you were the right person, I would have never asked you. You can do this."

"I really have to think about this, really weigh things in my head."

He nodded in understanding. "When can we talk again?"

She took in a deep breath and let it go. "Stop by in a day or so. I'll have an answer for you then."

"I hope your answer will be yes," he said, placing his napkin on the table and standing.

"We'll see," she said, as she watched him gather his belongings and head for the door.

He turned with his hand on the knob. "Thanks for a great meal—as always."

Jessica smiled with pleasure. "Anytime," she said, a bit more softly than she intended.

"Night, Jess."

"Night." She closed and locked the door behind him, her heart racing at an unnatural pace. She had five days to make up her mind—to decide if she was ready to step out into the world that her sisters insisted she enter or stay safe behind the counter.

It wasn't Wednesday and it wasn't Sunday, but she needed to see her Aunt Marie. Instead of going home, Jessica hopped on the A train and headed for Brooklyn.

"Chile, what are you doing here?" Aunt Marie said upon opening the door and seeing her niece. "Are you okay? Is something wrong with one of those sisters of yours? Well, don't just stand there staring at me, come in," she said all in one breath.

"Everything is fine, Auntie Mama," Jessica assured her. "I just need to talk, that's all."

Aunt Marie flashed her a questioning look as Jessica walked past her and into the house. "You're not sick, are you?" she quizzed as soon as she took a seat on the couch.

"Noooo, I'm not sick, just confused."

Aunt Marie folded her hands on her lap. "Is this about a man?" she asked, hope filling her voice and lighting up her eyes.

"Not exactly." She took a breath and launched into her story.

By the time Jessica finished, Aunt Marie's eyes and mouth looked like perfect circles. Then she suddenly let out a yell of delight and jumped up from her seat.

"Chile, chile," she hollered, waving her hands in the air, almost in praise. "I just knew good things were in store for you. In a magazine! A fashion magazine! Lawd, lawd." She beamed.

Jessica fought back her smile. "It's not that simple, Auntie Mama."

Aunt Marie stopped in her tracks and planted her hands on her hips. She tossed Jessica a hard look. "And why not? The man said he knows what he's talking about. He said you would be a star! For heaven's sake chile, what's the problem?"

"I have a business to run—employees and customers who depend on me. I can't just up and leave."

"Those are grown folks. They can take care of themselves, and if Melonie can't run that place after all this time, then you need to get rid of her. Humph!" She folded her hand beneath her ample bosom, then pointed a warning finger at Jessica. "Now you listen to me. This is your big chance, an opportunity that's not going to come around again. Don't you go getting foolish notions in your head about not doing this."

"But—"

"But nothing. You wanted my advice. Now you

have it. And you better use it, if you know what's good for you."

Jessica sighed. As much as she wanted to pretend to disagree, she was delighted that her aunt was so enthusiastic.

"What do you think Bernadette and Marcelle will say?" Jessica asked.

Aunt Marie rolled her eyes in Jessica's direction. "After they get over being shocked, they'll be happy. It's everything they've wanted for you and then some. Besides, this is about you, chile. This is your time to shine." She grabbed Jessica's hands in hers and squeezed them tightly. "You take it and run with it."

Jessica took her aunt's advice and let it simmer like a pot of good stew. She added the ingredients of change, possibility, and adventure; sprinkled it with the knowledge of leaving her friends and family, the business and customers she loved; and stirred it all with her aunt's wisdom and her own concerns. The pot bubbled and boiled through the night and when the lid was removed the following morning, Jessica peeked inside and there was her answer.

Chapter 7

As usual Jessica was the first one to arrive at Lip Smacking Good. But she wasn't alone for long. By the time she'd gotten out of her street clothes and into uniform, Herman, followed by Melonie and Iris, turned up. Jessica could not have been more surprised if she'd opened the door and found the Easter bunny.

Jessica placed her fist on her ample hip and looked skeptically from one face to the other. She arched her brow.

"Now unless I missed something, it's only six thirty. Melonie, you haven't gotten here before eight in all the time you've worked here. Herman, did your wife throw you out again? And Iris, the only explanation I have for you is that these two talked you into it."

Herman stepped to the front of the firing line.

"I got 'em here."

"Why?" Jessica leaned on her right leg.

"I've been keeping my eye on you, Jess. And you've been working yourself to the bone. I told these gals they need to do their part—starting today. We're all going to get here early and work late."

"Huh?"

"That's right, Jessica," Melonie chimed in. "There's no reason why you should carry the biggest load all by yourself." She glanced at Iris then back at Jessica. "If it hadn't been for you, I'd still be walking the street. You gave me a chance when no one else wanted to."

"Me, too," Iris agreed.

"And no one was willing to hire me," Herman added. " 'Cept you. We just want to return the favor."

Jessica felt the burn in her throat and her eyes filled with tears. "You guys are like family to me."

"And family sticks together," Herman said.

Jessica sniffed back her tears. Iris handed her a paper napkin.

"Thanks," she murmured.

"So we decided that it's time you took a vacation. Let us run things for a while," Herman said.

"But—"

"No buts. You deserve it."

"But—"

"You heard Mel," Iris said. "We have everything under control."

Jessica held up her hands. "If you all would hold on for a hot minute and let me talk, I have some news to tell you."

The trio stopped short and looked duly chastised.

"Thank you." Jessica took a breath. "Funny you all should think it was time for me to take a vacation. I've been offered this chance to model."

Everyone's mouth dropped open on cue then they all started talking at once.

"Say what?"

"Get outta here."

"Stop playing."

Jessica laughed. "I'm serious."

"Tell, tell," Melonie urged, pulling up a seat and sitting down.

Herman and Iris followed suit, giving Jessica their full attention.

"Well, yesterday morning . . ."

"I'll be . . ." Herman muttered when she'd finally finished.

"When do you start?" Iris asked.

"I'm not sure. All he said was soon. I haven't given him my answer yet. I wanted to talk it over with you all first."

"You are going to tell him yes, aren't you?" Melonie asked.

"Of course she is," Herman piped in. "Would you turn down something like that?"

"I've been thinking about it and . . ."

"If you're worried about the restaurant, you know we can take care of it," Melonie said.

"That's right. You don't have to worry about a thing except being famous!" Iris said with a broad smile.

"Well . . . I—"

"Look here," Herman said, cutting her off and pointing a warning finger at her. "You take the job. Enjoy yourself and let us do what you pay us for."

Jessica sighed heavily. "It's a big step . . ."

"Exactly!" they chorused.

"You go tell that young man that you'd be more than happy to take the job." He gave her a wink. "Perfect opportunity, if you know what I mean."

Jessica giggled. "Herman, I told you about that."

"Humph. Life has a way of working things out just the way they need to be worked out," he said. "All right, now. We done told Jess we can take care of this place, so let's get to it." He ambled off to the back.

Melonie got up from her chair and embraced Jessica. "I'm so happy for you, Jess. Make us proud." She stepped aside and followed Herman to the back to get into uniform.

Iris took Jessica's hands. "You've been my role model since the day I walked in here, Jess. This is just one more thing. Congratulations." She kissed her cheek and walked away.

Jessica stood in the center of the restaurant totally humbled by the love and support she'd received from her friends. They, just like her aunt Marie, believed in her, and so did Russell. But did she really have what it took?

The truth was she'd never been any farther than Manhattan and Brooklyn in her entire life. Her wardrobe consisted of shifts and Sunday dresses. Going to the hair salon was a treat and not a matter of course as it was for most women and the last time she'd had her nails and makeup done was for the sisters' marriages.

A part of her was thrilled by the possibility of what Russell offered and terrified that it may all come true. But in the meantime she had a business to run.

Before long the restaurant was overflowing with the usual morning rush. Periodically, Jessica peeked over heads and out the glass front door to see if she could catch a glimpse of Russell. However, by eleven A.M. when the crowd had thinned to a trickle, Russell was nowhere to be seen. From the many visits he'd paid to her establishment she was certain that if he hadn't arrived already, he wasn't coming.

Her spirits descended to her thick-soled shoes. Who was she kidding? He probably had a good night's sleep, thought about how ridiculous his proposition was, and was simply too embarrassed to tell her that it was all one big mistake.

Her eyes began to fill and her throat tightened. What a fool she'd been to fall for the okey doke. She knew she shouldn't have entertained the idea for a minute. To make bad matters worse, she'd told her aunt and her staff. Now they would be witnesses to her shame.

Mindlessly, she wiped down the tables with a damp cloth, reset the condiments, and headed to the back office, where she could be alone for a few minutes. She had to think of some graceful way to explain to everyone that the fantasy life she'd spoken of was going to stay just that—a fantasy.

Chapter 8

Eleanor Turner peered at Russell above her glasses, listening intently to his spiel about a restaurant owner who he believed was destined to be the new face of *Living Large International*.

"She has no experience in front of a camera," she finally said after he'd finished. "From what you tell me, she is reluctant to leave her business, and rightly so. Have you photographed her at all? How do you know she will come across with the look we need?"

For a moment, Russell was taken aback by Eleanor's negative response. He'd been under the impression that she wholeheartedly respected his abilities to spot the face she needed. But from what he was hearing, he'd been wrong.

"So are you telling me you don't want to use her, that you don't trust my instincts?"

Eleanor leaned back in her seat and removed her glasses. She looked him straight in the eyes.

"What I'm saying, Russell, is that she must be one helluva woman." She smiled broadly. "I trust your instincts implicitly. My only concern is her initial reluctance. I don't want to get halfway through this project and she has an attack of nerves."

Russell had worried about the very same thing. What if they were on location somewhere and Jessica got homesick or maybe her staff really wasn't capable of running the restaurant in her absence? His career was on the line with this one, and so was Jessica's. He knew he was going out on a limb. But deep in his gut he truly believed that Jessica could pull this off.

"I have to stand by my decision. I don't think there is anyone else, at least anyone that I've seen, who can give you what you're looking for. Especially given your deadline." He folded his arms and waited for Eleanor's reaction.

She exhaled, twirled her glasses on top of the desk for a moment, then looked across at him. "Okay. This is your shot. Don't disappoint me."

He released a breath of relief. "I won't and neither will she."

"One last question." She curled her mouth to the side. "Has she even said yes?"

"She will."

Eleanor chuckled and shook her head. "Go to work, Russell, and keep me posted. We don't have a lot of time."

He rose and picked up his ever-ready equipment bag. "Thanks."

"Don't thank me yet," she said, picked up her phone, and then stopped. "I hope you have a Plan B."

Russell took the elevator down to the studio and was quickly met by Brandon, who pulled him off to the side.

"What gives, man? You were up in the honcho's office for more than an hour."

Russell wasn't quite sure how to put it or how what he revealed would affect his and Brandon's friendship. He knew how much Brandon wanted Stacy to be the face that launched the new magazine. But the reality was Stacy didn't have what he was looking for.

"Was it about the mag?" Brandon pressed.

"Yes, it was," Russell admitted with reluctance.

"And? Did you pitch Stacy?" His eyes lit up like candles.

"Uh, no."

Brandon frowned. "But . . . I thought . . . Why not, man?"

"Listen, I know this might be hard for you to accept, but I found someone else."

"Someone else? One of the other women?"

"No, someone new to the business."

His voice deepened. "Who?"

"She owns a restaurant in Harlem."

"What! You've got to be kidding me."

"No. I'm not kidding. I think she's perfect."

"And being Mr. Know-It-All, I suppose Ms. Turner went for it, hook, line, and sinker," he said, his voice taking on a nasty edge.

"Hey, man, that's not fair and you know it. Some of the most famous models have been found in the oddest places."

"Yeah, right. Whatever." He started to walk away. Russell grabbed his arm.

"Look, this has nothing to do with friendship and favors, this is business. And you know that. We've been friends a long time. I trust your judgment as much as you trust mine."

Brandon's stiff shoulders slumped. He gazed down at the floor then at Russell. "Yeah, I know. It's just that I was hoping . . . Aw, hell. She'll be upset, but . . ." He grinned. "I'll just have to work real hard to make it up to her."

Russell smiled. "That's more like it. As a matter of

fact, I want you to meet her. And I can guarantee you will feel the same way I do."

They walked together into the studio. "I'd better," he grumbled good-naturedly.

Jessica spent the day in misery. Her aunt, her sisters, and even her sisters' husbands had been calling all day to congratulate her, telling her what a wonderful opportunity it was and how excited they were for her. Not to mention the chiming in by Herman, Iris, and Melonie, who felt it their duty to inform every customer who would listen. She didn't have the heart or the nerve to tell them otherwise. But by the end of the day she was totally exhausted with pretending that everything was great. All she wanted to do was to go home and cry.

After much debate, she was finally able to convince her staff to go home and that she would lock up. Just as she was about to turn out the lights, the loud rapping on the door nearly gave her a coronary.

Peering into the dark she was able to make out three figures. Cautiously she approached, shouting, "We're closed," along the way.

"Jessica, it's me, Russell!" he called out.

She halted in mid step. What was he doing here? And who was that with him? Did he need bodyguards to tell her what she already knew, that it was all one big mistake? With reluctance she turned the lock on the door and pulled it open, but didn't move aside to let them in. Quickly she gave the other two a once-over. They looked harmless enough. She turned her attention to Russell. "We're closed. I was getting ready to go home." She didn't mean to sound so curt but she couldn't help it. She was not in any mood for more disappointments.

"Can we come in? It will only take a minute. This is Eleanor Turner, the owner of the magazine and my boss, and this is Brandon Stokes, my partner."

The Eleanor Turner! Jessica swallowed hard. This was going to be worse than she'd imagined.

"Uh, sure, come in." She stepped aside and let them pass. "Can I get you all anything? As you can see we're done for the day, but I'm sure I could whip up something."

"No, I'm fine," Eleanor said, looking around before taking a seat in the center of the room. "Nice place you have," she commented, setting her purse on the table. "How long have you been in business?"

"Eight years."

"Then you must be pretty established in the neighborhood, regular customers and things like that."

"I would hope so." Where was all of this going? She glanced at Russell, who didn't give anything away in his expression.

"Good staff?" Eleanor continued with her third-degree.

"The best."

"Been with you long?"

"Pretty much since the beginning." She leaned on her right hip. She didn't want to be rude, but this woman was getting on her last nerve with all the questions. Why didn't she just spill it? Russell made a mistake.

"Do you have family . . . I mean a husband and children?"

"No. I don't. Do you?" she tossed back.

Eleanor grinned. "As a matter of fact I don't. I

haven't found a man who could put up with me long enough to marry me and have some kids. My career and making my magazine the best it possibly could be has taken up the better part of my life, I'm afraid to say. But that's a choice we make when we decide to let our careers come first."

Even though Eleanor tried to sound light and airy, Jessica could detect the underlying tone of loneliness, and the question of "What if" that was woven in between the words. For all she appeared to have, she was missing a part of life. Jessica understood that drive. She had it too. And many nights she lay alone in bed and wondered if her sacrifices had been too great.

Eleanor turned to Russell. "You were right," she said. "She's perfect." She turned back to Jessica. "I suppose you are wondering what all the questions were about. Part of it was getting to know you and the other was to watch the expressions roll across your face. Russell has done nothing but evoke accolades about you and I wanted to see for myself. He's right. You're just the woman I want on the cover of *Living Large International*."

Jessica nearly choked. "You . . . you do?"

"Absolutely." Eleanor stood and approached Jessica. She angled her head to the right and left, looked Jessica up and down. "Perfect. Your skin is flawless. Your bone structure screams 'Take a picture of me,' and your body epitomizes the whole living-large concept: that you can be a plus-size woman and still be beautiful, wear beautiful clothes, and carry yourself with style and grace."

Jessica looked at Russell, who was grinning as if he'd just won Lotto. She couldn't help but to grin, too.

"The only question I didn't ask, which I definitely

need an answer to, is: Are you willing to do the work to become the new face of *Living Large International*?"

Jessica's heart and mind were racing so fast she could barely breathe or think.

"Say, yes," Brandon urged, speaking up for the first time. "You have no idea what I can do with that smile and some great lighting."

Jessica covered her face with her hands, her new life and her old life flashing before her in rapid-fire succession. She took a leap of faith when she'd decided to open Lip Smacking Good in a less than perfect neighborhood, in a building that had needed major repairs. She'd hired less than top-notch employees by most standards and they had yet to disappoint her. She had the support of her friends and family. And maybe, just maybe she would really be good at this modeling thing.

Slowly she removed her hands and looked at Eleanor, then Russell, then Brandon. "Well . . . if you all really believe I'm the one . . . then . . . I'm in."

"Amen!" Russell said, relief flooding him. It had been risky bringing Eleanor to meet Jessica. She could have very well told them all to get lost, thanks but no thanks. But he'd been banking on his Plan B, which was the intuitive sense that Eleanor possessed. He'd gambled that her assessment of Jessica would turn the key, and it had. He'd bet and he'd won.

Jessica laughed and slapped her thigh. "I think this is cause for celebration." She looked from one face to the next. "How about some hot apple pie topped with vanilla ice cream, and my special smooth-as-cream coffee?"

"Now you're talking," Brandon said.

Russell looked at Jessica and smiled. Her eyes danced as she served her late-night guests and he quietly prayed that it would all turn out right. For all their sakes.

Chapter 9

The next few weeks were a blur of events for Jessica. Every morning at eight, she was in the studio being fitted, measured, made up, and photographed in a variety of settings, from casual day to nighttime flair.

She met with hair stylists who miraculously were able to give her an assortment of looks with her short do. The fashion consultant built an entire wardrobe specifically for her, including every accessory imaginable: earrings, bracelets, chokers, scarves, hats, and more shoes than she would ever wear in a lifetime. Anything she could possibly want was at her disposal, from bottled water to daily body massages, which she had to admit, she loved.

But the best part was seeing Russell for hours on end, watching him work. Seeing him in his element made him even more desirable. And just as hard as she worked in front of the camera, she worked to keep her feelings for Russell McDaniels in check, a situation that was getting more difficult by the day.

The entire experience was totally sensual in nature as he coaxed her with words of praise, cooed to her from behind the lens to get her in the mood, get the expression he was looking for. He was good at what he did and Jessica couldn't help but imagine what he would be like behind closed doors. Sometimes she would be so absorbed in pleasing him that she completely blocked out the fact that they were surrounded by lights, stagehands, and onlookers. When Russell eased up to her when she didn't think she had anything left to give, he would stroke her arm, tease her with a joke and make her smile, tell her how beautiful she was and that he knew she could give him just a little bit more. Oh, if only he knew, she'd muse. So she would dig deep inside herself and give Russell exactly what he wanted and the smile on his face was worth all the hours behind the hot lights.

Each day like clockwork, Eleanor would come down to the studio after the lunch break to check on everyone's progress and ensure that her "new star" was happy. Once per week Jessica met with an image consultant who coached her in how to walk, talk, hold her head, and carry on interviews. She had to read reams of material on the business, its concept and mission, as well as bone up on all the cities and countries she was scheduled to visit in the coming months. "If there is one thing I can't tolerate in this business," Eleanor said on numerous occasions, "is a model who doesn't know any more than her name."

At the end of the day, Jessica was more exhausted from the whole modeling thing than any day she'd spent in the restaurant. But it was an exhilarating kind of exhaustion, one that she shared with her staff and family. Every day, without fail, no matter how tired she was, she would stop by the restaurant to "check on things," but also to share her day. And when she went home she'd spend the next couple of hours on the phone with her aunt and sisters, bringing them up to date.

"So what's next?" Bernadette asked after Jessica's replay of her second week under the bright lights.

"When are we going to see the magazine?" Marcelle chimed in on the three-way phone call.

Jessica leaned back on her couch and kicked off her shoes. "Well, all I've been doing so far is learning the ropes, like I told you all before, and dealing with *this* artist and *that* specialist." She chuckled. "The pictures that they've taken so far have only been test shots. They did a contact sheet to get an idea of what works best for me," she said, using the new terms in her vocabulary.

"Like I said, girl, when is the real thing?" Marcelle asked.

"Everything takes time. They want to get it right." She was holding out the best information just to play with them a little bit longer. "It could be a few more weeks . . . or it could be next week."

"Next week!" her sisters squealed in unison.

Jessica laughed out loud. "Yes, ya'll, next Wednesday we do the real thing. I fly out to Paris, France!"

"Get out!" Bernadette screeched.

"Can you bring family? That's all I want to know," Bernadette said. "I have all the outfits and my passport is ready and waiting."

"Sis, you need to stop," Marcelle said. "You're the middle child. The youngest gets special treatment, and that's me."

"Just for the record, folks, neither of you will be going unless it's on your own. This is business."

"No harm in trying," Bernadette said. "And I heard you, Marcelle, with that middle child comment. Don't think I'm going to forget."

"I know you won't," Marcelle tossed back in good humor.

"Speaking of passports, do you even have one, Jess?" Marcelle asked.

"The magazine is getting it for me. It should arrive sometime this week."

"Wow, this is so awesome. I just can't believe it," Bernadette said with a sigh. "You are too lucky."

"But you deserve it, Sis," Marcelle said. "You've worked hard for a lot of years for everyone other than yourself."

"That's what Auntie Mama told me," Jessica said. "So I'm going to try this on and see how it fits."

"Speaking of fits," Marcelle said, "do you get to keep the clothes?"

All three sisters laughed then talked about Jessica's new life well into the night.

The following morning, Jessica arrived on time as usual, showed her pass to security and took the elevator to the second floor, but was surprised to find the studio dark and empty. She checked her watch. It was eight o'clock and she was certain that Russell said to be on the set by eight.

"Hello? Anyone here?" she called out into the shadows. Her voice echoed in the cavernous space and the white back drape cast a ghostly pall around the room.

"Where in the world is everyone?" she muttered. Maybe she should go back down and check with security, she thought, turning to leave.

Upon reaching the ground floor she walked up to the security desk and tapped on the window.

"Yes, may I help you, Ms. Morgan?"

"I went up to the studio and it's empty. Where is everyone?"

The security guard pulled out his clipboard and

scanned the daily schedule. "There's nothing scheduled for the studio today. Everyone is over at Rocke-
feller Center. I would have mentioned it when you
came in but I thought you were just going to pick
up something."

Jessica frowned for a moment and then her heart
started to race as reality began to take shape.

"The whole crew is over there. Mr. McDaniels and
Mr. Stokes came by about six to pick up extra equipment and lighting."

Jessica dug in her purse and pulled out her appointment book. She flipped to the current day, praying
it was a mistake. It wasn't. *Eight A.M. photo shoot
Rock Center.*

She slapped her palm against her forehead. How
could she have been so stupid? They'd all gone directly to the site, as she should have done. She was
so accustomed to routine, it didn't even enter her head
not to come to the studio first. She checked her watch.
It was already eight fifteen. If she caught a cab immediately she might be able to make it in twenty minutes,
if she didn't get stuck in rush hour traffic. She darted
toward the street hailing a cab.

A professional wouldn't have made this kind of mistake. They would have checked their appointment
book. She wasn't a professional, she was a restaurant
owner. Her head had been spinning with so much to
do lately. She hadn't paid attention. Now she'd really
messed up. By the time she arrived she was sure she'd
be fired on the spot. Fired before she ever began. And
then it started to rain.

The cab pulled up across the street from where
NBC's *Today* show was shot every day. Even in the
rain the crowd was gathered outside with umbrellas

and raincoats to catch a glimpse of Katie, Matt, and Al. Of course, she didn't have an umbrella and by the time she reached where the photography team was set up, she was soaked.

She looked around for some quick shelter feeling like a wet rag, and found refuge beneath an awning.

"Jessica! Over here."

Jessica turned toward the familiar sound of Russell's voice. He jogged across the space that had been cordoned off for the shoot, complete with an umbrella.

He smiled broadly. "Good morning. Don't you look like a damsel in distress?" He held the umbrella over her head and guided her toward the set director.

Jessica groaned. "Have they fired me yet?"

Russell frowned. "Fired you? Why in the world would you think that?"

"I'm late. I went to the studio instead of coming here. My hair is a mess. I'm soaking wet. Need I go on?"

He put his arm protectively around her shoulders and wished that they were alone, away from the inquiring minds and cameras, so that he could really hold her the way he'd dreamed about.

"That's why we have hair stylists, makeup artists, and fashion coordinators, all at your disposal, Madame." He made a half bow, caught her in the top of the head with the umbrella spoke, and they both laughed out loud.

"Sorry about that." He bit back his laughter.

"See, that's the kind of day I'm having," Jessica said, giggling and rubbing her head.

"Well, someone other than me will fix you right up."

"Will we still shoot in this weather?"

"That's up to Eleanor. But I'd say go for it. I actually think I can get some great shots out of this. I have some ideas in mind that I've been tossing around with Brandon."

Jessica curled up her lip. "Really?" she asked sarcastically.

"I got *skilz*, girl. Come on, let's get you to makeup and wardrobe and take it from there."

He hustled Jessica into the trailer where, as promised, everyone and everything she could need were waiting for her.

While the stylists and fashion consultant worked on her, a steady rain beat against the tin roof of the trailer. Eleanor peeked in the door.

"How much longer?" she asked, her tone brusque.

"Give us another ten minutes," Carolyn the makeup artist said, adding highlights around Jessica's eyes.

Eleanor gave Jessica a quick once-over. "Everything okay? Ready for this?"

Jessica swallowed. "Yes. I think so."

For the first time Eleanor smiled. "You'll do fine. The weather is horrible, but Russell insists that he can get the shots we need. I trust his judgment. If not, we'll be back tomorrow. Your passport arrived. When we're finished here today, I'd like to meet with you in my office."

"Of course," Jessica murmured.

"Have a good shoot." She shut the door behind her and was gone.

"You're one important woman," Leslie the hair stylist said as she spritzed Jessica's hair with sheen. "I've been working with Eleanor for years and this is the first time I've ever seen her come into the model's trailer and wish her luck."

"Really?"

"Yep," Carolyn agreed. "She's seen but not heard, unless it's to ball someone out."

"This is a big deal, Jessica. You're going to be the envy of every woman from sea to shining sea," Leslie said.

"I sure hope I'm up to it."

"You better be," Giselle, the fashion consultant said, stepping into the trailer with a lightweight copper-toned raincoat in a sweeping A-line fashion that did incredibly wonderful things to Jessica's complexion and hazel eyes. "This will be the perfect silhouette for the pantsuit," Giselle said. "I've had to rethink all of the outfits because of this weather," she complained in a sultry French accent.

"I can't wait to hop on that plane next week," Carolyn said, adding lip liner to Jessica's mouth. "You have the greatest skin," she commented. "A light touch is all you need."

"Thanks."

"Suck in your cheeks for me," Carolyn instructed and brushed blush across Jessica's cheekbones. She turned Jessica's face from left to right. "Perfect. I'm done here."

"Let me help you get dressed," Giselle said. "We are very much behind schedule. And I don't want to be a victim of Eleanor's wicked wrath."

All the women except for Jessica laughed. What she really wanted to do was run home. Everything was happening so fast. She worried constantly if she'd made the right decision and whether she was truly up to the task. Yes, it was terribly exciting and the chance of a lifetime, but what if she really blew it? Today was just a small example of how unprepared she was for this kind of fast-paced life.

There was a knock on the trailer door and Brandon stuck his head in. "We're ready for you, Jessica. Looks like the rain is easing up just a bit and we want to take advantage of it as quickly as possible."

"Okay." Jessica took a deep breath and stood. All of the assistants fluttered around her checking every inch of her body.

"Let's go," Giselle instructed, popping open an umbrella to hold over Jessica's head.

From the instant she set foot on the set it was non-stop activity. Flashbulbs popped continuously as onlookers gawked from the sidelines, and Russell barked out directions like a general ordering his troops. Jessica changed clothes a grand total of fourteen times. The sun came out and disappeared again only to be followed by more rain, then sun. Six hours later she had passed the point of exhaustion and was bordering on collapse when Russell finally shouted that it was a wrap for the day. She silently shouted hallelujah!

Somehow she managed to make it to her trailer and nearly fell out across the couch. No sooner had she sat down than Eleanor walked in.

She stood over Jessica and grinned. "Tough day, huh?"

"That's putting it mildly."

"This is only the beginning. I think we got some good shots."

Jessica groaned.

"I'll wait for you outside. How long do you think you'll be before you're ready to leave?"

"Uh, a few minutes. I need to get out of these clothes."

"Giselle will help you pack up. I'll see you in a few."

Jessica forced a smile. She had no idea what Eleanor wanted; she only hoped it wouldn't take long.

Chapter 10

"I won't take up too much of your time, Jessica, I know you must want to get home," Eleanor said as she moved around her office, then behind her desk. "Please have a seat."

Jessica did as she was instructed, and waited—for what, she wasn't sure. But when it came, she could have been knocked over with a feather.

"In this business, very often the models develop a . . . attachment to the photographer. They listen to all the words of love and praise and translate that into something that it's not."

Jessica's pulse began to beat a little faster.

Eleanor crossed her long legs and sat back in her leather chair. "I may not say much when I'm on the set, but I see everything." She looked at Jessica with a raised brow. "You're new at this, Jessica. I don't want to see you get hurt."

"What exactly are you trying to tell me?"

"Russell is very good at what he does. It's why I chose him for this particular job."

Jessica's stomach rolled.

"In other words, his words are just that: words to get you to do what he wants, *on* the set. If you make

it more than that you'll only be disappointed. He talks
to all the models the same way."

Jessica swallowed hard. "Of course. I don't take all
of that stuff seriously," she forced herself to say.

"Good. Glad to hear it. But I felt . . . woman-to-
woman that I should advise you." She smiled. "Well,
as I said earlier, I know you're tired." She reached
into her desk drawer and pulled out a small booklet
and slid it across the tabletop. "Here's your passport."
She stood, ending the audience.

Jessica reached for the passport. "Thank you," she
murmured.

"My driver is downstairs. He'll take you home."

"I can take a cab. You don't have to—"

"I'm sure you can take a cab, but why should you?"
Eleanor came from behind her desk. She sat on the
edge and folded her arms. "This is a whole new world.
You are going to have access to things that many
women only dream of. Enjoy it." She stood and
turned away. "Unfortunately nothing lasts forever.
Take it while you can." Eleanor faced her floor-to-
ceiling window, keeping her back to Jessica. "Have a
good night, Jessica. And I hope you'll remember what
I said."

Jessica drew herself up to her full height. "Good
night."

For the entire ride home, Jessica kept replaying Eleanor's comments in her head. What troubled her was
not what Eleanor said but what she didn't say. She
may be a bit naive, but she knew when one woman
was telling another to stay away.

She lowered her head, willing her heart not to
break. The deciding factor in taking this job had been

the idea of being closer to Russell, and that maybe he
would actually find his way across the line of friendship. It was true. She did believe that his words of
encouragement, the looks and the gentle touches were
just for her—not part of the daily routine, not what
he said and did to every other woman he worked with.

How could she have been so easily taken in? Did
she need the words of adoration so desperately that
she'd allowed them to cloud her judgment?

"Here we are, ma'am," the driver announced, pulling to a stop in front of her apartment building.

Jessica blinked and looked around, surprised to find
herself at her doorstep. The locks on the car disen-
gaged and the driver came around to open the door
for her.

"Good night, ma'am," he said.

"Good night. And thank you." She started to reach
in her purse to give him a tip.

"No, ma'am, that won't be necessary. Ms. Eleanor
pays me very well." He smiled gently.

Jessica pressed her lips together, nodded her head,
and hurried inside. *What else does she do very well,*
she wondered.

The moment she stepped into her bedroom the tele-
phone rang. She checked the caller ID and noted that
it was her sister Bernadette's number. By rote she
reached for the phone, then stopped. She wasn't up
to talking to Bernadette or anyone else for that matter. She knew her sister would want to hear every
detail of her day and she didn't want to lie. She didn't
want to tell her what a fool she'd been.

She stretched out across the bed until the phone
stopped ringing. Perhaps Eleanor was right—she was
new, she didn't know the ropes. Maybe this really

wasn't for her and what she should do was tell them
that they should find someone else. She turned and
spotted the contract that she kept on her nightstand
to remind her of how lucky she was, and realized she
couldn't back out.

Jessica sat up and reached for the document, looking over the words of agreement. She'd never quit
anything in her life and it was a little late to start now.
More determined than ever, she folded the contract
and set it back next to her alarm clock. She wasn't
going to be run off with some idle innuendo. If Eleanor had a thing for Russell, then so be it. He'd never
given her any indication that he had an interest in her
beyond her cooking and her face. She was the one
that fantasized and allowed herself to believe in something that didn't exist, but no more. She was hired to
do a job and that's what she intended to do.

Pulling herself up from bed she marched off into
the bathroom, took her nightly shower, said her pray-
ers, and turned in for the night. Tomorrow was another day. And as Auntie Mama always reminded her:
face every day and make it your own.

Jessica switched off the nightlight. Tomorrow was
hers for the taking.

When Jessica arrived at the studio the following
morning for yet another fitting, it was with a new attitude. If there was one thing Eleanor said that stuck,
it was that what she was being offered was something
that many women only dreamed of. She was no longer
going to go through her days with stars in her eyes
and quietly believe that she didn't deserve all this attention. She did deserve it, or she wouldn't be there.
It was as simple as that.

When she walked into her dressing room, she didn't walk in as if asking permission, as she had done for all the previous weeks, but as if it was hers and everyone else in it were *her* guests, not the other way around.

"I know we have another long day," Jessica said by way of a greeting. "I hope we can get started soon." She tossed her purse on the couch and turned to face the three musketeers: Giselle, Carolyn, and Leslie. She took off her trench coat and tossed that next to her purse. "I'd like to go over the colors. I wasn't all that crazy about some of the colors that were chosen."

Giselle and Carolyn wide-eyed each other while Leslie wheeled over the clothing rack with the outfits for the shoot.

Carolyn put her hand on her hip. "Everything in the lineup was selected specifically for you. We took into account your coloring, body type, and the types of fabric that—"

"That's all fine and dandy," Jessica said, cutting her off. "I'm sure a lot of thought was put into all of it. However, no one consulted me, asked me what I thought. Who would know me better than I know myself?"

Carolyn rolled her eyes and murmured "another diva" under her breath. "I'll be out front," she announced. "Call me when you're ready for me."

"Me, too," Leslie quickly added and followed Carolyn out the door.

"I want to start with the evening wear, if you don't mind," Jessica said, taking off her clothes until she was in her underwear.

"You seem different today," Giselle said as she measured Jessica for a cocktail gown.

"Different? How do you mean?" She gazed at her reflection in the full-length mirror.

Giselle bent down and pinned the hem of the teal-colored taffeta skirt. "I don't know." She looked up from her lowered position. "Almost as if you've suddenly grown up overnight." She laughed nervously.

"Maybe I have."

When Jessica stepped out onto the studio floor, Russell walked up to her and greeted her with his usual smile.

"How are you this morning, Jess? You look as gorgeous as ever."

She barely looked at him, determined not to be swayed by his sweet talk. "I'm fine, thanks. How long do you think this will take?"

Russell stopped in his tracks as Jessica walked by him and onto the set, not waiting for any response from him. He frowned. What was that about? he wondered as he strode over to the camera.

Brandon adjusted the lighting to mimic twilight set against the backdrop of Manhattan.

"Where do you want me?" Jessica asked.

"Right by the bridge," Russell called out.

Brandon moved one of the lights to reflect off Jessica's face.

"Perfect," Russell said from behind the lens. "Now give me some attitude. This is your night, baby. The town is yours. Let me feel you. Give me that smile that will make my heart melt."

Jessica cut her eyes in his direction for a moment. He wasn't going to work on her heart and head again. Not today. She draped her mink stole over her right shoulder and gazed into the camera.

The flashbulb started flashing and her day began. She went from formal wear to office casual and everything in between. She did a series of group shots with two of the other models. She listened to Russell's words of encouragement but she didn't really hear them. What she heard was Eleanor. "They are only words. The same words he uses on everyone." They mean nothing. They are not for me, she repeated over and over again like a mantra.

Finally the day was over. She was exhausted, physically and spiritually. And then Eleanor walked in.

"Gather round, everyone," Eleanor announced, clapping her hands to gain their attention.

"There has been a major change in schedule. We have pushed up the travel date to the day after tomorrow."

Everyone gasped "What?" in unison.

"I've just come out of an all-day meeting with our sponsors. They want the launch date of the magazine moved up and that means we have to move up all of our plans. I've already made all the necessary changes in the itineraries of everyone going. If this puts a crimp in anyone's plans, change them. You all have tomorrow off, but I expect to see each of you at the airport day after tomorrow." She opened a laminated folder and started handing out the adjusted itinerary to the crew. Then she turned to Jessica. "You'll be leaving with me and Russell in the morning. We need to get there and scout out the locations before the rest of the crew arrives. I'm sure that won't be a problem for either of you. Good night, everyone." With that she turned and left a room full of people with their mouths open.

*　　*　　*

Jessica packed up her belongings and went outside in the hopes of hailing a cab. Tomorrow! She had a million things to do. She wouldn't even have time to see her sisters and Auntie Mama before she left. According to the schedule that Eleanor gave her, the flight was at six A.M. She wasn't packed and didn't have a clue what she should take. She walked to the corner in a daze.

"Jessica! Jessica, wait."

She turned to the sound of her name being called. Her heart took a big jump in her chest.

Russell jogged up to her. "Can I give you a ride home?"

"No thanks. I can take a cab."

"But I thought we could get a chance to talk."

"About what?"

"Are you all right? You didn't seem like yourself today."

"Really? Who did I seem like?" she asked with an edge to her voice.

He frowned. "Just things in general. I miss our talks. Our breakfasts together."

She so desperately wanted to believe him. But of course she no longer could. It was just a job.

"I'm really tired, Russell." She stuck her arm out and a yellow cab screeched to a stop on the corner. She pulled open the door. "I have a lot to do to get ready for tomorrow." She looked at him before slipping inside the cab. "I'm sure you do as well. Good night." She slammed the door shut and the cab sped away.

For several moments, Russell stood there until the cab disappeared from view, and he wondered where the Jessica he'd known had disappeared to as well.

*   *   *

Jessica leaned back in the cab and closed her eyes. Immediately the face of Russell danced behind her lids. She didn't want to talk to him the way she had. It wasn't in her nature to be short and careless of other people's feelings. That's not how she was raised. But she also knew that if she was to keep her heart intact, she was going to have to harden it—harden it against the growing feelings she had for Russell that seemed to bloom in intensity with each passing day that they shared together. She was going to have to tune out his voice, turn off his smile, and just remember it was only a job. But heaven only knew if she had the willpower to pull it off. The next few weeks would be the test, starting with tomorrow.

Chapter 11

Jessica tossed and turned most of the night. Her dreams were filled with images of her and Russell sitting hip-to-hip in dimly lit Parisian cafés, strolling down the streets of London and wandering along the hills and valleys of Italian vineyards. But the images that heated her blood were those of her and Russell on the beaches of the Caribbean at high noon, with his bare chest glistening and muscles rippling against the sun. By night, white sand sifted between their toes as they frolicked in and out of the pale blue water beneath a blanket of brilliant stars. He would lay her down on a bed of palm leaves and slowly remove the sarong of burnt orange and lemon yellow that covered her total nudity beneath. He would stand above her, the beauty of his maleness pronounced by the evident arousal that she was able to create with a single smile, a gentle touch, the music of her laughter.

"You are exquisite, Jessica," he murmured, gently running his hands across her bare flesh until her body trembled with desire. "The most beautiful woman I've ever known. Let me love you. Let me make love to you in every way I know how." He then lowered his body toward hers, his mouth ready to capture her lips.

Jessica leaped to wakefulness at the sound of the alarm wailing against the break of day. She sat straight up in bed, her heart racing as if she'd been chased. Her entire body was damp and the dewy wetness between her thighs caused her to close her eyes, trying to recapture the memory, hang on to the sensations for just a moment longer. But as with all dreams they slowly dissolved until they were no more than a taunting memory.

She covered her face with her hands. Who was she kidding? She was just as crazy about Russell now as she'd ever been, even more so in the weeks that they'd been constant companions. It could only get worse when they would be spending time together in every romantic enclave in the world. She sighed heavily and pushed herself up from the bed. But Eleanor would be along to ensure that it never happened. What twisted her heart most was the notion that if she envisioned all the romantic possibilities, so could Eleanor. And it was made clear from day one, that what Eleanor wanted, Eleanor got. What Eleanor wanted was Russell McDaniels and Jessica didn't stand a chance.

*   *   *

The company car was outside waiting when Jessica came down with her bags. The driver loaded her suitcases and started out for the airport.

"Heading to Europe, I understand," the driver said.

"Yes, for two weeks."

"It's a beautiful place. Full of history. Is this your first time?"

"Yes, it is," she admitted, her pulse picking up its beat as anticipation began to creep through her veins. She leaned forward, bracing her palms on the front seat. "Where did you go when you visited?"

"I stayed in a little village in Paris. It's where I met my wife."

"Oh, how wonderful."

He chuckled. "We were both college students visiting for the summer."

"What did you study?"

"I was an art major. My wife was studying music history." He laughed again. "Trust me, we invented the term 'starving artists.' "

Jessica laughed. "But you had each other. That's what's important."

"I don't know what I would have done without her back then," the old man said wistfully. "It's important to have someone in your life, someone to come home to at the end of the day. Know what I mean?"

Jessica murmured yes.

"Pretty things like you shouldn't be leaving their husbands for too long."

"I, umm, don't have a husband. I'm not married."

He glanced up into the rearview mirror and looked at his passenger. "All things come in their rightful time and place. I bet you find the perfect man before you know it."

"Maybe."

"No maybe about it. Mark my words. I know about these kinds of things."

Jessica laughed. "If you say so." She shook her head in amusement. "You remind me of Herman."

"Who's Herman?" He made the turn onto the Kennedy Expressway.

"My conscience," she said jokingly. "He works for me at my restaurant."

"You own a restaurant," he said in surprise. "Well, I'll be. Good for you. So what are you doing running around the country if you have a business to run?"

"I've been asking myself the same question." She shrugged. "It was a big chance for me, and everyone I know says it's a great opportunity and that I should take it."

"So who's in charge while you are away?"

"Herman. He was one of my biggest supporters. He's always telling me what's best for me. He has the perfect man already picked out."

"Well, if he has any age on him, I'm pretty sure he knows what he's talking about. You should mark his words."

Jessica laughed again. "He says the same thing."

"So who's the lucky fella this Herman has all picked out for you?"

Jessica swallowed and gazed out of the window. "Just a guy that I've known for a long time," she said in a near whisper.

The driver looked at her in the mirror. "Hmmm. Sounds special to me." The corner of his mouth turned up in a half smile. "If he is, don't let him get away from ya. Happiness doesn't always come knocking more than once."

Jessica turned to find him looking at her in the mirror. Her face heated with embarrassment.

He pulled the limo into Kennedy Airport's International departure area, parked, rounded the car and took Jessica's luggage from the trunk.

"You have a safe trip. Make the most of it." He angled his head to the side. "I'd bet my next paycheck that the young man feels the same way about you." He tipped his hat and got back in the car.

"If only," Jessica murmured, watching the limo until it disappeared from sight.

"Can I help you with your bags, Miss?" an airline employee in a red cap asked.

Jessica blinked and focused on the man who looked young enough to be her son.

"Yes, thank you."

He loaded her bags onto a cart and led her through the revolving doors.

The terminal was bustling with people even at that unholy hour of the morning. Jessica went through all the high-tech security measures she'd only read about in the papers and heard about from some of her customers who'd had to nearly undress to get through the metal detectors.

Jessica followed the line that led to the X-ray machine and was advised to put all metal objects into a plastic tray. She stripped herself of her watch, earrings, and the silver locket that her aunt Marie had given her when she opened her restaurant, and stepped through the detector.

Horns, lights, and whistles flashed the moment she

crossed the threshold and two burly security officers were immediately at her side.

"Step this way, please," the bigger of the two instructed. "We need a female officer over here," he called out.

"But I didn't do anything," Jessica wailed.

"Over here, Miss," he said again.

Jessica did as she was told and took off her shoes, spread her arms and her legs as a female officer scanned her entire body with a metal wand, just like on television.

Jessica felt totally violated and completely embarrassed as the other passengers looked at her as if her face had been on a Wanted poster. But she could have died on the spot when she saw Russell standing there with a smirk on his face. The officer ran the wand over her body one more time then told her she could put her shoes back on and pick up her belongings. She gathered up her possessions with a huff just as Russell strode up to her.

"Good morning." He grinned at her.

"I really don't see what's so funny," she snapped and regretted her tone the instant the words were out of her mouth. "Do I look like a criminal to you?"

Russell bit back his laughter. "Don't take it personal," he counseled her as they headed toward their gate. "I've been through worse." For reasons which escaped him, he kissed her cheek, shocking them both.

Jessica's face felt as if it were on fire. Her heart pounded in her chest. She tried to look everywhere but in his eyes.

Russell swallowed hard. "Uh, let me get your bag." He took her carry-on from her hand.

"Thanks, but I can carry it," she said in a weak

voice but made no attempt to take it back. The truth was she was secretly thrilled—thrilled by his impromptu kiss and his show of gallantry. It reminded her of being a starry-eyed teenager and having the star basketball player carry her books home.

"How was your ride in?"

They stepped onto the escalator.

"Fine. Nice driver," she murmured, trying to regain her equilibrium. "I'm still trying to get used to all this. I'm accustomed to jumping in a cab or getting on the train."

"Well, get used to it. This is just the beginning. The weeks in the studio were just practice runs. Everyone is here to make your life as easy as possible."

She thought about Eleanor and frowned.

"Something wrong?"

Jessica glanced at him. "No."

"Can I ask you something?"

"Sure."

"Have I done something to upset you? You seem . . . different . . . distant."

The muscles in her stomach knotted. "W-why would you say that?"

They stepped off the escalator and began darting around would-be passengers as they all headed for their flights.

Russell was thoughtful for a moment. "I can't really put my finger on it—just different—and I was wondering if everything was okay. You haven't changed your mind about doing this have you?"

"Everything is fine . . . really. I suppose I'm just nervous, that's all. And worried that I won't do a good job."

Russell put his hand on her shoulder and a flood of heat ran through her again.

"Listen to me." He stopped walking and turned to her.

Jessica looked into his eyes and swore her heart did that little pitter-patter thing.

"I believe in you. I know it may be tough at first and sometimes I could kick myself for pulling you into this crazy world, but I know you can do this. You should see the shots," he added, his eyes lighting up with excitement. "They're incredible." His voice lowered as he looked into her eyes. "I know a beautiful woman when I see one."

His eyes danced over her face and for one crazy moment Jessica thought he was going to kiss her again . . . for real this time, the kind of kiss she dreamed about.

"There you two are."

They both turned as Eleanor walked toward them.

"I was wondering what was taking you both so long." She inserted herself between them and looked from one to the other. "So how are you feeling this morning, Jessica?"

"Pretty good, thanks."

"I know this is your first trip away from hearth and home, but we'll make sure you're well taken care of. Won't we, Russell?" she asked, stroking his arm and smiling broadly.

"I was just telling Jessica the same thing," Russell said, catching Jessica's eyes.

"Looked like you may have been telling her more than that," she said, a scolding tone to her voice. Her smile slowly faded as she looked at Jessica. "Well," she said on a breath, "now that Jessica is totally reassured everything should go smoothly." She snapped open her purse and pulled out a twenty-dollar bill. "Russell, would you mind getting us some coffee?"

"No problem." He put the bags down on an empty chair. "How do you want yours?" he asked Eleanor.

"Black . . . and sweet," she replied.

Jessica cringed.

Russell eyed her curiously and turned to Jessica. "What can I get for you?"

A skillet, she thought, *so that I can pop this hussy upside her head.* "Some orange juice would be fine for me."

Russell nodded and headed off to the concession stand.

Eleanor immediately turned to Jessica. "Wonderful man," she said.

Jessica didn't reply.

"Don't you think so?" she pressed.

"I'm sure he is, but I . . . don't really think about it," she lied smoothly.

"I don't see how you couldn't," Eleanor continued.

Jessica had about enough. If this was only the beginning of this unspoken battle, she wanted to get the details straight once and for all.

"Ms. Turner, no disrespect, but why don't we just get straight with each other."

Eleanor arched her brow and rested her hand on her right hip. "Straight?"

"Yes. Straight. I was hired to do a job. I'm not sure if I'm the perfect one to do it. But I'm damned sure going to try. And you may be the boss lady of this outfit," she said, her temper rising. "But I know how to run a show too. So if you have something you need to get off your chest then you should do it and stop beating around the bush." Jessica put both her hands on her wide hips and stared Eleanor down, waiting to be fired on the spot.

Slowly a smile crept across Eleanor's ruby polished lips, then she tossed her head back and laughed. "That's more like it," she said, pulling herself together.

Jessica frowned. "More like what?"

"More like the attitude you are going to need to survive in this business. You can't get through it with apology and uncertainty written all over your face and in your body language. We're going to make you the next diva for plus-sized women. I want to see it in your eyes, your smile, the way you strut into a room."

"Is that what this is all about?"

"Part of it." She folded her arms. "I want the best. I want this new magazine to blow folks away. I don't take losing lightly and I don't intend to." She looked at Jessica hard.

Jessica raised her chin. "What's the other part?"

"I want Russell McDaniels," she said matter-of-factly. "I have for a long time."

Jessica was taken aback by the bluntness of her admission. "I don't see what that has to do with me."

"I don't like interference, Jessica. But I love a challenge. May the best woman win."

"Here you go, ladies," Russell said, breaking up the stand-off.

Jessica's hands were shaking so badly she could barely hold the bottle of orange juice. This heifer had just thrown down the gauntlet, Jessica thought, fuming.

Eleanor smiled up at Russell. "Thanks so much."

"Now boarding flight 7682 to Paris," the attendant announced over the PA system.

Jessica watched as Eleanor took Russell's arm and began talking to him in whispered tones as they followed the line forming at the departure gate.

The corner of Jessica's mouth curved. It was on, now.

Chapter 12

Paris was more incredible than any magazine picture Jessica had ever seen. The historic sites, the cafés, the stylish men and women who frequented the restaurants and hotel lobbies were all real and now she was part of it. Excitement and awe filled her as she stared out the window of the cab, with Russell and Eleanor pointing out locations for the shoot once the crew arrived. Jessica worked hard at keeping her mouth from hanging open as they passed the Eiffel Tower, rode along the Champs Elysées. The day was a whirlwind of sights, sounds, and the mouthwatering scents of fresh-baked breads that wafted in the air like perfume.

That night they dined at Le Café Marly, one of Paris's most fashionable and most expensive French restaurants, Eleanor was quick to mention. And of course she spoke fluent French and seemed to take great pleasure in translating for Russell in intimate whispers while Jessica felt like a third thumb. It was Russell who finally took matters into his own hands and discussed the menu *in fluent English* with Jessica. She could have hugged him.

*   *   *

Eleanor was also quick to point out that they were staying at a true four-star hotel, the Chateau Frontenac.

"Only the best for the best," Eleanor said as the bellhop took their bags and escorted them to the elevator and on to their respective rooms.

The bellhop stopped in the middle of the corridor and slid Jessica's card key through the slot. He stepped inside, turned on the lights and put her bags in the room while Jessica stood in the doorway.

"Our rooms are at the other end of the hall, Russell," Eleanor said, emphasizing the word "our." "I arranged adjoining suites. I decided it would make it much easier when we need to meet." She turned to Jessica and gave her a smug smile. "Get some rest, Jessica. Tomorrow is going to be hectic when the crew arrives."

It took all of Jessica's home training not call Eleanor out of her name. But she knew better. Instead she tugged in a breath and put on her best "I'm only tolerating you for one more minute," smile. "Good night to you both," she muttered.

"See you in the morning, Jess," Russell said and Jessica would have sworn she heard a note of longing in his voice. His gaze caught hers for a moment before Eleanor's insistent voice snapped like a whip.

"You need your rest, too, Russell," she said, taking his arm. "And we need to talk before we turn in."

Jessica's mouth went dry but she maintained her cool.

The bellhop pushed on down the red carpeted hall and Russell and Eleanor followed. Jessica watched until their door was opened then shut behind them.

Slowly she stepped inside and closed her own door.

The opulent décor of her room went unnoticed as she plopped down on the bed. A blind man could see what Eleanor was doing and Russell seemed oblivious to her out-and-out taunting of Jessica.

Well, as of right that minute, the gloves were off. Had it been back in the day, she would have slapped some Vaseline on her face, took off her earrings, tied her hair back in a rubber band, and told Ms. Thang to meet her outside. Unfortunately she was a grown woman now and had to act as if she had some sense.

She puffed out a breath and took a look around for the first time. Nice, very nice, she thought, taking in the ornate molding, floor-to-ceiling bay window, the terrace that looked out over the city, her queen-sized bed, and a black marble bathroom that she could easily spend the rest of her life in.

"Well, Ms. Thang does have taste," she murmured, pulling open the closets and peeking in the drawers.

She sat on the side of the bed, pleased. Then she spotted the hotel directory on the nightstand and decided to do something she'd never done in her life: order room service. While she waited for her food to arrive, she ran a bath in the oversized tub and couldn't wait to wrap her body in the white, fluffy terry-cloth robe.

What she needed to do was go to bed and get some rest. But she was too wired. Perhaps the wine she'd ordered and the warm bath would do the trick, she thought, as she stripped and sank into the bubbles up to her neck. Before she knew what happened Russell was standing in the doorway of the bathroom. She gasped and tried to cover her nakedness with an infusion of bubbles.

"I want to see you, Jess," he said in a voice so deep it heated the room.

Her heart thudded in her chest as he stepped closer, taking off his clothes piece by piece with each step.

Jessica knew she was going to faint, faint dead away.

"I've been imagining this trip; you, me, together like this," he said as he kneeled by the tub, stuck his finger in the water and swirled it, creating little waves that danced up and down Jessica's breasts.

"But what about Eleanor?" she stammered as his hand sank beneath the waves and found the true center of gravity. Jessica's eyes fluttered and she moaned his name as he stroked her, leaning closer to kiss her lips.

Suddenly she was gasping for air and struggling to the surface of the tub like a woman tossed overboard reaching for a life jacket.

Bam! Bam! Bam!

She shook her head. Damn, another dream, she realized, coming to her senses.

Bam! Bam! Bam!

The door! Room service. She pulled her dripping self out of the tub and pulled on the robe that hung from a brass hook on the wall and hurried to answer the front door. Pulling the door open, she gasped out loud to find Russell standing on the other side. Water dripped into her eyes from her hair and she was sure that she had raccoon rings around her eyes. She tugged on the belt on the robe, which somehow seemed to push her breasts upward for closer examination. She didn't know what to do first—wipe the water from her face or cover her cleavage.

Russell was pretty confident that he'd died and saw

a piece of heaven when he set eyes on Jessica, knowing without asking that she had nothing on beneath that robe but what God had blessed her with. The swift and undeniable physical reaction to her made him inwardly groan as a teenage-like erection threatened to wake up the neighborhood. He started counting trucks in his head in the hope of getting himself under control.

"I, uh, really didn't mean to disturb you, Jessica." He handed her a small suitcase. "This was mixed up with my things. Thought you might need whatever was in here before morning," he added. He looked at her a moment and wanted to run not walk down the hall. As he was counting trucks he was praying that she wouldn't look down. He shifted his body just a little to relieve some of the pressure.

Jessica swallowed hard. Could he have actually seen her in any worse condition? Of course he would think that the only time she really looked decent was when someone fixed her up. He just can't wait to get away from me, she lamented, watching him shift back and forth with his eyes on the other end of the hall ready to make a quick getaway.

"Thanks," she murmured. "I appreciate it." She practically snatched the bag and held it to her chest, blinking rapidly between the water that dripped down her forehead, hung on the tip of her nose, then disappeared down the valley of her bosom.

Just then room service rolled up.

"You ordered, Madame?" the waiter asked in heavily accented English.

Russell cleared his throat. "Well, good night. I'll see you in the morning."

"Good night." She watched him hurry down the

corridor and shut his room door tightly behind him. Couldn't wait to get away, she concluded before turning into her room.

The waiter wheeled in the food cart, lifted the top that was covering a perfectly displayed arrangement of croissants and a bottle of wine, and took a bow as if he expected applause.

"Thank you. *Mercy*," she added in perfect Harlemese, and smiled.

The waiter flashed a look of disdain. "I believe you mean, *merci*," he said, the word flowing like music from his lips.

"That's what I said," she replied sweet as sugar.

"*Oui.* Good night, Madame." He draped his white towel over his arm and walked out.

Once he was gone, Jessica bolted the door behind him then took a peek at her order. But even as heavenly as it looked and smelled, she had no appetite for it. She'd totally humiliated herself in front of Russell. There was no telling what was going on in his head. From the strained look on his face and his body language he couldn't wait to make a beeline back to his room—and Eleanor.

Jessica sat down heavily on the bed. What was she going to do? Deep in her heart she knew she wanted Russell, but did she really stand a chance against Eleanor—a woman who had looks, money, *and* power? She pressed her lips together in thought. What she needed was a plan.

Her expression suddenly brightened. Her sisters may have been pains in the behind, but they knew a thing or two about catching a man, and her aunt Marie was no slouch either. She smiled. It was time for a conference call. She dialed the hotel operator.

Chapter 13

When the knock came on her door the following morning, Jessica was more than ready—at least on the outside.

She pulled the door open prepared to face Russell, only to find Eleanor, looking fabulous as always.

"Good morning. I know I should have called first, but I was sure you were up." Eleanor looked Jessica over as she stepped around her and inside the suite. She swung around to face Jessica, who still had her hand on the door. "I'm pretty sure you can take it easy today. Russell and I will scout out some locations this morning. The crew should arrive this afternoon and then we will complete the shoot tomorrow and leave for Barbados the following day. So it would be great if you could hang around to greet them when they get here."

Hmmm, so now I'm the official welcoming committee. "Sure. No problem." She came into the room, but left the door open.

"Thanks." Eleanor looked Jessica over again. "Did you do your own makeup?"

Jessica jutted her chin ready to catch the verbal slap in the face. "Yes, I did. I don't want to have to rely on someone for the basics. I've been paying attention to the products that Carolyn has been using."

"Great job."

Jessica hid her surprise behind a steady expression.

"Why don't you join us in the hotel restaurant before we leave?" She peered over Jessica's shoulder and noticed the food cart. "Unless, of course, you've already eaten."

"No, I haven't, actually." She laughed lightly. "I was trying out my ordering skills last night."

"Well I have an English/French dictionary I'd be happy to loan you." Eleanor's full lips curved into a grin. "I memorized everything important."

Jessica was taken aback once again in a matter of moments. So Eleanor wasn't Ms. Perfect after all.

"Do join us if you like." She started for the door then stopped. "Great outfit, too." With that she sauntered out.

Jessica stood in the center of the room for a moment, uncertain of what had just happened. She wished she could figure Eleanor out. One minute she was sweet as sugar, the next she was ready to meet you outside.

Bottom line, you need to keep one eye on her and one eye on that man, her aunt Marie had advised her during the late night powwow the previous evening. Her sisters had concurred, adding that if necessary, they would hop on a plane and straighten the whole thing out the old-fashioned way. Jessica had to laugh imagining Bernadette's new weave twisted around Eleanor's manicured hands and Marcelle's new boobs bouncing around in the fray. She shook her head. One thing she would agree with: she was going to keep her eye on the prize and when the right moment arrived—BAM! She snatched her purse from the bed and headed out. Plan A was in effect.

The moment Jessica walked into the hotel restaurant, she spotted Russell and Eleanor seated on the far side of the room, which was fine with her. She had no intention of being a third wheel, even if she was invited.

Although Russell was facing her direction he hadn't noticed her yet. Good. When the hostess in the form of a prepubescent teen walked up to her, Jessica asked to be seated at the window. From there she had the perfect vantage point. She could see clearly across the room without appearing to be watching, and the tinted window worked like a polished mirror.

"Would you care to order?" a waitress asked, appearing like an apparition.

"Some coffee and a glass of orange juice, please."

"Oui." The waitress walked off.

Jessica kept her eyes on the window, seeming to be doing no more than watching the passersby outside. But she was actually keeping her eye on Russell and Eleanor.

At every opportunity Eleanor made a point of touching Russell; his hand, his arm. Jessica cringed. And although Russell didn't respond in kind, he made no overt move to stop her.

"A beautiful woman such as you could not possibly be eating alone."

Jessica glanced up and a flesh-and-blood superhero was standing in front of her, tall, handsome, and dressed to impress.

"Actually, I am," she replied, deciding to be bold. Today was a new day.

"Do you mind if I join you?" he asked in halting English. "No meal should be eaten alone." He smiled and the dimple in his left cheek winked at her.

She extended her hand toward the empty seat and he sat down.

"My name is Jon Alexander. Yours?"

"Jessica."

"American," he stated more than asked.

Jessica smiled shyly. "Yes, I am."

"Are you here on business or pleasure?"

"A little of both. This is my first time."

"Oh, I see. Well perhaps you will do me the honor of allowing me to show you around town while you are here."

"That would be nice, but I'll probably be very busy. I'm only here to do a photo shoot. I fly out day after tomorrow."

"Photo shoot?"

"Yes, I'm a model for a fashion magazine."

His cobalt blue eyes widened. "A model? Well, I've never met a real model."

Jessica giggled. "I'm pretty new at it."

"Then you must let me take you to dinner or lunch while you are here so that you can tell me all about this modeling that you do."

"Do you live here?" she asked, darting the invitation.

"Part of the year."

"What about the other part?"

"I travel."

Jessica raised a brow. "That's what you do for a living, travel?"

Jon laughed. "I suppose you could say that."

The waitress returned with Jessica's coffee and orange juice. "Anything for the gentleman?" she asked with a brilliant Colgate smile.

"I will have what my lovely companion is having, *s'il vous plaît*."

"Oui."

"So, my lovely model, are you here in romantic Paris all alone?" he asked once the waitress was gone.

"No. I'm here with the owner of the magazine and . . . the photographer."

"How interesting."

"Yes," she answered vaguely, as she watched Russell and Eleanor in the window.

"If I am not being too forward, may I ask you a question?"

"I can't guarantee that I'll answer but you can ask."

Jon tossed his head back and laughed. "I so admire American women. They always speak their minds."

"What is your question?"

"Who are the man and woman to you?"

Jessica blinked rapidly and felt her face flood with heat. "I beg your pardon."

"I've sat exactly where you are on many occasions to do just what you are doing." He tilted his head to the side. "Am I right?"

Jessica pursed her lips and was prepared to tell him just where he could go, but there was something sincere in his voice and in his eyes that stopped her.

"The woman is who I work for."

"And the man is who you would prefer to be sharing your coffee with."

"You seem to have it all worked out. So why ask me?"

"Simply testing my powers of observation." He was thoughtful for a moment. "May I make a suggestion?"

"I get the feeling that you will no matter what I say." She took a sip of her coffee.

"My companion has decided that they would prefer to be with someone else. So I am at loose ends right now. And you seem to be as well. Perhaps we can help each other."

Jessica frowned as a million news-flash horror stories ran like a bad movie through her mind. But her curiosity got the best of her. "Help each other how?"

Jon smiled mischievously and leaned forward.

Russell fought valiantly to keep his attention focused on what Eleanor was saying, but what he really wanted to find out was who the man was that seemed to be charming Jessica right out of her pantyhose. Inwardly he fumed. She'd been here only overnight. When did she have time to meet anyone? He'd been ready to go to her table and ask her to join them when he saw the man walk up to her and sit down.

She looked more incredible than usual, he mused, dying to hear what was making her laugh and bring a sparkle to her eyes. All night he'd envisioned showing her the sights of Paris, but Eleanor and her demands put a halt to that. She'd mentioned that she'd stopped by Jessica's hotel room and invited her to breakfast. Obviously Jessica had other plans.

"We'd better get a start to our day," Eleanor said, breaking into his thoughts. "I want to have a good list of locations so that we don't waste a lot of time tomorrow. Perhaps we can get some night shots this evening," she suggested.

"Sure," he murmured, not really listening or caring.

Eleanor picked up the check, slid her platinum card into the leather folder, and signaled for their waitress.

Moments later the waitress returned with her card.

"Ready?" Eleanor asked and stood.

"Sure," he mumbled again.

Eleanor turned in the direction of Russell's intent

gaze. "Oh, there's Jessica. Seems that she's found someone to occupy her time." She took her purse from the tabletop and headed toward their table.

"Jessica. Here you are. We were worried about you. Weren't we, Russell?" she asked, slipping her arm through Russell's. "But I see you're just fine." She turned her attention to Jon and flashed him a smile. "Eleanor Turner," she said, extending her hand.

Jon stood, took her hand, and kissed it. "Jon Alexander. Jessica was telling me all about you." He looked at Russell. "And you."

Russell's gaze darted in Jessica's direction and she smiled sweetly. "Really," he grumbled.

"I understand you are here to shoot photos for your magazine. I hope you will allow me to be a quiet observer. I would love to see Jessica in action."

"We'd be delighted," Eleanor chirped. "I'm sure Jessica can give you all the details. Well, we must be going. Nice to meet you, Jon."

He nodded his head as the duo walked off, then he sat back down.

"My dear, you have nothing to worry about. She doesn't have a chance." He raised his glass of orange juice and tapped it against Jessica's.

Chapter 14

Jon did exactly as he promised: stuck to Jessica like glue. When the rest of the crew arrived in the afternoon, he was there right along with Jessica to greet them. When they all went to dinner, he was there at Jessica's side, treating her like royalty. And Russell did everything in his power to keep from snatching Jon's arm from around Jessica's waist. Everyone thought he was so charming and how lucky Jessica was to meet such a wonderful man. Russell thought otherwise.

Thankfully the night was finally over and Russell worked hard to maneuver some time alone with Jessica. After everyone had gone to their respective rooms, Russell slipped out of his and headed down the corridor to Jessica's suite and knocked lightly on the door.

"Yes?" Jessica called out from behind the closed door.

"It's Russell."

Jessica covered her mouth to contain her glee, straightened her shoulders, and walked to the door.

"Is something wrong?" she asked sweetly when she opened the door.

"No. I was just . . ."

"Yes?"

"I was just wondering, if we have some time tomorrow after the shoot, if . . ."

"Yes?"

"If, uh, you'd like to take a tour of the city before we leave." There, he'd finally gotten it out.

"That would be nice. You could join Jon and me."

He gritted his teeth. "Maybe you two should go alone. I don't want to interfere."

"You wouldn't be. I'm sure Jon wouldn't mind and neither would I."

"I'll think about it. Well . . . have a good night, Jessica."

"You too, Russell," she said a bit more wistfully than she intended.

He pressed his lips together, nodded his head, and went back to his room.

Slowly Jessica closed the door. Her heart told her to call him back, ask him in so they could talk like they used to. But her womanly instincts and all the advice she'd received from her aunt, sisters, and Jon told her otherwise. Confused and disheartened, she prepared for bed and the events that faced her in the morning.

The day started off in a whirlwind. At five A.M. Carolyn, Giselle, and Leslie were at Jessica's door ready to get started. By six Jessica was on the set of TV5 French International Television, which had recently become available in the U.S. Her interview was her first appearance on television and she had to admit that she was totally thrilled by the experience. That was followed by a five minute interview on CNN. By ten the entire crew, including its newest member, Jon, were in front of Notre Dame for the first of a dozen shoots for the day. Then it was off to the Louvre. Somehow, Eleanor had obtained permission to shoot inside of the famed museum. After more than two hours they moved on to the Eiffel Tower, broke for lunch, and then they took the final shots for the day in front of Chanel, before Jessica's interview with a local French newspaper.

Although Jessica and Russell worked side by side, the intimacy that they'd shared before this trip was missing and Jessica's heart was breaking. Maybe she'd taken it a bit too far and turned Russell off completely . . . if he'd ever been turned on at all.

Depressed and exhausted she bowed out of dinner with the crew and an evening stroll with Jon deciding instead to hide out in her room and call home. She needed a pick-me-up.

"We saw you on CNN this morning!" Marcelle screeched into the phone the instant they were all connected.

Jessica giggled. "You did? Did I do okay?"

"Girl, you were fabulous and you looked incredible," Marcelle said.

"You know you are living large now, Sis. You go with your CNN self," Bernadette said with a hitch of pride in her voice. "I told everyone who would listen that you were my sister, the soon to be famous supermodel and you were on CNN! Honey, let me tell you the folks at my job were about sick of me today!" She cracked up laughing. "And your darling niece told all the toddlers in day care that her auntie was *infamous*!"

Jessica beamed with delight.

"Well, how did it go with Russell?" Bernadette, Marcelle, and Aunt Marie asked all at once.

"It didn't," Jessica moaned, suddenly crashing back to reality.

"What happened, chile?" Aunt Marie asked.

Jessica replayed the day for her family.

"Girl, you have him just where you want him," Marcelle said at the end of Jessica's monologue.

"That's right," Bernadette agreed.

"But it doesn't feel like it, does it baby?" Aunt Marie asked and Jessica nearly burst into tears.

"No! It doesn't." She sniffed loudly.

"Well, what about that Jon guy?" Bernadette asked.

"I think he's just making matters worse." She

paused. "To be truthful, I think he's taking his role too seriously."

"What do you mean?" Marcelle asked.

"I mean, he acts like he really likes me."

"Maybe he does, silly," Bernadette said.

"Why is that so hard to believe, chile?" Aunt Marie wanted to know.

"It's just that . . . well . . . it was only supposed to be for fun. Keep each other company. And . . . maybe I'm imagining things."

"You remember what I told you, chile. The quickest way to a man's heart is through another man. Mark my words," Aunt Marie pronounced.

"Amen!" her sisters chorused.

"Do the French really wear berets?" Bernadette asked out of the blue and they all broke into laughter.

More than an hour later after a nice hot bath and some light reading Jessica was finally ready to call it a night. She thought about her aunt's words as she slid between the cool cotton sheets. *The quickest way to a man's heart is through another man.* She wasn't too sure anymore how true it was, but if so, what if it worked both ways?

Eleanor had conveniently on purpose booked herself and Russell in first class and the rest of the crew, including Jessica, in coach for the trip to Barbados. Jon had accompanied Jessica to the airport and promised to stay in touch.

"You are on your way, *cherie*," he'd said as they stood in the departure terminal. "Don't forget your roving French companion when you get rich and famous." He kissed her cheeks. "It has truly been my delight to spend these few days with you. Perhaps both of our hearts will be better for it. Yes?"

Jessica smiled and realized that she would actually miss Jon. "I hope so," she said. "And thank you for everything."

"For what?"

"For being a friend."

"I wish I could be more," he admitted and Jessica's heart leaped to her throat.

"Sadly, distance and the great seas separate us. But perhaps we will meet again someday. You may need a friend." He gave her a gentle smile. "Bon voyage."

With that he turned and left.

Now sitting between Carolyn and Giselle, who talked incessantly about clothes, manicures, and makeup, she wished Jon *was* there—at least she wouldn't feel so alone.

Barbados was like heaven on earth, Jessica thought as they drove from the airport to the hotel. Lush green flora dotted the landscape and the clear sky seemed to meet and kiss the crystal blue water. Barbadians of every shade moved in an almost sensuous dance down the narrow streets and the aromas of Caribbean food wafted through the air.

Eleanor had secured the crew a string of bungalows a stone's throw from the water on the edge of town in the province of St. Michael. Jessica had to admit when she stepped into her new temporary digs that even though Eleanor worked her last nerve she knew how to do things in style. She could definitely get used to this.

She unpacked her suitcases, changed into a light

orange and yellow print sundress of gauze with a matching overjacket that brushed her ankles, and decided to take a stroll along the beach. She stood at the water's edge and let the warm water splash against her bare feet. Her life was changing, she thought as she gazed out onto the horizon—for better or for worse she couldn't be sure. Everything was happening so quickly. A part of her missed her life at the restaurant and interacting with her customers and the neighborhood characters. But another part of her wanted to rise to the challenge of doing something she'd never imagined could happen to her.

"It's quite beautiful, isn't it?"

She spun around at the sound of Russell's voice and her heart beat like a tribal drum in her chest.

He held up his camera and took her picture against the backdrop of glistening ocean water and a brilliant orange sun that was setting behind her.

"Yes, it is," she whispered. "I thought everyone would be resting after that long flight."

"I couldn't. Too wound up." He walked up to stand beside her. "What about you?"

She sighed deeply. "Just came out to think." Suddenly she turned to him. "Remember when you asked me if there was one thing I wanted to do and one place I wanted to be what was it?"

He smiled. "Yes."

"Well, I have to admit that dreams do come true. I want to thank you for that."

"You deserve it, Jessica. I meant every word of what I've told you. You're a beautiful . . ." He stepped closer. "A desirable woman."

Jessica swallowed hard as Russell eased closer. Her

eyes fluttered with expectation of the kiss she knew was coming.

"And I . . ."

"Oh, there you two are."

They both turned. Eleanor was making her way toward them, decked out in a white linen pantsuit and strappy white sandals.

"I went to your room, Russell, and couldn't find you." She looked at Jessica. "How is your room?"

"Everything is wonderful," she answered in a shaky voice, her pulse still pounding.

"Good. Well, Russell, if you have a few minutes, I'd like to talk to you about the plans for tomorrow."

"Sure." He turned to Jessica. "We'll talk later," he said, looking into her eyes.

Jessica nodded and watched them walk back toward the bungalows. *Does the woman have psychic powers or what?* Jessica turned back toward the ocean, annoyed but inwardly thrilled. It was there in his eyes, she realized. He did care for her. And she hoped it wasn't the romantic setting, the sun hanging over the ocean, or the intoxicating scent of the sea and sand. During the few encounters she'd had with the other models back in the States she'd heard them talking about how it was cause for dismissal to get involved with the crew and vice versa. Was it policy that kept Russell from making a move? Was that the thing that held him back and the noose that Eleanor had around his neck? Then why ask her to be a part of a world that was set up to keep them separated? She kicked the sand in confusion then looked up to the heavens as if the stars that were beginning to glow against the midnight blue sky would provide her with the answers she longed for.

Turning, she headed back to her bungalow. There had to be a way around this without ruining her career and his. She'd made up her mind. She wanted Russell Mc-Daniels more than she'd ever thought possible. And as determined as she was about everything else in her life, she was just as determined to have him as well.

Chapter 15

The following morning was a full day of activity. It began with a fabulous island breakfast of flying fish and callaloo then it was on to the beach for the first set of shots. Eleanor had also flown in Stacy and Nicole as background models. The perimeter that Brandon and Russell had set up for the shoot was rimmed with curious onlookers who took their own photos, applauded and whistled at the wonderful outfits and actually came up to Jessica after the first break to ask for her autograph, both women and men. The men paid her much more attention than Russell had a stomach for, but what could he say?

Jessica seemed to bloom beneath the umbrella of adoration and the flashing lights. Russell, used to working with beautiful women, was completely mesmerized by her. Each outfit, each setting only brought out more of her radiance. She didn't seem to need his coaching words to come alive in front of his lens.

"It seems that our star has caused quite a stir with the native men," Eleanor said coyly during a break in the action.

Russell looked up from his camera equipment to see Jessica surrounded by an array of island men who seemed bent on gaining her favor. What were they asking her? What was she saying? What made her toss her head back and laugh in that delightful laugh of hers?

He grumbled something deep in his throat and went back to adjusting his equipment.

"Does it bother you?"

His head snapped in Eleanor's direction.

"Does what bother me?"

"The fact that the once very simple restaurant owner will soon be a face that people around the world will recognize. That her goals and dreams will be bigger than the square feet of space on a Harlem street."

He swallowed. "No. Why should it? Everyone is entitled to be happy."

"What about you, Russell? Are you happy?"

"Yeah. Sure I am."

"But you would be happier if Jessica was the Jessica you once knew, wouldn't you?"

"I don't know what you're talking about."

"Of course you do. You're an intelligent man. That's why I hired you for this project. But I didn't expect you to fall for the star. It's unfortunate, especially since any relationship between staff and the models is cause for dismissal and I would hate to see Jessica lose everything she's gained for a fling. Wouldn't you?" With that she turned, clapped her hands, and informed everyone that the break was over.

For the balance of the afternoon, Russell could barely keep his mind on the job. Several shots had to be taken over and everyone was getting hot and tired. All that kept running through his mind was Eleanor's veiled threat: go after Jessica and she would lose her job and he'd lose his. He couldn't do that to Jessica, especially after what she'd told him on the beach about finally living her dream. He wouldn't do that to her no matter how much he wanted her, no matter how much he found himself falling deeper in love with her.

The balance of the week in Barbados was more of the same, long hours inside and outside and more pictures than they would ever use. There were interviews with the local newspapers, a spot on a morning radio show, and one of the cable stations came out to tape the photo shoots and interview the models. The evenings were filled with open pit barbecues on the beach, R&B and jazz playing in the background with a little reggae thrown in. Laughter danced in the air and emotions were high as they celebrated a successful week and the impending launch of the magazine.

Eleanor stood in the middle of the gathering with firelight blazing behind her and held up her glass of wine. "A toast," she said over the chatter and laughing. By degrees the group quieted. "I want to make a toast to each and every one of you for all your hard work, for tossing your personal lives to the side to make this project a success. We could not have done it without each other."

"Hear, hear!" they cheered and clinked glasses.

"In two days we head home and in less than a month all the fruits of your labor will hit the stands." She turned to Jessica and raised her glass in a salute.

"To Jessica, the face that will launch *Living Large International.* And to Russell who can make anyone a star."

Another round of cheers and applause filled the night. "Enjoy the rest of your evening. Tomorrow you all have the day off. See the sights and have a good time."

One by one the group slowly dispersed and the flickering flames died down to sparkling embers.

Jessica paced back and forth in her bedroom, debating about the veracity of the decision she'd come to. She thought of the possibilities, the chance she was taking and the outcome. She felt as if she were standing on top of a cliff, looking down at the rushing waters and praying that she wouldn't hit rock when she dived off. The advice of her aunt and sister taunted her. The words of Mr. J and Herman back in Harlem scolded her, and the subtle warnings of Eleanor dared her.

She looked at the door. It was now or never.

Russell sat staring at the television, not really seeing but needing the inane program to keep him company. What was he willing to risk? If it was only him to consider, he wouldn't give it a second thought. He could easily find work. He had credentials. Sure, Eleanor might make it difficult for him at first, but he'd squirreled enough money away to be able to survive until something else came along. It was Jessica he was concerned about. How could he act on his feelings if it would cost her dream? There was only one option. He shook his head. He should have thought of it earlier. Yes, he knew what he had to do. He grabbed a light jacket from the coat rack and headed for the door, when knocking from the other side slowed his step.

He pulled the door open.

"Hello, Russell. Surprised to see me? You shouldn't be." Eleanor stepped in and shut the door behind her.

"What is it, Eleanor?" he said with an edge to his voice.

She turned toward him and ran a hand down his chest. "Isn't it obvious?" she cooed, stepping closer.

"Yes, it is," he said, taking her hand from his chest and putting it at her side. "You seem real comfortable using your power to get what you want no matter the cost to anyone else. You don't want me, Eleanor. You had no interest in me until you realized I had an interest in Jessica. You made it clear that if we got together everything we worked for would go down the drain. But you know what, Eleanor, that's okay."

She stepped back and frowned. "What are you saying?"

"I'm saying you can't threaten me anymore. I don't have anything to lose. I've done what you hired me for. And I'm finished. It's over." He walked to the door and opened it. "Good night, Eleanor."

She walked to the door and stopped. "I hope you realize what you've done."

"I'm willing to take the chance."

Eleanor stalked out leaving the door hanging open.

Chapter 16

Jessica stepped across the threshold of her bungalow and ran smack into a hard body.

"Russell . . ."

"I had to see you."

"I was coming to see you."

"You were?"

"Yes." She took his hand and pulled him inside shutting the door behind him. She looked up into his eyes. "I don't care what Eleanor says," she murmured.

He cupped her face. "Neither do I. I just quit."

"So . . . what does that mean?" she asked, her heart thudding in her chest.

"It means this . . ." He lowered his head, seemingly in slow motion until his lips met hers, tentative at first and then with the assurance of a man who knew his way around a woman's hot spots.

She sighed against his mouth as he gently opened hers with a flick of his tongue and slid his hands down her back, pulling her close, melding his body with hers.

"Jessica," he groaned, the years, weeks, and months of longing coming to a close. He felt her shudder and he held her tighter before finally releasing her mouth.

His eyes ran over her face, igniting her with the passion she inflamed in him. "I want you, Jess. I've wanted you for so long."

"So have I," she said, breathless and trembling.

"But I never thought you were interested in me . . . this way."

"Oh, baby." His fingers unzipped her dress, pushed it off her shoulders and down her body. He stepped back to look at her from the light of the moon that cast the room in an ethereal glow. "You are a goddess," he said on a strangled breath. "Exquisite in every way." He reached out and tenderly caressed her breasts. "A perfect specimen of woman. Let me love you, Jess. Let me show you what I've been dreaming of."

She took his hand and on legs that seemed almost unable to hold her, she led him to her bedroom.

Item by item they played a game of removing each other's clothing; tit for tat, right down to Jessica's teal thong.

As she lay with him on her bed while he put on a condom, she didn't know which was more deliciously torturous: his tongue exploring every inch of her body, his fingers making a haven in the wetness of her sex, or the anticipation of him filling her and her capturing his loving deep within her.

Russell braced his weight above her on his forearms, and gazed into her eyes. "This is no one night stand, or a wild moment of lust." He spread her thighs with his knee and pressed himself against her opening. "This is about me loving you, Jess." He pushed against her until her body gave way and admitted him.

She gasped and her eyes widened as he pushed deeper, seeming to know that although he may not have been the first, it had been a very long time since the last. He moved slowly until she picked up his beat, rotating her hips in a way that made him holler and beg her to stop before he exploded.

He lifted her hips to meet his building thrusts and lowered his mouth to suckle a taut nipple, praying that it would take his mind off the incredible sensation that her body was giving his. But pleasuring her only seemed to fuel the fire, giving added life to the passion that was on the verge of eruption.

Jessica throbbed with each downward stroke and felt her insides gripping and releasing his length of its own volition. Her body shuddered and bucked against him and all she could think was that she never wanted this to end. Never. She raised her legs higher up his back to allow him deeper entry and he cried out, his fingers leaving their imprint on her shoulders and he pushed into her one final time, throwing them both over the edge.

"Ahhh, Russ . . . ahhh . . . yessss . . ."

He held on and dove in and out of her until he had nothing left to give.

They lay in each other's arms totally satiated and content, talking in whispers and giggles like two teenagers afraid of being caught by their parents.

"I love you, Jessica," Russell said, stroking her cheek. "I have for a very long time."

"And I love you. But what are we going to do about Eleanor, your job, the magazine?"

"If there is one thing I've learned about Eleanor, she won't let herself fall. The magazine is set to launch. Nothing can stop that now. My job with her is over. And since I am no longer in her employ I can fraternize with the models," he said, squeezing her behind.

She lovingly slapped his hand. "She'll probably kick me to the curb too," she said.

"You are a moneymaker for her, doll. And when the magazine launches you will have your pick of jobs. If that's what you want to do."

She turned onto her back and stared up at the ceiling. "I've been thinking about that. I mean I love all that I've been exposed to, the excitement and glamour of it all, but . . . I love what I do, Russell." She turned to face him. "Can you understand that?"

"Of course I can. But what are you really saying?"

"I'm saying that this was nice while it lasted, but my world won't end if I never do this again."

He smiled, relief easing the weight that had rested on his chest. "I prayed that you would say that, that I hadn't ruined it for you."

"Baby, just like you were coming for me, I was coming for you. We both made a decision. For the best." She pressed her lips to his and kissed him slow and gentle.

"Hmmm. Now you know I'm an old-fashioned kind of guy," he said, caressing her inner thigh. "Meaning when I say I love someone, it's not just words. It's not love them and leave them."

"Russell? What *are* you saying?" she asked, her heart suddenly racing.

He leaned over her. "Remember when you said you wanted to send a picture back to your sisters?"

"Yes?"

"Well, I have an idea for a picture that will really blow them away . . ."

The following afternoon, in front of the justice of the peace, standing beneath a palm tree with the sea at their backs, Jessica and Russell took their vows to

be man and wife. While the crew looked on, Brandon
acted as photographer and captured every moment.

"What do you think your family will say when they
see this?" Russell asked that night as he showed her
the pictures of them sealing their vows with a kiss.

Jessica giggled with delight and held her husband close.

Chapter 17

When Jessica returned to New York with a brand-new
husband and a new attitude, Herman, Iris, and Melonie
decided to throw an old-fashioned party to celebrate the
nuptials. All the folks from the neighborhood attended:
old Mr. J, who immediately said, "I told you so," Mr.
and Mrs. James from the Truly Saved and Delivered
Baptist Church; Ms. Millie the hairdresser; and, of
course, all of Jessica's customers were invited. Even
Mr. Wilson took time out from his chair on the corner
of 135th Street to attend. First to arrive were Bernadette and Marcelle, their husbands, and Auntie Mama,
who couldn't stop crying until Jessica threatened to
send her home in a cab.

Food flowed like water and Brandon brought a case
of champagne along with Stacy, who clung to him like
a second skin. But the big surprise of the evening was
the appearance of Eleanor bearing gifts.

She walked up to the happy couple.

"Congratulations to both of you," she said, looking
humble. "I was wrong. I have no right to dictate any-

one's happiness or threaten their livelihood. I guess it took the two of you standing up to me to make me realize that love is not something you can buy, it's something that grows." She handed Jessica a small envelope. "For both of you." She looked at Russell. "How long are you going to be honeymooning? I need my best photographer."

Russell smiled. "Give me about six weeks."

"And you know I can't let my star slip through my fingers. Whenever you're ready, Jessica, come on back. I mean it."

"Thank you, Eleanor." She leaned forward and kissed her cheek and could have sworn she saw tears sparkling in Eleanor's eyes.

"Well, you two, enjoy your evening. And have a happy life."

"Wonders never cease," Jessica murmured as she watched Eleanor walk out.

"You got that right." Russell kissed her forehead. "Well, my lovely bride, let's boogie." He took her hand and they danced the night away.

When *Living Large International* hit the newsstand three weeks later, Jessica Morgan-McDaniels was an instant star. People who were bold enough stopped her on the street, and the shy ones pointed and whispered behind their hands. Eleanor's PR campaign hit every area imaginable from print media, to radio to television. Jessica was being bombarded with calls for interviews and job assignments. Someone even called the restaurant and wanted to do her biography: *From the Kitchen to the Runway*, they wanted to call it. Jessica just laughed and hung up the phone. But then an idea hit her.

"You know my first love has always been the res-

taurant," she said to Russell that night as they lay
nestled in bed.

"Hmmm."

"Well I was thinking if Eleanor can put me on the
map, maybe I can use *me* to put the restaurant on the
map. With your help of course."

Russell sat up. "What do you mean?"

"I mean let's use our connections and take what we
already have and turn it to our advantage."

"What's going on in that head of yours?"

"This is what I was thinking . . ."

Within the week all the players had been assembled.
Jessica and Herman fixed some of her favorite dishes and
set them out picture perfect on the tables, which were all
occupied by the models from *Living Large*, decked to the
nines. Brandon set up the lighting and Russell took the
photographs while his old college buddy Vincent Flem-
ing, the food editor for the *New York Times*, took notes
and interviewed all the patrons. When the story hit the
papers that Lip Smacking Good was the hottest spot in
Harlem, Jessica simply stood back and let the good times
roll as customers from all over and out of the city
flocked to her restaurant. Jessica was so busy that she
hadn't thought twice about going back to modeling, and
the *Times* was so impressed with Russell's photography
that they asked him to come on staff. In six months she
was able to lease the vacant space next door and start
renovating so that she could expand, and Russell
couldn't have been more proud of her.

They lay in each other's arms in the four-story
brownstone that they'd purchased, and relished in
their love and the blessing of finding one another.

"You know, sometimes when you go looking for happiness or that extra something, you really don't have to go searching," Jessica whispered.

"I know. Often what we are looking for is right in our own backyard."

"Exactly. Not over the rainbow." Jessica stroked his bare chest, running her fingers along the elastic band of his pajama pants. "I've been thinking," she cooed in his ear.

"What's that, baby?" he asked, feeling his nature rise.

"Maybe you could get me a job posing for *Maternally Yours* magazine. That is, if you have any connections."

The grin on Russell's face lit up the darkened room as he pulled the lush body of his wife to him. "As long as I'm the only one taking the pictures," he said, and kissed her long and hard.

Tempting Fate

 Brenda Jackson

Tempting Fate is dedicated to Selena Hodge of Selena's Secrets (SelenasSecrets.com), who gave me the inspiration for this story and who owns an Internet business that proves that *sexy* doesn't have a lingerie size.
Thanks for making it sexy.

We toss the coin, but it is the Lord who controls its decision.

—Proverbs 16:33

Chapter 1

There's no place like home.

For at least four weeks anyway, Blake Savoy thought, glancing around the bedroom where he would be staying for a much needed vacation. Although he totally enjoyed the work he did for a living, after consistently traveling around the world for the past two years he was glad to be back in Alexandria, Virginia.

To him this was home.

His parents had moved away some twenty years ago when he'd been twelve, but he had managed to convince them of his need to come back every summer to visit his grandmother and the mass of cousins he had left behind.

Speaking of cousins, his gaze moved to the one who had picked him up from the airport and who was now nervously pacing around the room while he unpacked. He had known Tonya long enough to know when something was on her mind, and whatever it was, he would give her time to work it off.

In the meantime, he would think about the rest and relaxation he planned to get during the next month. Around family he could chill and be himself. His relatives accepted him for who he was. To them he was merely Blake, Cleophus and Christine's boy, another one of Thelma Savoy's grands and cousin to all those zillion other Savoys. He smiled, thinking just how much he appreciated that.

Blake thought about how others viewed him. Some said he was cold, unapproachable, and unsociable. Personally, he didn't consider himself any of those things. He merely lived his life the way he wanted and only associated with those he wanted to be around.

There were those who thought he was born with a camera around his neck or at least with one in his hand. That was the only explanation for his being a master craftsman with the ability to capture wildlife subjects and scenes through a lens the way he did.

His business was photojournalism and he was proud to admit he was very successful at what he did and had numerous awards to prove it. Over the years he had made a name for himself. His work had been featured in numerous wildlife documentaries for National Geographic and several other television shows, and his books on animal photography were bestsellers with millions of copies in print.

But one of the things people could not figure out about him was how with all his notoriety, fortune, and fame, he still maintained a level head and hadn't let his accomplishments swell it.

His smile widened as he closed his luggage. Those who spent their time pondering why success hadn't spoiled him had never had Thelma Savoy for a grandmother. She always had instilled into each one of her children and grandchildren—and was probably preaching the same message to her great-grands—that no

matter how successful, rich, and famous you got in
life, you never forgot your roots. That was her most
important rule, a rule that had stuck with him. No
matter how much money he made, he much preferred
living a simple life. A private yet simple one. He enjoyed having nice things but treated them as a luxury
and not a necessity.

He thought of another one of Gramma Savoy's
rules: A Savoy was always to be there for another
Savoy. Therefore, although he didn't want to ask the
question—not knowing what his cousin Tonya's answer might be, and remembering she had a history of
asking favors that got him in trouble more often than
not—he stowed his garment bag in the closet, turned
around, and asked, "Okay, Tonya, what's going on in
that pretty little head of yours?"

He watched as she stopped pacing and smiled. She
had cut her hair into a short Afro that she had dyed
honey blond, which looked rather good with her
creamy brown skin and the Savoys' trademark hazel
eyes.

"Since you've asked, there's a tiny favor I'd like to
ask of you, Blake."

Blake had expected as much. Of all his girl cousins,
he felt closest to the one standing across the room
staring hopefully at him. Although there was a six year
difference in their ages—she was twenty-six and he
was thirty-two—they had always had a close relationship. He had heard through one of his cousins that
she had started some sort of Internet sales company
last year, but he was unclear as to just what type of
business it was.

"What's the favor, Tonya?" he asked, leaning back
against the wall and crossing his arms over his chest.

She met his gaze. "I know you only came home to relax, and I really hate to impose."

He smiled. "You're not imposing, now what is it?"

"I started this Internet company called Tonya's Temptations."

He lifted a brow. "Tonya's Temptations?"

"Yes, it's a lingerie company that caters to full-figured women."

His forehead furrowed in confusion. His five-three, barely one hundred and twenty pounds, slim and trim cousin was anything but full-figured. "Why?"

She knew just what he was thinking. "Because there's a need. I did a lot of research and sadly discovered that a lot of the well-known lingerie shops only sold merchandise up to a certain size. I thought they were making an unfair statement that full-figured women don't want to be sexy so I decided to change that. I'm proud to say I've only been in business for a year and sales have been tremendous. I'm shipping out orders all over the country. Although the U.S. is my primary market, I'm steadily getting orders from places like Africa, Australia, and Japan. A few months ago I decided to quit my job at the bank, step out on faith, and expand the business. Starting next month I'll be working full time for Tonya's Temptations dot com."

He nodded, proud of her accomplishments and her decision to become self-employed. "So what do you need from me? Another hand at stuffing boxes?" he asked, grinning.

"No, it's something a little more involved than that."

"What?"

"I'm doing a major overhaul to my Web site, since

that's how I get my sales. The new site is supposed to be up and running at the end of the month, but the photographer who was taking the photos for the site was called out of town unexpectedly due to a family emergency before the last model was photographed, and I need those photos in my Webmaster's hands right away. So, I was wondering if I can impose on you to take the remaining photographs for me."

Blake looked at her surprised. "Photographs of a model?"

"Yes, only one model and Justice is a natural and will be easy to work with."

"Justice?" he asked, thinking the name was unusual.

"Yes, Justice Manning. I don't think you've ever met her but I believe you know her brother, Bryan Manning. He's a good friend of Tyler."

He nodded, thinking of his cousin Tyler, who was his age and a veterinarian. He recalled Bryan Manning and had heard from Tyler a few years back that Bryan was working for the FBI. Blake also recalled something else: for as long as he could remember, Tonya had a major crush on Bryan Manning.

Blake sighed deeply. "I usually don't shoot human subjects, Tonya. I mainly stick to wildlife and wilderness scenes, but if you're sure you can't get someone at this late date and—"

"I can't."

"And if you're certain this Justice person won't be difficult to work with—"

"She won't be."

"Then I guess I can do that small favor for you. It shouldn't take any more than a few hours to get some decent photos done."

Tonya's face broke into a huge, relieved smile and

she quickly walked across the room to hug her cousin. "Thanks, Blake, I knew I could count on you. I'll talk to Justice and make all the necessary arrangements, and you can use the basement at my house. The other photographer I hired said the lighting was rather good there."

"All right. I'll check things out tomorrow to make sure."

Tonya's smile widened. "You're the greatest and I owe you one."

"Justice, why are you being difficult?" Tonya asked as she reached for her wineglass.

Justice Manning picked at her salad and mumbled. "I'm not being difficult."

"Aren't you?" Tonya asked, her hazel gaze fixed straight on Justice's face. The two of them were having lunch at a restaurant located on the third floor of a renovated eighteenth century building that housed the temporary staffing agency Justice owned.

Tonya had known Justice since high school and although they had attended different universities, their close friendship had spanned more than ten years. In her opinion Justice was simply beautiful, with her slanted dark eyes, straight nose, soft feminine curvy mouth and flawless sable-colored face. With her fashionably short hairstyle and expertly applied makeup, she could grace the covers of *Essence* with ease.

Seconds passed before Justice placed her fork down and met Tonya's gaze. "You told me a woman would be photographing me."

"And I just explained the last-minute change and the reason for it." A slight frown marred Tonya's smooth forehead. Justice was certainly not acting like herself today. Everyone was entitled to PMS days but for some reason Tonya had a feeling there was more behind Justice's mood.

"Okay, girlfriend, what's the real deal here? And I don't buy the change of photographer from a female to a male has gotten you this agitated. So level with me, Just. What's going on?"

Justice sighed. Tonya knew her too well so there was no need to lie and say there was nothing going on. She reached into her purse and pulled out an envelope and slid it in front of Tonya. "This came in the mail yesterday."

Tonya lifted an arched brow as she picked up the envelope and pulled out the card inside. It was a wedding invitation. After reading it she released a quick hiss and met Justice's gaze. Shocked. "Harold is getting married?"

Justice shrugged. "So it seems."

Tonya glanced back down at the invitation. Harold Roberts was the guy Justice had dated exclusively for two years. Last year he had asked Justice to marry him and she had turned him down, telling him she wasn't ready to make that sort of commitment yet. Upset at being turned down, he had walked out of her life.

Tonya reached out and laid a hand over her friend's. "He asked you to marry him and you turned him down, Just. You knew how much marriage and having a family meant to Harold. He was a good catch. Sooner or later some woman, willing to give him anything and everything he wanted, was bound to reel him in."

Justice sat silently for a moment. Tonya was right. She had wanted a relationship with Harold yet at the

same time had been fearful of the big C—
commitment. The minute he had begun talking marriage, she had begun getting cold feet. "I know and
now I can't help but feel this tremendous sense of
loss."

Denying herself love because of being afraid of taking
a chance had done nothing but cause her plenty of
lonely, sleepless nights. Over the past year she had read
as many self-awareness and love-and-understanding-
yourself books she could get her hands on, but still,
the simple truth was that when it came to men she
had lumped them together, seeing the danger of failure and heartbreak in all of them.

She wished she had someone in her life who wanted
to make her happy and whom she would make happy
in return, but she wasn't sure that was possible. The
main reason she was suffering from commitment pho-
bia was because divorces ran in her family. Her
mother had been married three times and her two
aunts were also on their third husbands. When it came
to marriages, people weren't as strong, dedicated, and
committed. At least it seemed that way in her family.
In her opinion there didn't seem to be such a thing
as "till death do us part."

Tonya handed her the invitation. "Do you plan to
go to the wedding?"

Justice leaned back in her chair and gave Tonya a
forced throaty laugh. "You know I ought to go just
for the hell of it." Then her pretend amusement faded.
"But a part of me thinks I should leave well enough
alone. I didn't want Harold and he found someone
else who did. I should be happy for him and accept
that things wouldn't have worked between us
anyway."

"If you feel that way then why the 'I'm pissed off' attitude?"

Justice grimaced. "Although I believe I did the right thing by not jumping into another relationship when things ended with him, you know as well as I do the biggest challenge for a single woman is meeting a good available man. The only ones out there seem to be emotionally handicapped or just not interested in anything but one night stands."

Tonya took a sip of her wine and smiled. "Hey, we're only twenty-six years old so let's not get depressed or begin feeling hopeless. We have a few years left before the big thirty and I happen to believe in fate. There's someone out there for both of us. At the moment, I happen not to be looking since my heart is still set on getting your brother to notice me one day. As for you, move on; start going out more and try new things. Sitting home every night will not open the door to meeting a potential mate. But my strongest advice for you is to work on overcoming your fear of commitment and stop avoiding relationships, Justice. You should consider putting into place a plan of action that starts with realistic expectations of a relationship. When you do, everything else will fall into place the way you want it to."

Realistic expectations of a relationship . . .

A flood of emotions tore through Justice as she contemplated it.

Since she feared she would never be able to fully commit to any man, she wasn't looking for someone who was husband material. Nor did she want to become involved in an exclusive relationship again where the man assumed marriage would eventually be the outcome.

She wondered if she could somehow become one of those women who could date just for the sheer fun of it? In other words, could she settle for nights of passion rather than for a long-term relationship since in her book no one was ever truly happy together forever?

She sighed deeply. First, she needed to find a man who appealed to her and then take it from there. Instead of sitting back fantasizing about a fun, short-term relationship with a man, one she could accept, it was time she made things happen.

Chapter 2

"Sorry I'm late."

"Don't mention it," Blake said without glancing up from arranging the camera equipment. Although truth be told, he had begun getting a little annoyed that the woman he was supposed to photograph hadn't thought enough to be on time. Already she was causing problems and he distinctively remembered Tonya saying she wouldn't be difficult. The only thing he wanted to do was snap the few pictures and leave. He had made plans to meet with several of his cousins to play basketball later.

"Tonya said that you're here visiting on vacation for the next month and doing this as a favor to her. I think that's really nice of you since the last photographer left her in a bind."

Blake frowned. This was all he needed; a subject

that talked. He hoped it didn't become a constant thing. He was used to focusing his viewfinder on animals and scenes with no noise and chatting. He sighed, thinking he might as well get this show on the road.

He turned around.

Desire. The kind he'd never encountered before immediately hit him in the gut and stoked a fire deep inside of him, evoking a need he had conveniently forgotten about until now. For a moment he gave in to the pure pleasure of staring at the woman who was now too busy checking out the pieces of lingerie Tonya had laid out for her than to notice him staring. He knew it was impolite but his only excuse was that he was human and definitely male. She was reminding him of the latter with full force.

The woman was dressed comfortably in a pair of denim shorts and a T-shirt that boldly advertised Tonya's Temptions. The cotton material of the shirt stretched over a pair of luscious breasts that sat high and looked so large and firm that he had to take a deep breath.

Triggered by a surge of male hormones he hadn't dealt with in over a good year, his body launched into a quick, sudden case of hard-on. He was glad he was standing behind the tripod, but to play it safe he pulled down the hem of his shirt and lowered his camera in front of him, which kept his state of arousal from being so obvious. He took a quick look at her hands. No rings. Then with a disgusted mental jab recalled that with some women, the presence of rings didn't mean a damn thing.

He took another deep breath and tried to bring his body and mind under control and found the task not easy—especially while looking at such a nice pair of hips and thighs, not to mention a real nice-looking rear end.

Voluptuous. Stacked. Curvy.

"Oh, Lawd."

Blake blinked when he realized the exclamation hadn't come from him but from her.

"Is Tonya out of her mind? There's no way I'll be photographed in these things."

It was then that she turned around and met his gaze. Even with a frown marring her forehead and a deep blush darkening her face, he thought she was simply beautiful, then quickly decided there wasn't anything simple about it.

Her features were stunning. She was definitely a head-turner, sexy as all outdoors. Indoors as well. She would be an ideal person to capture on film. His lens would love zeroing in on every aspect about her, from the striking features of her face to the voluptuousness of her body.

It was only at that moment, while his hormones continued racing into overdrive, that he noticed the sudden hush that had taken over the room, and that she was staring at him just as hard and steadily as he was still staring at her.

Oh, Lawd, Justice thought for the second time. Great. On top of everything else, all she needed was a good-looking man to drool over—and one that was a Savoy. But still, she couldn't take her eyes off the broad lines of his shoulders and chest that were clearly defined beneath a gray shirt whose tails hung low outside of his pants.

She swallowed, wanting to say something but at the moment not knowing what to say without making a fool of herself. She moved her gaze from his chest to his velvety nut brown–colored face. His chiseled jaw and the sharp angles of his features had her catching her breath and she was tempted to go fan herself. Then there were those hazel eyes that all Savoys were blessed with. Electric eyes, ones that could give a woman a tantalizing shock upon first glance.

Just like she was getting now.

She felt her knees actually shake and decided not to make a further fool of herself. She'd never been one to lose her cool over a man but she figured there was a first time for everything and the one standing across the room was most deserving.

Justice caught her lower lip between her teeth and took a deep breath. Now she had two reasons to kill Tonya.

"I take it that you're Justice Manning," Blake said, stepping forward, making sure his shirt was hanging low enough to cover his aroused state. He extended his right hand. "I'm Blake Savoy."

"Nice to meet you, Blake," Justice said after clearing her throat and taking the hand he offered, although she wasn't sure that comment was true yet, especially when she felt a slow heat build in her stomach the moment their hands touched. And he looked even taller standing in front of her than he had when he'd stood across the room.

Blake Savoy.

She'd heard a lot about him from Gramma Savoy, Tonya, and his other cousins. It seemed everyone in the Savoy family was proud of him. She knew he was a well-known and successful photographer who traveled the world, but everyone had failed to mention that he was as handsome as he was successful.

It had been over a year since a man had thrown sparks, heat, and strong sexual chemistry her way and her body was responding in an irregular fashion. She'd never thought of herself as the type of woman who could get turned on by just looking at a man, but her body was proving just the opposite. She was beginning to feel a bit crazy.

"Sorry, I got detained on a call," Tonya said, coming down the steps and smiling brightly. "But I see the two of you have gone ahead and introduced yourselves."

Tonya's cheerful voice brought back the real world, and with it, Justice's sanity returned. She heaved a small sigh, feeling totally disgusted with herself. She was simply pathetic, not to mention downright hot and bothered. And it didn't help matters that she hadn't made love to a man in an awfully long time, which had to be the reason all of her senses were heightened to the third degree. She was too fazed to act otherwise but was determined to pretend. And the best way to do so was to focus her concentration on something else. Namely, the lingerie Tonya had laid out for her to be photographed in.

Justice frowned and her attention slid from Blake to Tonya. "Yes, we introduced ourselves but I have a question for you, or rather a statement. I hope you don't expect me to be photographed in those outfits."

Tonya chuckled. "Of course I want you to be photographed in them, Justice. Why are you surprised? You know the type of outfits Tonya's Temptations sells."

"Yes, but I thought those other models would be the ones photographed wearing the skimpier outfits. I thought I would be wearing the full-length bathrobes and things less revealing."

Tonya shook her head. "No, that hadn't been my plan at all. I think those outfits will look good on you. You're the perfect person for them." She glanced at Blake. "Wouldn't you agree?"

Blake preferred not getting involved in Tonya and Justice's disagreement. Besides, Justice Manning sounded annoyed, definitely peeved. He hadn't taken a look at the outfits Justice would be wearing but a part of him was sure, more than fairly certain, that whatever the woman put on her body would look good. Since another one of Thelma Savoy's rules had been not to lie, he couldn't help but say, "Yes, I agree."

It was times like this that Justice wanted to strangle Tonya. Did her friend honestly not have a clue what was going on here at this moment with her? If not, then she was determined to make things clear. She delivered a pointed glance in the direction of the boxes Tonya had placed on the table. "We need to talk about this, Tonya." She turned to Blake. "Please excuse us for a moment."

Quickly walking across the room, Justice grabbed hold of Tonya's hand and pulled her into the room Tonya had converted into an office. Once the door was shut behind them, Justice released Tonya's hand and glared at her. "You better make this fast and quick, Tonya. What the hell is going on?"

Tonya lifted a brow and crossed her arms across her chest. A smile touched her lips. "I'm the one who should be asking you that question since you seemed kind of hot and bothered around Blake when I arrived."

Justice sighed. Tonya *had* picked up on things, and Justice wondered if Blake had picked up on things as well.

Tonya read her question. "No, I doubt Blake picked up on anything. I found out in dealing with your brother that most men are slow when it comes to detecting how a woman feels. I'll bet a hundred dollars Blake doesn't have a clue that you were attracted to him." Even as she said the words Tonya knew they weren't true. She knew her cousin well enough to know that sexual interest had stirred his blood as well. The evidence had been in the hazel eyes that had stared at Justice. "Blake's a nice guy and there's nothing wrong with being attracted to him."

Justice's frown deepened. "But I don't want to be attracted to him or any man. I don't have the time."

Tonya's smile widened. "And maybe your body is telling you in a nonsubtle way that you need to make the time. I think you should make it a point to listen to what it's saying."

Justice rolled her eyes toward the ceiling. "Yeah, and I can just imagine the kind of trouble I'll get into if I were to do that. Tonya, I haven't been intimate with a man in over a year, so how am I supposed to handle Mr. Testosterone who's waiting outside that door?" She refused to acknowledge that just a couple of days ago she had decided to make things happen. In her book making things happen didn't include a man as good-looking as Blake.

"I'm sure you'll manage the same way I've managed whenever I'm around your brother."

"Yeah, but you've never paraded in front of Bryan wearing lingerie; and speaking of lingerie, why do I have to wear something as outlandish as those outfits?"

Tonya shook her head. Although Justice never seemed to notice, whenever the two of them were together, it was usually Justice who got all the male attention. To a brother, there was just something about a woman with ample breasts, big legs, and a lush, curvy behind.

"Because the whole purpose of Tonya's Temptations is to show full-figured women that they have a right to be sexy and feel sexy, too," Tonya said, determined to make her point. "Other lingerie shops focus their attention on slim and petite women. You're a perfect size sixteen and those outfits I've chosen for you will focus on that. I want all full-figured women to picture themselves wearing any of those things for their man. You owe it to them to show that they are totally feminine, sexy, and sensuous."

Justice sighed, knowing there was no way she could get out of posing in those outfits since Tonya's mind was dead set on her doing it and she had promised her that she would. But still, she couldn't help but think of the man standing on the opposite side of the door. "And what about Blake?" she asked. She could just imagine those gorgeous hazel eyes leveled on her even through the lens of a camera, and didn't want to think about that chiseled mouth her gaze had stared at earlier. The man had perfect bone structure and his features would make any woman wet her panties.

Tonya lifted a brow. "What about him?"

"What will he think with me wearing those outfits?"

Tonya's mouth curved into another smile. "I explained the aspects of my Internet business to Blake.

Although he's not used to photographing human subjects, I'm sure he'll adjust. And don't worry about him getting out of line with you because he's a professional. Besides, he wrote off women years ago."

Justice's interest was piqued. "He did? Why?"

"He got married right out of college. When he landed a job that required a lot of traveling, his wife, who didn't like to travel, stayed home to run the gift shop she opened. Blake discovered her real reason for wanting to stay back when he returned to town unexpectedly and caught another man in his bed. He hasn't been serious about another woman since his divorce and that's been over seven years ago."

Justice shook her head sadly, thinking how easily some people refused to accept the vows they made to others. Her father had been that type of man. But then her mother's second husband hadn't been any better.

At least her current stepfather, Donald Spears, was different. Like her mother, he was in law enforcement and he was everything she thought a father, stepfather, and role model should be. She was happy that after the third try her mother seemed to have finally gotten it right.

"So are you going to do it, Justice?"

Tonya's question brought Justice out of her reverie. She met the hopeful gleam in Tonya's gaze and knew how much her Internet business meant to her. And Tonya was right. It was time somebody focused on the needs of the full-figured woman. Most of the women on her mother's side of the family were tall and full-figured, and she'd always thought her mother and aunts were simply beautiful, gorgeous statuesque amazons. They had proven to her over the years that a person's beauty was not measured by the size of one's body but by the love and loyalty one carried within one's heart. A part of her knew that she owed it to all full-figured women to show they had it going on and had something to offer a man just like any thin woman. And more than anything she wanted to show they weren't lacking when it came to the qualities that made a woman sexy and feminine.

"Okay, I'll do it," Justice finally said. When she thought of Blake Savoy she just hoped that she wasn't making a big mistake.

Chapter 3

"We got everything settled and are ready to start things rolling now, Blake."

Blake turned when Tonya and Justice reentered the room. His cousin had a confident smile on her face but Justice still seemed unsure about things. Evidently like him she had decided pretty much to just go with the flow.

He smiled but his amusement faded the moment his and Justice's gazes again met and held. Just thinking of how Justice Manning would look wearing those outfits made the air between them hot.

Not liking where his thoughts were going, he scowled and shifted his gaze to Tonya. He said, probably a bit too briskly, "I'm glad we're finally getting started since we wasted valuable time already. I'll get things set up while Miss Manning changes into her first outfit."

"Justice."

His gaze shifted back to the woman and watched as her dark brow arched expressively. "What?" he asked.

"It would be easier for you to call me Justice instead of Miss Manning, don't you think? Especially since you introduced yourself to me as Blake earlier. Besides, there's no reason for such formality since I feel a part of the Savoy family."

Blake shrugged. If she thought saying that would make him feel better she was dead wrong. Because of her close friendship with Tonya, she might feel like she was a part of his family, but the truth was that she wasn't. His body knew that point and he was having a heck of a time getting it under control.

"And I apologize to have wasted your valuable time, Blake," Justice added.

He frowned at her statement of apology and couldn't help but note the almost-smile that touched her lips. Tonya had said this woman wouldn't be difficult but already she was trouble in more ways than one. However, he would deal with it. He placed an almost-smile on his lips as well and said, "Apology accepted. Now if we can get this show on the road I'd appreciate it."

Ten minutes later Justice stared at herself in the full-length mirror of Tonya's basement bathroom. Although she had supported Tonya in her business venture by making a couple of purchases, her buys had always been what she'd considered practical items such as robes or long gowns. When she thought of sleepwear for herself, her mind reflected on her supply of extra-large T-shirts and not the sexy, risqué outfit she had on. It was a jaguar print chemise of stretch mesh and lace with matching G-string panties. It had a sexy Tarzan "Jane" hemline that hit high on her upper thighs with a crisscross low-cut back. She thought it fitted her body well—too well.

"Girl, you look good in this," Tonya exclaimed walking around her, giving her the once-over and smiling brightly. "This outfit has your name written all over it and is one of the most popular items in my jaguar series of lingerie. You look absolutely stunning."

Justice shook her head, wanting to groan out loud. Stunning? In her opinion the outfit made it hard for her to even recognize herself. Could displaying your stuff in such an outfit have that much effect? Evidently it did. The print of the outfit made the color of her eyes appear a deep coffee brown and a part of her couldn't help but wonder what Blake would think when he saw her.

Good grief, she thought, tugging at the neckline of her outfit. It was no use. The way the lingerie was made seemed to deliberately nest her breasts so the cleavage showed in a wanton fashion; a deliberate open invitation. She met Tonya's gaze. "I don't know about this," she said doubtfully.

Tonya chuckled and shook her head. "Hey, don't worry, like I said you look great and as far as Blake is concerned, he's a professional. But then he wouldn't be a man if he didn't notice you at first so don't sweat things. If I were you I would enjoy the attention. Now get your butt in gear and go on out there. I'll let Blake know you're almost ready."

After Tonya slipped out the door, closing it behind her, Justice buried her face behind her hands, peered through the gap in her fingers to look at herself in the mirror again, then softly said, "Oh, Lawd."

*   *   *

"I'm ready, Blake."

Blake turned and gave Justice's face a quick glance before zeroing in on the rest of her. Pulse leaping, his body reacted immediately and he was grateful that he'd had the sense to make sure his shirt was still hanging low.

He breathed in deeply and at the same time wondered if somehow he was dying a slow death. No woman should look that good in an outfit she was supposed to sleep in. The way he saw it, this was an outfit a man was supposed to take off a woman with thoughts of making love to her on his mind. He liked sex, especially the uncomplicated kind, and hadn't given much thought to just how much he liked it until today.

He frowned. That was a discomforting notion, especially when he thought of the last time he'd made love to a woman. It was hard to believe it had been over a year ago while on a photo shoot in Australia when he'd had an affair with Earlene. She'd been a reporter on assignment for CNN.

Dragging his mind back to the present, Blake took a deep breath and tried to keep his focus off the lower part of Justice's body as he wondered how he was going to keep things on a strictly professional basis.

"Where's Tonya?" Justice asked, glancing around.

He sighed. Evidently she was as uncomfortable with the strong sexual chemistry flowing between them as he was. "Someone was at the door. A delivery, I think," he responded.

Justice nodded as she glanced over to where reflectors, umbrellas, and a camera in a tripod were set up.

"Well, I'm ready when you are," she said, not meeting his gaze. "What do you want me to do?"

Don't ask, Blake thought as he walked over to the tripod to remove the camera. *Trust me when I say that you don't want to know.* "I think Tonya wants a natural effect," he said, taking the camera firmly in his hand. "And since you're definitely photogenic, that shouldn't be a problem."

Justice lifted an arched brow. He thought she was photogenic? Her gaze flickered to him and she watched as he went about readying the equipment and felt her pulse rate increase as he bent over to adjust something. His jeans stretched tight, doing amazing things to his thighs and butt. There was just something about looking at a well-built man.

She cleared her throat. "Did Tonya say how she wanted me to play out this scene?"

He glanced at her over his shoulder. "Yes, she wants the sexy look on all the pictures. She wants photos of how a man would see you if you were in the bedroom waiting for him and dressed in one of those outfits."

Tilting her head on the side Justice chuckled. It had been a long time since she'd been waiting for a man in her bedroom. "That may be hard to do."

He turned to face her and wondered why but decided it would be safer not to ask. "We're going to use that bed for the first prop. How about reclining on it, close to the edge."

Justice walked across the room and sat on the bed, and did as Blake instructed. She watched as he aimed his camera and focused on her through the viewfinder. Seconds later he lowered the camera.

"You look too stiff and your smile appears forced. Try to relax. And each time I snap a picture, slowly change positions, something smooth and easy that won't necessarily focus on your change of movement but on the outfit you're wearing. If it will help, think of something pleasant. Something you would like to have."

Justice smiled, thinking that would be easy since she would definitely like to have him—short term and for the fun of it. For some reason this man made her feel very, very aroused. She blinked, wondering where that thought had come from, then accepted it had come from the innermost workings of her mind and couldn't be denied. He was an attractive man and she was a woman, one who was strong and independent. She was also a woman who hadn't been intimate with a man in quite some time—although she didn't plan to do anything about it. But still, there was nothing wrong with having fantasies and she could imagine one in particular—a single shattering night of passion with the man looking at her with his camera.

Just like he had instructed, each time he triggered the flash, she moved her body, twisting this way and that, smiling seductively and giving him on film what she hoped was a perfect picture of a passionate woman. She tried to convince herself that the reason she was putting everything she had into it was for the women who would purchase the lingerie off Tonya's Web site, but deep down she knew she was doing it for Blake Savoy.

As he moved back and forth in front of her, she watched him, fascinated by his proximity and swift movements and wondered if he would have similar movements in the bedroom. For some reason she couldn't push away the carnal thoughts from her mind. Although in front of her he was fully dressed, she was able to drum up images of him naked, his dark skin showing smooth muscles and strong, long limbs.

And she detected the masculine scent of cologne she hadn't encountered before. It was something woodsy and seductive, a scent that would linger long after the man was gone.

She bit her bottom lip, thinking that she was certainly losing it.

Perfect, Blake thought. *The woman was perfect at this.*

Perspiration formed on his forehead as he clicked away with his camera, capturing her at different angles, shot after shot, and getting more aroused by the second. He felt the huge bulge in his pants and his breath was coming in faster and faster as ideas popped inside his head, one more hot and erotic than the next. His pulse was beating almost out of control but he was determined to capture the very essence of what he was seeing through the lens of his camera.

He wondered what Justice was thinking to have such a sensuous look on her face? He didn't have to prompt her to move any particular way since she was doing a hell of a job on her own. In fact she seemed to enjoy posing for the camera and playing the role of a temptress in the outfit she was wearing.

He could imagine being the man who came home to find her dressed this way. She would definitely drive a man wild with desire. No man in his right mind would be able to get enough of her beautiful body. Full hips, plump and ripe breasts and voluptuous thighs that would give you a hard-on for days if you didn't do something about it. And he had a feeling that she would be a fantastic lover in bed. A man would want to keep her on her back for hours . . . days, he thought, as he continued to click the shutter to the camera rapidly, in quick succession, the same way he would want to take her.

He breathed in deeply knowing he had to end this session before he ran out of film, or really did something stupid like explode in his pants. Slowly, he brought the camera down away from his face. "That's enough for that scene. You can go change into your next outfit," he said huskily. "You were great."

He watched as she blinked twice as if coming back from wherever she had gone and he couldn't help but wonder where that place had been. It must have been one hell of a sensuous trip and he would have loved to have gone there with her. He wondered if she had a steady man in her life? A lover? Would there be someone special to see her in the outfit she was wearing? What about all the others she planned to be photographed in? Would some man see her in those too?

He shrugged as he watched her sashay off to the room she was using to change in. It wasn't his concern if she was involved with someone or not. And to be quite honest, he wasn't really surprised with the way his body was responding to her. He'd experienced lust before, numerous times. He was a hot-blooded male and a Savoy at that.

He sighed deeply, wondering where in the hell Tonya was and what was taking her so long to return. He needed her as a buffer; someone to take the heat off things. With her around he could keep his mind focused on the photographs he was supposed to be taking and not on Justice's luscious body.

"I'm back. Sorry it took so long," Tonya said as she came down the steps.

Blake smiled. Luckily, someone had heard his prayer. Now there was hope of getting through the evening.

"Okay, I'm ready."

Hearing Justice's voice, he glanced around the moment she came out of the room wearing . . .

Ahh hell.

His heart thumped in his chest and he wondered, Where was a bottle of Jack Daniel's when a brother needed it?

Chapter 4

"Hey, man, you okay?"

Blake looked up into the face of his cousin Tyler. Sweat was pouring down Tyler's face as well as his own. He and four of his cousins had just finished playing a mean game of basketball and they were all tired, sweaty, and out of breath.

"Yeah, I'm fine. Why do you ask?"

Tyler grinned. "Because your game could have been better. So what's going on? Woman trouble? Or were you in the Australian outback too long?"

Blake leaned back against the bench and took a huge swig of water. "Neither," he replied moments later, lowering the water bottle from his mouth and meeting his cousin's gaze. "The reason my game is off is because I'm still trying to get adjusted to the different time zones."

"Hey, I can understand that," Tyler said, wiping sweat from his face with a towel. "Are you interested in coming to my place tonight to watch a couple of videotapes? I got some action-packed flicks that hit Blockbuster this week."

Blake shook his head as he stood. "No, I think I'll pass. I need to get busy developing those photographs I took for Tonya today. Otherwise, she'll be all over me tomorrow."

Tyler nodded. "How did things go with that?"

Blake shrugged. "They went okay but we didn't finish like I thought we would. I was hoping we could finalize things tomorrow but Justice has several business appointments so we won't be able to finish up until Friday." A part of him wanted to ask Tyler what he knew about Justice Manning. Specifically, he wanted to know if she was involved with anyone.

After Tyler and his other cousins left, Blake went inside his grandmother's house. She had gone to visit a sick friend at the hospital and had left his dinner warming in the oven. He smiled. His grandmother enjoyed cooking for him whenever he came to visit although he'd told her when he'd first arrived that she didn't have to. But she did so anyway.

Before sitting down to eat he took a shower and decided that if he wasn't too tired when he finished developing the photos, he would call Tyler to let him know he'd be coming over after all since there would be nothing for him to do later.

For as long as he could remember, the small windowless room in his grandmother's basement had always served as his darkroom for developing film, and over the years it had remained pretty much intact.

In the dark he worked briskly to bring to life the

photographs he had taken that day. A photographer was always eager to see what he had captured on film, the finished product. However, in this case there was more than eagerness that gripped him. He had an urgent need to see Justice again even if it was only in print.

Under the rays of the amber lights, he took a sip of a beer after one set of negatives was developed and hung to dry. Arching his back and stretching his shoulders, he set his attention to the next set, his thoughts already on the prints he would produce.

Less than an hour later he was sliding the film proofs under the enlarger, his breath catching in his throat. Letting go of the ease he'd always found when developing pictures, tension flowed through him as he quickly and methodically went through each frame. He brought the magnifier closer. It seemed each shot of Justice was more beautiful than the one before it . . . and more magnificent.

His favorite was of her posing in a huge recliner chair wearing a red satin slipdress that was tailored to fit her body. The outfit had been both simple and sexy, and with her wearing it, it had also been a total turn-on. The way she had gazed into the camera had clearly showed the passionate woman he believed her to be. No woman could have such a look and be otherwise. Then there was the tattoo of *Lady Justice* on the upper part of her left leg. He had angled his camera so he wouldn't capture the Lady and her scales on film for Internet viewing, but he had managed to get a few close shots for himself. These copies were his and his alone.

Neither Tonya nor Justice had seen the burning intensity in the eyes that had looked through the lens, holding Justice in their view. And neither had known the heavy pulse of his body with every click of his camera as he captured her on film wearing lingerie guaranteed to catch a man's eye. She had worn lingerie whose sole purpose was to stimulate and project the self-assurance that what you saw is what you got.

He swore and a tremor quivered through his body. As far as he was concerned each photo was perfect and there were none to eliminate. Each in its own way had a story to tell. He had used his expertise to capture the woman and all her sensuous flesh, and how the sheer material could caress and accentuate everything feminine.

In the span of one day the woman had amused him with her witty conversations with Tonya, stimulated him whenever he heard the sound of her voice, and razzled and bedazzled his mind and body every time she modeled a different piece of lingerie.

Heat blazed his eyes as he continued to study the proofs. The lighting had been perfect, striking her at just the right angles, making her skin appear a golden brown. Then there were her fluid movements. With practiced ease she had shifted her body with each flash and had smiled sensuously into the camera while fire had licked through his blood. Each outfit she'd worn was designed to show the voluptuousness of her hips and thighs, rounded curves as well as the fullness and ampleness of her breasts. He had been filled with thoughts of taking those breasts into his mouth, tasting, sucking and with the moist stroke of his tongue and the gentle scrape of his teeth, driving her, as well as himself, deliriously insane.

The sound of the doorbell snapped him out of his erotic haze. Leaving the darkroom he made his way up the stairs out of the basement and to the door. He did a double take when he looked through the peephole. He immediately felt a tightening in his gut and the hot, jagged edges of his senses escalated to full awareness. Justice Manning was standing on the opposite side of the door.

He took a deep breath as his pulse kicked hard. He couldn't help but wonder what the hell was wrong with him. No woman had ever made nerve-ending heat rush through his veins with such intoxicating speed before, and he didn't quite know what to make of it. As far as he was concerned, no woman was worth all this fuss and lust.

So he wanted her. Big deal. He'd wanted other women before and all of them he had found incredibly sensual. But even as he accepted those thoughts with shattering intensity, a part of him was forced to admit that when it came to Justice Manning, there was more than a longing to touch, taste, and devour. This had to be the most erotic person he had ever known. Then there was also a need he hadn't counted on: an intense, potent need for a woman he'd only met that day. With a mental grimace, he shook his head thinking that *had* to be the craziest thing.

When she rang the doorbell again he inhaled a deep breath. "Stay in control and accept lust for what it is," he murmured low in his throat before reaching for the doorknob. While he may enjoy the fantasy elements that visions of Justice evoked, he had to deal with reality, and the reality of it all was that the last thing he wanted was an involvement with any woman.

Justice checked her watch. Usually Gramma Savoy would be home and she couldn't help but wonder if perhaps she had stepped out awhile. She was about to turn to leave when she heard the sound of the door opening slowly.

And then he stood there staring, the depths of his hazel eyes making her senses leap. Blake Savoy. The man who had occupied her thoughts most of the day. It had been the first time a man had outright fascinated her and he had a definite way of reminding her she was a woman.

A woman with needs. Some tapped. Most of them not.

The awkwardness of the moment was somewhat downplayed by the chemistry openly flowing between them to the point that it would be a waste of time to pretend things were normal. But still she knew they would try like hell anyway.

"Justice, this is a pleasant surprise," Blake finally said.

His words coaxed a smile from her. They eased the tension a bit, but definitely not enough. The sound of his voice, low and husky, sent a warm ache flowing through all parts of her body. And it didn't help matters that he looked good enough to eat with the snug pullover shirt he was wearing and a pair of jeans. He'd worn jeans earlier that day but a different pair. The ones he had on now were well-worn and even more a perfect fit. And they seemed to radiate body heat since she could definitely feel warmth emitting from his body.

"Would you like to come in?"

It was at that moment she realized she had been staring and had not responded to his greeting. "Oh, hi, sorry, but I'm surprised to see you here," she said, giving him a truthful excuse as she entered the house when he stepped aside.

He closed the door behind her, crossed his arms over his chest, and leaned against the door and lifted a brow. "Why are you surprised? My grandmother lives here."

"Yes, but I thought you'd probably be staying with Tyler or one of your other cousins while in town."

"No, whenever I come to visit this is where I stay. I don't think my grandmother would have it any other way." He moved away from the door and came to stand directly in front of her. "If you're here to see her, she stepped out and I can't tell you when she'll be returning. She's at the hospital visiting a sick church member."

Justice nodded as she tried to ignore the flutter in the pit of her belly caused by his nearness. This, she thought, had to be the epitome of sexual chemistry since it had been boiling over all day.

"The photographs came out great."

His statement came midway through some naughty thoughts she was forming and she felt the need to leave quickly. "They did? Then I'm glad. Tonya wanted to get the new Web site finished and up as soon as possible."

Blake nodded. He wasn't sure just how he felt about those photographs being on Tonya's Web site for everyone to see, especially men. One look at her in those outfits and any man in his right mind would immediately visualize naked skin and rustling sheets.

But then, Tonya had fully explained that that had been the whole intent behind Tonya's Temptations: to prove that full-figured women could hold their own in the sexy department. He would definitely not argue with that because the woman standing before him didn't lack anything. In fact, he liked the very thought that she was so well stacked in what he considered to be all the right places.

His gaze slowly and thoroughly raked in all of her. She had changed from what she'd been wearing earlier and was now dressed in a blue skirt and a white blouse. The outfit was casual as well as seductive. And then there were these cute little sandals that she wore on her feet. Speaking of feet, hers looked good. He'd always gotten a good, hard throb looking at a woman's feet and hers were smooth and her toes were neatly trimmed and polished a sultry red, the same color as her fingernails.

"Well, I'd better be going."

He returned his gaze to her face. Evidently his close scrutiny of her had made her nervous because now she was in a hurry to leave. But a part of him wanted her to stay, if only for a little while. And he would love to show her his darkroom.

He cleared his throat. "Would you like to see the photographs?" he asked, thinking that was one way to get her downstairs. He could imagine being alone with her in the dark and at the moment would find just about any excuse to get her there.

"I'd better not. Tonya prefers seeing the photographs before anyone else and she likes picking out the ones she wants without any of the models' input." Her smile widened. "Probably because she knows that if we had our say, we'd probably balk about the ones she thinks are good."

His lips parted on a smile, thinking that very well sounded like Tonya. "All right. Would you like for me to tell my grandmother anything other than the fact that you came by?"

"No, there's nothing else to add. She knows I drop by occasionally just to sit and chat."

He nodded and seeing no reason to hold her up any longer—at least no reason that he thought she would go along with—he walked her to the door. "I'll let her know. And I'll be seeing you on Friday."

"Yes, I have business in Baltimore tomorrow and won't be back until late tomorrow night. But I promise to be at Tonya's on time. Good night, Blake."

"Good night, Justice." After he closed the door behind her, Blake spent several minutes leaning against it, trying to get his emotions back in balance and his mind back in focus. He could stand there all night and debate why he shouldn't feel such an attraction to Justice Manning, but it would be a complete waste of his time because he did feel an attraction to her and had from the first. The question of the hour was how he would control it and not let it go any further when she was so damn irresistible.

He puffed out a heated breath and knew he had to figure out some answers. Seconds ticked by and the only thing he could come up with was that he wouldn't have to come in contact with her any more after Friday. He should be able to wrap up all the photography work by then and afterward there was no reason their paths should cross for the remaining three weeks of his stay in Alexandria.

He would stand his ground and no matter how much chemistry flowed between him and Justice, he would bottle it and keep the lid on tight. Chin high, confidence raised, he walked away from the door thinking he had everything in full control.

*   *   *

Justice's heart and blood and mind were still racing as she swung her car into her driveway less than twenty minutes later. Cutting off the ignition she inhaled deeply then blew out a long breath. Tonight would be another night that she spent alone. At any other time that thought would not have bothered her in the least, but that was before she'd gotten a good look at Blake and he had reminded her of just what she was missing out on as a woman.

As she walked into her house and closed and locked the door behind her, a sheen of perspiration began soaking her skin. It would be one of those nights when a vigorous shower would do wonders. But she knew that nothing would relieve her from the rare chemistry and that soul-sizzling connection she had with Blake Savoy.

Moments later after removing every stitch of her clothing, she stepped under the cool spray of the shower and tilted her head back. The water drenched her face, body, and skin. She sighed as she washed away some of the day's stress, but none of the temptations that had plagued her. For some reason she couldn't let go of the images of Blake's smile tonight.

When she turned off the shower and stepped out to towel off, she knew she had to think about the reason her mind was still filled with thoughts of Blake. Maybe it was time that she "lightened up" and continued with her plan to check out a brother for something short-term and fun.

Over the past week or so she'd been trying to convince herself that she should, and now that the opportunity had presented itself, maybe she should take full advantage of it. In a way it made perfect sense. There was no doubt in her mind that she needed a fling—

badly, so why not turn her attention to Blake while he was in town, which meant something short-term? And there was no doubt in her mind that she would have fun. Things would be harmless as long as they both knew what they wanted—what to expect and what not to expect. Tonya had made it pretty clear that he wasn't interested in a serious relationship, and neither was she.

But she was definitely interested in a nonserious one.

She smiled and decided to let nature take its course—and if it led a path straight to her bedroom, then so be it.

Chapter 5

"You're early."

Justice blinked at Blake's statement. The man had been playing havoc with her common sense as well as her emotions for the past two days. This was the second time he had surprised her and opened the door at someone else's home.

She tightened her grip on her shoulder bag, trying to ease the tingling sensation that suddenly swept through her body. "Where's Tonya?" she asked when he stepped aside to let her in.

"She had a couple of errands to run but said for us to go ahead and get started. The scenes I'm supposed to be shooting today are for the bridal collection. She left everything laid out for you in the basement bedroom."

Blake decided not to add that he'd taken a peek at the outfits, all five of them, and already his libido had kicked into gear.

"I need a few moments to change," Justice said, following him down to the basement.

He smiled at her over his shoulder. "Of course."

A few moments later, alone in the bedroom, Justice checked out the outfits she was supposed to be photographed in that day—bridal lingerie. With no plans to ever marry, this was probably the closest she would come to wearing such attire. The first piece of lingerie that caught her eye was a black three-piece pegnoir set. It was a downright sexy, intimate ensemble made of Chantilly lace and consisted of a baby doll top, a sheer short coat and G-string panties.

She smiled. This particular piece spelled seduction with a capital S and would definitely capture Blake's attention, which is what she wanted.

As she began undressing, she was swept with a sudden case of nervous tension, and wondered just what kind of woman would plan the outright seduction of a man? She quickly decided it was a woman who was intensely hot and suffering with a bad case of unrequited lust.

Namely her.

And it was a woman who had finally decided to be brave, bold, and uninhibited. Men took the initiative and came on to women all the time, so what was wrong when a woman felt empowered to do the same thing? Besides, there was something about Blake that summoned her on a primal level, a level she hadn't known existed until the first day she'd seen him. It had certainly never come through with Harold or any of the guys she had dated in college.

Reclaiming her courage, she slipped into outfit number one and was determined that by the time she was down to outfit number five, there would be no doubt in Blake's mind just what she wanted.

"I'm ready, Blake."

He glanced up from loading film in the camera and met her gaze. His own gaze took a slow, thorough sweep of her outfit. "Yeah, I can see that," he said. Although his tone was light and teasing, she had a feeling he was dead serious. "This set of photos ought to be interesting," he added.

She smiled. *Interesting was definitely the word.* "Yes, I'm sure they will be." She should have felt uncomfortable with the way he was looking at her, although he was pretending not to by fiddling with some gadget or other, but she didn't. By no means was she a woman who made it a habit to parade in front of a man wearing such skimpy attire, but neither was she a woman who was ashamed of how she looked in it. She was a full-figured woman, tight and stacked. Although she wasn't into any type of fitness program, she did make a habit of going walking every day and always concentrated on eating the right foods. She never worried about how she looked since she always made it her business to look good. And from the way Blake was looking at her, he evidently thought the same thing.

"Sorry if my staring makes you uncomfortable," he finally said, breaking eye contact and looking down to adjust something on his camera. "But you look good in that outfit."

His compliment pleased her. "Thanks. I'm not uncomfortable." Struggling with her good judgment to take things slow—well, at least as slow as she could handle—she inhaled deeply. At the moment she felt a little bit dizzy, as if just being in the same room with him was making her feel hot.

She cleared her throat. "So what do you want me to do today? I noticed the bed is gone."

Was that disappointment he'd heard in her voice? Blake wondered. "I thought I'd use that loveseat over there for some of the poses and for others we can use the backdrop screen. We don't want to be repetitious with the scenery. You and what you're wearing should be the main focus."

She nodded and walked over to the loveseat and immediately noticed a beautiful arrangement of cut flowers sitting on the small table next to it. "Oh, these are beautiful. Are they part of the scenery?"

"Yes, they can be but that wasn't their intent. They're yours."

Justice's attention jerked from the flowers to Blake. "Mine?"

His dark head lifted from whatever he was doing to his camera and met her startled gaze. "Yes, yours."

"From Tonya?"

At first his lips twitched. Then white teeth flashed in a sinfully handsome dark face when he said, "No, they're from me."

Disbelief, surprise, then pleasure flooded across Justice's face. She picked up the vase and inhaled the flowers' scent. She loved flowers. "Thanks, Blake."

Blake thought she made a beautiful picture standing there dressed in that outfit with her face tilted low, and he felt compelled to capture it on film. He lifted the camera to his face and stared into the lens and caught her, just as he saw her—beautiful and breathtaking. Her attention was so focused on the flowers that she hadn't realized he had clicked his camera.

Moments later she glanced over at him and what he saw was a woman who was truly touched by what was a very small gesture on his part.

"I just love them but you didn't have to get me flowers, Blake," she said softly.

Blake shrugged. A part of him wanted to go to her and pull her into his arms and tell her that for some reason, yes he did. Instead he said, "I know I didn't have to but I wanted to."

What she didn't need to know and what he wouldn't tell her was that she had filled his dreams all last night and had been the first person he'd thought about upon waking that morning. He hated admitting it but he'd been anxious to see her today. And when he'd seen the florist shop on the drive over to Tonya's place, he couldn't help but stop and make a purchase. Why he'd done it, he couldn't exactly say, other than it had been an impulsive move. But then people who knew him would be quick to say he wasn't an impulsive person. He usually thought things through thoroughly before doing anything. But not this time and not with this woman.

"You did real good the other day," he decided to add when the room got quiet. "I enjoyed working with you and, like I told you last night, I got some great shots. Tonya was pleased."

Justice placed the vase of flowers back on the table. "She's seen the proofs already?"

Blake gave her a throaty chuckle. "Yes, and luckily my favorites were also hers. The ones she picked are over there on the counter if you want to take a look at them."

"Maybe later. I'm ready to get things started if you are."

Blake gripped the camera and didn't speak for a few moments as he adjusted the lens. "Busy day?" he asked. What he really wanted to know was if the reason she was in such a hurry to get things going was because she was meeting someone later.

A smile lit her eyes. "My days are always busy. But then that's all a part of owning your own business. Since I was out of town yesterday my desk is loaded with paperwork today."

"Yeah, I imagine it would be."

Justice glanced over at him, trying to decipher his mood from the expression on his face and the tone of his voice. Even when she had thanked him for the flowers she hadn't been able to determine if anything other than appreciation had motivated him to buy them. It had been a long time since someone had given her flowers and she was touched by such a kind gesture.

"You can stand in front of the screen for this first go-round."

Blake's words forced Justice from her thoughts and back to the situation at hand. "All right."

The room got quiet, too quiet. Blake decided to make small talk, which would open the opportunity to find out more about her. "I understand you own a temp agency," he said, pulling more film out of his camera bag. He had a feeling he would use every single roll.

"Yes," she said. "I do."

"Business going okay?"

"Yeah, for the most part. It keeps me pretty busy but I enjoy that."

He lifted the camera and focused, checking out the

lighting, the distance. Checking out her. "I bet your boyfriend's not too happy about that."

"I don't have a boyfriend."

Blake couldn't stop the smile that touched his lips. "That's too bad."

He lowered the camera. "Okay, let's get rolling. I think we should start off with various poses. We'll take a few shots of you in a standing position before moving over to the loveseat."

"All right."

He lifted the camera again and focused. "Okay, Justice, do your thing."

And she did.

With minor prompting from him she looked straight into the lens as she moved her body in a way that made it easy for him to capture the essence of what she was wearing as well as the full effect of the lighting that fell on her face.

He clicked the shutter repeatedly and felt intense heat with every shot. Moments later, he paused, wanting a close-up, and walked over and crouched a couple of feet in front of her. "Turn a little to the right, Justice. I want to focus in on how the outfit compliments your hips, breasts, and thighs," he said in a professional voice—which, considering the circumstances, was hard to do.

Following his instructions, she shifted her body and placed a hand on her thigh in a pose that he thought was sexier than any pose had a right to be. Sexy and sensual. He felt the hand holding the camera tremble and noted the exact moment the pattern of his breathing changed.

A few minutes later he stood. His chest was heaving as he lowered the camera. "Now for the loveseat."

"Do you want me to change outfits first?"

"No, I like this particular one and want to take at least two more frames. I don't want you to sit on the sofa but lean against it."

She nodded and did what he asked.

"Okay, tip your head to the right," he called out to her as the camera flashed once, then twice. "Now to the left." A couple of more flashes. "Now give me the look of a woman who's looking forward to her wedding night."

Justice went rigid and a sudden frown appeared on her face. Blake picked up on her reactions immediately through the lens. He brought the camera down and stared at her. "What is it? What's wrong?"

Justice gave a forced laughed. "If you're trying to get a happy look out of me then you'd better think of something else since I'm not a woman looking forward to her wedding night," she said, then added, "I don't have plans to ever marry."

Blake lifted a brow. "Why?"

"I'm not the marrying kind."

Over the years Blake had heard several men banter that fact but never a woman. Until now. He wondered what had happened to turn her against the thought of marital bliss. "I thought all women had dreams of a wedding day."

Again she gave a forced laugh. "Not in my family, if you're smart. Three seems to be everyone's lucky number for marriages. And because I'm a person who doesn't take failing at anything too well, I've decided the best thing for me is to remain single."

He shrugged. "Who knows, you might get lucky on the first try."

"Yeah, and I might not. I'm not willing to take a chance."

He paused. His heartbeat thudded in his chest at the panic he heard in her voice. He met her gaze. "And what if you want kids one day?"

"Then I'll have them. I don't need a husband for that."

He nodded. That was true. She didn't. But still, it would make things easier on a child. He'd always felt blessed that he was raised in a home with both parents. He sighed, deciding he didn't want to talk about marriage or children with her any longer. "Okay, Justice, don't think about the wedding you won't ever have. Think about something else and whatever you think about, make it sexy."

She laughed, a genuine laugh this time. "Make it sexy?"

He gave her a lazy grin. "Yes, make it as sexy as it can get."

Her eyes met his and moments later he saw her gaze become filled with desire as she stared at him. She tilted her head back at an angle that kept him within her scope while showing the sexiness of her neck, the fine lines of her breasts and the smallness of her waist in proportion to the size of her hips. A seductive smile touched her lips as she continued to stare at him.

He felt the bulge in his pants as he lifted the camera to capture her intense sensual look. "Nice. Very nice," he whispered, his voice rumbling low. He moved around, clicking shots of her at different angles as she watched his every move.

She was giving him just what he had asked for. She

was making it sexy and seeing her looking that way was more of an aphrodisiac than anything could ever be. And if he didn't know better, he'd swear she was deliberately trying to seduce him.

His camera clicked as she took her tongue and moistened her lips. The gesture was a colossal error in judgment on her part. He shivered and felt his own tongue tingle with the urge to taste hers, to mingle his own in her mouth. He was a man who enjoyed the rewards of an intoxicating kiss, one that went straight to your head, not to mention other parts of your body.

Slowly, he lowered the camera and watched her throat tighten as she swallowed. Heat, the need for sex, stimulated the air. At this point Blake didn't want to consider that this wanting, this desire was all one-sided. No woman had ever looked at him that way and he refused to believe he was imagining things.

He saw the warm flush that touched her cheeks. He saw how her nipples had hardened against the sheer material of the pegnoir. She licked her lips again and his groin tightened. Instinct told him to pull back and regain the professionalism he'd lost when she began making it sexy, but he knew it was too late. The invitation in her gaze told him all he needed to know, all he wanted to know . . . for the moment.

Justice noticed Blake had stopped using his camera and was staring at her. "That's it for now?" she asked nervously, licking her lips yet again.

He shook his head and slowly closed the distance separating them. He lifted her chin with his finger to hold her gaze to his. "Yes, that's it for now."

Then he lowered his head and kissed her.

Chapter 6

This isn't going to be a kiss, this will be torture, Justice thought the moment she felt Blake's tongue touch the very center of her top lip, stroking it gently and making her mouth open for his.

Her body shuddered when she tasted him, breathed him in as her tongue willingly and eagerly mingled with his. But he didn't let her take the lead and refused to give her control. It soon became evident that he was determined to play a game of slow seduction, making her concentrate on every aspect of what he was doing to her mouth.

Like she could think of anything else.

Their mouths were in perfect alignment, opulent harmony. The sensuous slide of his tongue tasting her everywhere, exploring her fully, possessed a tantalizing heat that took the act of kissing to a whole new level for her. She was not just being kissed, she was being absorbed, tasted senseless, and consumed. He was taking his time, lingering, not rushing. It was as if he intended to learn everything about her, starting with her taste.

She couldn't stop the moan that escaped her lips when he deepened the kiss, intensifying the flavor, heat, and desire. When he pulled her closer to him, shifting his hips slightly in the process, she felt the hard length of him press through the Chantilly lace.

Her body trembled at the contact that seared her

like a molten flame. Red-hot sensations poured through her bloodstream, making her incapable of doing anything but staying latched to his tongue the same way he was latched to hers.

No telling how long they would have stayed that way, kissing, absorbing, tasting, if they hadn't heard the none-too-subtle sound of someone clearing their throat. Too fired up, too overcome with desire to care that they'd been caught kissing, both were reluctant to stop and slowly released their mouths, but not before Blake's tongue touched the center of her lips one final time. This time the soft stroke wasn't a form of torture but a promise of more to come—later.

They both turned and met Tonya's smiling hazel eyes. She had caught them kissing and seemed pretty damn pleased about it.

"So, how far did the two of you get without me?" she asked glancing around the room with a smirk on her face.

"Not as far as we would have liked," Blake replied in a voice that bordered on annoyance for his cousin's lousy sense of timing. As far as he was concerned, tasting Justice had changed everything. Whether she knew it or not, the kiss had only fanned the flames between them and had not put them out.

"I guess we should get back to work," Justice said softly.

"Yeah," he said, detecting the disappointment in her voice. She wanted more like he did and he decided they both would get it. "How about going out to dinner with me later?" he asked, ignoring Tonya, who had the decency to pretend she was busy studying the proofs again.

Justice smiled and it was a smile that tempted him

to pull her into his arms and kiss her again. "I'd like that, Blake."

"Good. Will seven o'clock be okay?"

She nodded. "Yes, that will be fine. I'll give you directions to my place before I leave."

"All right." He forced his gaze from her mouth and picked up his camera before he was tempted to kiss her again. "I guess you can go change into another outfit so we can start up again."

She met his gaze. "Okay."

He watched her walk away, appreciating the sway of her hips. Usually it didn't matter to him if he got to know a woman mentally before things got physical between them. In fact he usually preferred it that way. Things became less personal. He had a preference for getting into a woman's body and not her head. And he hadn't wanted anyone this bad since . . . hell, come to think of it, he hadn't ever wanted anyone this bad, so a night of rolling between the sheets should be a satisfying conclusion.

But for some reason with Justice he wanted things to be different. There was something about her that pulled at him, something besides wanting to devour her mouth again that made him want to get to know her better. He was curious as to what she liked and what she didn't like. What turned her on and what turned her off besides the thought of getting married.

He didn't want to rush things, which really was crazy since he had only three weeks left in Alexandria. In fact, he was willing to let her set the pace between them. She would definitely let him know when she thought he was going too far, too quickly. No doubt the time they spent together alone would be hot, intense, and passionate.

But there was more. She had the ability to stir his emotions each time their eyes met and when he had kissed her, she had unleashed within him secret desires and hidden pleasures that he'd never before shared in a kiss. Why? And what kind of woman had the ability to break down his defenses that way?

He sighed deeply. Starting tonight he would find out.

Justice looked at herself in the full-length mirror and thought, *This is unbelievable*. No, not the length of her dress, which she had to admit was unbelievable, too, but what she was thinking about was the fact that in less than ten minutes Blake would be arriving to pick her up for dinner.

What was so unbelievable was that for the first time ever, she felt she was dating a man outside of her element, a man completely outside her scope of experience. No man had ever bestowed a kiss on her that had taken a full twelve hours to calm her racing heart and make her change her panties twice just thinking about it. If this kept up she would have to carry a spare pair around with her.

Luckily for her things had gotten real busy after she had changed outfits and had returned to continue the photo session. But still, there had been something about watching him move around with that camera, seemingly concentrating on her with the same intensity she was concentrating on him, especially when she'd studied his mouth knowing she'd gotten a real good taste of it. Heat had settled deep down in the pit of her stomach each time their gazes had met.

She jumped at the sound of the phone and quickly wondered if perhaps Blake was calling to cancel.

Maybe he'd thought over things and decided he didn't want to become involved with her after all. She quickly picked up the phone. "Yes?"

"Boy, don't we sound anxious?"

Justice's brows arched. She wanted to be annoyed with Tonya but couldn't be. Although they hadn't had a chance to talk, Justice had recognized a set-up when she saw one. Tonya *had* set her up. "If I do sound anxious it's all your fault," she said, not being able to keep the smile out of her voice. "I don't know whether to thank you or strangle you."

"Go ahead and thank me. Besides, I thought I would be doing you both a favor, especially after I saw the flowers Blake bought you and listened for five full minutes to the lame excuse he was giving me for getting them. I figured the two of you had it bad and didn't need me around for a while. I would have stayed away longer had I known things had started heating up."

Justice giggled. "Yeah, your timing was pretty lousy."

"Evidently. Trust me, I didn't relish walking in on the two of you with locked lips, but I figured you had to come up for air sometime. Now, enough of that. Tell me what you're wearing tonight."

After telling Tonya about the outfit she had chosen to wear, Justice wasn't surprised that her friend had clapped with approval. When the two of them had gone shopping a few weeks ago, it had been Tonya who had seen the scarlet red, curve-fitting mini dress and had talked her into buying it.

Justice had thought the dress was beautiful but way too short for her, but Tonya had convinced her that there was nothing wrong with showing her legs since she had such a gorgeous pair. She hoped Tonya was right because she would definitely be showing her legs tonight as well as parts of her thighs. In fact she would have to make it a point not to bend over since the dress was just that short. But a part of her had to admit she looked good in it and her high heels complimented the outfit.

"Okay, I got to run. Blake will be here any minute," she said, suddenly feeling nervous.

"All right, and remember what we talked about the other day."

Justice frowned. The two of them talked often and about so many things that she wasn't sure just what particular conversation Tonya was alluding to. "What did we talk about?"

"How we would start dwelling on realistic expectations of a relationship."

"Oh, yeah, that's right." But what she had failed to tell Tonya that day was that her expectations of a relationship were quite different from Tonya's. Tonya was in love with Bryan and always had been, and deep down Justice believed her brother loved Tonya as well, but he just hadn't recognized those emotions for what they were yet. No doubt Tonya's expectations involved getting Bryan to realize that she was meant for him and only him.

As far as Justice was concerned, she wasn't meant for anyone. Unfortunately Harold had assumed she was meant for him and had asked her to marry him. She'd known that one day he would realize she had really done him a favor and get on with his life, and from the looks of things, evidently he had.

She sighed. Her only expectation from the relationship she wanted with Blake was sex. For some reason she was tired of being a shy, good girl who played it safe and protected her heart.

Justice considered herself a lot smarter than that. She knew the score and was ready to be bold and adventurous. She wanted excitement and a hot encounter that would send her up in smoke and still have her insides sizzling long after Blake left town. After twenty-six years, she wanted that. She deserved that.

And from the way the area between her legs was quivering, she needed that.

When she heard the sound of the doorbell, indicating Blake's arrival, a part of her was determined to get that.

Talk about making it sexy . . .

Nothing, Blake thought, could have prepared him for the woman he saw when Justice opened the door. She had looked gorgeous all the other times he'd seen her, and had certainly raised his temperature while modeling all those outfits during the photo sessions, but nothing, and he meant nothing, could be more sensuous than seeing a full-figured woman in high heels and a mini dress that fitted her voluptuous body to a T. The sight had his breath coming out slow and tortured.

"Would you like to come in for a drink before we leave?"

He blinked upon realizing Justice had spoken to him. He cleared his throat, knowing he had to refuse her invitation. Once inside her house alone with her, and he doubted he would be able to leave. And he had made reservations for them at B.

Smith's, an exclusive restaurant near Union Station in D.C.

"No, I think we need to get going to avoid traffic. Are you ready?"

Justice smiled. "Yes, just let me grab my purse."

A few moments later he was walking her to the rental BMW that he was using during his time in Virginia.

"Nice ride," she said as he opened the door to let her slip inside.

Nice set of thighs, he thought when he glanced down at how the already short dress had ridden up when she'd gotten into the car. He suddenly felt perspiration forming on his forehead. "Thanks, I like it. It delivers a smooth ride."

As soon as he'd spoken the words, he wished he hadn't. An image suddenly formed in his mind of her giving him just as smooth a ride in the bedroom. He would bet all the camera equipment he owned that a BMW's performance would not be able to match hers.

He closed the door and quickly moved around the car to the driver's side as he struggled to breathe. He needed to get to the restaurant fast. He was suddenly having a snack attack and what he had a taste for was a woman by the name of Justice.

Now how unjust was that?

Chapter 7

"So, what do you think are the Redskins' chances of winning the Super Bowl next year?"

Although Blake asked the question, he really didn't give a royal flip. He merely enjoyed watching Justice's mouth move. They had enjoyed what he thought was a succulent meal and were now drinking a cup of coffee. The taste of the coffee was good but not nearly as good as he knew her mouth tasted.

"Umm, I'm not sure but I would have thought the Savoys' allegiance would have changed now that your cousin Lance is playing for the Dolphins."

Blake smiled. "It has changed to some degree but we're hoping he gets traded next season to Washington." He felt comfortable, relaxed. The photo sessions he'd committed to for Tonya were over and now he could enjoy the rest of his vacation.

"Where are you headed when your vacation is over?"

Justice's questions reclaimed his attention, not that she had ever lost it. Over dinner they had discussed a number of things such as the state of the economy, the recent war with Iraq, and how much they each enjoyed what they did for a living, although he'd seen that wistful look in her eyes when he'd told her of all the places he had traveled to.

"I'll be flying back to Texas for a week or so to go

through my mail and check on my parents. Then I'm off to Canada for a while."

"Canada? I've heard there's a lot of beautiful country up there."

"There is and I enjoy photographing it. If you ever decide to check it out, let me know. I very seldom get visitors while traveling."

"I'm surprised you would want them. Wouldn't that take the focus off your work?"

He chuckled. "I doubt anything can take the focus off my work, but then I know how to work and I also know how to play. The only time I feel pressured is when I'm up against some kind of magazine deadline."

"Does that happen often?"

"No, not too often." It surprised him that she was interested in his work. Most women he took out always cut to the chase and inquired about his financial worth.

"So tell me, Justice, why aren't you involved with anyone?" He decided to cut to the chase himself and ask the one question that nagged at him. He could tell that the question had surprised her. She wasn't expecting it. He watched as she took a sip of her coffee and for a while wondered if she would even answer it. Then she did.

"Sometimes it pays to be by yourself and not have to answer to anyone. The last guy I was involved with, we dated exclusively for over two years and he assumed a lot, like the fact that we would eventually marry."

He lifted a brow. "After two years I would think that was a reasonable assumption to make."

Justice shrugged. "Maybe for some women, but not

for me. Like I told you earlier today, I don't intend to marry."

He nodded, thinking he wouldn't ever forget that piece of information she'd shared. "Had you not told him at some point that his expectations weren't yours?" he asked.

She sighed. There was that word again—*expectations*. It seemed to be creeping into her conversations a lot lately. "Yes, I thought I had but I guess he figured he knew me better than I knew myself."

"Or maybe he thought he could get you to change your mind."

"If that was the case then it was a complete waste of his time."

Blake felt compelled to ask the next question. "Do the two of you still communicate?"

"No. In fact he's engaged to be married in a few weeks."

His hands stilled as he tried to detect anger, hurt, or regret in her voice and he resumed breathing normally when he didn't. He wondered what the hell was wrong with him. Why would the thought of her carrying a torch for an old boyfriend bother him?

"And I wish him the best," she added.

He watched as she took a sip of coffee, thinking she may wish her ex-boyfriend the best but as far as Blake was concerned, the man had lost the best when she refused his offer of marriage. At the moment he couldn't think of anything or anyone being better than her.

Blake leaned back in his chair. The last thing he needed was to be swayed by a beautiful face and a gorgeous body. His ex-wife had shown him that both could cause a man nothing but misery. But he was smart to know that all women weren't alike. There were too many good, honorable women in his family to believe otherwise. However, he was cautious and accepted that the hard job was trying to find a woman who was true and honest to the things she believed in and held sacred.

"More coffee?"

Blake glanced up at the waiter who'd come back to their table. "No, that's it for me." He glanced over at Justice. "What about you?"

She shook her head. "No, that's it for me too."

After the waiter left Blake met Justice's gaze. "Ready to go?"

He watched as she swallowed nervously. Like him she wasn't sure just how this night would end for them. "Yes, I'm ready."

First, Blake decided as he drove away from the restaurant, he wanted to seduce Justice's mind. By the time he reached her house he wanted her to have decided what their next move would be. If they didn't make it to the bedroom tonight that would be all right with him since there would be a next time. Already he was considering another date with her, which would be a damn good reason to let the chemistry sizzle and build, and whenever they did come together, he could count on one really big explosion.

He had no qualms about taking a woman to bed on their first date as long as he kept things safe. One-night stands never bothered him, but for some reason the thought of a one-night stand with Justice did and it had nothing to do with the ties she had with his family. They were both of legal age and consenting adults and what they did was nobody's business.

"You're quiet."

He glanced over at her when the car came to a stop at a traffic light. It was time for the mind seduction to begin. "I'm thinking."

She lifted a brow. "About what?"

"What might or might not happen when we get back to your place."

He heard her swift intake of breath. His candidness had surprised her. She hadn't heard anything yet.

"What makes you think anything might happen? There's a strong possibility I might not invite you in."

He chuckled. "And I'm thinking it might be a damn good idea if you didn't. You're a nice girl and maybe I should try to keep it that way. After all, you're close to my family."

She frowned. "Your family nor mine has anything to do with what we decide to do."

He nodded, glad to hear they shared the same opinion on the matter. Now back to seducing her mind. "I'd like to come in tonight," he said, meaning every word.

"For coffee?" she asked, turning slightly in the seat to meet his gaze while they were stopped at another traffic light.

"No, for you."

His words hung between them in the close confines of the vehicle, making the interior sizzle. From the illumination of a streetlight, he could see her features and read the anticipation in her eyes as well as hear the irregular breathing coming from her lips. Lips he couldn't wait to taste again.

"You're pretty straightforward, aren't you?" she asked when the car started moving again.

"Yes, I don't like playing games. I believe I know

and understand what we both want. Are you going to deny it?" His hand tightened on the steering wheel as he waited for her to respond.

"No, I won't deny it."

He released a deep breath; she had been honest with herself as well as with him. That meant a lot. He reached out and inserted a CD he had borrowed from Tyler into the CD player, thinking times like this called for a little Marvin Gaye. When "Let's Get It On" kicked into play, he glanced over and noted she had eased the seat back and with any preliminaries out of the way and a clear understanding established between them, she had closed her eyes and was enjoying the ride home.

He smiled.

"Justice, wake up, you're home."

After bringing the car to a stop, he'd been tempted to kiss her awake but had decided not to give her neighbors anything to talk about. He watched as her eyes slowly opened and wondered if this is how she would look waking up in the mornings, irresistibly sexy.

"Sorry, I fell asleep on you."

"That's no problem."

She glanced to her porch where she'd left a light burning. She returned her gaze to his, then paused, obviously giving herself time to get out the next words. "You still want to come in?"

"Definitely," he said easily. He saw her throat tighten when she swallowed and wanted to lean over and kiss the spot.

"All right."

He got out of the car and walked around to open

the door for her. Moments later they were walking side by side up to her door. He took a step back while she opened the door then followed her inside.

Justice's pulse quickened when Blake closed the door. She hadn't been able to keep her eyes off him all night. Awareness and male appreciation had consumed her the moment she had opened her door to find him dressed in a nice-looking blue shirt and a pair of navy trousers. The sight of him had literally taken her breath away. The man was simply gorgeous.

She turned and watched as he stopped in front of the vase of flowers he had given her that now sat on the table in her living room. She couldn't help wondering what he was thinking as he studied them and a delicious warmth settled low within her as she studied him, unable to look away.

He had told her a lot about himself at dinner and she had enjoyed his company. Like all the Savoys she'd gotten to know over the years, he came across as someone who would stand up for what he believed in, was loyal and dedicated to those he loved, and was a person who strongly believed in doing what was right.

Justice thought his attitude was a good reflection on the way he'd been raised. His parents should be given credit for such an outstanding accomplishment, and then there was Gramma Savoy, who played a vital part in all her grandchildren's lives. Justice's own grandmother had died when she'd been too young to really know her and she cherished the part Gramma Savoy had in her own life. She'd always thought that Thelma Savoy was a person who was the ideal grandmother anyone would want to have. She praised you when you did something good and wouldn't hesitate to give you a good old-fashioned dress-down if you did something bad.

As she continued to study Blake he slowly shifted his gaze from the flowers to her. She licked her bottom lip, feeling heat churning through her. Heat and desire.

"Thanks again for the flowers," she said, getting more heated by the look in his eyes.

He covered the few steps separating them. "You're welcome. I saw those particular ones and thought of you."

She glanced over at the arrangement. "Really? Why?"

"Besides their beauty, I got the distinct impression that no matter how bleak the outlook of things may seem, they have the ability to brighten anybody's day."

The corners of Justice's lips tilted into a smile. He had given her a touching compliment. "Like everyone else I do have my days."

He chuckled, unable to deny that, since he'd seen her in action that first time. "All of us do," he assured her. "But it didn't take much to notice that you know when to give in and let go."

Like I'm about to do now, she thought, as she watched him studying her mouth as if it was a treat he was dying to have. She breathed in a slow, deep breath, remembering their kiss that day and how she had longed to kiss him again. "Well, after hanging around Savoys long enough, a person gets smart. Tonya and I have been friends for years, so I learned quick."

"And why haven't our paths ever crossed before now?"

"Mainly because by the time Tonya and I were in

high school your family had already moved away. The only time you came to visit was during the summers, and that's when I had to spend time with my dad since my parents were divorced."

He nodded. "And why didn't Bryan have to go away during the summers?"

She smiled, remembering those times. "Because he always managed to snag a summer job, so he got to visit Dad during the holidays."

Blake didn't want to talk about her and her brother's summers any longer. In fact he didn't want to talk at all. As far as he was concerned, they had talked enough already. But there was something he wanted to ask her, something he needed to know. "Did you have a good time tonight?"

She smiled. "Yes. Dinner was delicious and the atmosphere was . . . great." She had started to say the atmosphere had been romantic because it had been. The table they'd been given had been in a private area with lit candles all around. She'd wondered if they'd gotten it by luck or had he asked for it.

"I'm glad because I wanted to make a good impression."

"Well, you did," she said softly, still not understanding why he would want to. It wasn't as if they would be engaging in something long term.

"There's one more impression that I want to make tonight," he said, taking a step closer to her, coming so close she could smell his heated scent.

"And what impression is that?" she asked as a shiver coursed through her. His voice was low and husky and his proximity made goose bumps form on her arms and he hadn't touched her . . . yet. But she knew he would. He had to.

"This impression," he said, gently pulling her into his arms and capturing her mouth, angling her head for better access. Their first kiss had been steamy; this one was definitely hot, Blake thought, mingling his tongue with hers. Unlike earlier that day when he'd taken his time, tonight he was in a hurried frenzy as he fought not to totally devour the mouth he was convinced had been made just for kissing.

Just for kissing him.

Somehow that thought leaped into his mind and he had a feeling that it wouldn't go away anytime soon, if ever. There was something about his attraction to her that didn't make sense and hadn't made sense since he'd first laid eyes on her. A warning signal buzzed in his mind letting him know he was damn close to losing it if he hadn't lost it already. Sexual chemistry was some strong, heady stuff.

Slowly, he shifted positions to wedge his leg between hers, wanting her to feel how hard he was for her, and when he readjusted their bodies, he caught her womanly scent. It was stronger than it had been earlier which meant she was aroused and her body was letting him know it.

He deepened the kiss and placed his hands on the contours of her lush behind, fitting her even better to him and she followed his lead and curved her hand across his backside as well, as they continued to partake in the wet heat their mouths generated.

When breathing became necessary, he reluctantly pulled back and ended the kiss but his hand remained where it was. He couldn't break the contact. He had to touch her.

She stared up at him and he didn't know if the astonished look on her face was surprise that he had ended the kiss or if she was amazed at what they had just shared, which in his opinion had been even more hot and heavy than the kiss they'd shared earlier over at Tonya's place.

Before giving her a chance to say anything, he leaned down and kissed her again, cutting no corners and giving no slack. And when he felt her knees weaken, he held her up, determined to see this through.

Without breaking the kiss he leaned slightly and began inching up the hem of her dress as a fierce and compelling need ripped through him. He wanted to touch her, feel her wetness, and wondered if she would allow him to take such liberties and knew there was only one way to find out.

He slowly eased up her dress and shifting his body once again, he was able to continue the kiss while slowly caressing her. He made a low, guttural sound when he eased his fingers under the elastic of her thong and found what he wanted, her feminine core.

Her tongue jerked his in response at the exact moment of contact and he swallowed her moan of pleasure. She was wet and hot and his fingers went to work to send her completely over the edge.

And he did.

Her body came apart in his arms and he continued kissing her, refusing to release her mouth even for the scream she wanted to make. He could have lived a lifetime and not known a woman this passionate, this sensuous, this classy.

He removed his fingers from within her when her tremors began subsiding, and he slowly ended their kiss. He hugged her tight, not wanting to let her go. Giving her pleasure that way had meant a lot to him. When she no longer had to struggle for every breath she took, he eased back and lifted her chin to meet his gaze.

The flush that darkened her cheeks made her even more beautiful and desirable and she seemed dazed by what had just transpired between them. Dazed but not sorry. And he was glad of that.

"I want to see you again," he said huskily. "I promised Tyler that I would go with him to Philly tomorrow and we'll be gone for the next couple of days. But when I get back, may I come to see you? Take you out again?"

She breathed in deeply and he could tell she was pondering his words. "Blake, I'm not looking for anything serious," she said softly. "I have a thing with commitments."

He'd gathered as much from their earlier conversations. "And I'm not looking for anything serious either," he said quietly, although conflicting thoughts were tumbling in his mind. But this was neither the time nor the place to try and figure things out. He would have two days away from her and her temptation to do that. "I'd like to spend the rest of my time with you while I'm here in Alexandria." He saw a glimmer of uncertainty come into her eyes, then moments later it was gone. She knew what he was asking for. A vacation fling with no strings attached.

Justice thought of what he was offering, which technically was what she wanted. "All right, then. I'd love to see you when you get back," she said.

He released a breath he hadn't realized he'd been holding. He had two days to get himself together and get his head back on straight.

Two days.

Chapter 8

It had been over two days and he hadn't gotten himself together and his head still wasn't back on straight.

And he'd made the mistake of taking one of her photos with him to Philly, the one of her dressed in that black pegnoir, inhaling the scent of the flowers he had given her. Each time he gazed at that photo, something deep and profound would well up inside of him. It was something he didn't understand and finally chalked it up as being a case of overpowering lust.

"You look nice. Are you going someplace?"

Blake smiled when his grandmother entered the room. She would be seventy-five years old her next birthday and to his way of thinking, she still got around pretty well. "Yes, I'm taking Justice to a movie."

His grandmother smiled. "Now isn't that nice. She's such a nice girl."

Blake lifted a brow. He knew, thanks to Tonya, that his grandmother, as well as his cousins, had gotten wind of the fact that he'd given flowers to Justice. And there was a good chance they also knew that he had taken her out and had plans to see her again. Tyler had even teased him about the possibility of him falling in love with her. He had laughed it off as being one of the craziest things he'd ever heard. Once he had recovered from laughing, his response had been that he wasn't falling in love with anyone and had merely thought Justice was a nice person to spend some time with while in Alexandria. End of story.

He sighed. Evidently his grandmother was going to make sure it wasn't the end of story. "Yes, she sure is nice, Gramma."

"And she's big-boned and strong. The kind of woman who'll give her husband a lot of babies. Too bad she's against ever marrying."

Blake almost told his grandmother that Justice had it all figured out that she didn't need a husband to have babies, but quickly decided not to. Besides, he was surprised his grandmother knew about Justice not wanting to ever marry.

"You know she doesn't want to get married?"

His grandmother's smile widened. "Of course I know. I consider Justice like one of my own."

Blake nodded. In that case it meant she knew all Justice's business, even things Justice probably didn't want her to know. He was a living witness that you couldn't keep anything from Thelma Savoy. Sometimes he often wondered if she was psychic.

"And just what do you know?" he asked, definitely interested.

"I know she thinks she can't commit to a man because of her mother and her aunts."

Blake raised a dark brow. "What about her mother and her aunts?"

"They've been married three times each and Justice looks at that as failing and she doesn't ever want to fail at a marriage. She sees that as the ultimate collapse of one's ability to hold on to something or someone."

He shook his head, thinking he could see how she would think that way. At one time, so had he until he'd learned to move on. "But just because her mother's and aunts' marriages didn't last doesn't mean hers won't."

"But you'll never convince her of that."

He shrugged. And why would he want to? Thinking that way was her hang-up and not his. He checked his watch. "Well, I'd better go. Since Justice has a late meeting, we decided just to meet up at the theater."

His grandmother nodded. "Give her my love and tell her to try and make it this Sunday for dinner. It's Tyler's birthday and I plan on baking him a cake."

Blake licked his lips. He looked forward to eating a piece of his grandmother's mouthwatering cake. "All right, I'll tell her."

The movie had been good but for the life of him he couldn't remember much of what he saw, Blake thought as he followed closely behind Justice's vehicle with his own. They had met at the theater to see Eddie Murphy's current flick. Blake had been there waiting for her when she pulled up, and had been so glad to see her that he had walked over to her and kissed her; glad the kiss she returned indicated she'd been glad to see him as well. And they had sat in the movies holding hands and sharing popcorn.

Her laughter at the scenes on the movie screen had turned him on and he'd sat there seeing everything, yet really not seeing anything. Instead his mind was preoccupied with all the things he wanted to do to her once they got to her place.

He took a deep breath when she pulled into her driveway. He was close on her taillights and pulled in right behind her and immediately shifted the automatic gear in park.

Quickly getting out of the car, he walked over to hers to open the door and silently, they strolled up the walkway to her front door. Just like before, he stepped back to give her space to open the door and once she did, he followed her inside. She turned on all the lights and his gaze immediately went to the flowers. They weren't as vibrant as they had been that first day, but in his opinion they still looked good and were holding their own.

He closed the door and his gaze then shifted to Justice. She was wearing another dress, this one longer in length but it looked just as sexy on her. Man, she had some gorgeous legs and those thighs and hips were to die for. And he didn't want to think about her curvy behind.

"I missed you," he decided to say, breaking the silence in the room. "I know it might sound crazy but I couldn't wait to get back. Tyler thinks I'm crazy because I kept rushing him to finish up his business." He chuckled lightly. "I must be coming down with something."

Justice smiled. "Well, whatever it is, it must be contagious because I've caught it. I missed you, too. So bad that I ached from it."

His face went from amused to serious in a blink of an eye. He'd felt those same aches. "Are you serious?"

"Take a step over here and I'm willing to show you just how serious I am." Justice didn't want to analyze anything. All she knew was that she *had* missed him something awful. She had missed him to the point of being miserable. How could she possibly agonize for a man she'd only met a mere week ago? She had never missed Harold when he would frequently go out of town on business trips. At the moment she didn't want to rationalize just what that meant. The only thing she wanted was Blake, here, in her arms, and kissing like there was no tomorrow.

Blake didn't hesitate in closing the distance to her. He pulled her into his arms and immediately captured her mouth, kissing her the way she wanted to be kissed, the way he wanted to kiss her. The heady sensation of her taste rocked him to the core and he deepened the kiss, eliciting a sensuous response from her.

Their tongues mated, clashed, sucked, each trying to get the taste they craved. Suddenly, she broke off the kiss and slowly began walking backward to her bedroom. Taking his hand she tugged him along with her. Once in the bedroom, she motioned for him to sit on the edge of the bed. He did so and opened his legs and pulled her to stand in the space between his spread knees.

He hooked both arms around her hips and pressed his face to her belly, closed his eyes and inhaled her scent.

The womanly scent of her shook him to his bones and he knew more than anything, that he wanted her. All legitimate concerns for whatever emotions he was feeling for her were tossed aside.

He lifted his gaze and met hers. "I want you."

Justice heard the deep desire in his voice and knew it matched her own. "I want you, too."

He didn't want to rush things if she needed more time. "Are you sure this is what you want? It's only been a week."

As far as Justice was concerned, it was a week too long. "It's what I want, Blake."

He heard her loud and clear and she took a few

steps back as he stood. His hands skimmed her voluptuous hips, remembering what his grandmother had said earlier and thought of them as childbearing hips.

Hips to bear his child.

A shudder went through him, not knowing where that thought had come from and tried to quickly dismiss it from his mind. He lowered his hands past the hem of her dress to her smooth stockinged legs, liking the feel of them, too. "I think it's time for this dress to come off," he said, slowly removing the garment from her body.

"Oh, Lawd!" he moaned, barely catching his breath. She was wearing the sexiest undergarments he had ever seen. Her matching lace bra and panty set was black and the bra fit her breasts snugly while the panties provided more temptation than coverage. He knew it was just the thing Tonya's Temptations would stock and he bet that's where she'd gotten them. She was definitely making it sexy.

"You're beautiful," he said huskily, meaning it. She was everything any man could possibly want in a woman. And tonight, he wanted all of her.

He wondered how long it would take to completely undress her since he wanted to touch every part of her body, but she hurried him on and as soon as he undressed her, she undressed him.

His breath became shaky as he watched her stretch out on the bed on her back waiting for him and knew, although he didn't want to think about it now, that this wouldn't be just an ordinary mating. He would be making love to her, really making love to her, in a way and with a degree he hadn't made love to a woman before. He felt like a different man than the one who had stepped off the plane when arriving in

Virginia. He had different wants and needs and knew
that she was a woman who could fulfill all his desires.

Justice read the deep longing gaze in the depths of
Blake's hazel eyes before her gaze took in all of his
nakedness. When she lowered her eyes to his midsec-
tion, she took a quick intake of breath. The man's
body parts were put together rather nicely and there
was no doubt in her mind that tonight he would put
them to good use. She watched as he put on a condom
from his wallet and appreciated his efforts to keep
them both safe.

The bed dipped as he climbed next to her on his
knees. "Do you know how much I wanted you that
first day I laid eyes on you and how much I want you
now?" he asked her, his voice low and seductive.

"No."

He smiled a very sexy and sensuous smile. "Then
let me show you."

He leaned down and kissed her, capturing her
tongue in his and greedily tasting her to the point
that her body shuddered from the onslaught. They had
kissed a couple of times before, but never with this
degree of passion and all she could do was wrap her
arms around his neck and return the kiss with equal
fervor, glorying in the searing heat of his tongue as it
explored every part of her mouth.

Blake knew he had to ignore the coils of sexual
tension inside of him and go slow, although the need
to mate with her was almost driving him crazy. He
had to take his time and savor everything and she had
a lot for him to savor. He doubted if he would ever
get enough of her and felt her desire in the way she
was returning his kiss.

He lifted his mouth from hers and immediately went

to her breasts, capturing the nipple of one gently between his teeth, holding the hard nub hostage while his tongue bathed it, sucked on it, lightly nibbled as she arched her back, squirming under his attack. Without missing a beat, he moved on to the next nipple, delivering the same torment. Deciding to check to see how ready she was for him, he moved his hand downward to her feminine core and his fingers found her so wet that he groaned deep in his throat.

He kissed her again, hard and deep, at the same time he placed one leg over her hips to straddle her, bringing the tip of his erection close to the juncture of her thighs. It took all his willpower, every bit of his strength, not to thrust right on in, but he wanted their first joining to be slow and easy. He wanted to feel every delectable sensation while going inside of her. He wanted to experience her every tremor as he journeyed deep, seeking the pleasure he knew awaited them both.

He broke off their kiss and their gazes locked. He felt her arms tighten around his neck but neither said anything. At this point words weren't needed. Slowly, knowing he couldn't do it any other way, he eased into her warmth while his gaze held hers. He groaned when he felt her tightness, and his chest heaved with the effort to strain forward. His body tense, his muscles flexed as he moved deeper.

He knew the instant he had gone as far and as deep as he could go. He felt her inner muscles clamp on to him tight, squeeze him, and felt her thighs beneath him tremble with the effort to hold him. And he wanted as much as she did this intimate, unbroken connection. But when he felt her muscles begin milking him, he couldn't stand it any longer.

After a long, still moment, he began moving with all the strength and desire that he felt. Sliding his hands downward he held her thighs and hips in place while he established a rhythm. She eagerly met his thrust each and every time he increased the pace to assure the deepest and quickest penetration. He heard her breathing escalate and knew the same raging fire consuming him consumed her.

She clenched his buttocks as he continued to thrust in and out, rocking against her, building pleasure one stroke at a time. She released a scream when a climax hit, which triggered his own need for release. With a low, guttural growl he tossed his head back as every muscle his body exploded. He cried out her name and knew at that moment she was giving him everything and for the first time in over seven years, he was greedily taking it, surrendering all. But not to just any woman. This woman. Justice. A woman who definitely knew everything about making it sexy.

In the moments that followed, while he held her in his arms, a part of him felt contented, no longer confused although he wasn't sure when lust had turned into love. But frankly, he didn't care. No matter what had happened in his past, now, on this very night, he had been found guilty: guilty of believing he could never care for another woman. But he had been proven wrong.

Justice had been served.

Chapter 9

Blake stood next to the window and looked out. It was two days before he was scheduled to leave and Gramma Thelma had gathered all the Savoys together for a little party in his honor. The backyard was crowded and his heart swelled at the sight. They were loud and rowdy but then they were Savoys, and right there in the midst of his family was Justice.

His heart ached when he looked at her, beautiful as ever, as she played volleyball with his cousins. She was wearing a T-shirt and cutoff jeans and he felt himself getting hard just looking at her.

They had been an item ever since the night they had made love. They would go out and then return to her house and make love until it was time for him to leave to get back to Gramma Thelma's house at a decent hour. Although he was more than sure his grandmother knew the score, in no way did he want to devalue her opinion of Justice by spending his nights over at her place, although more than once he'd been tempted to do so.

He inhaled deeply as he thought of all the nights they had spent together, the talks they had and the lovemaking they'd shared. She had promised to come visit him in Canada in six months and he was looking forward to that. Since he knew how she felt about commitments, he had decided to keep his feelings for her to himself. The last thing he had wanted to do was to cause friction between them and if she knew he had fallen for her, and fallen hard, she would drop out of the picture fast. So, he had settled for seeing her whenever he could and hoped and prayed that eventually she would come to love him as much as he loved her.

"So, you're going to leave without letting her know how you feel?"

Blake didn't turn around since he knew who was standing behind him and asking the question. "Leave it alone, Tonya. It's not your fight."

"And it doesn't appear to be yours. I can't believe you're not going to tell Justice that you love her."

Blake slowly turned and met his cousin's frustrated gaze. "Dammit, Tonya, you're her best friend. You of all people know how she feels about commitments. If Justice knew that I had fallen in love with her, she'd cut me out of her life quicker than quick, and right now I don't want to let that happen. Leaving this way at least assures me that she'll come visit me in Canada in six months."

"But will that be enough, Blake?"

He shrugged. "I don't have a choice. It has to be enough." He walked over to his cousin and hugged her tight. "Hey, don't worry your pretty blond head about me. I'll survive." Even as Blake said the words, deep down he wasn't sure.

Justice looked around for Blake and noticed her brother looking around for Tonya. Smiling, she walked over to him. "Having fun, Bryan?"

He returned her smile. "Yeah, I'm having a blast."

"Good, and if you're wondering where Tonya went, I believe she went inside the house to make a phone call. I'm sure she'll be back in a few moments."

Bryan frowned. "What makes you think I'm interested in Tonya's whereabouts?"

"Because you are. And maybe you ought to take my advice and stake your claim before someone else does."

He shook his head. "I don't know what you're talking about."

"Don't you? Think about what I said."

When she started to walk off, he grabbed hold of her hand. "Hey, you're a fine one to talk. I don't see you staking a claim on Blake."

Although she hadn't mentioned anything to Bryan about her relationship with Blake, she wasn't surprised that he knew. After all, her brother and Tyler were best friends. "I have my reasons."

Bryan rubbed his jaw. "Oh, yeah, I forgot. You still have your hang-ups about committing your life to someone."

"Yes, I do and it seems to me that you're suffering from the same plight."

"But not for the same reason as you. The only reason I haven't made a move on Tonya is because of my work with the Bureau." He looked around again and smiled when he saw Blake and Tonya coming outside to rejoin the others. "But maybe it's time to get my priorities straight." He glanced back at her. "And maybe it's time for you to have a long talk with Mom."

Justice's gaze lifted. "Mom? What on earth for?"

"Just talk to her, Justice. And she will explain everything."

"Everything like what?"

"The reason why she, Aunt Katy, and Aunt Lois had problems with their marriages."

Justice frowned. She already knew the reason why.

Evidently Bryan read her thoughts because before she could reply, he said, "You don't know everything. Do yourself a favor and talk to Mom."

Justice sighed as Blake cupped her cheek in the palm of his hand and gave her a slow, drugging kiss. He pulled her into his arms, and shifted their bodies to settle down in the comfortable bed. They had just finished making love and she was too depleted for anything other than this, and wanted nothing more than to spend the next hours in his arms. And it seemed she would be getting her wish.

He had told her when he'd arrived that his grandmother assumed he would be spending the night with Tyler but he had plans to stay all night with her. She had smiled when he'd told her. He had only two more days and then he would be gone. Although she had made plans to visit him in Canada for Christmas, that was almost six months away and to her it seemed like eternity.

When she heard the sound of his even breathing, she knew he had slipped into sleep, which she understood. The party his grandmother had given him that day had been taxing enough, yet he had made love to her with a passion and strength that had nearly taken her breath away. Her nipples grew hard and tight just thinking about it.

There was something else she was thinking about, everything that Bryan had said. What could her mother tell her that she didn't already know? She decided that the best thing to do was to go pay her mother a visit tomorrow.

She snuggled closer to Blake's warmth, closed her eyes, then joined him in sleep.

*   *   *

Justice really liked Donald Spears, her mother's third husband. She smiled when he opened the door. Since he was dressed in his policeman's uniform, she knew he was either on his way to work or returning from work. He was a bear of a man and immediately and automatically she walked into his outstretched arms for the hug she knew awaited her.

Her biological father had moved to Ohio and remarried within a year of her parents' divorce. He and his new wife had started another family and although Justice would visit him every summer, somehow she felt lost in the shuffle of their growing family and hadn't received the love and attention she'd wanted from her father. Donald had more than made up for it during the five years he had been married to her mother. Justice's nightly prayer to God was, considering her mother's marital history, for their marriage to last.

"You're going or coming?" she asked him when he released her.

"I'm going, but Marie's in the kitchen. I told her I thought that was your car I heard pull up." He grabbed his jacket off the sofa. "I got to run since we're having a meeting before the start of my shift. I've already kissed my woman good-bye, so I'm out of here." He leaned down and kissed her on the forehead. "Love you, Lady Justice," he said, grinning.

She grinned back at him. From the first day her mother had surprised her and brought him to her college dorm for the two of them to meet, he had called her Lady Justice. "I love you, too, Don."

She stood at the window and watched as he got into his car and drove off. He was a man who really loved her mother and Justice knew her mother loved him, too. It was evident in the way they interacted and Justice didn't think she'd ever seen her mother happier.

"Justice, honey, I'm in the kitchen. Come on back," her mother called out to her, claiming her attention.

Justice stopped dead in her tracks in the doorway of the kitchen. Her mother was standing at the sink dressed in a long, Bohemian print gown that had spaghetti straps, sexy side splits and a daring low-cut back. The material was sheer and looked soft and draped her mother's curves. It was a great outfit for casual lounging, especially if you had your man around, and evidently her mother had, up until a few moments ago.

Justice shook her head, smiling. She wondered if she would ever come to terms with the fact that the woman who had a thirty-three-year-old son and a twenty-six-year-old daughter was still so beautiful, and it seemed her marriage to Don had brought out all the beauty her mother hadn't thought of exposing for years. Justice knew for a fact, since she often helped Tonya stuff boxes to fill her orders, that her mother and aunts were three of Tonya's Temptations's most loyal customers, and she knew the outfit her mother was wearing was one she had ordered from Tonya's company.

"Hi, Mom," Justice said, crossing the room and giving her mother a warm hug. She loved her mother and thought they had a wonderful relationship. They didn't get to spend time together as much as they used to but she knew her mother was there if she needed her and vice versa. But she always managed to come for dinner every Sunday, right along with Bryan.

Her mother had become a police officer a couple of years after getting divorced but recently decided to come off the streets and work within the school system, protecting the children who came to school each day.

"And how is my favorite daughter?"

Justice smiled. "Mom, I'm your only daughter," she replied to her mother's usual greeting.

"And what's this I hear about you having a boyfriend?" Marie Spears asked, grinning from ear to ear as she put the huge pot of spaghetti she was making on simmer.

Justice frowned. "I guess Bryan's been talking again."

Her mother chuckled as she turned to give Justice her full attention. "No, it wasn't Bryan. I happened to run into Thelma Savoy, and she told me that you've been spending a lot of time over at her place—more so than usual—and that her grandson, who's visiting, has been spending a lot of time over at yours."

Justice picked an apple from the fruit bowl and took a bite. "Guilty as charged."

"Then why haven't you brought him to dinner? Don and I would love to meet him."

Justice sighed. And she would love for them to meet him, too. "I didn't see the need since he was only going to be here for a short while."

"Oh."

A part of Justice knew that response hadn't satisfied her mother's curiosity, but Marie wouldn't ask or push the issue. She believed in letting her kids live their own lives and keep their privacy if they felt they needed it.

"Mom?"

"Yes, sweetheart?"

"Why did you, Aunt Lois, and Aunt Katy get married so many times before the three of you could truly be happy?"

Marie tossed the dishtowel aside as she watched her only daughter study the apple she had already taken a big bite out of. Her heart immediately went out to her. She had an idea of what was bothering Justice and what issues were plaguing her. Over the years she had hoped and prayed that she would come to her about it so the two of them could talk. On several occasions she had brought up the subject herself, but each time she had tried talking about her past marriages, Justice hadn't wanted to hear anything about them. Evidently things were different now and after her conversation with Thelma Savoy, she had an idea why.

Marie came to the table and took the chair next to Justice. "When I think about the reason, it seems real simple now but to me, Lois, and Katy it wasn't then. Your aunts and I were raised believing that sex with any man was dirty and deplorable. Our mother instilled in us the belief it was something awful and degrading."

Justice's eyes widened. "Why?"

Marie shrugged. "Probably because she was a single mother with three daughters and worked a lot, both day and night. I think she saw telling us that was her way of making sure we never made the same mistakes that she did by getting pregnant in our teens. Her intent was good but the message was damaging since the three of us grew up hating the very thought of having sex."

Marie paused, thinking about that difficult time in

her life and what it had cost her. "When we got married our feelings about sex didn't change, so I can't fault your father for looking elsewhere for needs he had to have filled. He put up with it for as long as he could and then he just couldn't take it anymore. I never blamed him for leaving me, Justice, you know that."

Justice nodded. She had never understood why until now.

"Then with Frank Hill, I thought I could be different, but I couldn't," Marie continued. "The moment he touched me I would freeze up and freak out, no matter how gentle he was. Pretty soon he got fed up and started looking elsewhere for satisfaction since he wasn't getting it at home, so I couldn't blame him either."

Justice leaned back in her chair, hearing but not wanting to believe what her mother was saying. She'd always thought her mother and aunts were the sexiest and most sensuous women on earth. Although they never went out of their way to flaunt it, in her mind they certainly looked the part.

"What made you decide to take a chance on Don?" she asked softly, reaching over with her finger to wipe away a tear that threatened to fall from her mother's eye.

Her mother chuckled softly. "Maybe you should be asking what made Don decide to take a chance on me. He'd been asking me out for months and I kept turning him down but I knew deep down that I was falling in love with him. Then one day I woke up and realized I had a problem and needed help. I called Lois and Katy over and we talked and realized we had pretty much the same issues which were the reasons we could not get anywhere in the intimacy department. So the three of us decided to get help. A lot of folks see getting therapy as an admission of weakness, but for the three of us, we saw it as survival, a way to have a better and more rewarding life. After a few sessions we knew getting therapy wasn't a weakness but a strength. It's not easy to admit when you have problems and it's harder still to be willing to do something about them. We did, and over time we were strong enough, self-confident enough, and determined enough to get our lives on the right track. Lois met and fell in love with Carl, Katy met and fell in love with Joe, and I finally acknowledged my love for Don, and today my sisters and I are very happy with the men in our lives."

A radiant smile touched Marie's lips. "Don is wonderful and everything I need. With him I glory in the fact that I'm a woman, a very sensuous woman, and it's like I've never had any hang-ups about sex at all. I told him everything and he understood and was there to help me turn things around. He is the best thing to ever happen to me and I am truly happy."

Marie reached out and took her daughter's hand in hers. "Just like I want you to be happy, sweetheart. I didn't turn you against sex like my mother did me, and I hadn't realized until you turned down Harold's marriage proposal that you had a problem with committing your life to anyone. I tried to bring the subject up a few times but you didn't want to talk about it. I'm curious as to why you wanted answers now."

Justice closed her eyes. She was willing to admit to her mother something she hadn't yet admitted to herself. She loved Blake. She couldn't refuse to believe that fact anymore. It didn't matter to her that they had met less than a month ago, what really mattered was how she felt.

She opened her eyes and met her mother's gaze. "The reason I wanted to know is because I've fallen in love with Blake Savoy. I didn't want to love him but I couldn't help it. From that first day I saw him he touched my heart. I tried to convince myself it was all physical but deep down I knew that it wasn't. And you're right. I don't have a hang-up with sex so that's not an issue. The issue was whether or not I could commit to anyone and until you told me what you just did, I didn't think I could. But now I truly believe that I can try. I appreciate your sharing this with me. It really explains a lot, Mom."

Marie smiled. "So now that you understand, what do you plan to do?"

Justice wiped a tear away from her eyes when she thought about what she was about to lose. "I don't know. I really don't know."

Chapter 10

Justice inhaled deeply as she pulled into Thelma Savoy's driveway. Cars were everywhere and when she recognized the one belonging to her brother, she remembered the Savoy cousins were playing basketball this evening.

Blake would be leaving at noon tomorrow, flying out to visit his parents for a week in Texas. Although he had told her he would be coming by and spending time with her tonight, she needed to see him now and say what she had to say. She had no idea how he felt about her but she intended to tell him how she felt about him. She wanted him to know that the nights she had spent in his arms had meant more to her than just sex.

Taking off her sunglasses she decided not to disturb Gramma Thelma by going to the door but would walk around to the back of the yard since she knew that's where the guys were. Her breath caught in her throat the moment she rounded the corner and her gaze immediately latched on to Blake. He was shirtless and the gym shorts he was wearing blatantly showed all the attributes of his athletic body. He was unadulterated male and the sight of him made her pause. But that didn't stop her heart from beating faster in her chest as she saw the sweat that covered his dark skin.

Her gaze moved to his broad shoulders and she remembered the bite mark she had put there the night before. He'd been on top of her, thrusting in and out, driving her insane, wild, out of control, determined to give her the most incredible orgasm she'd ever had and when he'd succeeded, she had tried smothering her scream in the blade of his shoulder and had unintentionally bit him, leaving her mark. He'd been too wrapped up in his own release to notice the pain and when he did, smiled and simply said she had branded him.

She smiled at the memory, thinking that Blake Savoy was the most incredible lover and the most caring, sensitive, and giving human being that she knew. During their talks he had shared with her some of the foundations he had put into place to help underprivileged kids and how closely he worked with the Historically Black Colleges to assure that deserving students had a chance for a college education.

"Hey, Blake, your woman's here."

Tyler's statement got Blake's attention, as well as reclaimed hers. He stopped playing in the middle of a pivot and caught her gaze. He smiled, turned, and made a perfect shot into the basket then shouted, "Time out and if I'm not back in five minutes continue without me."

It seemed that all his cousins watched with interest as he made his way across the yard. The moment he reached her, he pulled her into his arms and kissed her, not caring who was looking. In a way it seemed that he was staking his claim, letting his family know without a doubt that she meant something to him, and that's what she needed to know—just what she meant to him. For all she knew, he was only sharing a vacation fling with her since that's how things originally started out. But a part of her wanted to believe that Blake felt more for her than that although he'd never said so. And the bottom line was she had to find out.

A smile touched her lips when he released her mouth. "Hi."

"Hi, sweetheart. You're a pleasant surprise," he said huskily.

"Thanks. I hate to take you away from your game but I was wondering if we can talk for a few minutes."

He lifted a brow. "Sure. Come on inside the house. Gramma went to Richmond with Aunt Bessie and won't be back until late tonight."

Justice nodded as he opened the back door for her and she stepped inside the house. "Where's Bryan? I saw his car out front."

Blake shrugged. "Umm, I don't know. He was playing with the rest of us and suddenly called time-out and came inside. We figured he took a bathroom break but that was over fifteen minutes ago."

"Oh," she said. She followed Blake down the hall that led to the basement. "Why are we going to the basement?"

"That's where the darkroom is located, and I thought you'd like to see the photos we took at the party yesterday."

She glanced up at him. "I'd love to see them." As soon as they reached the bottom step to the basement they stopped. It seemed the huge room was already occupied. There stood Bryan and Tonya, wrapped in each other's arms kissing like there was no tomorrow.

Justice smiled. Evidently her brother had taken her advice like she had taken his. "Should we clear our throats to let them know that we're here, Blake?" she whispered.

Blake chuckled softly. "I doubt it will do any good at this point," he whispered back. "What you see has been a long time coming and I'm glad they've finally gotten things together. For a while the cousins and I thought we would have to beat the crap out of your brother to make him see the light, and we regretted the thought of doing that since he is such a good friend and all."

Justice giggled. "Bryan has always loved Tonya. He told me as much, but he was afraid the type of job he has would interfere with a relationship with her. Evidently, he got things worked out."

"Well, all I can say is that it's about time."

Justice had to agree. When Blake took her hand in his, he led her through an area where the darkroom was located. The room lived up to its name since it was truly dark. After closing the door behind him, he switched on a small lamp in the corner.

"So, what do you want to talk to me about?" he asked, coming to stand directly in front of her.

Breath rushed out of Justice's lungs in a nervous sigh. She didn't know where to begin. "I need to know something, Blake."

He heard the nervousness in her voice and met her gaze as he gently released her from his embrace. "All right. What do you want to know?"

She inhaled deeply. "What we shared the past three weeks, I need to know what it means to you."

He lifted a brow, confused as to where she was going with things. He searched her face intently. "Maybe I should be asking you the same question, Justice."

"Yes, but I asked you first."

Yes, he agreed. She had. And she had definitely put him in a dilemma. If he told her the truth, that he loved her senseless, would she back away because of her fear of commitment? And if he lied and pretended he viewed what they shared as nothing but a no-strings affair, would that make her happy although it would make him miserable?

He sighed and decided he would make a decision with a flip of a coin. He reached out and picked up a quarter that had been left on the table. Heads she got the truth and tails he would lie.

Blake knew Justice was confused with what he was doing but he flipped the coin and it landed on . . . tails.

Damn.

He closed his eyes tight, refusing to believe that the outcome meant he had to lie to her.

"Blake? What is it? What's wrong? Why did you flip that coin?"

Justice's question made him reopen his eyes and the only thing he could think about was the fact that he could not and would not lie to her. He had to tell her the truth no matter how she took it, even if it meant she put distance between them by not visiting him in Canada for the holidays. Honesty and not lies had to always be between them. Hadn't his grandmother preached that one lie only led to another, then another?

He met her confused gaze. "The reason I flipped the coin was trying to make a decision that I didn't want to make and thought I needed help. Well, the outcome wasn't what I wanted, so I'm going to do what I know is the right thing and what I should have done in the beginning and follow my heart, no matter how things turn out, because I believe in the end the truth will win."

Justice nodded, although she was still confused and getting more confused by the minute. "All right. Now will you tell me what these past three weeks have meant to you?"

He pulled her back into his arms and met her gaze after inhaling a slow, deep breath. "These past three weeks have meant more to me than you'd ever know, Justice, because I found something that I thought was lost to me forever," he whispered softly.

Nervous tension swirled around in her belly. "What?"

"Love. Don't ask me how or why. All I know is that we may have started out with one goal in mind but somehow along the way my emotions rebelled and I fell in love with you. In truth, I believe I fell in love with you the first moment I saw you that day, in Tonya's basement. I never believed in love at first sight until that day."

Justice blinked back the tears that gathered in her eyes. Acceptance unfolded within her as her mind consumed Blake's words. She gazed into the depths of his hazel eyes and saw the truth in what he'd said. "I'm glad to hear that Blake, since I've fallen in love with you, too. I had issues to work out that were keeping me from committing my life to anyone and now I'm resolving those issues. And I'm free to love and to admit my love and I want to admit loving you. I believe I fell in love with you that day in Tonya's basement as well."

That's all Blake needed to hear and he knew she had spoken from her heart the same way he had. "Does that mean that sometime in the near future there will be a Savoy-Manning wedding?"

Justice laughed throatily as she swiped away the tears from her eyes. "Yes, possibly more than one if I know my brother. Now that he's staked a claim on Tonya, he won't waste any time getting her to the altar. But as far as we're concerned, if marriage is what you want then marriage is what you'll get."

"Yes, it's what I want, among other things," Blake said, kissing the corner of her lips. "I also want to be the father of all your babies and if you're not willing to leave here and travel with me, I'll understand."

Justice shook her head. She knew Blake's first wife wouldn't travel with him and she refused to take that same position. Besides, her business was at a point where her office manager could run things quite efficiently. "But I am willing to travel with you, Blake. I'd love to visit all those places as your wife, your soul mate, and the mother of your children."

Filled with happiness beyond belief, Blake framed

Justice's face in his hands and lowered his head and kissed her, long and deep, and with all the love in his heart. They both had tempted fate and with a flip of the coin, had lost. But a Higher Being had interceded and decided it was meant for them to join their lives together forever.

And everyone knows that He has the last word.

Epilogue

Four months later

It was decided that there would be a double wedding since it wasn't every day that two Savoys married two Mannings.

It was a beautiful day for a wedding and the church had been packed. The brides, best friends for life, had chosen well and knew they would spend the rest of their lives happy with their mates.

Bryan and Tonya had made plans to go to Bermuda on their honeymoon and Blake and Justice would spend a week in Hawaii before heading for Canada. Justice was excited about the trip and looked forward to going. Bryan and Tonya had promised to visit them the first opportunity they had now that Bryan was no longer an FBI agent out in the field but had taken a teaching position at the Bureau's academy.

It was time for the bridal couples to leave the reception to embark on their honeymoons, and the brides had escaped to change clothes.

Tonya placed several beautiful gift-wrapped boxes in Justice's arms. Justice smiled, recognizing the red box and black bow as the traditional signature packaging of Tonya's Temptations. Anyone ordering from the Internet company received their merchandise in the beautiful package. Justice also knew that once she opened the boxes, in each one she would also find the traditional red silk rose lying atop the black tissue paper.

"Should I guess what's in here?" she asked Tonya.

Tonya laughed. "In those boxes are items you thought you'd never wear since you would never marry but I happen to know of one particular man who would love seeing you in them . . . again."

Justice giggled, knowing that was true. She had recently discovered that Blake had kept copies of every photo he had turned over to Tonya to use on her Internet site. She had also discovered he had made a few of his own that neither she nor Tonya had known about. They were photos that he claimed were only meant for his personal collection.

The two women hugged. They were no longer just best friends, they now belonged in the same family, doubly so.

Moments later when Justice walked out of the room she was temporarily blinded as a flashbulb went off in her face. As soon as she got her sight back she met her husband's gaze as he handed the camera back to Tyler. He pulled her into his arms and whispered, "I couldn't resist, since no matter what you wear, you definitely have a way of making it sexy."

When Wishes Come True

 Monica Jackson

Chapter 1
The Wish

The waiter placed the spectacular two-tiered cake studded with thirty candles at the center of the table. Four women sat around the table, a yearly ritual since childhood. They'd tell one another that they never had big birthday parties, they had birthday squares; four points of the compass, one for the each of them. They wanted only each other at their birthday celebrations.

"This cake is simply too fabulous." Topaz said, smiling at her sister and two best friends. She was a striking woman whose eyes looked like huge pools of melted chocolate fringed by long, thick lashes. Her natural hair flowed down her back in a soft, frothy African cloud touched with golden highlights. Velvety, copper skin covered rounded, plump curves carried with womanly confidence.

"It's your big three-oh. You deserve it," Cherice said. Cherice was big, brash, and beautiful, the owner of one of the most successful hair salons in the city. She was a honey-skinned beauty with startling blond locks that on second glance suited her perfectly. They matched her golden cat's eyes and the single elegant, black beauty mark perched to the left of her heart-shaped ruby red lips.

Topaz's sister, Rosaline, a pediatrician, nodded in agreement over the glow of the candles. Rosaline and Topaz had roughly the same plump body structure, but the likeness ended there. Rosaline was casually dressed in a pantsuit, her hair pulled back at the nape of her neck in a bun. She was a classic beauty with even, bronzed features and minimal makeup.

"The cake is honey-vanilla with whipped cream frosting and real butter," Brandy said. "I hope y'all left your diets at home." Brandy was the only one of them who wasn't heavier than average, and the only one who wasn't a raving beauty. She was totally unself-conscious about her looks. She never wore makeup and wore her hair in low-maintenance braids. Brandy anchored the evening sports for a Kansas City network affiliate and wrote a syndicated sports column, a coup for someone both female and young. She was a natural tomboy, athlete, and sports lover extraordinaire.

It was good to be back in Kansas City, Topaz thought. She'd cut tours short, left recording sessions, and canceled concerts to rush home for one of their birthdays and she knew each one of them would do the same for her.

Their yearly birthday rituals included more than cake with sugary frosting, burning candles, and presents with brightly colored paper.

"Since it's your big three-o, you better make this wish count," Rosaline said.

One of the most important things in their lives was the trailing wispy smoke of their birthday wishes. Somehow and in some way, when the four of them came together, their birthday wishes really came true.

Topaz stood. She blew out the candles with one big

breath. It was her time again: another year, another wish.

"You have to name it to claim it. What is your Heart's Desire?" they asked her.

That was her cue. It couldn't be a secret wish; the wish had to be spoken. They'd tried wishing secretly one year when they were in junior high and their hormones were running amok. The results had been woefully disappointing.

They never knew exactly how their wishes would come true, and often they didn't turn out quite how they'd planned or hoped. Some things didn't work at all. You couldn't wish for world peace or a cure for cancer, for instance. You couldn't wish to win the lottery or wish something that would affect someone else unattached to you. Heartfelt, sincere personal wishes that did no harm were always fulfilled.

"My Heart's Desire is to find true love," Topaz said fervently, eyes closed, passionate love scenes running through her mind. Was it her imagination that she heard rustles and the whisper of wind in the background?

It was tradition that nobody questioned your Heart's Desire once it was spoken, but she could feel her companions' raised eyebrows.

"Yep. That's what I want," Topaz said in answer to the unspoken question.

"Shouldn't you be more specific?" Rosaline fretted.

"What's more specific than true love?" Cherice asked.

"Shoot, my dog loves me, and he gives me less headaches than my boyfriend," Brandy said.

"That's a point," Cherice said. "I hope you don't get a dog."

"That's a new sort of wish," Rosaline said, still frowning slightly.

"Every year we get together and wish for material successes and happiness and health, things like that. But we never wish for what our women's hearts need most."

"Gurl, you've been singing too many looooove songs," Cherice said, fanning herself with a napkin.

"Maybe so, but haven't you ever wondered why we don't wish for love?" Topaz asked. "What are we frightened of? Maybe I have a little of Rosaline's scientific mind after all. I got to thinking that in spite of all the love songs and the love scenes in the movies and the romance novels . . . Well, maybe that sort of love doesn't exist after all."

"What?"

"Maybe love-ever-after is something that was made up to tell stories, like monsters and things that go bump in the night."

"I don't know about that," Cherice said. "I wouldn't want to do without a regular dose of good lovin'."

"That's lust, honey," Brandy said, examining the cake with longing. "Aren't y'all hungry?"

"I'm not talking about lust or infatuation," Topaz said. "Cherice, your record is about three months before you kick a man to the curb. That's not true love. That's more like being a female dog in heat."

Cherice's perfectly arched eyebrow lifted. "It works fine for me," she said.

They all cracked up at Cherice's serious expression.

"At least the girl knows she's a dog, unlike some men out there," Brandy said.

"I suppose it doesn't hurt for some men to know

how it feels to be on the other end of the leash once in a while," Topaz muttered.

"I can't argue with that," Rosaline agreed. "But what's the difference between true love and wishes coming true?" she continued. "We see magic happen in our lives all the time. So how can you say there is no such thing as fairy-tale endings, passion, and romance-ever-after?"

"That's what I want to find out. I want to know if that sort of love exists, and more important, if it exists for me."

They were all silent for a moment.

"You're preaching to the choir," Cherice said. "We've all lived our own fairy tales in one way or another every year our entire lives. I can't wait to see what happens for you."

"Yeah, Sis, if happily-ever-after-love exists, it'll come to you."

"Remember when that investor for Cherice's salon walked up to our table before she'd hardly got her wish out?" Brandy said.

"I about fell out of my chair that day," Topaz said.

"Or when we got that call about Brandy's mother?"

They got quiet and more than one pair of eyes misted. They couldn't save the world or cure the common cold, but they could save a life or make a small difference. Rosaline's wishes almost never concerned herself, but rather some child to whom she'd become attached. But somehow Rosaline always had whatever she wanted and needed. There was a glow about Rosaline. Often she seemed more blessed than the lot of them.

"What is this you're giving me?" Topaz asked Brandy.

"It's a knife. Cut the cake, chile."

They'd barely managed to put a dent in the cake before Brandy exclaimed, "Look over there! Look who's being seated!"

"Where?"

"Over there! It's Ray Gaines, in the flesh. How long has it been since he's been back in town?"

"Years. Since we graduated from high school," Cherice said.

"Didn't he go pro?"

"He went more than pro, chile," Brandy said. "He went to the Super Bowl." She turned to Topaz. "And he used to be your man. Weren't those the days, Topaz?"

The fork with a piece of cake on it had frozen halfway to Topaz's mouth. Ray Gaines. Star football player. Her high school sweetheart. Her prom date. Her . . . first. So Ray Gaines was going to be her true love? He had to be. The Wish. She hadn't expected that this quickly . . .

"I'm getting his autograph," Brandy said, rising from her chair. "What am I thinking? I'm getting an exclusive interview. C'mon, Topaz. You're my entrée. He'll be happy to see you again. C'mon girl. Topaz!"

"Brandy, calm down. Don't you see the girl is in shock?" Cherice said.

"The Wish," Rosaline whispered.

"Ohhh. The Wish. Oh, yeah. Ray Gaines. I remember. Dang. That was quick," Brandy muttered.

"He got bank too. And a Super Bowl ring. My, my," said Cherice. "You're one lucky lady, Topaz."

"I just want my interview," Brandy said.

Rosaline dipped her napkin in ice water and was dabbing her sister's temples with it. "Topaz? Topaz!

Snap out of it. Put your fork down. You're going to be okay."

"There goes Brandy," Cherice said. "She's headed over to his table. I wonder who that is with him. That other man is too fine."

"They're getting up," Rosaline hissed in Topaz's ear.

"Here they come. I wonder if that guy with Ray played in the Super Bowl too," Cherice mused.

"Ray's coming to our table and you're rubbing my makeup off? Are you nuts? Quit it," Topaz said, pushing Rosaline's hand with the wet napkin away.

"I see that Topaz has pulled herself back together," Cherice said, as Topaz hurriedly fumbled for her compact.

Topaz clicked the compact shut just as Ray, his friend, and Brandy reached the table.

"Ray had to come over and say hello when I told him you were all here," Brandy said, looking very excited.

"Topaz," Ray said, extending his hand.

"Ray, it's good to see you again."

"You haven't changed a bit. You're quite a success. I hear your music on the radio every once in a while."

"And you're quite a success too," Topaz said, unable to keep from glancing at the huge Super Bowl ring on his finger.

Ray looked the same, only fatter, but his voice didn't sound quite like she remembered it, or maybe it did and that was the problem. It still seemed high pitched and crackly like an adolescent boy's voice, out of place on such a big man. His hand was surprisingly cold and sweaty. Topaz had to restrain herself from wiping her hand off on the napkin after she retracted it.

"You remember Jonathan Bynum?" Ray said.

There was a simultaneous pause as four pairs of eyes swung toward the tall, slim man that Ray introduced.

"This is your cousin, Jonnie?" Topaz asked faintly.

"The same," Jonathan answered, putting out his hand. "I remember you well, and I have to agree with Ray that you're more beautiful than ever."

Unlike Ray, Jon's voice had changed along with him. His voice was soft and silky as buttery leather and his lashes were as long as she'd seen on any man, almost as long as her own. He wasn't as beefy as Ray, but he was as tall, easily six feet three, long and lean. His hair lay in the distinctive crisp black ringlets that many of her classmates had envied. She was happy that it wasn't too short. It would have been a shame to cut off those curls.

Yes, Jon had grown into a more than handsome man. She remembered the tall, bespectacled kid who constantly trailed them. They tolerated Jonnie because he regularly did Ray's homework and whatever other errands and chores they could think up for him to do. Come to think of it, Johnnie regularly paid for most of those meals at Micky D's they enjoyed. He'd written more than his fair share of her essay papers too.

"We always stuck you with our homework, I remember," she said.

Jon took her hand and it seemed as if the room tilted sideways for an instant. Must have been all that sugar in the cake she'd just eaten.

"Jon always did like schooling. He's been doing more than his fair share of it all these years. I think it's his hobby." Ray clapped a hand on his cousin's back. "I bet you don't know what you're going to do with yourself now that you're finally done."

"I just finished my surgical residency," Jon said to them. "I'm taking some time off, and then I've accepted a fellowship in the San Francisco Bay Area."

"Isn't that more school? See, I told you. This guy will never quit," Ray barked.

She could feel Rosaline's attention perk up and she could almost hear Cherice behind her drooling.

Jonathan still held her hand. His thumb circled on her palm and it felt as intimate as a kiss. Her heart pounded and she looked up into the deep, dark pools of his eyes and it was as if there was a thunderstorm brewing there, with lightning and hail and swirling clouds. She was lost there for a moment.

Then Ray said her name and brought her back to the now, and she withdrew her hand and turned her attention back to where it belonged, to Ray Gaines, her Wish come true in the flesh.

Chapter 2
Gathering Clouds

Excitement rose within Topaz, filling her throat, making it hard to breathe. Her Wish, immediately followed by the man who had been her first lover so many years ago had to be more than coincidence. Her old high school flame, Ray, had to be the One—her dream lover. She swallowed hard.

So why did Topaz feel a touch of jealousy when Cherice leaned over *Jon*—her generous breasts brushing his arm—and handed him her personal card. Jon had grown into a mighty fine man, but it should be Ray who was drawing Topaz's eye, not Jon.

"I'm having a get-together for Topaz tonight," Cherice purred. "I'd really like for you and Ray to come. It'll be like old school days." She turned and winked at Ray. "Speaking of old school," Cherice continued, "there'll be a band. We'll try to get Topaz to sing you one of those old school love songs she likes so much."

Ray hesitated. "We have plans—"

"That we can reschedule," Jon interjected smoothly. He took the card from Cherice's fingers.

He gave his cousin a sideways glance and Ray coughed and subsided into a sullen silence. "We'll be there," Jon said.

Jon's eyes widened as he pulled into the grounds of what he would have to call an estate.

Ray whistled. "You sure you got the right address, cuz?" he asked.

"This is where she said she lived," Jon answered.

Cherice Givens grew up with all of them in the poorest neighborhood in Kansas City, Kansas, but Cherice started doing well all of a sudden around elementary school, maybe a little after the time that Topaz and Rosaline's mother died in that car accident. "I heard her mother must have won the lottery or something like that," Ray said.

"Looks like Cherice kept on winning," Jon murmured, as he pulled up to Cherice's opulent home.

Uniformed tray-bearing waiters met them at the

door with drinks and they were guided through black-and-white marble hallways lined with a luxuriant and fragrant jungle of green plants to a ballroom where a band played soft jazz and couples slow-danced.

"We were looking out for you." Brandy approached Jon and Ray with a grin. "Meet my boyfriend, Jackson." Jackson was a dark-skinned affable man with dreadlocks hanging to his shoulders. Jon liked him immediately.

"Cherice is over there," Brandy announced. Jon looked around to where she pointed. Cherice was dancing with a slim, extremely handsome man who looked vaguely familiar.

"Ray, there are tons of people dying to meet you." Brandy dragged Ray away.

Jon exchanged a few more pleasantries with Jackson, before making excuses to go and freshen his drink. What he wanted to do was to find Topaz. That was who he'd really come to see. She was as beautiful as he remembered her from high school. He'd had a crush on her for years, one of those all-encompassing, obsessive, adolescent crushes. Topaz was the hopelessly unobtainable girl of his dreams.

He'd dreamed of her, thought of her, and wanted her with white-hot intensity. Years had dulled the memories and other women had sated his yearnings. Jon thought that time had healed his desire. Then he saw her and it all came rushing back as real as yesterday. Everything and nothing had changed. He wanted her as much as he ever had.

The new fullness of her body only enticed him more. She'd always been a big girl, but now she was more womanly. She embodied femininity to him, curves upon curves, crevices and secret sweet womanly spaces.

But the best part of Topaz was what hadn't changed, what couldn't change: her generosity of spirit, her quick laugh and humor, her tenderness, the way she smiled up at his cousin, her eyes glowing with warmth and affection.

He would have cut off his right arm to be the recipient of that smile. She was smart and snappy, not sappy and dull. When he touched her hand, even after all these years he knew that Topaz was still everything he ever wanted in a woman.

And she still had eyes only for his cousin. Was fate destined to repeat itself? Maybe not. Maybe for once, she'd see him for the man he was. And maybe she'd see the woman that he saw in her. But where was she?

There was a riff from a horn and there she was with a microphone in front of the band. Topaz wore a short gold dress that clung to every full-bodied curve without a bit of self-consciousness or shame. Her hair flowed down her back in a wild riot. She was big, fabulous, sexy, and all woman. When she let it loose, shook, and shimmied, Jon had to lean against the wall and stick both hands in his pockets.

Topaz was enough to make a skinny woman break and order a steak and French fries with a side of Ben and Jerry's ice cream. *Lemme at that fat!*

Topaz lifted the mike and opened her mouth. Jon had bought every CD she recorded, but he'd never heard her sing in person. Her voice soared, and whispered, and cried, and hollered, and laughed within the moments of the song and took all of them on the wild ride with her.

Her talent was incredible, not raw, but polished,

perfected, and controlled. Topaz was a true artist, seasoned at her craft. He felt his eyes moisten. She was more than magic. She had power and range, but most of all, she had emotion.

Topaz. What a rare jewel. More than he realized. What would he do if he couldn't have her for his own? What could he possibly do?

Topaz finished the set with the familiar feeling of exhilaration and exhaustion she always had. She always put her all into singing whether it was for a small intimate gathering such as this one or a concert hall of thousands.

She walked off the makeshift stage. Cherice was waiting for her with a towel and a glass of ice water. Topaz took both gratefully. "Thanks girl, you knew just what I needed. Did Ray and his cousin show up?" She didn't know why it was important to her that Jon came too, it simply was.

"They both did. Right before you started singing."

"Good."

Topaz eased the high-heeled shoes off her feet. "I'm taking a quick shower. Occupy them. I'll be out in fifteen minutes."

The hot water ran over Topaz's body like a benediction. She tried to dredge up old feelings of passion for Ray, but couldn't. They'd been long forgotten, even before that fateful prom night. How long did she and Ray date? It must have been since ninth grade. She was head cheerleader and he was the star football player. They'd settled into a comfortable habit, sort of like old married folk.

Did she ever have one of those teenage crushes on him?

She didn't think so. She was the one who decided that it was time to lose her virginity and picked the traditional time to do it on prom night. She'd made all the arrangements. Sometimes it seemed that Ray had been in the whole relationship merely for the ride.

She made sure that she was protected and got the hotel room and the mandatory sexy lingerie. She had to strain to remember the act. The impact of the whole night was, unfortunately, *"Was that all?"* Well, at least it wasn't an unpleasant experience as she heard it could be. As far as she was concerned, it barely registered as an experience, period.

Speaking of experience, she was sure that Ray had plenty of it since then and he must be much better. She sure hoped so.

Topaz turned the water off. Ray must have had to improve a *great deal* because he was her One True Love and fireworks would explode, tides would roll in, and mountains would rumble, as so vividly described in that awesome novel she read last night. She was quite sure that would be the case.

Not one single firework had exploded yet. Not one. It didn't seem quite fair that she was still in the snap, crackle, and pop department. Ain't been no tides crashing in her life either; more like pond ripples. And mountains rumbling? Please. More like gas passing. She knew her Wish had to do her far better than that. It was way past time.

When Topaz entered the party, she first ran into Rosaline. "Have you seen Ray's cousin or Ray?" she asked.

"Jon was asking after you. I told him you usually like to shower after performing. He's over there.

That's a nice man, Topaz. Far brighter than Ray ever was."

"You interested, Ros?" Topaz asked, that strange jealousy cutting at her.

"No, he's not for me."

"What do you mean?"

"He's not my type. There's somebody else for me," Rosaline said, looking somewhat mysterious. "Speaking of Jon, here he comes."

"Hello, Topaz."

She felt shy in his presence. "It's good to see you here."

"You were great up there. I hadn't heard you sing in person before. I was awed."

Topaz looked into his eyes and saw that hint of storm. It disturbed her and she looked away toward the floor where couples were dancing to Smokey Robinson.

"Do you want to dance?" he asked.

"Sure," she said. Anything to keep from losing herself in his eyes again, she thought. But when he took her into his arms she realized what a big mistake she'd made.

His body was hard and firm. He smelled of sandalwood and leather and good clean soap. His arms held her firmly and just right, not too close or too far away. They swayed in time to the music, and she could imagine their hearts settling to beat as one.

Warmth started to rise between them and she felt an irresistible urge to raise her head and lift her lips toward his. If only . . .

"Dancing with my woman, cuz?" Ray's voice cut between them.

The spell was broken. Jon's arms dropped and he

melted away and Topaz felt bereft. Ray took her into his arms, too roughly. "Just like old times," he said, two-stepping out of beat to the music.

Topaz wanted to sigh. A memory had returned. Ray had always been out of step with the music. He never could slow-dance. "Just like old times, Ray," she said.

Topaz, Cherice, Brandy, and Rosaline sat on the stage with full plates of catered canapés, watching the dancers as the night grew late, the drinks flowed freely, and the party grew wilder.

"Gonna close down soon?" Brandy asked Cherice.

"Yes, it's about time before somebody breaks something and I get pissed off," Cherice replied around a chicken wing.

"Where's Jackson?" asked Rosaline.

"He went home and went to bed," answered Brandy. "He's got to get up early for a race in the morning."

"And look where Tyree has been for the past forty-five minutes," said Cherice, her eyes narrowed.

Tyree and Ray were whispering in each other's ears.

"Looks like they've hit it off," Rosaline said.

"They've hit it off a little too well," Cherice said.

"Feeling possessive about your man, Cherice?"

"Tyree isn't my man. It's something about those male models. I never did like a man to be prettier than me and know it. It's a turn-off."

"The man gets paid big bucks for people to take pictures of him," Rosaline reminded her.

"Have you seen that man in front of a mirror? He acts like he's posing for *Vogue* magazine twenty-four seven. It's sissy-looking."

"Really?"

"He puts more cream on his face at night than I do."

"Dang!"

"And he wears makeup."

"Are you kidding?"

"They call it special fixatives for men, but I looked at it and I call it by what it is. The stuff is makeup. He won't leave the house without it."

"Nooo!"

"Maybe Ray and he are exchanging eye-shadow tips," Cherice said.

Brandy tried to stifle a giggle. "Girl, stop it."

"Or how to put on the mascara without sticking the wand in your eye," Cherice added with a resentful sniff.

"You need to quit," Rosaline said, her tone serious.

"Where's Jon?" asked Topaz.

"He's over there," Rosaline said.

"What's he doing?" Cherice asked.

"Looks like he's watching us watch him," Rosaline said.

"Let's wave," Brandy suggested.

He waved back.

"He's so fine," Cherice mused.

Topaz jumped to the floor. "Party's over," she said. "Cherice, why don't you go and announce that everybody go home like you always do. Brandy, go over there and turn the lights on."

As the partygoers were moving out Cherice's door, Topaz headed over to Ray. It seemed as if the next move was going to be up to her. "I wondered if you'd like to come over for dinner at my place tomorrow," she asked him. "We didn't get a chance to talk very much today."

Ray looked down at her, bemused. "Your place? I didn't think you lived in KC any more than I do."

"I don't. But I keep a condo here because I visit frequently. This is my home and where my friends and family are."

"We've come a long way, haven't we, Topaz? We're both public figures now. We have public careers and public images."

"I suppose so."

Ray's eyes narrowed. "We can really help each other out; we've always been one of a kind, Tope."

Topaz winced. She hated it when he called her that.

He nodded as if he'd made a decision. "We shouldn't go to your place, what we should do is go out on the town. I'll pick you up at eight. What's the address? On second thought, give it to Jon." Ray gave her a quick nod of dismissal before he turned and walked after Tyree.

Chapter 3
Weather Alert

"What the hell?" Topaz muttered as she saw the long white limo pull up in front of her condo. She glanced at her watch. Eight o'clock on the dot. It had to be Ray. Why didn't he drive? What was with the ostentatious limo? It wasn't her style at all.

Topaz had decided to dress simply and elegantly with classic velvet black dress and pumps and her favorite diamond earring studs and necklace nestled in the cleavage of her generous breasts.

There was a honk, and Topaz sighed. She always hated that Ray never came to the door like a gentleman, but instead leaned on the horn. She didn't think that he was driving the limo, but he was certainly giving the instructions.

She carefully applied ruby red lipstick to her lips, then squared her shoulders, surveying the results, and wished with a touch of melancholia that she felt more . . . excited. What was wrong with her? She should feel grateful, blessed. That was the word, blessed. She was very blessed.

The horn blared again, and she closed her eyes, trying not to let the rush of irritation replace the gratitude she was nurturing. Topaz slipped on her black leather coat and picked up her bag. Then she hurried out the door.

The chauffeur opened the car door. Ray was lounging in the seat with what looked like a martini in his hand.

"It took you long enough," he said.

"You look nice too," Topaz answered.

Ray had the grace to look shamefaced. "You look great. Very classy."

"Thanks."

"Where are we going?"

"There's this restaurant called La Plata. My publicist says it's very trendy. Then we're headed to the Station for a little partying."

"Your publicist said? And I'm not really dressed for that sort of dancing."

"You look fine. We don't have to stay long. We just need to get in a few photo ops. The problem is that this is Kansas City. There really aren't that many places to be seen."

"I don't want to be seen, Ray. I wanted to spend an evening with you."

He patted her hand. "We will, we will. We're going to have a great time."

That night, Topaz dreamed about windswept plains, jagged lightning and stormy nights against a background of thunderous wonder somehow mixed up with endless deep brown eyes. The thunder rang out again and clashed with the sound of their hearts . . . The phone. She reached for it blindly, her heart pounding, her dream already fading into that forgetting place where dreams always go. She tried to stop it, but she couldn't and it felt as if she'd lost something precious.

Topaz said, "Hello," her voice hoarse with sleep.

"You and Ray really kicked your heels up last night and didn't waste any time letting the whole world know about it. Good going, girl. Nice pics."

She yawned. "It was Ray's doing. He had photographers waiting, the works."

"Looks like his publicist must have had the copy written too. Listen to this: 'Ray Gaines and his old high school flame, Topaz, ignite Kansas City. Will wedding bells ring?' How trite."

"Brandy, is that what she really wrote, wedding bells?"

"Yeah. Pretty sorry, huh?"

"I don't give a damn about her writing skills. I'm interested that she's predicting marriage for Ray and me. I was having doubts about the Wish. There just doesn't seem to be any chemistry between Ray and me, but maybe—maybe, I'm mistaken."

"Our wishes always come true. With Ray showing up like that, you have to admit that it's more than a coincidence. You did lose your virginity to him."

"There is that. Things like that have shown to have certain significance."

"It's got to be Ray. It has to be the Wish. We have to just go along with the flow. Leave our own will out of it," Brandy said.

Topaz had to agree. One of the first things they'd learned was that magic had rules like everything else. They knew to heed the obvious way, and realized quickly that what they thought they wanted wasn't exactly what they were supposed to get.

Topaz bit her lip. Sometimes you gotta have faith that everything was going to turn out all right. "Yes, Brandy, you're right. It has to be Ray," she said.

Topaz had barely hung up the phone from speaking to Brandy when it rang again. It was her publicist. "Why didn't you tell me that you and Ray Gaines are hooking up? I want to be the first to give my congrats. This is fabulous. You and that big, brawny, masculine, gorgeous football player look great together. And high school sweethearts to boot. Wonderful PR for you. Don't worry, I'm working it."

Topaz put the phone in the receiver with a sense of resignation after her publicist finally said good-bye. Apparently it served Ray's purposes that everybody from God on down knew that he and Topaz were now an official couple. But he had yet to kiss her cheek. It was a strange situation, and she didn't know quite what to make of it.

If she and Ray were going to be a couple, it served her own purposes that she and he come to some sort of a more physical understanding. Hopefully a satisfactory understanding. A *very* satisfactory one. She wanted some fireworks, dammit. She believed that that old clause was null and void long ago, but if there had to be some legal paperwork before she got some satisfaction, well, Ray would have to make a trek on down to city hall. But she doubted it. From what she'd heard, true love had been moving and shaking the earth for folks for decades without a shred of paper signed or a single "I do" muttered.

A week had passed and still Topaz hadn't managed to get Ray alone. She loved her friends, but they were starting to feel like an entourage. She didn't know quite what to make of Jon. They tried to stay in opposite corners of the room. It was best that way. She didn't dwell on why. It was best that way too.

They'd decided to meet at Beanie's for dinner. Jon had offered several times to cook for them, but nobody had the heart to take him up on it. Actually, they were afraid that they'd be expected to reciprocate. Topaz knew where the kitchen was, but she tried to avoid entering it much. She didn't even think Cherice thought about the kitchen as a functional room. Brandy knew how to operate the microwave and Rosaline knew how to pick up the phone and order out. Culinary arts were never high on their agendas.

Why should it be, when there were places like Beanie's, that served the best soul food in town—serious down-home, stick-to-your-ribs eating, served up with real professionalism?

There were no long waits, and woes betide you if you were more than ten minutes late for your reservation. Beanie didn't believe in CPT and cut no slack for colored people's time no matter what the excuse.

If you were late for your reservation, you didn't get a table, period. It didn't matter if you were Colin Powell in the flesh. If Bill Cosby was late he wouldn't get a table either, and Denzel's grin would get him nary a rib if he operated on the CPT principle.

Beanie got cussed out regularly and needed the employ of two burly security guards to enforce her no-nonsense stance. Nevertheless, her place was always full, no matter the time. Good food, good service, and getting in and getting fed without a ridiculous wait made Beanie's restaurant one of the best and most profitable in Kansas City.

Brandy, Rosaline, and Cherice were already there when Topaz entered the restaurant. "Sorry I'm late. There was an accident on Four thirty-five, and traffic was hellacious," she said.

"Where's Ray?" Rosaline asked.

Topaz shrugged. "I haven't heard. I thought he'd be here by now."

She settled down in her chair, poured herself a glass of iced tea from the pitcher, and helped herself to some of the delicious-looking appetizers arrayed on the table.

She smiled at her friends. True, she wanted to get Ray alone for practical purposes, but she loved this group of people. She'd been working all day on a particularly hard song, a tune that stuck in her mind, but somehow the right notes eluded her. The work was creation—taxing but pleasing—and it was nice to come at the end of the day and unwind with this group and a good meal.

"Rosaline, is that you? Long time, no see!" A very thin white woman streaked across the room. Rosaline embraced her.

"I'd never thought to see you in a soul food restaurant, Susie," Rosaline said. "Aren't you a die-hard vegetarian?"

Susie averted her eyes away from the feast of spare ribs, neck bones, and hot wings at the table and shuddered. "That I am. I let Leroy talk me into this." She gestured to the tall black man who had moved beside her. "This is my friend. He thought I should have some new experiences."

Rosaline peered at Leroy and her eyebrows disappeared into her hairline. "It appears that you are," she said. "Nice to meet you, Leroy. This is my sister, Topaz, and my friends Cherice and Brandy."

Leroy's eyes widened and he took in Topaz. "The singer?" he stammered. "I'm honored to meet you."

Topaz, used to the reaction, smiled easily and extended her hand. "I'm honored to meet you also, Leroy."

"Rosaline and I were thick as thieves in med school," Susie said.

"She was forever trying to get me on some wild diet," Rosaline said with a laugh.

"Remember when I made that bet and got you to run that marathon?"

"Crawl that marathon, you mean."

"You finished a marathon?" Brandy said to Rosaline, disbelief in her voice.

"I don't know if I would consider it exactly finishing."

"If you cross the finish line I think they consider that you finished," Susie said.

"You dragged me," Rosaline reminded her.

"I wouldn't exactly call it dragging," Susie said.

"If the bottoms of your feet aren't touching the ground, it's dragging," Rosaline clarified with a laugh.

"Nobody can argue that the Sinclair sisters are the running type. Not unless chased—and it's questionable then, 'cause I think they both might simply turn around and coldcock the SOB in preference to doing the sprinting thing," Brandy said.

Susie surveyed both Rosaline and Topaz. "Nope, I guess they aren't running types. I'm really into preventive health," she said with enthusiasm. "I'd love to work with you both. I know weight loss is hard, but with a little dedication—"

"Who said that anybody wanted to lose weight?" Topaz interjected.

"Well, for health reasons."

"I'm perfectly healthy. Are you? Notice that I asked first before I made my assumption," Topaz said pleasantly.

"Okay. Uh. Well, I'd better go," Susie said, looking down and her voice trailing off.

"Susie, it was good to see you," Rosaline said, darting a sharp glance at Topaz. "You keep in touch."

Susie and her boyfriend said their farewells and made a quick exit.

"There was no need to scare her off, Topaz. She was just trying to be nice," chastised Rosaline.

"She pissed me off. She has nerve to tell somebody with her scrawny, behind that they need to lose weight and that they're unhealthy. She doesn't know a thing about the state of my innards."

"You know that many of those white women are brainwashed from near-infancy," Rosaline said to Topaz. "You should have cut her some slack."

Brandy said, "You could have all been skinny if you wanted, but you never wanted to waste a Wish."

"Because we are fine enough already, quite healthy,

and also, we like to eat," Cherice said, picking up a rib and taking a delicate bite.

"Amen," Topaz said. "According to the laws of physics, supply and demand, yada, yada, yada, there is no such thing as being thin and eating what we like. We would be forced to eat boiled eggs, water-packed tuna, and cottage cheese. And for what? So I can look bony and underfed enough to fit into some homo-fashionisto's outfit whose ideal of beauty is based on a fifteen-year-old boy's body? Please."

"True enough. But Susie's certainly not interested in fashion. You saw how she dressed. Everybody in her family is thin, it's natural for her. Anyway, she's a vegetarian, not the chronic dieter type. She eats stuff like sprouted beans and soy milk," Rosaline said.

"Worse yet," Cherice said with a shudder.

"I think that stuff can be made somewhat edible—if you like to cook," Rosaline said. That sent a collective shudder through all the women.

Brandy sniffed. "Suddenly I'm feeling downright puny."

"You are nowhere near puny. You wear a size ten and have the dimensions of a real human woman, not an adolescent boy. Hollywood and Madison Avenue would pronounce you fat as a pig and have nothing to do with you," Rosaline said.

"Get over it, chile," Cherice reassured Brandy. "Go eat something."

The waitress picked that opportune time to bring their plates. "So what's going on with you and Ray? Have you managed to get him alone yet?" Rosaline asked Topaz.

"Getting alone with that man is harder than trying to sneak in a bite of a Twinkie at a Weight Watcher's meeting. There's always some event or party to go to. You all shadowing our footsteps doesn't help either," Topaz said.

"We try to leave you alone, but he's not helping. He seems to want people around him all the time," Rosaline said.

Topaz sighed. "Ray's always been like that. He's a people person, that's for sure. One of those types who never could be alone for an instant. I'm forced to turn to subterfuge."

"What do you have planned?" Rosaline asked.

"I'm going to sing at Jazz In Blue tonight. Ray thinks it's going to be a party, but it's going to be just us for once. And afterward . . ."

"Finally," Cherice drawled.

"Lawd, yes," Topaz said.

"It's about damned time," Brandy said as she laughed and high-fived Rosaline.

Chapter 4
Raindrop Kisses

Jazz In Blue was perfect for Topaz's purposes. It was a small, intimate supper club and she knew the owner from way back. He'd make sure Ray was seated with his favorite drink, a dry martini, at the table with the best view of the stage.

She had the evening all planned out. She'd sing her heart out to him, get him worked up, then they'd have a romantic candlelit dinner and retire to the hotel room she had reserved.

Somehow, tonight felt strangely reminiscent of prom night. She'd booked the hotel room and placed her sexy lingerie there, planned the romantic dinner and cuddly breakfast in bed the next morning, and taken care of all the details in between, from the flowers to the scented candles. She could only hope that Ray had a better grip on the physical events that happened between the sheets than he did so many years ago. Her mind skittered away from what she would do if he didn't. That would be impossible. Ray was no longer a boy, he was a man, and her Wish come true.

She'd spoken to Ray earlier about how important to her this date was and he'd assured her that he would be there on time. She smoothed her moist palms against her gown. She was wearing black silk tonight. There was something about silk that soothed her soul. Something about tonight felt special. It had to be a turning point. She'd been feeling serious doubts that Ray was the One, and it was causing her deep-seated worry, because doubting Ray felt like doubting her Wish, and that seemed fundamentally wrong. Maybe tonight would set everything straight.

She didn't have the song she was working on finished. She really wanted to have it ready for tonight. It was a song for her fairy-tale prince, a song about wishes coming true. For some reason, the exact melody was eluding her. But no matter, she had plenty of music to choose from.

For her first number Rufus and Chaka Khan's "Sweet Thing" seemed particularly appropriate. Topaz stepped out onstage. As usual, the lights blinded her, but as soon as she touched the microphone, she felt at home. This was one of the places on earth she truly belonged. Then the music started and Topaz's voice rose to meet it.

Jon stared at Topaz, a vision in black. She'd started out with familiar soul tunes, but now was crooning her own neo-soul ballads, love songs that made him want to satisfy every single desire she moaned into that microphone.

Unlike the glamorous sexy diva look she donned at the party, Topaz had transformed into a sultry siren. She steamed up the stage, and there was no way that Jon could believe that there was a man in that place who didn't desire her, at least momentarily.

He couldn't see how Ray could have stood her up. He didn't fathom the fool. Topaz replaced the microphone to thunderous applause. "One more song," cries echoed.

Topaz hesitated, and then picked up the microphone once more. The room hushed to a soulful rendition of "Over the Rainbow."

"Somewhere over the rainbow, skies are blue, and the dreams that you dare to dream, really do come true . . ."

And the way Topaz sang, the song wasn't as wistful as sometimes it could be. Her eyes twinkled and sparkled, and it seemed as if the other side of the rainbow was a place she often visited.

The waiter had placed a sumptuous feast in front of him while he was transfixed by her song. "I didn't intend to eat," Jon said.

"Ms. Sinclair ordered. She'll be joining you shortly. A martini, sir?"

"No, water is fine." He hoped that Topaz wouldn't

be too upset that he was sitting where she was expecting Ray to be sitting. Ray had just asked him to pass on a message, but when he complained to Jon about the effort that Topaz had gone to for this evening to ensure that he'd be present, Jon wanted to know what was it that was so important that he couldn't bother to show. "I have other plans, man," Ray had whined. "She didn't give me enough advance notice. Take care of this one for me, cuz, and I swear, I'll owe you a big one."

"You owe me more than one already," Jon muttered. But since it was Topaz—and more important, Topaz's feelings—he couldn't just let this go. He gave it one more try.

"Ray, you need to cancel whatever your appointment is. Topaz is supposed to be your lady, and this obviously is important to her. You should be there."

"Give it a rest. I said I didn't want to be bothered. If you don't want to help me out, I'll just call and leave a message." Ray started to pull out his cell phone.

"All right. I'll show up. But you're no damn good."

Ray grinned at Jon. "I knew you wouldn't let me down."

"Where's Ray?" Topaz asked, looking shocked at the sight of Jon.

Jon stood and pulled out the chair for her. She sank into it slowly. "He couldn't make it."

"But why? Why didn't he call me? He knew how important tonight was to me."

"He was busy. He asked me to come instead."

Topaz bit her lower lip and looked away. Jon longed

to punch Ray in the face at that moment. How could he hurt this woman?

"I know I'm a very poor substitute," he said. "But I'm willing, if you'll have me."

Topaz smiled at Jon, her eyes moist. "Of course. You're very kind to come. Could you excuse me for a moment?"

He nodded and stood while she left the table. Sometimes he hated claiming that ignoramus as a cousin. How could he risk messing up what he had with a woman such as this? Incomprehensible.

Jon kept the conversation light but interesting over a delicious dinner of prime rib. It was a skill cultivated over years of dating. He liked women a lot, and frequently dated. He'd had a few, a very few, long-term relationships, but in general he was leery of commitment. He was still waiting for the right one. Everyone said he was naive, but something within him still believed in magic, in soul mates, and in the sort of love that lasts forever.

Being with Topaz told him his wait hadn't been in vain. His cousin was not only inconsiderate, he was foolish. Jon had basic morals. He'd try not to make a move on his cousin's woman, but the fool was sending in a hungry shark into the mermaid's lair. It was going to take everything he had not to take a bite.

"Would you like to come in for coffee?" Topaz asked Jon at the front door to her condo. She enjoyed his company so much, she wasn't ready for the evening to end.

He seemed to hesitate.

"Please. I have some nice blends that I think you'll like." She smiled at him.

"All right." He smiled back at her and she felt a flutter in the vicinity of her stomach. It should be against the law for a man to be that handsome.

She opened the door and led him into her living room. She'd decorated it in white. She loved the cool expanse of white and indulged herself since she was a single woman with multiple homes and a cleaning service. She gestured toward a soft and supple white leather sofa. "Make yourself at home," she said. "I'll go and put on the coffee. How do you like it?"

"Max cream and sugar. I like all the good stuff."

Topaz was pouring the coffee grinds into the coffeemaker when she heard the tinkle of notes from her white baby grand. When she recognized Percy Sledge's "When a Man Loves a Woman," she felt her heart pound. She knew beat and meter and not a key was hit out of place or time. She imagined his long, sensitive, brown surgeon's fingers flying over the pearly white and ebony. The lyrics rolled along with the music in her mind: *'Cause baby, baby, baby, you're my world* . . . Would that be how it would be with Jon?

Topaz's hand had a slight tremor as she stirred in the cream and sugar. She didn't want the forbidden thought to cross her mind, but as unwanted thoughts often do, it lodged there anyway. *Because it sure wasn't that way with Ray.*

She set the coffee mugs on a tray and entered the living room. He was playing Sinatra's "Under My Skin."

"I didn't know you played," Topaz said.

"Years of forced practice." Jon stood and crossed the room to sit beside her.

"All the while we were in school together?"

"Yes." He took a sip of coffee. "This is good."

"Thanks. There's a lot I don't know about you, it seems," Topaz said.

"Maybe, but I'm not very mysterious. Years of schooling mainly, as Ray puts it."

Topaz frowned at Ray's name and set the cup down.

"I'm sorry, it was thoughtless for me to have brought his name up."

"No. It's not you. I'm thinking I've been a little foolish myself," Topaz said.

"In what way?"

"In a lot of ways. More coffee?"

"Please."

She took his cup and hers too and returned with mugs of freshly steaming brew.

"You like the old love songs too, I see."

"Yes, I do."

"They certainly don't make them like they used to," she said, going through her CDs.

"You're trying to."

"Yes, I can only try," she said.

Topaz turned over a CD in her hands. Should she? It was almost as close as a direct invitation to seduction as one could get. She tried the exact same CD on Ray and it was like trying to start a fire in the middle of a sodden swamp with soggy matches. But even though she might chalk it up to a too-fine, too-nice man and her hormones getting the best of her, she would. She opened the CD case and snapped out

the Smokey Robinson CD. *Turn the lights down low,
baby come close, let dreams come true for me and
you* . . . Smokey crooned.

Jon blinked once, but didn't miss a beat. He stood
and drew her to him for a slow dance, a slow, delicious dance.

Ah, that's how it should be, Topaz thought and
struggled not to go utterly boneless against Jon's hard,
masculine body, enveloped with the scent of sandalwood and clean soap that she remembered well. He
glided perfectly to the beat.

He pulled her closer against his body and inhaled
against her hair. His hips and thighs moved with the
music, causing her heart to race and pulse to pound
in an inner music of their own. His arms held her
tight and strong. She felt their hearts thudding
against their chests and the incremental pressure as
their bodies unconsciously strained together with the
fundamental need to merge. Her breath quickened
as she felt Jon's hand move her hair aside and his
lips touch her neck.

She buried her face against his throat, feeling his
rapid pulse echo her own. His lips were firm with
warm, hard sensuality.

Past all thought, she lifted her head and Jon's mouth
covered hers. His tongue traced the soft fullness of
her lips, and then explored the recesses of her mouth.
Intense and hungry kisses, all male, demanding
satisfaction.

Topaz's insides turned to liquid silk, pourable and
about to be spilled. When he pulled her against his
male hardness, liquid silk transformed to molten lava
demanding eruption.

At the point just before touch and sensation pass boundaries of no return, Jon lifted his head. "I can't," he said, his voice husky with desire. "He's my cousin, family. There are some lines you don't cross."

Topaz closed her eyes in what felt almost like pain. But she understood. She took one of the hardest steps in her recent memory and moved away from the circle of Jon's arms. "I understand."

She didn't really. Her body couldn't understand a damned thing but the need to have Jon in her bed, preferably inside her more intimate territory right this second. She almost fainted at the thought.

But having second thoughts before screwing your cousin's supposed girlfriend . . . she guessed it was reasonable. "You better leave," she said. "Quickly."

Jon nodded, a distant storm in his eyes. He turned and fled.

Chapter 5
Flash Flood

Topaz was on a plane with Ray on the way to Los Angeles. She was expected to show for this acting awards ceremony, and show she would, with Ray by her side. He'd managed to show up for this engagement, unlike their appointment last night. She felt herself flinch at the thought of last night.

She touched her lips. Her head was still spinning

from Jon's kiss yesterday. *What if?* Yes, what if? Dangerous thoughts, those. She refused to think about what might have been, only what was.

She glanced over at Ray, who was predictably swilling down martinis and snapping his fingers to blessedly inaudible music through his headphones. In much the same way as James Bond preferred his martinis shaken, not stirred, Ray's musical tastes seemed to lean to rap, screamed rather than sung.

It also seemed the more ugly and misogynistic the performers, the better Ray liked them. There was no individual rapper with any star power of that stripe. That type seemed to have to populate the stage in packs, all with their own microphones, to create their hellish cacophony to a sample and a beat. Different strokes, she supposed.

The pilot announced the landing of the plane and she snapped her seatbelt shut. It would be a long evening indeed with Ray by her side. One thing she needed to do, as soon as possible, was to get some things straight between them. This was getting ridiculous.

On the ground a few hours later, from the backseat of the limo, Topaz took a deep breath. She wasn't crazy about this part. The door was opened for her and she exited the car, Ray at her side. Fans erupted with cheers as she stepped onto the red carpet. It was a bigger cheer than last year. Her CD sales had been good.

Lo and behold there was Jean Livers and her daughter—Hollywood's formidable viper-tongued twin spokeswomen for anorexia—headed over her way. Topaz looked over her shoulder for bigger stars behind her—Michael Douglas or Tom Cruise's latest women maybe—but no, the Liverses were definitely headed toward her.

"Here's Topaz, and Ray Gaines on the carpet! We're hearing rumors of weddings. Care to give us the scoop, Topaz?" Jean thrust the microphone in her face.

Topaz said a few noncommittal words and perused Jean's face close-up. Topaz was fascinated and truly concerned that Livers's grin might crack something; her skin was pulled that hard, shiny, and tight.

"You are getting quite a name for wearing large-sized women's fashions with flair. I bet you have an entire silk harvest set aside for the wedding dress." The Liverses poked each other in the ribs and yukked it up at the lame joke.

"Are you done?" Topaz asked patiently.

"Of course dear, do you have anything to add? Maybe an extra factory of weavers, or a boatload of seamstresses or so?" Jean asked, obviously trying not to bust what she had for an excuse for a gut on that new quip.

"Not at all. I just wanted to know if you were done with your dry-as-a-bone-sorry-ass jokes so I could go ahead and go in and get me a drink and something to eat. But if I need a couple of toothpicks to clean my teeth afterward, I'll be back out, because I sure do know where to find those." She nodded pleasantly at the Liverses and headed toward the door. "C'mon, Ray."

The air was stale and smoky at the noisy after-party at the ritzy hotel. The air-conditioning filters might need changing or the vents cleaning, Topaz thought.

The awards ceremony had been as long and tedious as always. Ray predictably disappeared early into the party.

Topaz made her rounds, and then she got to thinking. Strange that Ray was spreading all these hints about the impending wedding but responded to no hints that it was past time that he make his move on her.

What was wrong with the man? It was past time that she found out, and now was as good a time as any. She found the concierge and whispered in his ear. Then she went hunting for Ray with a Seven and Seven in hand for the ordeal ahead.

There he was, stuck in some corner, as usual, with some cronies. "Ray, c'mere," Topaz called.

"What?"

"I advise you to do what I ask," Topaz said, her voice soft and dangerous.

Ray stared at her and came toward her. "What do you want?"

"I want you to come here. Follow me."

Topaz glided to a hotel room, and opened the door with the magnetic key the concierge had slipped her. She closed the door behind them and turned to confront Ray, first taking a sip of her drink.

"Don't you think it's as strange as hell that we've been dating for weeks and you've never kissed me?"

"Is this what you had me come all the way out here for? I'm leaving."

"Touch that doorknob and we are done. I mean it!" Topaz said. "You're not running away this time, buddy. I want to know what the hell is going on."

"What are you talking about?"

"You've never made a move on me and we've been

dating for weeks! What's the matter with you? You were sorry in bed as a teenager—I hope you've improved. That's not the problem, is it?"

Ray looked around. "Shush! Will you be quiet?"

"Not until you tell me what your deal is. So why haven't you even attempted to put some lovin'—?"

"Topaz, you're drunk."

"I'm not drunk. I'm only slightly tipsy. I never get drunk. But I am pissed. I asked a simple question, and what I want is a simple answer."

"Okaaaay." Ray pulled her to him.

Topaz raised an eyebrow and shrugged. "This could be a promising start." She squeezed her eyes shut. "I'm waiting."

"Topaz, what you want me to do is . . ."

"I'm waiting. Take me, you fool."

Ray sighed heavily. Then he bent his head and gingerly kissed her.

He lifted his head. Topaz hadn't moved a muscle from her original position.

"Are you satisfied now?" he asked.

"Uh . . . is that it?" she asked.

"Well, yeah."

"Well, I suppose that wasn't much of a test. I'll give you another chance." She squeezed her eyes shut again.

"What?"

"Hey, it took me three drinks to strengthen my resolve this much, so I'd say you'd best get to it before the buzz wears off."

"Topaz . . ."

She opened one eye. "All I can say is that I hope you improved a hell of a lot since high school."

"What?"

"Because you were one sorry soul in the sack, I cannot tell a lie."

"You're not inspiring me here."

Topaz opened both her eyes, sighed, and picked up her drink again. "I suppose not. Why are we supposed to coddle male egos like y'all are made of greased porcelain, but we females beat ourselves up for our relationship performance all the time. Makes no sense." Topaz frowned and looked at her watch. "Are you procrastinating, Ray?"

"What?"

"Never mind, because after that kiss, which managed to be both boring and slimy, I have no desire for you to touch me again anyway. That's a bad sign to have for a guy you've been dating almost a month, you think?"

"What?"

"And your unconcern and unresponsiveness show definite indifference, which add up to triple-digit deficits on your part. But the *hardest* thing for a lady to overlook is your lack thereof . . . At least in high school, I did note some wood sometimes, but now you might have a boiled noodle down there for all I know. All bad signs. I think we better call it quits now."

"What?"

"Is there an echo in here?" Topaz knocked on Ray's forehead. "Empty, as I suspected." She wheeled. Just as she was leaving she turned and called over her shoulder, "Close your mouth, Ray. You're not trying to catch flies."

"I want to talk to you about Topaz," Jon said to Ray.

"About what? That bitch is driving me crazy."

"What did you call her?" Jon's temper flared. He didn't like women referred to disrespectfully and hearing Topaz called that . . . Ray had best stay sitting down because if he stood up, he was going to hit the floor.

Dim knowledge seemed to dawn of Ray's impending danger. "I didn't mean nothin' by it, man," he said, not moving a muscle. "I've been stressed. It ain't working out between us."

"I can tell. So you won't mind if I see her?"

"Why not? You've been sniffing after her for years. Sure, go after her now that she actually has something to offer."

Jon lunged after him and grabbed him by the collar of his sweatshirt.

"Let me go, man. Damn, for a skinny guy, you're strong," Ray whined.

"Topaz always had something to offer your silly, sorry ass and don't you forget it."

"Chill, cuz, I said I didn't care if you saw the woman. For a doctor you sure can get fired up."

Jon tightened his grip. Ray coughed, and fear crossed his face momentarily.

"Don't ever let me hear you speaking disrespectfully of her. It wouldn't be healthy for you," Jon said. He released Ray and brushed his hands off on the front of his jeans, turned, and walked toward his car. Ray stared down the street at him with something like admiration in his gaze.

Chapter 6
Cataclysm

Cherice was helping Topaz finish packing for another flight to Los Angeles. Tonight was yet another awards ceremony, but much more significant to her than the previous one she attended with Ray. It was for one of the biggest annual awards given in the music industry, and one in which Topaz was actually nominated for a major award.

"You should have wished to win this one," Cherice said.

"Honey, if you have to wish to get an award, it doesn't count," Topaz said.

"I suppose you have a point," Cherice said, "but think, what if you win? You get to glide up to the podium all dressed up with all those television cameras pointed toward you. Then you can oh-so-graciously accept the award. And you get to give a speech!" Cherice paused, considering. "Where's your acceptance speech? How many times do you thank me?"

Topaz grinned at Cherice. "Just once. Don't think this is all that much fun. I've done it before remember? I didn't win, but I remember the most predominant feeling when my name was read was worrying that I was going to heave, and trying not to show it."

Topaz looked at her watch and frowned. "We better get going. Missing this flight is not an option."

"Where is everybody?" Cherice asked.

"Rosaline and Brandy are catching the later flight where I booked seats for everybody."

At that moment Brandy burst into Topaz's condo waving a newspaper. "Is it true?"

"Is what true?" Topaz said.

"Is it true that Ray dumped you?"

Topaz lifted an arched eyebrow. "Ray dumped me?"

"That's what I hear. The *Enquirer* interview said that he had enough of your prima donna ways and tantrums."

"Let me read it."

Topaz perused the gossip rag. "That dirty dog," she said. She folded it and laid it on the coffee table where Cherice retrieved it and read the article avidly.

"You do know how to throw an excellent fit, but you never spread them around among the undeserving. You also don't have a prima donna bone in your body. More like down-home. You're a country girl at heart. Maybe a little ghetto around the edges," Cherice commented.

"Thanks for your vote of confidence and your reassurance that I'm still maintaining that ever-so-important ghetto factor," Topaz said, her tone dry.

"You're welcome, sweetheart. Anytime," Cherice murmured absentmindedly, still reading.

"I really didn't want to talk about it, but I called it quits with Ray. There was simply no heat there, no passion."

Cherice glanced up from the magazine. "Somehow I'm not in the least bit surprised," she said.

Brandy looked stricken. "I know you have to get to the airport. But I'm so sorry, Topaz. Ray was your

Wish. This is just a bump in the road or something like that. Everything will have to work out. I'll see you onstage tonight, and we can talk later. I'm wishing you all the luck in the world." Brandy brushed a kiss on Topaz's cheek and rushed out the door.

Seated at the awards ceremony, Jon loosened the tie at the neck of his tuxedo. This was a new experience for him. He glanced around at all the people that he'd seen only on television or in photographs before. They looked so ordinary, and many seemed as uncomfortable in formal togs as he did.

The evening seemed interminable. He was too far away from Topaz. She had her agent and her sister next to her in the front, near the stage with the other music award nominees. Jon glanced at his watch. He had a little more time to bide.

Ray and Topaz were through. Jon almost smiled at the thought. Rumors were flying about how Ray dumped Topaz. Jon didn't believe them for a minute because she gave Ray entrée to places like this. Ray was a football player and a good one, but he wasn't on Hollywood's B list, as Topaz modestly put herself. That's the only reason that Jon could think that Ray would be using Topaz. Because it was evident that his cousin didn't want her for the obvious and usual reasons a man wants a woman.

Finally, the words rang out from the stage: "... *and the winner is . . . Topaz Sinclair for 'What a Woman Really Wants.'* "

Topaz made her way to the stage. She wore a simple shimmering silk topaz dress that clung to her ample curves. It had long sleeves with a deep V in the front and back and a mid-thigh length slit, modest by Hollywood standards, and was set off by baroque jewels of her namesake stones set in gold.

Jon's heart swelled with pride as her song came up and she accepted the award, thanking first God who makes all things possible and all wishes come true.

Then a short time later came her performance, and she started singing "What a Woman Really Wants." The tune swelled and crested and gently turned into something else, something new, something wonderful . . . "When Wishes Come True." Topaz sang about what all little girls dream about and women sigh over and old women yearn for, remember, or regret. She sang an enchantment of fairy-tale princes, raindrop kisses, magical love, and happily never-ending. She sang of excitement, fireworks, and storm and the drama that made life worth living.

Jon knew that Topaz had another hit on her hands, this one probably even bigger than "What a Woman Really Wants." And from the applause and ovation the crowd gave her, they knew it too.

Afterward, there was the party, the photo ops, the interviews.

Then a moment came when the crowd faded away. Topaz and Jon stood alone as if by magic. "Let's get out of here," she said.

They rushed outside. There was a light Los Angeles rain, full of night breezes and fragrant with desert flowers. The drops glistened in Topaz's hair like diamonds. He wanted to kiss each one off her, drink it like nectar.

"Did you make plans?" he asked.

"None whatsoever," she said.

"Sometimes that's the best way," he answered. He hailed a taxi and helped her inside.

"Where to?" the driver asked.

"A villa on the beach," Topaz whispered in his ear.

Jon gave the taxi driver the name of one of the ritziest hotels in Beverly Hills. "They have those, except I believe they call them bungalows. And if they're full, for an award winner, the concierge will surely find us someplace else suitable."

The hotel didn't have a bungalow available, but they had the most wonderful room, which Topaz and Jon couldn't resist.

Half an hour later he laid her softly across the bed. "Happy?" he asked.

"Very," she answered.

And he did what he'd been aching to do, and touched his lips against her hair. He inhaled a sweet aroma, honeysuckle and sweet peas, waving grasses and meadow flowers. Topaz wasn't a desert flower, but a Kansas one, well-nourished and healthy, used to thriving in rich black soil.

His lips trailed across her burnished temples to settle home on velvet lips. Her soft sigh at his kiss unleashed his passion like a dammed torrent.

His tongue invaded the depths of her mouth, learned her, tasted her, knew her, and learned her again. Her body writhed under him, stiffening him.

Jon raised his head. He looked into her eyes, gauging her need. He raised his hand and unfastened her dress. It slid off and her brown skin gleamed through gold silk lingerie.

He groaned at her beauty. He trailed kisses down her neck and traced his tongue damply through fabric to the areola of her nipple, one then the other, back and forth, teasing them into stiff peaks.

Topaz arched her back, reaching for him, making incoherent sounds.

"We've got all night, baby," he whispered.

He pulled away from her and took off his tie and dropped his jacket to the floor, then his shirt.

She reached for his cummerbund with greedy fingers. She eased his pants and briefs over his hips, her eyes widening when she saw his package. She blinked rapidly like a kid faced with more candy than she could eat at once.

He rolled over to the side of the bed, got a condom from his pants pocket, and rolled it into place. Then he took Topaz's hand and guided it to the topic of discussion.

She licked her lips. Jon, unable to resist, followed the pathways of her tongue with his against her lips. His hand touched the soft V of tangled curls under the silk and traveled down to the dampness between her legs. He parted the wet silk with his fingers and slipped it into the depths of her well to wet it more. He spread the slick fabric between her secret crevices around her stiff nub and spread it over and around in a ceaseless unchanging rhythm.

He felt her flutter and pulse under his fingers, climbing, tensing, with every muscle taut and craving release. She moaned and whimpered, her hips writhing. Not yet.

He withdrew his fingers and pulled the wet silk down over her hips, fitting his rock hardness to her. She bucked and pushed, trying to force him in.

"You want me?" he asked, needing to hear it. He rubbed the swollen head of his penis against her wet clit.

"I want you," she whispered.

He pushed himself home, slowly, holding his breath, holding control. She was tight, so tight. Warm and wet. Sweet like honey. He closed his eyes with the ecstasy of it.

She was working her hips against him, bucking and pushing. Delicious friction, pushing him over the edge of control. He took a breath. Control. He withdrew to her very edge and almost out completely. She gasped in protest.

"I need it all, now, ohhhh . . ."

He wanted to see her lose it, give it all up to him. Now.

He gave it to her controlled, pushing and driving, grinding, in and out.

"You like it like that, baby?"

She was past speech. But she liked it like that, he could feel it building within her, like a storm, and again and again and . . . she . . . exploded. With the power of her contractions and the sounds of her pleasure he lost all control. A force beyond reckoning took him to that place where nothing but sensation ruled.

"We better go home," Jon said.

"I never want to leave," Topaz answered.

"Neither do I. That's why I said we better go now before they put out APB's on us. If we stay any longer, it's going to be too difficult to go."

Topaz sighed. "You're a smart man, Jonathan Bynum."

"I hope I didn't take out all those school loans for nothing," he said.

"How long have we been here?"

"All night, the next morning, working the next afternoon."

"My goodness, that long?"

"That long."

"We haven't slept."

"No, we haven't," Jon replied.

An hour later, they snuggled in the back of a taxi.

"LAX," Jon told the driver.

The plane ride to KCI was three hours of excruciatingly sweet foreplay. Topaz never knew that a look, a caress, could move her as much as the most intimate act.

Exhausted, they shed their clothes on the way to bed and fell asleep curled in each other's arms like kittens.

Early afternoon sun peered through Topaz's sheer curtains. She stretched and opened her eyes to the masculine glory of Jon's nude form. He was on his side hugging her pillow. If she had paint and canvas, she would have wanted to paint him. There was no way he was breaking and running this morning. Screw Ray. Or as was the case, not.

She headed for the shower.

She'd rinsed her hair when she felt the shower door open and knew Jon had joined her.

She felt him move her hair to the side and she closed her eyes in pleasure. "How did you sleep?" he murmured in her ear.

"Fabulously."

"So did I."

"Let me do that." He took the soap and washcloth from her nerveless fingers and washed her.

She did the same to him, slowly learning the crevices of his body.

They bathed in silence, the slippery soap over silken skin, and warm water showers a meditation, a tantric exercise in control. Their breathing quickened; arousal held at abeyance.

And then Jon took her in his arms under the spray and tasted her lips. His hardness pressed into her stomach, and they both were trembling with need. They left the shower and dried off with her large white bath sheets. Jon laid her on the bed and unwrapped the towel from her hair.

He kissed her lips and worked down her neck to her breasts.

"Be right back, baby, stay right there on simmer. Don't move, all right?"

Topaz nodded. Jon grinned at her and padded out of the room. Then she heard the strains of Smokey and laughed. Apparently that CD had really gotten him going.

He traced her lip with a finger. "Ready?"

"Never readier."

"Have you ever tried a horizontal slow dance?"

"I've never heard of such a thing."

"Listen." He kissed the valley in between her breasts and slowly circled one nipple then another to the sensuous beat of Smokey.

"Jon?"

"Shhhhh, listen."

He kissed her down the lines of her body and when he reached south of her navel she curled her fingers in his hair. "Jon," she whispered.

But his lips and tongue never stopped their ceaseless beat.

It was a series of tremors, like those firecrackers that go off all at once in a packet. Soon she was making mindless noises in her throat while her fingers clutched the sheets and her head lashed back and forth on the bed. "I want . . ."

Jon eased up the length of her body. "What do you want, baby?"

"You, I want you. Oh, lordy, please."

He fastened his mouth on hers, hard, and eased his knees in between her thighs.

"Your wish is my command," he said as he slid home. He filled her up all the way, pleasure peaking into urgent mindless need.

She'd needed it bad. No matter how much he satisfied her, she wanted him more. She didn't think she'd ever have enough of him. Topaz heard an incoherent voice moaning and knew it must be hers. She'd lost control of her body and it bucked wildly around his male hardness. It was as if a cliff moved toward her, faster and faster and she had to jump or she would die. She felt Jon surrender to that same precipice as he drove into her again and again, sweaty, slick and wet and hard, grinding together, until she fell all at once, slamming into what was surely an earthquake.

Tidal waves crashed over her body, quivering, and crashed again and again. She felt Jon stiffen and call her name and sparkling fireworks exploded behind her eyes.

Moments later, Topaz exhaled in slow satisfaction. Now *that* was how lovin' was supposed to be.

Chapter 7
Tornado Warning

The day after the awards show when they had all flown back to Kansas City, Brandy filled Rosaline in on Topaz's trials and tribulations with Ray.

"Oh, no!" Rosaline cried, her hand touching her lips.

"And that's not the worst of it," Brandy said. "The way she tore out of L.A. last night . . . Ray didn't show—you know she had to be absolutely heartbroken. And she hasn't answered any of our calls."

"We have to do something. It was her Wish. Sometimes the road is a little rocky and—isn't that Ray?" Rosaline asked, pointing.

Brandy stopped, turned, and stared. "Nah, it couldn't be. He has his hand on that man's tushie." Then she looked again, her eyes narrowed. "I think it is Ray. Most of those men in front of that place have their hands on each other's tushies. I think it's that sort of place, if you know what I mean."

A frown appeared on Rosaline's lovely brow. "It's probably an athletic club. Those football players are always patting each other's tushies on television. They do that." Her frown grew deeper. "I'm tired of Ray dangling Topaz on the hook like this. He's her Wish and it's time it came true. I'm going to put a stop to this right now!"

Brandy looked at her, alarmed. "What are you going to do?"

"Some men need a little push, you know. I wouldn't call it an ultimatum or anything, but more like some incentive to commit. Ray has been a bachelor for a long time."

"Um, Ros, maybe there are good reasons that Ray . . ." Brandy said, her voice trailing as she looked over her shoulder in consternation at Ray, now with his arm around the man's waist.

"Oh, yes, there's more than enough good reasons. There's all that money he has and all those adorable women throwing themselves at him. Well, a man has to grow up and settle down sometime. I'm just going to help him out a bit."

"Oh, Ray got into a taxi with that guy. I suppose it's too late," Brandy said, relief evident in her voice.

"We need to make a call on Ray. Topaz made her Wish and it simply has to come true. What if there was a reason we saw Ray standing there squeezing that man's tushie and we failed to help? We have to make Ray understand the need for him to have Topaz in his life."

Brandy shook her head and sighed.

"Don't you dare touch my Honey Crème Whip. I order that special. You can use that cream over there."

Tyree pouted and gave a longing look at the cream, but withdrew his hand and reached for the other jar instead. "Honey Crème Whip, that name fits you so well. Can I call you that from now on?" Tyree asked.

"Hell, no," Cherice said.

"Why do you let me hang around, Ma Cherie? It

hurts my feelings terribly that you no longer fancy me." Tyree batted his long lashes at her.

"What can I do to get you to call me by my correct name?" Cherice muttered. "I keep you around because you're turning out to be a very good salon manager. I don't fancy you because you're flaming, darlin', and frankly that trait turns me off. Also I want to keep an eye on you."

"Just because I like men doesn't mean that I can't like you too," Tyree purred.

"Please. We got too much in common. And even I can figure out that I like to chow down on beefcake too much to have a concurrent overwhelming craving to lap up some sushi."

Tyree crowed with laughter. "I assume you're also keeping an eye on me in case I drop some gossip about our mutual acquaintance, the hunky football player, Ray Gaines?"

"You assume correctly, dearie."

Tyree settled back on the chaise longue with a grin. "I'm happy there's at least one girlfriend with a brain cell to figure it out."

"We all have plenty brain cells. But I work in a beauty salon and I'm accustomed to sissy types. Believe me, it's not brain cells it takes to figure y'all out. More like a certain lack of innocence, if you know what I mean."

"It didn't take you long to figure it out."

"I can't deny that."

"But you're making a futile effort, my little Honey Crème Whip," Tyree said.

"I told you not to call me that. Why do you say I'm making a futile effort?"

"Ray Gaines is nothing but a slut."

"Say what?" Cherice's eyes narrowed and she drew in a breath, resolute.

"Listen, I have something that I need you to do for me whether you like it or not," Cherice said in measured tones. "We are going to Topaz's house and I need you to tell her what you know about Ray."

Tyree pulled back. "I'm not in the mess," he said.

"Ouch!" Tyree squeaked. "Why did you pinch me? Bitch! Why don't you tell her?"

"I can't tell her because I'm her best friend, and best friends don't get into their friend's business like that. It always backfires. You gotta let your friends figure it out on their own. But this is getting pitiful." Cherice sighed. "I can't tell Topaz that the man she's pinned all her hopes and dreams on is a sorry, lying slut. But you can."

Ray's hotel room was dark when they arrived, but two trays were outside. Rosaline's mind was made up so they knocked loudly on his door. "Yes?" said Ray's muffled voice. "Can I help you?"

"Please open the door, Ray," Rosaline answered. "It's important."

"Can you come back later? I'm a little busy now."

"No, I can't. This is urgent."

There was a hesitation. "Okay, one moment."

They heard rustlings and in a few minutes the door opened, and Ray poked his head out. "What's going on?" he asked with a frown once he saw the two of them.

"Can we come in?" Rosaline asked.

"Well . . ." Ray hesitated.

Rosaline pushed her way past him and clicked on

the light. Ray had a robe wrapped around him and surprisingly skinny legs for such a big man.

She saw she needed to get to the point, so she wasted no time going there. "Brandy and I saw you on the street with that man earlier."

Ray's eyes widened and a look of panic came over his face.

"We think that we were meant to see what we saw. At first it looked like you were a sissy. I'm sure you could understand how it could be taken like that." She paused.

A sound that could be mistaken for a wheeze came from Ray's throat.

When it was evident that he wasn't going to say anything intelligible, Rosaline continued. "But we got to thinking about the situation with Topaz and how fate was working things out. It's time for you to step up to the plate, Ray."

"Step up to the plate," he echoed faintly

"Take hold of the reins," Rosaline said.

"The reins?"

"Yes. Take command of the situation. Topaz is waiting on you."

"On me?"

"This has been dragging out way too long. Let's get this over with. We'll make it easy. Show up at Topaz's place tonight at eight o'clock sharp. We'll make sure she'll be there." Rosaline sighed with satisfaction. "You need to say it with extreme humility and tenderness, not to mention romance and passion in the best true-love tradition."

"What?"

Rosaline's eyes and demeanor hardened. "Be there at eight sharp or you will regret it. Do you understand me?" Ray looked over his shoulder toward the bedroom door and nodded.

Rosaline stood. She pointed upward. "More than the fates of two people are riding on this. It's destiny and magic." Her voice lowered to a whisper. "It's the Wish."

She crossed the room to the door. Ray stared up to the ceiling where she'd pointed, in bafflement.

"Oh, and Ray," she said.

"What?"

"It's best to keep your hands off other men's tushies. It looks funny."

Chapter 8
Duck and Cover

"Have you ever wished that a day would never end, that it could simply stretch out to infinity?" Topaz said.

Jon pushed a stray lock of hair from her cheek, and a hot ache grew in her heart from the tenderness of his touch and the pure love shining from his gaze. The storm clouds were gone, transformed into sunny skies and flowering meadows flecked with fairy dust.

"As long as I'm able to spend all of it with you," Jon said. "And all of the tomorrows after today."

Tears sprang to Topaz's eyes. "I wasted so much time. You were always there, and I was so blind."

"Deluded, maybe, crazy, possibly; but blind? I doubt it."

Topaz shook her head. "Here I was thinking you were going all out for the full fairy-tale prince romantic love scene, but you had to go and ruin it by a smart-ass remark! You almost had me in tears for a moment there."

He gave her a wicked, boyish grin. "Sorry, I couldn't resist. I can only sustain the romantic maudlin momentum for so long."

Topaz laughed. "That's okay. What's important is that you can sustain the more fundamental elements to our lovemaking long enough."

"I have no problem there. I can do both. And to prove it, I vote we engage in hot and horny, raunchy sex again."

"I wonder as the years march by, if romance tends to last longer than the raunchy sex?"

"I hope not! At least until we hit our nineties. Maybe not even then. Who knows what they'll have invented? Hot and raunchy sex is a top priority in political circles, I hear."

"I heard that they approved Viagra in Japan before they approved birth control pills."

"See, I told you."

"How did our topic of conversation move from fairy-tale romance to Viagra?" Topaz asked.

"It was a natural progression, sweetheart," Jon said, tenderly stroking her hair.

The doorbell rang.

"Do you think we should answer the door?" Topaz asked.

"It's been two days. We could get dressed."

"I suppose we could."

Topaz sighed, reluctant to let the world intrude on

what she was beginning to think of as the cocoon that enshrouded her and Jon.

The doorbell rang again, insistent. "Hold up," she called and pulled on a white robe.

She got a scarf to tie back her loose hair. "Who is it?" she called.

"Your long-lost homies."

Topaz grinned. She should have figured that her girls would be frantic about her disappearing for so long.

She pulled open the door, and to her surprise, not only did Rosaline, Brandy, and Cherice tumble through, but they also had Ray and Tyree in tow. Topaz frowned. This was certainly not the time.

"Ray," she started to say, fully intending to ask him to leave.

"Ray has something very serious to ask you," Rosaline said, turning to glower at Ray.

Topaz's hand crept up to her throat as Ray awkwardly took her other hand. She saw Rosaline surreptitiously kick him.

"Topaz, I want to talk to you about our relationship . . ." Ray intoned.

"Time out," Cherice cried. "Rosaline, I saw you kick him. Did you put him up to this?"

Rosaline shuffled her feet. "I prompted him gently," she finally said.

"You'd have to do more than *gently* prompt him," Tyree said with a laugh.

Tyree sobered when Cherice cleared her throat loudly. "Topaz, there's something you need to know . . ." Tyree's voice trailed away as everyone turned to look at him. He tried again. "I want to tell you—" Tyree finally threw his hands in the air and said to Ray, "Why did you play Topaz like you did? She never did anything to you. You shouldn't lie about who you are, man. It'll catch up with you. Believe me, I know."

"What's all this about, Ray?" Topaz asked.

"This fag doesn't know what he's talking about," Ray said, sneering.

Tyree stared at Ray and shook his head.

There was a click in Topaz's mind as all the pieces slid into place. Of course. Why didn't she guess before?

She rounded on Ray. "So your cowardly behind was just using me."

At that moment Jon walked out of the bedroom, pulling on a shirt, obviously fresh from the shower. He moved beside Topaz, taking in the scene. "Fill me in," he murmured to Topaz.

"Apparently your cousin is gay and was using me merely to stay in the closet."

Jon's eyes widened. "Ray, is this true?" he asked.

Ray's gaze darted around as if looking for an escape, and then he sighed. "Yeah, I'm gay."

"Always been?"

"I guess so."

Jon merely looked exasperated as he ran his hand over his hair. "Why didn't you say something, for heaven's sake? Nobody would have tripped as much over the fact that you're gay as you seem to be tripping."

"It's not the family, it's my public."

Jon rolled his eyes.

"I gotta go."

"Please, do," Jon said.

Ray turned and left. Jon looked after him and shook his head. "That man needs help," he muttered. "It's pathetic when somebody goes to such lengths to hide from himself."

"Amen!" Tyree said. "Well thank goodness that's over."

Cherice leaned over and smelled his breath. "You smell like a distillery. You haven't been drinking, have you? You know you can't hold liquor."

"Drinking I have been. You want me to come over and break hearts free of charge; I need fortification, all right? I took a taxi. You have to drive me home," Tyree said. Then he pulled a card out of his pocket and handed it to Jon with a puppy-dog smile. "You can call me anytime, day or night."

Jon's upper lip curled in distaste as he handed the card back. "I won't need this," he said.

"Keep it," Tyree said. "You never know. They say your new girlfriend's snatch is 'Hazardous to a man's sexual orientation.' See what it did to Ray."

Topaz felt all the blood drain from her face, fall down to the pit of her stomach and roar back up to her ears. She still had a core of basic sexual insecurity, down deep. The past month had simply been too much. She'd dealt with an old flame and a new attraction. She'd revisited failure from the past, and started an incredible relationship with the usual accompanying fears. She'd released years of pent-up sexual frustration, followed by what she saw as direct sexual humiliation in front of her new love.

Tyree's words brought up her worst fear—that something was wrong with her, that it was her fault that she couldn't make it work with Ray, that she hadn't made it work since with another man and that she wouldn't make it work with Jon. Tyree's comment was the drop that sent her cup flowing over.

"Get out of my house, every single last man of you, out, out, out of my house! Now! Move. If I see one man in my house in one second I swear I'm going to get my butcher knife and start bobbitting!" Topaz yelled before storming into her bedroom, slamming the door behind her, and locking it.

"Don't worry about me," Tyree said while moving rapidly toward the front door. "I'll have them call me a taxi from the bar across the street."

"Maybe you should leave," Rosaline said to Jon.

He ignored her statement. "I'm begging you to tell me. Why did you want Ray to be with Topaz?" he asked.

"It was the Wish," Rosaline said.

Jon raised an eyebrow.

"Topaz wished for her true love on her birthday," Rosaline continued. "Ray showed up right afterward, so we knew it had to be him fulfilling her Wish. We were all helping."

Jon stared at Rosaline blankly.

"Is that it?" he finally asked.

"Well, yes."

"So you are telling me that in addition to my cousin being gay, you all are crazy?"

"Hey, we aren't crazy. We simply believe in birthday wishes coming true," Cherice said.

"They always have and always will," Brandy added.

"Oh," Jon said.

"Listen, I know Topaz," Rosaline said. "This has been a lot for her. She needs some time to cool down and some space."

"She doesn't need space. I know what she needs; she needs me," Jon said.

"I'm not denying that she needs you; I'm just giving you a lesson in Topaz 101. When she's upset, back off a little. And when she says something, she generally means it."

Jon frowned, walked around Rosaline, and knocked on the door to Topaz's room. "Topaz, let me in right now. We need to talk."

"What we need to talk about is what letters of the words 'Get Out' do you not comprehend?"

"Open the door, please," Jon asked, his voice growing stern.

The door swung open, and Topaz emerged in her white robe looking like a plump, angry angel. "This is my home, and I made two requests for you to leave the premises. The third I'll make to the proper authorities. Just because you—"

"Topaz—" Rosaline raised a hand and touched her sister's lips. "Don't say something in the heat of your emotions that you'll long regret. You have a tendency to do that."

Rosaline turned to Jon.

"Okay, I'm leaving," he said, sounding disgusted. He stopped at the door and looked back at Topaz. "I don't like it that you won't talk to me."

Topaz held up a hand. "Give me some time, dammit."

Jon sighed and shut the door behind him.

Chapter 9
Blown Clear to Oz

Topaz sank down on her sofa and cradled her head in her hands. "Can you believe I mentioned something this morning about this awful day lasting forever?" she said to no one in particular.

Cherice, Brandy, and Rosaline sank down on the sofa beside her. "We're sorry," Rosaline finally said. "We were only trying to help."

Cherice shook her head, looking miserable. "I never should have asked Tyree to tell you about Ray. I got sick of biding my time. I knew the rule, I should have stuck to it!" she almost wailed.

"What rule?" Brandy asked.

"The one where you never tell your friend directly that her man is cheating on her or that he's gay."

"I didn't know that was a rule. I'd want someone to tell me," Brandy said.

"No, you wouldn't. It always backfires on the person who tells. The friend ends up hating her."

"I think at some level the person knows already, and by telling, you're not necessarily enlightening her, just forcing her to acknowledge and deal with it," Rosaline said.

Cherice nodded. "That sounds about right."

Topaz cleared her throat loudly. "I hate to interrupt your philosophical discussion, but weren't you supposed to be comforting me with comfort I didn't need until you decided to come over and bust my idyllic fairy-tale ending all to hell?"

"See what I mean?" Rosaline said, indicating Topaz.

Cherice nodded sagely. "Ray was gay before we told you about it, Topaz," she reminded her friend.

"I don't think Ray is the problem," Brandy said. "She's got Jon now. I always thought he knocked Ray out of the running as far as fine-looking men go anyway. Damn, he looks good." Brandy fell back on the couch, fanning herself.

"Collect yourself, girl," Cherice said. "It does look like a mistake has been made, and Jon is the Wished One, not Ray. So why are you sitting there looking like the dry cleaner's ruined your favorite dress, Topaz? This is a good thing. At least Jon isn't gay."

Rosaline brightened. "True. And I always thought he was so much better than Ray all along."

"If I can't hold on to him, what does it matter?" asked Topaz, her voice rising to a wail gracefully and dramatically as only a singer's voice could.

"Can't hold on to him? Are you tripping, chile? That man's nose is wide open for you," Cherice said.

"She's right," Brandy added. "You're one hell of a woman."

"What's gotten into you? Was it what Tyree said? You're not seriously worried that you made him gay?" Rosaline said.

Topaz snorted. "Not hardly. But my track record with men is awful. I'm wondering . . . If all goes like it usually does, the relationship with Jon will end up disappointing me from week two and going downhill from there. I don't know how I'll stand that."

"Oh, honey, those weren't the men for you. Jon is

the right one for you. Anybody can see that. You don't have a thing to worry about," Rosaline said.

"And if all else fails, there's always the Wishes," Brandy said.

"By the way, I told Jon about the Wishes," Rosaline said.

"What did he say?" Topaz asked.

"He thought we were crazy."

Topaz shrugged. "Figures."

"It does sound crazy, honey," Cherice said.

"I have to agree," Rosaline added. "C'mon, a Wish coming true every year for each of us? Notice when it all started—right after our mother was killed when Topaz and I were kids."

They all grew silent at the memory. It was a time only Topaz or Rosaline was allowed to bring up. Losing a mother at such a young age was still a raw and painful memory.

"Maybe it's not Wishes that are making our dreams come true. Maybe it's us, and only us," Rosaline said.

"How could that possibly be? Look at us! Look at all we have and all we turned out to be," Cherice said.

"Exactly," Rosaline said. "Look at us."

"But we need the Wishes," Brandy said.

"Maybe we don't need Wishes. Maybe the seeds to everything our hearts desire are right here." Rosaline spread her arms and hugged them—all her sisters, in so many ways.

Jon couldn't remember enduring a longer twenty-four hours. But she'd asked for time, and her sister let him know clearly that Topaz was a woman who needed space when upset. He expected folks to respect his space, even if they didn't always fully understand his need for it at the time. So he had to do the same.

It was a new thing for him. He had never had to exercise self-control to allow a woman time or space before. Generally it was the other way around, and he had to jealously guard his own reservoirs of space and time from feminine invasion and encroachment.

He was developing a new awareness of the female psyche, because this was driving him out of his mind. He wanted to talk, to share, to be with her. But she wanted her space, to crawl in her cave, to be with her buddies! He'd picked up the phone at least a thousand times.

He was staring at it when it rang. He let it ring twice before he grabbed it.

"Missed you," her voice crooned into his ear.

"Missed you, too," he whispered.

"I'm on my cell phone looking at your front door. Are you going to open it?"

He almost tripped over his own feet.

He pulled open the door, and there stood Topaz in jeans and a sweatshirt, looking contrite. "I'm sorry for the way I carried on last night. I was really upset about what Tyree said."

"I can't imagine why," Jon murmured. He pulled her inside and shut the door. He was famished for the feel of her.

When he kissed her, her sweetness tasted like ambrosia to a starving man. Her sweetness did nothing to sate him. But he could wait.

"We need to talk," he said with a sigh.

"I know," she agreed.

"Do you want some tea, water? It's all I have here to drink—but I can offer hot or cold."

"Whatever you're having is fine."

He brewed a pot of green tea. They sipped from small cups, leaning against each other on the sofa. The silence, the tea, and simply being together was enough for right now.

Topaz took a deep breath. "We decided we weren't crazy," she announced.

Jon chuckled. "That's always a reassuring decision."

"Our mother was killed shortly before Rosaline's birthday when I was in the second grade."

"I remember," Jon said. "It was a sad time. I couldn't really relate; the fact that a classmate's mother had died was so shocking. It was a terrible impossibility for a child."

"Since our father had never been in the picture, our grandmother raised us the best she could, bless her heart. Cherice and Brandy were our best friends and classmates. Rosaline had a quiet birthday that year because of the tragedy. That's when it started. We'd make a Wish each year and that Wish would come true, but only if there were just the four of us, like at that first party. The interesting thing was that our Wishes always came true."

"Always?" Jon asked.

"Always."

"Even if you wished that an elephant appeared in the middle of the room, it would appear?"

"Well, no, because that would be against the laws of physics. What would the elephant be made of and how would it be transported? And most important, why waste a Wish like that? You only got one a year," Topaz explained.

"So there were rules, such as the laws of physics," Jon said.

"Yes, lots of laws. Magic is very logical."

"That doesn't make sense."

"What doesn't make sense?" Topaz asked.

"If magic is logical, it isn't magic. It's science."

"That doesn't make sense," Topaz said.

Jon looked at her. "Does it seem sometimes as if your mother is granting these wishes, like a fairy godmother?" he asked.

Topaz looked away. "Sometimes."

"So if you give up the concepts of Wishes, you give up something you kept of your mother. Maybe something precious."

"But my mother has been long gone."

"You needed her. And so did your sister. Maybe this is the way she's helped you. You, your sister, Brandy, and Cherice have been phenomenally successful. You are all relatively wealthy women. I can see where you'd believe you wished it so."

Topaz turned away, something deep inside gnawing at her, unable to relinquish the reality of the magic . . . *of her mother?*

"Wishes come true for you," Jon was saying. He tapped her on the forehead. "Thoughts create reality, Topaz. And I don't think there's any greater magic than that."

"You don't think we're crazy, that I'm crazy?"

"No. And I was wrong to say what I did in the first place. My pride was hurt, and I was confused. But I'm clearer myself now. I know what I want," Jon said. He took Topaz's hand and ran his thumb in thoughtful circles around her palm. "I want to make your Wish come true more than anything in the world."

"Jon?"

"Can I be your fairy-tale prince, your Wish come

true? I'm not saying that I'll be that great at it. But I'll always try."

Topaz touched his lips with something like wonder. "I told you that my Wishes always come true," she whispered.

He enfolded her in his arms, and there was no more need for words as he took her to that enchanted fairy-tale place of happily never endings.

Epilogue

Topaz and Jon got married a few months later in an enchanted fairy-tale setting amid the morning mists of an ancient redwood forest in San Francisco. Topaz later gave birth to a healthy baby boy. Jon promptly cut his patient load in half and devoted himself to house-husbandly duties.

Ray Gaines appeared on the cover of *Coming Out* magazine for the Modern, Proud Gay Man.

Brandy and Jackson married on the field of Arrowhead Stadium at halftime on one of the rare occasions that the Cardinals actually made the playoffs.

Cherice and Rosaline are doing just fine and are still wishing for a story of their own one day.

The Wright Woman

 Francis Ray

Chapter 1

She had done it again.

Michael Dunbar looked around the elegant two-story atrium of the Wyndham Anatole Hotel near downtown Dallas in search of his missing mother. With several retail shops lined up on his right, there were a lot of possibilities. The only thing his mother liked better than visiting and trying to marry off her three sons was shopping.

Michael swiped his calloused hand across his clean-shaven face and barely kept from groaning. Why had he let Stevenson waylay him as he and his mother were coming out of the elevator on their way to lunch? The answer came almost immediately. Stevenson was the executive manager of the hotel, and the man Michael had to answer to if the landscape project he had been contracted to do wasn't up to the company's exacting standards. Measuring up was one worry Michael didn't have. He wasn't being egotistical or a braggart when he said he was one of the best landscape designers in the business.

He'd studied hard and worked harder to establish a growing clientele in the past five years, using his ability to turn vague or all too often completely unrealistic ideas into landscapes that pleased the eye and soothed the senses. He'd do the same with the Anatole. The hotel's landscape would go through a complete transition under his direction.

He had gone after the job with a vengeance after driving by on countless occasions and noticing that the hotel's grounds could use a little lift in welcoming guests and visitors. It always surprised him that home and business owners thought nothing of redecorating where they lived or worked, but seldom thought of doing the same thing to the grounds surrounding the structure.

The only shrubbery remaining would be the two elephant topiaries at the entrance of the hotel's towers. They were as much of a landmark as the gold domes atop the towers.

Michael glanced around the busy atrium again and accepted the inevitable. He'd have to go in search of his mother. He'd seen the gleeful expression on her face when Stevenson asked if he could have a word with him. She'd excused herself before Michael could get a word out, then hurried off.

Of course Stevenson had wanted to go outside and check on the progress of the two-week-old project. Since the austere manager admittedly didn't know a weed from a flower, Michael had to run through the basics . . . again.

Stevenson, a snappy dresser, had stood far enough back from the proposed azalea bed not to get any dirt on his immaculate black pin-striped suit while Michael dug in the rich bed of loam and acid mixture they'd plant the flowering shrubs in to ensure they thrived in the hot Texas climate and naturally sandy soil. Michael saw no reason for the landscape to consist of ordinary hedges. He liked the extraordinary; liked rounding the corner and seeing the unexpected. Guests and visitors of the Anatole would see beauty long before they entered the hotel's elegant and richly decorated lobby and saw the Ming Dynasty art.

After finishing with the manager, Michael had gone to the bathroom to clean up. He couldn't have been gone more than fifteen minutes, but it had been more than enough time for his shopaholic mother to disappear.

He started toward the first store, a clothing boutique. She certainly wasn't going to stop shopping and come look for him. He knew that from personal experience. She forgot everything when she was "on the hunt" as she called it.

Even as he reluctantly neared the double glass doors of the store, an indulgent smile tugged the corners of his mouth. She had a right to shop like there was no tomorrow. There'd been a time when she wasn't sure what the next day would bring. It hadn't been easy being mother and father to three young children.

After their father died when Michael was ten, she had done without things some women took for granted. With three growing boys to feed and clothe, she usually ran short of money before she could buy herself a new dress or a pair of shoes. As the oldest of the three boys, Michael remembered the hard times more than his younger brothers, Neal and Brody. Raising them on a census clerk's salary had been rough, but their mother had done it. And not once had Michael ever heard her complain.

Years later, when he was grown and on his own,

he'd overheard her tell a friend of hers that there had been times she wouldn't spend thirty-five cents on a soft drink for fear one of her boys would need it. The next day he'd had a soft drink machine stocked and delivered to the house her sons had bought for her.

Although her successful, college-educated sons were scattered over three states, that had never bothered Corine Dunbar. She'd always encouraged them to follow their dreams. It probably helped that whenever the urge struck she could visit him in Dallas, Neal in Florida, or Brody in New Mexico. She always stayed in a hotel, insisting that she didn't want to invade their privacy. With Brody and Neal, who were seldom without a woman in their lives, she might have been right. With Michael that might have been true once, but not anymore. At least not since April.

April Carter had been beautiful, successful, and a gold digger. A month after they'd started dating he'd come up behind her with the glass of wine she'd asked him to get and heard her bragging to her girlfriend about all the money he spent on her. She'd gone on to say that she only dated men with money. She just hated that he didn't dress more fashionably and that he insisted on working like a common laborer with his men. Too angry to speak, Michael had tapped her on the shoulder, given her the wine, then left her standing there with her mouth hanging open.

Since April wasn't the first woman he'd dated only to find out later that she liked his money more than she cared for him, he had to accept that he had lousy taste in women. He wasn't wasting his time on another woman until he knew that she saw the "real" him— rough hands, blue jeans, and all.

There *had* to be a woman like that out there. Someone he could have fun with. He wasn't looking for a wife—heavens, no!—he just wanted someone who'd be good company, someone he could share a little affection with, someone he could trust.

Reaching for the gleaming brass handle on the door, Michael dismissed April and all the other dishonest women from his mind. Two steps inside the brightly lit store he saw a mannequin clad in a heavy white lace peignoir in the back of the store. He almost backed out. One of his old girlfriends used to drag him with her shopping for lingerie. She obviously thought it would be a turn on for him. It had had the opposite effect.

He'd always felt a little embarrassed . . . just as he did now, and the mannequin's attire wasn't anywhere near as racy as those he'd seen with his ex. He was seriously considering trying the gift shop next door when a woman came around the corner. Thoughts of leaving evaporated from his mind.

She was simply gorgeous. She looked cool, elegant, and lush in a tangerine-colored suit with a straight skirt. The winsome smile on her chocolate brown face—as if she'd heard a joke and couldn't wait to share it with you—captivated him. He wasn't aware of an answering smile on his face. "Hi."

"Hello," she greeted, stopping a few feet in front of him beneath a crystal chandelier. Her rich chocolate-colored eyes sparkled. "Welcome to Texas Chic."

Her voice was soft and alluring with a faint trace of huskiness, as if she'd just climbed out of bed. Michael thought he'd like to take her straight back there.

"Is there something I can help you with?"

You leaped into his mind, but luckily stayed locked behind his teeth. He cleared his throat. He wasn't sure what was happening here. He didn't usually react to women so quickly. Maybe sleeping single for the past six months was finally beginning to take its toll on him.

"I'm looking for a woman," he said, then listened as laughter flowed from lips painted a soft-coral color. He had the strangest urge to brush his across hers, before belatedly realizing how misleading his statement must have been. "I can't find my mother." He groaned at the inanity of a grown man saying that.

The beckoning laughter faded and he missed the sound until she spoke again. "We get men in here all the time looking for women." Her eyes twinkled in a face that lured him as much as her voice and the rest of her. "If your name is Michael, you've struck pay dirt."

"My mother's here?"

She nodded, a smile curving her lips again. "She's in the dressing room."

That statement brought him back fast. "How many outfits did she take in?"

"Six. The maximum," she answered.

Michael shook his head and wondered if he'd have to buy her another suitcase or ship the clothes back as he had the last time she'd visited, three months ago. He never understood why women needed so many clothes. "You don't sell shoes, do you?"

"No, I'm sorry."

"I'm not," he said relieved. A dress and shoe store on the premises would be too much of a temptation. "Maybe she'll only buy half the outfits," he mumbled to himself and tried to remember if one of the two suitcases she'd brought with her for a three-day visit seemed lighter than the other.

"Our sale starts tomorrow," she said.

Panicked, Michael quickly looked beyond the woman, hoping he wouldn't see his mother. She'd really go berserk if she heard the word "sale."

"If your mother finds anything she wants, I'd be happy to hold it for her until tomorrow," she offered helpfully as two other women nearby looked through a rack of suits.

It took Michael a second to realize she thought he was worried about the amount of money his mother would spend. He could hardly blame her since he was dressed in scuffed work boots, well-worn denims, a white shirt, and a black Stetson. He didn't have to look at the price tags to know they would be steep. Upscale hotel shops always were. He could afford whatever his mother wanted, as she very well knew . . . if she'd let him pay for once.

He reassessed the woman before him, looking past the outer trappings of beauty and sensuality that had captured his attention and peaked his interest on first sight. In Michael's opinion she was a rarity: a woman who wanted to save a man's money instead of spending it.

"Or not," she added, obviously worried that she had offended him because he was silent so long.

Before he thought, he reached out and gently touched her arm in reassurance. He was surprised by the little jolt of awareness. From the sudden widening of her eyes, she had felt it too. "Thanks for the offer, but I knew she was coming, so I'm prepared."

Her smile blossomed again, showing beautiful white teeth. "I can show you where to wait and bring you a cup of coffee if you'd like."

"I'd like that. Thanks."

She turned away and he slowly followed, admiring

the shapely curve of her body and the brisk no-
nonsense way she moved. He was disappointed when
they arrived at their destination so quickly. He took
a seat in one of the four white leather tub chairs surrounding an oval-shaped glass coffee table with several fashion and men's magazines on top.

"I'll be right back with your coffee."

"You know my name. What's yours?" He hoped he
didn't sound too eager.

"Stephanie."

Had she actually blushed? He hadn't seen a woman
blush since high school. Another intriguing surprise.
He found himself wanting to say something corny like
"a beautiful name for a beautiful woman," but an
older gentleman sat down across from him. "It fits,"
he said simply.

She gazed at him a moment longer, as if trying to
figure out if he was just being nice or if there was
more to it, and then she was gone. Michael settled
back in his chair, a small smile playing across his
mouth. Who would have thought that he'd ever be
glad his mother had gone into a dress shop.

Stephanie could float, she felt so light.

She almost giggled at the thought of a woman her
size floating. She was a perfect size twenty . . . all
right, twenty-two in the hips. But seeing Michael had
made her feel almost light-headed. *He was hot.* What
made it so special was that he seemed to think she was
hot as well. Unable to help herself, Stephanie gave a
little impromptu wiggle of her ample hips.

Picking up the carafe of coffee she'd made an hour
earlier, sudden doubts assailed her. She pushed them
away as a more pressing matter entered her mind. She

hadn't asked him if he wanted cream and sugar. But she had been so surprised and pleased when she'd seen him that she'd almost squealed with joy. Despite her knocking knees she hadn't hesitated in going to greet him.

She'd seen Michael a couple of days before as she was coming to work through the back entrance by the tennis court. He and three other men were loading onto a truck one of the ten-foot crape myrtles they'd apparently dug up. Afterward he'd taken off his white T-shirt and wiped the sweat from his face and chest. She'd been so transfixed by the flex of muscle, she'd actually felt her heart flutter.

If another hotel employee hadn't spoken to her at that moment, she wasn't sure how long she would have simply stared at him. That morning, for the first time in the six months she'd been the assistant manager at Texas Chic, she had been late for work.

And if she didn't get moving, he'd start wondering what had happened to her. Grabbing a gold-rimmed china cup and saucer, she finished preparing the tray and hurried back out.

Michael glanced up, tossed the magazine he'd been flipping through on the table, and stood with an easy strength and grace. Stephanie's heart did a somersault. What a man! What a man! He was six-feet-plus of mouthwatering muscles. As she neared she caught a whiff of his citrus cologne and noted that, with her high heels, their mouths were mere inches apart. Her body heated; her hands began to tremble. The cup and saucer clinked on the tray.

"Please, let me take that," he said.

"Thank you."

Their fingers brushed and the awareness that flowed

between them was even stronger than it had been before. This time the jolt didn't stop in her nervous stomach, but went all the way to her tingling toes. Helplessly, she stared into his narrowed black eyes and felt as if the oxygen was being squeezed from her lungs.

Moistening her dry lips, she said, "I-I brought cream and sugar."

"Thanks, but I take it black." Finally his gaze moved away from her mouth and, although she could breathe easier, her hands remained unsteady.

She'd never reacted so strongly to the mere touch of a man's hand or from the way he looked at her. What would happen to her if he actually held and kissed her? Her stomach took a dive. Needing to gather her thoughts, Stephanie busied herself moving the magazines aside so he could set the tray down, then she poured a cup of coffee and handed it to him.

The cup looked small and fragile in his large, powerful hands . . . hands that she knew could easily shatter the delicate china. Would his touch be as gentle and restrained on a woman's tender skin or fierce and demanding? Would she ever learn the answer?

Suddenly she remembered something vitally important. She tucked her lower lip between her teeth to keep from groaning.

"What is it?" he asked in concern, setting the cup back on the table.

Stephanie stopped chewing on her bottom lip and glanced again at his coffee cup before looking at him. "The shop was extremely busy until about an hour ago and we ran out of coffee. I had to make the second pot while Rose was on break. I'm not very good at making coffee."

He smiled into her worried face, then reached for his cup again. "I'm sure it's fine." He raised the cup to his mouth. Stephanie saw his throat move, his eyes go wide.

She considered jerking the cup out of his hand, or running away and hiding, but she couldn't seem to do either. Then the impossible happened. His throat moved again. He had taken a second sip of her coffee! Coffee that was known throughout the hotel as perhaps the worst in the state. Rose, the store's manager, always teased her and said she'd bet motor oil would taste better.

Michael turned away slightly and set the cup down. When he faced her again there were traces of water in the corners of his eyes. "It—" His voice cracked. He cleared his throat and tried again, "W-wasn't so bad."

If two customers hadn't walked by just then, Stephanie might have kissed him. Her voice was tremulous when she spoke. "I'd heard men in Texas were gallant, but now I know it's really true. Thank you."

"The Stetson gave me away, eh?" he said, a smile trying to materialize on his strained features.

That hat, the molasses-dipped voice, and the way you're wearing those jeans, she thought. "Your mother said you lived here and she was visiting from your hometown of Houston."

"That's right. Where are you from?" he asked.

Stephanie was glad that his face looked almost normal and that his voice was no longer hoarse. "Seattle," she answered. "I better go check on your mother."

She started for the dressing room located in the curve of the U-shaped store. Just before turning the corner, she glanced over her shoulder in time to see

Michael make a mad dash for the front door. She sighed. He was either heading for the water fountain a couple of doors down or the open café across the way.

She hoped he didn't keep on running. She'd really like to see him again.

Chapter 2

Stephanie saw the smile on Mrs. Dunbar's face as she exited the white louvered doors of the dressing room and knew she had a sale. She had liked the smartly dressed, effervescent woman immediately. "You found some things you like," she commented.

"Too many," Mrs. Dunbar replied, her smile warm and open.

Laughing, Stephanie took the assortment of suits and separates from her. "Michael should be happy that you're ready to go. I got the impression he was thinking about bolting for the door before I stopped him."

Mrs. Dunbar stared into the floor-to-ceiling mirror at the end of the dressing area as she adjusted the short sky blue jacket of her suit. "He does hate shopping. Thank you."

"My pleasure," Stephanie continued. "I enjoyed talking with him."

The other woman stopped and studied Stephanie with shrewd eyes. "He's a wonderful man *and* he's single. Are you single, Stephanie?"

Stephanie felt heat flush her cheeks. That's what she

got for rattling on about Michael and calling him by his first name. "Yes, ma'am," she admitted and went to the rack at the entrance of the dressing room where unwanted clothes were hung until she or one of the other three women working there had a chance to restock them. "Which of these would you like to purchase?"

When no answer came, Stephanie glanced over her shoulder. Frown lines radiated across Mrs. Dunbar's forehead. "Is there a problem?"

"If Michael sees that I want those two suits, he'll insist on buying them," she said with a shake of her stylishly cut salt-and-pepper hair. "He and his brothers grumble about me shopping, but they won't let me pay for anything when I'm with them. If I didn't insist on using my government ID to book my flights and hotel rooms, they'd pay for that too. As it is, they always find a way to stick money in my luggage before I leave."

In Stephanie's opinion, any man who spoiled his mother was definitely worth knowing better. "He said he'd saved up for your visit."

Mrs. Dunbar studied her again. "You two must have gotten along well. He's usually not so talkative. A woman would have a hard time finding a better man."

Stephanie's cheeks heated again. "Oh, well . . . that's obvious," she said. She couldn't help thinking how she'd always heard that if you wanted to see how a man would treat his wife you should find out how he treated his mother. Of course, all she had in mind was a fun date or two with him. That is, if her coffee hadn't scared him off. "You must be a wonderful mother and you're blessed to have such loving sons."

The lines disappeared from the older woman's forehead, leaving her round face bright and full of pride. "That's what I tell my friends all the time . . . even when they don't want to hear."

Both women laughed.

"I have an idea," Stephanie said. "Since you're staying at the hotel I can deliver the items you want later this afternoon or put them on hold until tomorrow when we have the sale. You can pick them up then."

"Sale!" Mrs. Dunbar's eyes glittered. "How much?"

Since Stephanie frowned on paying full retail herself and loved bargain shopping, she quickly told Mrs. Dunbar how much the clothes would be dismounted. "Rose and I are doing the markdowns after the store closes at seven," she finished.

"That's put a different light on things," Mrs. Dunbar said. "Please hold everything and I'll return first thing in the morning. It's so hard to find stylish clothes since I gained weight and now wear a size sixteen."

Stephanie, who had heard similar words so many times in the past, nodded. "For women my size it's even more difficult." She shook her head of black hair. "Don't get me started," she said with a sigh. "You better go before Michael comes looking for you."

"Did I mention that he'll be working on the landscape for the hotel for some weeks?" Mrs. Dunbar asked in a conversational tone.

Stephanie moistened her lips. "Uh, no, you didn't." She was not going to mention to his mother that she had seen her son hot and sweaty at work and had gotten pretty heated and worked up herself.

"Chances are you'll be seeing each other again. I

certainly hope so." The older woman stuck the Prada envelope purse that exactly matched her shoes beneath her arm. "Thanks for all your help. I'll see you in the morning. Good-bye."

"Good-bye," Stephanie replied. "I'll see you tomorrow."

Stephanie fought the urge to hang the clothes up and see if Michael had returned. The only reason she didn't was fear that another customer might take his mother's garments. Women shopped the return racks as hard as they did the racks on the floor. Instead, as always, Stephanie put the customer first and went through another set of white louvered doors to the holding and office area in the back of the store.

"A few more customers like that and we won't have that much merchandise to mark down tonight," drawled a feminine voice layered with Southern charm.

Stephanie hung up the clothes on the rolling rack and turned to see her boss and friend, Rose Athens. She had the smooth unlined skin of a woman half her age, and wore a size six, the same size she'd been since she was eighteen. As always, she was fashionably dressed, in Oscar de la Renta black and ivory crepe pants and a black silk T-shirt and a natural embossed jacket. Her black silk head wrap was intricately knotted just above her left ear, completely covering her short natural hair.

"That's what you hired me for." Stephanie grabbed a pen and paper to tag the clothes.

"Darn right," Rose said, then took Stephanie's arm when she finished. Together they walked back toward the front of the boutique. "I saw you were wasting your talent on accessories in that specialty shop. You know what looks right on a woman. You can't buy that kind of instinct."

"But you tried," Stephanie countered with a smile, remembering Rose's daily pilgrimage to where she had worked, each time upping the ante a little more for her to leave and come work with her. She'd recently been promoted to the manager of Texas Chic and needed a savvy assistant to take over her old position. Together she hoped they could build the store's reputation so that customers would come by choice and not by chance.

Stephanie hadn't been so sure she wanted to walk away from her job and deviate from her plan, which was to gain as much experience as possible before opening her own boutique. Since graduating from college four years before with a degree in fashion merchandising, she'd worked in some of the most fashionable stores in the country and had come away with one indisputable fact: women who wanted stylish clothes past size fourteen were overlooked and underserved. One day she planned to change that.

"I knew you'd make a great assistant," Rose said.

"Just as I knew having clothes for full-figured women and enlarging their dressing area would draw in more customers," Stephanie countered. It had been a deal breaker and chancy. Her previous employers had turned the idea down flat.

"You drove a hard bargain, but it paid off," Rose replied, glancing around the busy store again.

"Yes, it did." Stephanie's gaze followed Rose's noting the fresh flowers, mirrored glass, the comfortable seating area, the spaciousness where shoppers could easily browse without bumping into a clothes rack or each other. They were all her ideas. She was the creative one. Rose's talent lay in ensuring they stayed on budget. They complemented each other beautifully.

"When you decide you're ready to open your own shop, you're going to do very, very well."

Stephanie took the compliment to heart. Rose didn't blow smoke. Stephanie had the money left to her by her aunt in an interest bearing account and she was gaining experience. She simply had to decide when she was ready to step out on her own. The thought was exhilarating. Almost as exhilarating at the idea of seeing Michael again.

His mother was about as subtle as a sledgehammer, Michael mused as he cut into his inch-thick bloodred prime rib. She hadn't stopped talking about Stephanie since they left Texas Chic. The more she went on and on about what a sweet and thoughtful young woman Stephanie was, the more determined he became that he wasn't going to follow through on his earlier plans of seeing her again . . . no matter how much he might agree with his mother. You'd think, after raising three sons, she'd know that there was an unwritten rule that men never dated the women their mother picked for them.

"What time did you say your plane leaves Wednesday?"

"Today is Monday, Michael. Are you trying to get rid of me after only one night?" His mother paused in adding ground pepper to her grilled chicken salad. "Even Brody and Neal don't get restless until the third night."

Michael twisted in his seat and hoped she didn't get started on the subject of his brothers' sex lives. "You know we all love having you."

"And I love seeing you. It's just that I'd feel so much better knowing you were each married to some nice young woman." She picked up her tea. "Didn't you think Stephanie was nice?"

"She makes the worst coffee I've ever tasted," Michael answered with a chuckle. She'd been so endearingly embarrassed. He'd wanted to comfort her, *and* to pour out that coffee to save the next unsuspecting person.

"Since you're smiling it couldn't have been that bad."

Luckily Michael had gone back to his food and had his head down so she didn't see his start of surprise. Just thinking about Stephanie made him smile. Bad. Very bad. Especially since his mother had a one-track mind and such keen eyesight. Time to bail, and fast, before his mother started matchmaking again. He didn't want a wife, just a nice trustworthy girlfriend.

Casually he lifted his head. "My advice is that, if you go back in the store again, shop only for clothes. Now, how are the new water lilies in your fishpond doing?"

His mother shrugged, smiled, and began talking about the three well-stocked fishponds in her backyard. She was death on a houseplant, but her fish and the water plants thrived. He relaxed as they dined and she didn't bring Stephanie's name back up. Apparently she'd taken the hint and given up trying to match him up with Stephanie. He just wished he could forget about her as easily.

*   *   *

Michael had a problem.

His mother hadn't brought Stephanie's name back up since yesterday's lunch, but that didn't seem to stop him from thinking about her. Getting out of his truck Tuesday night, he crossed the well-lit parking lot of the hotel to pick up his mother for dinner and a movie. She had an early flight out of Love Field the next morning.

Nodding to the doorman, Michael entered the lobby with every intention of continuing to the elevators on his immediate right. But somehow his feet kept walking . . . toward the row of ritzy shops. Getting mixed up with a woman your mother tried to push in your path was doomed from the start. He knew that. So why didn't he turn around and head for the elevator? Why had he looked for her as he worked outside? It was getting so bad the men thought he'd developed a nervous tic.

Still fighting the need to see Stephanie again, Michael reached for the brass handle on the glass door of Texas Chic, pulled and found it wouldn't budge. Transfixed, he stared at the offending door, then at the discreet gold lettering listing the hours of business. The store closed at seven on weekdays. He couldn't believe it. After all the mental acrobatics he had been going through, she wasn't there.

He'd known she'd be trouble.

Out of the corner of his eye he caught a glimpse of movement. Stepping closer he peered through the glass, unaware that his hand tightened on the door handle.

A petite woman finally emerged from behind a rack of clothes with one of those radar-looking guns he'd seen salespeople check merchandise with. She laughed and glanced behind her. Michael's nose pressed against the glass as he stepped even closer. Moments later he saw Stephanie, as beautiful as ever and smiling. She certainly didn't appear to have lost any sleep over him, the way he had her.

He scowled. Women!

Unfortunately Stephanie chose that moment to look in his direction. Her eyes widened. Her hands flew to her mouth. The gun-thing in her hand fell heedlessly to the floor.

Instantly contrite for scaring her, Michael called out, "It's just me, Michael. I'm sorry." He received more than a few curious stares from people passing by. He sent them an innocent smile, hoped no one would call security, and then gave his attention back to Stephanie.

Stephanie picked up the price-check gun and started toward the door only to stop short. The woman said something to Stephanie, then she hurried out of sight. Michael held up his hands, palms out, to indicate that he was harmless. He hoped Stevenson was on duty to vouch for him if the woman was calling the police.

Stephanie didn't move until the woman reappeared. For once she wasn't smiling. Michael felt like a heel for frightening her. As soon as she opened the door he began to apologize again. "I'm sorry. I didn't mean to scare you or the other woman."

"You didn't scare me, not really," Stephanie said, going outside the shop instead of letting him inside. "I was just surprised to see you."

He nodded toward the other woman who was still staring at him. "Did she call the police?"

Stephanie moistened her lips. "No. That's Rose, the store manager. She went to turn off the alarm. I forgot and almost opened the door. It's wired to security, the front desk, and the police department. I don't see how I could have forgotten."

"Oh." That bit of knowledge and the puzzled look on Stephanie's face went a long way in soothing Michael's wounded pride. Maybe she *had* thought about him. "You're working late. It's almost eight."

"After a sales day the clothes are always a mess. Rose and I were trying to put some of them away before tomorrow," she explained. "I'd invite you in, but it's against store policy once the store closes, unless security is on the premises."

"That's all right. I understand."

A large group of laughing women with badges proclaiming them to be with the Romance Slam Jam conference were headed in their direction. Michael took Stephanie's arm and drew her into the little alcove by the door. It was as good an excuse as any to give them a little privacy. For what reason, he wasn't sure. At least they'd be out of Rose's line of vision. She hadn't taken her eyes off them since Stephanie had come outside. "I just wanted to thank you for helping my mother yesterday."

Stephanie thought it wise not to mention all the clothes his mother had purchased that morning. "I wish all the customers were as pleasant to deal with. She told me she's leaving in the morning."

Michael propped his shoulder against the wall and stared down at Stephanie. He just liked looking at her. "I'm on my way to pick her up for dinner and then we're going to a movie."

Once again she was struck by how considerate he was. "She said you and your brothers spoil her."

"We try, but she can be stubborn. Guess that comes

from raising us by herself after dad died," he told her. "Is your family in Seattle?"

"Yes. I'm next to the youngest of seven," she said and watched his eyes round as most people's did when she told them she came from such a large family. "My parents were here visiting last weekend and wanting to know when I planned on coming back."

Another frown crossed his face. "You're leaving?"

"No, but that doesn't stop them from hoping."

Michael absorbed the answer, unaware that he was holding his breath while he considered her words. "I'm glad you're staying."

"Me too," Stephanie said, and they stood smiling at each other. "Do you plan to be here in the morning?"

"I'm picking Mama up at six to take her to the airport."

She shook her head. "No. I mean to work on the landscaping. I thought we could . . ." Her voice trailed off as his eyes chilled.

He straightened. "You know about my job?"

The smile slid from her face. His scowl was fiercer than when she'd seen him watching her through the store window. She didn't think it would help the situation for her to admit the first sight of him had made her practically drool. She cleared her throat. "Your mother said you were working on the landscape for the hotel."

"I see." His voice matched the aloofness of his face. "Well, I've got to go. My mother's waiting. Good-bye, Stephanie." He turned and strode away.

Completely baffled, she stared after him and wondered what she had said that made him turn so cold.

Chapter 3

Michael was in a mood. A very bad one.

The broad side of the pick he wielded bit deeply into the earth around a five-foot crepe myrtle behind the screened wall of the tennis court at the Anatole. He didn't pause and swung the pick again. His muscles had long since heated and loosened. He had thought the strenuous work would drive Stephanie from his mind. He'd been wrong.

The pick tore out another chunk of earth. Women. Whoever said they could mess up a man's mind surely spoke the truth. It had been all he could do not to ask his mother exactly what she had told Stephanie about him. But any indication on his part that he was the least bit interested in her and his mother would be ready to send out wedding invitations.

The trouble was, not asking left him completely in the dark. He had no way of knowing if she'd mentioned to Stephanie that he was *working* on the hotel's landscape or that he owned the landscape firm. Without the answer, he had no way of figuring out if she'd been putting on an act since they first met or if she was genuinely interested in him and was as warm and open as she appeared to be. And he wasn't likely to find out.

Dirt flew. It had been his experience that, when women found out that he had a little money, their attitude toward him changed. Stephanie probably wasn't any different, but thoughts that she might be had his thinking about her more than he should have.

He wanted her to be different. He had easily forgotten April and the other women like her. He didn't seem to be able to do the same with Stephanie.

Laying the pick aside, Michael went down on his knees with a spade to work around the crepe myrtle. He planned to uproot the stunted tree and transfer it to an inner city park in South Dallas. With proper care and nutrients it would grow twelve to fifteen feet. He'd save what plants he could and transport them at his own expense to places where they were needed and would be appreciated. The rest, he'd turn into mulch.

"Hello, Michael."

He froze. He'd recognize that husky, midnight voice anywhere. He glanced up, knowing Stephanie would be standing there. He hadn't counted on how seeing her would send a punch straight to his gut. His gloved hand tightened on the short wooden handle of the spade. She wore a raspberry suit that fit perfectly. The wind shifted, bringing with it the scent of the soft fragrance she wore. It made him think of a secluded grove filled with flowers, and the two of them locked in each other's arms.

He rammed the spade into the dirt. "Hello."

Her smile wobbled. Weariness entered her eyes. "I-I didn't mean to disturb you."

The hurt in her voice and in her face made him feel like he had jerked the wings off a butterfly. "You're not."

Nervously she moistened her lips and when her tongue slipped back inside her mouth he wished his could follow. "I-I'm not sure what I said to upset you the other day, but I've been worried that it might have something to do with your mother, maybe something I misunderstood." His mouth compressed into a thin line. "I can see from your expression that it does. I just wanted to say that I'm sorry."

"Doesn't matter," he said with a shrug. "I'm kind of busy here."

She would not let herself be hurt that he didn't want her around him. She'd finish what she had to say then leave. "I just wanted to tell you that your mother loves you and your brothers very much. I hope my telling you what she said hasn't put a strain on your relationship. It's all right to be upset with me, but please don't take it out on her." He didn't say anything, just continued to stare at her. "That's all I wanted to say. Good-bye, Michael." She turned to leave.

"My mother likes you."

The words were muttered so begrudgingly that Stephanie wanted to weep. "I like her too," she said, her back still to him.

"What's in the Thermos?" he asked.

Stephanie lifted the gallon Thermos by its plastic handle. She'd forgotten she carried it. She faced him. It wasn't his fault that she had read more into their reaction to each other than she should have. "I brought you something to drink."

He frowned. "Coffee?"

Her smile reappeared. "No. I wouldn't do that to you. It's lemonade."

He found himself wanting to believe she had no ulterior motive for seeking him out. What if she liked him for himself, not the prospect of a rich date? The only time April went out of her way was to find reasons to spend his money. "It's supposed to get in the nineties today. I appreciate it."

She handed him the Thermos and belatedly remembered the red plastic cups in her other hand. Around Michael she'd forget to breathe if it weren't automatic. "Here are some extra cups in case you want to share."

"Thank again. The other guys will be grateful for this." He pulled off his glove and unscrewed the top. "I'll bring this back before I go home."

Her fingers laced tightly in front of her, she glanced toward the roped-off parking area near the convention site a couple of hundred feet away where several men were working in the flower beds. "Do you think you should ask one of them to help you or would your boss mind?"

The plastic cup stopped midway to his mouth. "What?"

She swallowed, then decided to plunge ahead. If she was going to upset him again, it might as well be for his own welfare. "I saw you last week, taking these trees away, but there were four of you."

Michael felt the vise around his chest ease. She'd been watching him, and she didn't know he owned the landscape firm. The day had taken a dramatic turn for the better. "I can manage." He'd tackled the job by himself because he was in a foul mood and needed to work it out on the dirt and not on his men.

"I didn't mean to infer that you couldn't," she quickly said.

"You didn't." He took a deep breath and raised the cup to his mouth, determined to drink the lemonade no matter how bad it tasted. "This is good!"

The surprised look on his face made Stephanie laugh. "It's only coffee that I've never been able to make. My parents didn't drink it and I never learned how."

He took another drink of the sweet lemonade with just enough bite. "Then I'll have to show you sometime." She blushed and he made up his mind to take a chance. "Would you like to go out sometime?"

She tilted her head to one side. "Are you asking about next week, next month, next—"

"Tomorrow night," he interrupted, coming to his feet. She was within arm's length and much too far away. He took a step closer. "How about it?"

Her eyes rounded. She licked her lips. One day soon he was going to do that for her. "I-I'd like that."

"Good. I'll get your address and phone number when I bring this back." He held up the Thermos. "For now, you better go so I can go back to work."

Nervously she glanced around. "Is your boss here?"

"Yes." He told himself he wasn't being deceptive. If it lasted for more than a couple of dates, he'd tell her the truth.

She glanced around as if trying to pick out the man, then nodded. "I better go. The store closes at seven. Bye."

"I remember. Bye," he called as she hurried back inside the hotel. He watched her every step of the way. He hadn't been completely honest, but he hadn't lied. He waned to see where things would lead with Stephanie without worrying if she had any ulterior motives for dating him. There was nothing wrong with that, he told himself, but he couldn't shake the vague uneasiness that he was being as dishonest as April.

He was late.

Stephanie tried not to become worried as the grandfather clock near the entrance struck half past seven. What if his boss had seen them talking and gotten upset with Michael? If he had gotten into trouble, it would be her fault. She caught herself chewing on her lower lip and made herself stop. She was letting her imagination run away with her.

She'd straightened the clothes on the mannequins in the display windows at least three times while trying to keep an eye out for Michael. She'd had to clean the glass twice from getting nose and fingerprint smudges on it. Waiting had never been her strong suit. Then another thought struck. What if he wasn't coming?

Initially that afternoon he hadn't been pleased to see her. That stung after all the hours she had spent thinking about him. She debated for three days before seeking him out. She'd written his mother a thank-you note for shopping at Texas Chic, careful not to mention Michael. Not for anything would she want to be the cause of any bad feelings between them.

She caught herself with her nose almost to the glass again and straightened. This was silly. She'd never been this anxious over a man showing up in her life. Either he came or he didn't. Her life would go on regardless. The same applied to Michael. She wasn't waiting on him any longer.

Determined steps carried her to the office to say good-bye to Rose and get her bag. As she entered, the older woman looked up from behind her desk.

"Maybe he got tied up," Rose offered, removing her half-glasses.

Stephanie shrugged, but her face showed how disappointed she was. She'd told Rose all about Michael.

"It isn't the first time I've been stood up. I'm going home. I have a test coming up next week and I need to study."

"You'll pass it like all the others. I don't know how you have the energy to take online courses after you get home. I'm pooped when I leave here," Rose said, coming to her feet and stretching.

"You have a husband to care for." Stephanie removed her Michael Kors black oversized bag from her desk drawer. "It's just me and my betta fish."

Rose shut down the computer. "I finally finished the accounts. We're still racking up major sells and putting the store on the map."

"I knew we could do it," Stephanie said, unwilling to let Michael not showing up damper her enthusiasm for how well the store was doing. "The executives should be pleased when they make their on-site visit next month."

"That they will." Rose picked up her Gucci alligator briefcase. "I've been doing some snooping and we're way ahead of any of the other hotel properties' retail clothing stores. We'll finish the quarter number one."

The women slapped palms. Everything was finally coming together. "We'll have to celebrate with dinner."

Rounding the desk, Rose asked, "How about tomorrow night? We can go to Fogo de Chão. You'll love it."

Stephanie had long wanted to go to the Brazilian themed restaurant where waiters dressed as gauchos served a skewered variety of meats that had been cooked over an open fire. "Michael asked me out for tomorrow night, but I'm not sure we're still on."

"You can let me know in the morning. We'll still have time to make reservations." Rose straightened her desk. "Always keep your options open."

Stephanie didn't know if she had any, but she nodded in any case.

"Good. I'll walk out with you."

"All right." At least with Rose along she wouldn't be tempted to go looking for Michael. "Where did you park today?"

The other woman smiled impishly. "In front."

"Same here." Employees were "encouraged" to park in the back. She hadn't wanted Michael to think she was stalking him, so she had parked in front.

After setting the alarm, the women left the store and started toward the front of the hotel. They were almost to the revolving glass doors when Stephanie heard her name.

"Stephanie."

Michael. She whirled and watched him sprint toward her. He'd come! Wild exhilaration swept through her. Then she recalled the past thirty minutes of doubts and worry. Did she really want to become involved with a mercurial man like Michael Dunbar? A man she could tell could easily damage her heart?

Or should she walk away now while her heart was still intact?

Chapter 4

"That is one fine brother," Rose said. "Care to toss for him?"

Stephanie didn't have to think long for the answer. The moment Michael had walked into Texas Chic, she'd ceased to have a choice. "No, because if you won, I'd have to hurt you." She never took her eyes off Michael as he moved toward her. Nothing worth having was without risks.

Rose chuckled. "I'll take off then. See you tomorrow."

"Don't you want to meet him?" she asked as Rose headed for the door.

"There'll be another time," Rose said. "Have fun." With a wave over her shoulders she was out the door.

Stephanie definitely hoped she was right. She turned just as Michael stopped in front of her. He wasn't even winded. Stephanie wished she could say the same thing about herself. Her breathing became off-kilter each time she was near him. He had the strangest effects on her.

"Hi. Sorry I'm late," Michael said. "I got held up and then I wanted to clean up before I returned this."

She took the Thermos, felt the lingering heat from his hand. "I would have waited, if I had known."

He smiled. "That's good to know." She blushed and his smile widened. "Do you have time to sit down and have a drink?"

"Sure. A few minutes," she said and started for the open atrium with seating in a courtyard atmosphere.

"What would you like?" He pulled out a padded white cushioned chair at a white wrought-iron table for two.

"Water is fine."

"Two waters coming up." He went to the kiosk and returned with two bottled waters and cups. "Big plans for tonight?"

"Not really. I'm taking a couple of online courses and one of them is on tonight," she said, unscrewing the bottle top.

"What are you taking?"

"International Business and Marketing Made Easy," she told him. "I have a degree in fashion merchandising, but I want to learn even more."

He propped his arms on the small round table. "I can see why you'd want to go into fashion." His gaze ran appreciatively over her. "You always look like you stepped off the cover of a fashion magazine."

"Thank you," she said, thrilled at the compliment.

"Me, I hate dressing up." He took a swig of water. "People around us are probably wondering what a beautiful woman like you is doing sitting here with me wearing jeans."

Stephanie simply stared at him. His casual compliment had gone straight to her heart. Didn't he realize how impossibly sexy he was in those blue jeans and that white shirt?

"I didn't mean to embarrass you," he said with a hint of self-derision in his voice. "I scare you, then I embarrass you. That's not what I had in mind."

Stephanie wished she had enough nerve to ask exactly what he had in mind, but decided that was too bold. "Clothes don't make the people, people make the clothes. I'm happy that we finally have a chance to talk."

"So am I," he said, meaning it. When he'd seen that it was fifteen minutes until seven he had been on the other side of town, hot and sweaty after replanting the crepe myrtles. He'd rushed home, showered, and hurried back out to his truck. "How was work today?"

"Busy, but that's a good thing." She poured water into the clear plastic cup. "Rose told me tonight that our store is tops in sales of all the stores in the Wyndham chain."

"Congratulations. This calls for a celebration with a little more than water," he said with a smile.

"Rose said the same thing," she admitted. "She wanted me to go out tomorrow night with her and her husband."

Michael stared at her intently. "And what did you tell her?"

Stephanie stared right back. "That you had asked me out, but I wasn't sure anymore."

His hand closed over hers on the table. "You can be sure of me, Stephanie. I'd like for us to get to know each other better."

"So would I."

He breathed easier, reluctantly releasing her hand. "How about if we double date? Then I could offer my apology personally for scaring her the other night."

Stephanie's face glowed. "That would be wonderful."

"Good. Come on, I'll walk you to your car." He stood and reached for her chair.

Standing, she dug into her purse and handed him a buff-colored business card. "My phone number and address are on the back."

"Thanks." He slipped the card into his shirt pocket, discarded their trash, then came back to take the Thermos in one hand and her arm in the other.

His touch was gentle, yet she could feel the strength beneath his calloused fingers and palms through the fabric of her stylish cardigan. What would his hand feel like on her bare flesh? She shivered, not in fear, but anticipation.

"You cold?"

"The temperature in here is always a little chilly," she quickly said by way of explanation.

Without missing a step, he slipped his arm around her shoulders, bringing the heat and hardness of his body against hers. "Better?"

"Y-yes." His nearness made her knees a little weak, her head light. She didn't even care if the employees who worked the front of the hotel were all watching as they continued to her car. Taking out her keys, she deactivated the lock to her Volvo.

Michael opened the door for her and put the Thermos on the passenger seat. "What time shall I pick you up?"

"I'm not sure," she told him, tossing her purse on the seat next to the Thermos. "Rose planned on making reservations in the morning."

His dark head tilted to one side. "I'm glad you waited and gave me a chance to explain."

"I almost didn't," she said honestly.

"Why did you?" Pushing the car door shut, he stepped closer to her.

Staring up at him, anticipation zipped through her

veins like quicksilver. She felt as if she were on the precipice of something unique and wonderful. "Because I wanted to believe I could trust you."

"Believe," he said, his dark head slowly descending toward hers.

She lifted herself on tiptoes and met him halfway. The first touch of their lips was light, as if both wanted to prolong the moment, remember it, savor it. The second brush of their lips demanded more as their mouths heated and softened, each learning the shape and taste of the other.

His arms went around her, lifting her, pulling her closer to him. No kiss had ever taken him so far, so fast, and he knew the ride wasn't over. He dove into the madness, giving more, asking more until his control was stretched to the limits. Slowly, reluctantly, he pulled back, simply holding her until some part of sanity returned to both of them.

Their breathing was rough and ragged as they stood shivering by her car. Her arms remained locked around his neck; his hand continued its relentless sweep up and down the curve of her back.

"I-I . . ." She shuddered.

"Yeah," he breathed, his hand flexing on her back.

Finally she looked at him. The light from the nearest security lamp was too far away for her to see his eyes, but his face was taut with passion, the same passion she had felt sweeping through her like wildfire. She *never* kissed on the first date. Good grief! They hadn't even *had* their first date, and here she was, wrapped around him and clinging for all she was worth. She wasn't sure what was happening here, but whatever it was she was certain her life would never be the same after that night.

"Stephanie."

Hearing her name on his lips caused her to shudder again. Had it been a curse or a plea? "Yes?"

"Never mind." Michael let her go, then stepped back and opened her door again. "Go home while I'm still thinking straight."

She didn't have to ask what he meant. She got in the car.

"You all right to drive?" he asked.

Her hands clamped around the steering wheel, she nodded.

"You're a better woman than I am a man. My knees are knocking."

Her head jerked toward him, not sure what she expected. She saw wonderment in his dark gaze. She saw a man self-assured enough to express himself in order to help her in an awkward situation. "I wonder if yours are playing the same tune mine are."

His laugh was short. He hunkered down by the car. "Stephanie," he said again.

This time she heard appreciation in his voice. "Michael."

"The moment I saw you, I knew you'd be different."

"I thought the same thing about you." Cars zipped past on the nearby freeway, but they were in a world by themselves.

"How long does it take you to get home?"

"Twenty minutes."

"I'm calling you in twenty-five. Drive carefully." He rose to his feet and shut the door.

Starting the car, Stephanie pulled away. It wasn't until she was on the freeway, heading for her home in Oak Cliff, that she recalled that Michael hadn't given her his phone number.

Michael had made an error in judgment.

No, not the simple kiss that had practically incinerated them. Not even his admitting how shaking the kiss had left him. His error was in not telling her he owned Evergreen Landscaping. Now what did he do?

He gunned the Dodge Ram and zoomed up the snaked driveway of his trilevel house on the rocky cliffs on the east shore of Joe Pool Lake. He made the trip in record time. Activating the garage door, he jumped out and raced through the garage. Unlocking the back door, he headed for the cordless phone in the sleek stainless steel kitchen.

Grabbing the slim black phone, he pulled out Stephanie's card and dialed her home phone number. If she had Caller ID "blocked call" would show up and not "Evergreen Landscaping" as it would on his cell. Worse, if he gave her his cell phone number and it went into voice mail she'd hear his voice and hear him say he was the owner.

"Hello."

The sound of her voice jolted him again. "You made it home all right."

"Yes. Did you?"

"I just walked in. How long before your course begins?"

"About five minutes."

"That doesn't give us very long to talk," Michael muttered. Opening the refrigerator, he pulled out a bottle of carrot juice and bumped the door closed with his elbow.

"I know."

He heard the sigh and regret in her voice, and wanted her there with him. He glanced around the state-of-the-art kitchen that led to the spacious living area on the second floor then up the stairs to his bedroom with its skylight over the bed and a balcony looking out on the lake. How could he bring her there when she thought he was nothing more than a landscape worker?

"Michael?"

"I'm here." Unscrewing the top, he wandered up the short stairs to a living room done in creamy beige and chocolate. "Which course is on for tonight?"

"International Business. I have to develop a plan for a business for my assignment."

"I guess I better let you go." Unlocking the French doors, Michael stepped out onto the stoned-terraced floor. He heard the gurgle of water coming from the fountains and waterfall in back. "I'll call you tomorrow around noon and find out what time to pick you up. I hope I don't have to wear a tie."

She laughed. "You don't, but you may have to leave the jeans at home."

"That would be interesting," he said, unable to keep the seductive teasing out of his voice. She laughed again and once again he wished she were there so he could see the expression on her beautiful face. He took a seat on the chaise longue and listened to the night sounds. "Where're we going?"

"Fogo de Chão. I've never been there, but I understand the array of meats is wonderful."

And a bit pricey. Not including drinks, the single-priced meal for two people, including the minimum tip, would cost a hundred bucks. He had planned to take April there the night after they broke up.

"Michael, you're not a vegetarian are you?"

No, but he just might be a fool. Too restless to sit, he came to his feet. "No."

"Good. You had me worried." He easily heard the renewed happiness in her voice. "Rose suggested the restaurant because she knew I had never been there and wanted to go. It's a favorite of hers and her husband Stan's. They go there every couple of months."

His hand tightened on the phone. Damn! He'd done it again. Measured her with the same stick he had other women. "If you want to go, that's where we're going," he declared.

"Thank you." She sighed. "I have to go. Class just started."

"Night. See you tomorrow."

"Good night, Michael."

Turning off the phone, he sipped his juice, and began to plan.

Chapter 5

Stephanie was ready twenty minutes before Michael was scheduled to pick her up for their eight o'clock dinner reservations, leaving her plenty of time to brood.

Needlessly fluffing the silk pillow on the sofa in the living room, she did what she always did when she was nervous or worried, chewed her lip and paced. Her high-heeled sandals were soundless on the white carpet in the white and gold room. Why hadn't Michael given her his cell or home phone number? Moving around so much she may not have dated a great deal, but she had read women's magazines and listened to other women talk about their relationships.

A man who didn't give you his number was either hiding another woman or didn't want to be bothered with you until he was ready. She reached the end of the white chenille sofa and whirled, sending the handkerchief hem of the multicolored silk chiffon dress swirling around her legs.

Michael's mother apparently thought he wasn't involved with anyone, but that wasn't saying much. With five brothers, she was well aware of the games men played. The question was, was she being played now or had he simply forgotten? Or was she making too much out of something minor? Growing up in a testosterone-filled house, she knew men thought and acted differently about certain things. She hadn't told him she wanted his phone number. Maybe he was waiting on her to ask.

The doorbell chimed and she started for the door, then remembered the pillow she was holding and tossed it toward the sofa. Opening the door, she didn't see Michael, but she did see a huge, decorative clay pot filled with spectacular blooms that spanned wider than her open hand. Charmed, she stepped outside and knelt. Sniffing was mandatory as she touched a single French-manicured nail to one of several blooms that had a dark red eye encircled by a ring of rose pink, a ring of ivory, and finally, an edging of butter yellow.

She sensed Michael before she saw him. "They're beautiful."

"So are you," he said, stretching out his hand to assist her in standing.

Her heart fluttered. She placed her hand in his, felt a little zip, and came to her feet. He certainly made her feel beautiful and desirable.

"I hope it makes up for my poor behavior. Because of its flamboyance the hibiscus has been compared to Versace or Armani clothes, but it can't rival you." ·

Her heart went crazy again. "Thank you. You look very nice yourself. Isn't that Hugo Boss?"

His broad shoulders shrugged carelessly beneath the expensive wheat-colored sports coat. "Mother bought it on one of her shopping sprees," he said. "I'm glad you like the hibiscus."

She glanced at the beautiful blossoms swaying in the warm evening breeze. "I do, very much. But I have to tell you, Michael, I'm death on plants."

Smiling, he circled her waist with his arm. "So is mother. I'll help you. Tomorrow I'll bring over some plant food and instructions. In the meantime we better get a move on or we'll be late."

"I'll just get my purse." Going inside she picked her small bag up from the sofa, then came back out. His arm around her waist again, they started down the curved walkway.

Michael's attention to Stephanie didn't waver as they neared the curb where his truck was parked. He'd had an idea how she would react and she proved him right.

Her mauve-colored lips curved upward as they rounded the front end of the bright red Dodge Ram. "I've seen more trucks since I've been in Texas than I have in the past ten years."

Opening the passenger door, he assisted her inside. "Some women don't like going on a date in a truck."

"You haven't met the right woman." At his lifted

eyebrow, she blushed. "Oh! That sounded so . . . so forward."

"Why?"

"Well, because my last name is Wright."

He smiled. "Stop worrying. It never crossed my mind." Closing the door, he came around the truck and got in.

He started the truck and headed down the heavily wooded street with its well-tended yards. "You live in a nice neighborhood."

"Thank you. A month after I moved to Dallas, I knew my wandering days were over and contacted a realtor." Relaxing against the leather seat, she continued, "We looked all over the city, but the other parts of town were too flat. They lacked the character and maturity of Oak Cliff with its hills and trees."

He thought of his home hewn from the side of a cliff, a mere seven minutes away, and wished he could take her there. "How was work today?"

"Wonderful." She twisted toward him. "We're not going to slack off because we're ahead in sales. When the execs come in a month we want to blow them away. How about you? Will the landscape be ready?"

Michael jerked his head around to stare at her. It took him a moment to realize she was talking in general about the project. "Most of it. We're about five or six weeks away from completion."

"Take it easy out there. It's hot and the temperature is supposed to go up next week," she told him.

Michael stopped at a signal light. He didn't like the idea of her worrying about him. "I'll be fine. I've been at this for a long time."

Stephanie wasn't convinced. "Then you shouldn't have been working by yourself yesterday without help."

Michael shifted gears and pulled off when the light changed. "I usually don't. I was taking out my bad temper on the dirt instead of on the men. I'm in charge of the project."

Her eyes rounded. "Michael, that's wonderful!"

He had thought a long time about the next thing he was going to say. "You don't mind dating a man who does manual labor?"

"Why should—" Her eyes widened. "Is that why you became upset when I mentioned that your mother told me you were working on the landscape? You thought I was that shallow?"

Michael answered the only way he could. "I didn't know you then."

His answer seemed to appease her. "I'd rather you be honest about what you do. Some men make up stuff about what big shots they are. I can't stand a phony."

Michael gulped.

"If a man is happy doing what he does, that's all that matters," she told him. "I've known men and women with six-figure salaries who are miserable. The bottom line can't be money." She turned toward him. "*Do* you enjoy your job?"

He hadn't expected that question, but he had an answer. "Very much. My dad died when I was ten and we had some lean years. The man next door had a garden and I used to help him. I found I liked having my hands in dirt, liked watching things grow. I can't imagine doing anything else."

"Then that's all that matters," she said simply.

Michael glanced at her and read the truth in her direct gaze. He took her hand in his and it felt right. She felt right. "I'm glad we're going out."

"So am I, Michael. So am I."

* * *

Rose and Stan were waiting by the fireplace at Fogo de Chão when Stephanie and Michael arrived. After introductions were made, a friendly waiter showed them to a window table draped in white linen, then presented them their menus.

"Since the waiters bring you all the types of meats, you won't need that except for the dessert," Rose said, looking lovely in a black Dior knit dress with a cowl collar. "And, of course, the good sense to turn your token from green to red so they'll stop serving you."

Everyone at the table laughed. Stephanie wished she could join them. Her eyes were glued to the menu prices.

"Stephanie, are you all right?" Michael asked, a frown wrinkling his brow.

"Yes," she told him, wondering how she could get out of this gracefully. Since Rose had chosen the restaurant, she had no idea if Michael knew how much the dinner would cost. She didn't want to take a chunk out of his paycheck or embarrass him.

The waiter appeared and explained how the meal was served and asked about drink choices. It didn't surprise her to hear Rose and Stan order wine. What snapped her head around was Michael ordering a bottle of chardonnay to celebrate the success of Texas Chic. A quick look at the wine's price list made her blink: $79.

"That isn't necessary, Michael." She sent her friend a beseeching look. "Is it, Rose?"

Rose frowned across the table at her, then caught on. "Stephanie is right." She turned to the hovering waiter. "Please change my order to iced tea. My husband will have the same."

"What?" Stan asked, staring hard at his wife. "You know I always have wine with my dinner."

"Tonight, you're having tea." Rose started to stand and another waiter pulled out a chair for her. "Come on, let's go to the salad bar."

Stan, reed thin and dressed in a tailored navy blue Armani blazer, went after his wife, grumbling that he wanted wine.

"I'm not very hungry." Stephanie handed the waiter the menu. "I'll have the vegetarian meal and water with lemon to drink."

"Sir?"

Michael handed the waiter the menu, his gaze locked on Stephanie. "The lady will have the regular meal, as will I. Please bring the bottle of chardonnay."

"Excellent choice, sir. Please help yourself to the salad bar."

Michael stood and reached for Stephanie's chair. She came to her feet, chewing on her lip. He'd seen through her ruse and now he was upset with her. She was trying to think of a way to explain when they kept going past the salad bar and out the front door.

"Michael?"

"In a minute." He didn't stop until they were behind the restaurant. The parking area was full of cars and they were alone. "Did you think I wouldn't catch on to what you were trying to do in there?"

She didn't even think of trying to evade. "Rose chose the restaurant and made the reservations. I wasn't sure if you were prepared for the prices. I happen to like salads, and wine can give me a headache."

"You were trying to save me money." He tossed out the words in accusation.

"We could eat out for a week at some restaurants

on what you're going to spend tonight," she said, un-
willing to back down because of some silly male pride.
"That's not counting what you spent on my hibiscus.
You work too hard for your money."

Michael was caught between exasperation, admiration, and a lie of his own making. There was only one
thing to do. "Come here."

She went into his open arms without hesitation. "I
really do like salads."

He chuckled. Stepping back, he took her face in
his hands and stared into her eyes. "I have it covered. Let's just enjoy the meal and, if you want, for
all of our future dinner dates we'll go to Jack in
the Box."

Hearing him say "future" made her insides tingle,
but she wrinkled her nose at the thought of eating
junk food all the time. Her hips and her arteries would
scream in protest. "I don't think we have to be quite
that drastic."

"Thank goodness." He kissed her on the forehead,
then slid his hand down her arm to clasp her fingers.
"Let's go enjoy ourselves."

After a stop by the salad bar, they went to their table
where the wine steward was ready to serve them. When
their glasses were filled, Michael lifted his. "To the
lovely ladies sitting here and to the continued success of
Texas Chic." Glasses clinked and wine was sipped.

"I'd like to make another toast." Rose held her
glass in the air. "To Stephanie, a wonderful friend and
the best assistant manager in the business. You make
Texas Chic what it is."

"Thank you," Stephanie said, her voice tremulous.
"And thanks for giving me a chance."

"I'm just glad I got you while you were going up," Rose told her.

Michael stared at Stephanie. "I didn't know you were the assistant manager, and what's this about going up?"

"Didn't she tell you?" Rose asked. At Michael's blank stare, she continued. "I tell her all the time she's too modest. She plans on opening her own boutique."

"You never mentioned it," he said with a frown.

"It hadn't come up," she said.

Michael recalled her telling him she didn't like phonies and braggarts. She would never fit into either category.

"That's why she lived in so many of the top fashion cities . . . to gain experience," Rose said, her voice and face animated. "It was a lucky day for me when I went into Leslie's looking for a pair of shoes and saw Stephanie. I stole her right out from under their noses."

Stan laughed and hugged his wife. "She was like a general going into battle. I'm so proud of her."

"I realized immediately she had what it would take to help me make Texas Chic into what it is today," Rose said, lifting her glass in a salute to Stephanie. "I'll hate to see you go, but I'll be cheering for you all the way."

"So will I," Michael said.

"I appreciate the vote of confidence," Stephanie said. "But the Wright Solution is still in the planning stages. I'm using the ideas I have for my boutique to develop a prototype for class." Humor touched her lips. "We'll see if my instructor agrees with you."

She was as modest as Rose had said, Michael thought. She was also down to earth, beautiful, and fun to be with. She had so much going for her and yet she had wanted to go out with him, the hourly wage earner, not the millionaire owner. "You're amazing."

"If you and Rose don't stop, my head will be too big to go through the door," Stephanie replied, but Michael could tell she was touched.

"Can't have that." Michael picked up his fork and began eating. Stephanie was proving to be more open and charming than he'd ever dreamed a woman could be.

Dinner was superb, the wine delicious, and the service impeccable. Stan and Michael hit it off immediately. It helped that the wine Michael ordered was one of his favorites. Stephanie didn't think she'd ever enjoyed herself more on a date.

She probably would have worried about the check, but she went to the ladies' room with Rose and when they returned the bill had been taken care of and the men were finishing their wine and discussing Stan's grass, which was dying in spots.

"I'd be happy to come out and take a look if you'd like," Michael offered.

"He's the project manager for the landscaping at the Anatole," Stephanie said proudly.

"The lawn is well-lit. How about now?" Stan asked. "We live about five minutes from here."

Michael looked at her. "Is that all right with you? I think I know the problem, but I'd like to see his lawn and make sure."

"Of course I don't mind," Stephanie said. "Maybe I'll learn some pointers about my own yard."

"It just needs some fertilizer. I'll do it tomorrow when I come over," he said easily.

"I wasn't suggesting you do my yard," she protested.

He smiled into her worried face. "I know. That's why I want to do it. That and I can't stand seeing a yard in need."

"Well, mine just might make you cry." Stan chuckled and they all joined in.

Michael followed behind Stan's Lincoln. Stan stopped in the circular driveway in front of a two-story home in an upscale neighborhood. Michael eased to a stop, then opened the door for Stephanie. "I'll get a flashlight out of the trunk and we can take a look."

The two men walked across the lawn, stopping every now and then to hunker down and talk. Stephanie and Rose wandered behind them. Stephanie was amazed by the amount of knowledge Michael had about plants and their care.

"I like him," Rose said. "Do you think he's a keeper?"

"I certainly hope so. He kissed me and fried my brain circuits," Stephanie admitted.

Rose whooped, drawing the men's attention. "We're going inside to make coffee."

"She means *she* is," Stephanie clarified, and shared a smile with Michael. Any man who drank her horrible coffee, kissed like a dream, and brought her beautiful plants was definitely a keeper.

"I can certainly see why your boss values you," she said when they were walking up the driveway to her home.

"It was easy to see Stan's problem was grub worms."

"Stan couldn't, and his yard man couldn't," Stephanie said as she unlocked the front door. The crystal chandelier in the foyer cast a golden light over them. "Do you want to come in?"

He brushed her hair behind her ear. "I want to, but perhaps it's best that I don't."

She hated to admit it, but he was right. Common sense went out the window when he was around. "I'll see you tomorrow, around twelve. You can come for lunch."

His eyebrow arched. "You cook?"

"Don't worry. My mother loved to cook and she taught all of the children. I'll have you licking the plate."

Michael knew exactly what he'd like to lick. His hand flexed on her arm.

Her voice trembled. "Michael?"

"I like hearing you say my name. As if it's every dream you've ever dreamed."

"It is."

Something clenched inside him. He dropped his forehead onto hers, aware if he kissed her, he might not be able to stop. He knew it was too soon in their relationship for intimacy. "I'll see you around twelve." He stepped back. "Good night."

"Good night." Reluctantly, Stephanie went inside and shut the door softly behind her.

Michael slid his hands into the pockets of his dress slacks and went to his truck. He wanted Stephanie very badly, and he wondered how long he could control the desire to make her his.

Chapter 6

Stephanie hurried home from early morning church services, changed into a sunny yellow sundress, and set about preparing lunch. She wanted something elegant but light in calories after the heavy meal last night. As she bustled around the kitchen, she could only hope Michael agreed. She had long since accepted that she'd always be full-figured, but she intended to take care of herself as much as possible.

She worked smoothly and efficiently. She hadn't lied about her cooking skills. The Wright household loved good food and, with so many of them, there had been a whole lot of cooking going on. Since her parents were both barbers and worked long, erratic hours, all the children pitched in to help. They had fussed and argued about duties, but working together made them close. If they got too out of hand, one of their parents would leave the shop and come home to settle matters—something none of them wanted. She missed her family, but hoped to have her own.

Her hand paused in mixing the greens for their salad. Before Michael, she always thought love and marriage were in the distant future. Her feelings for him were more than sexual attraction. Something about him called to the woman in her. She was falling in love with him and saw no way to stop . . . even if she wanted to.

The doorbell rang. *Michael!* Giving the kitchen table

a quick once-over she went to answer the door. As always the sight of him left her a little weak in the knees.

"Hi, come in."

"Hi." Stepping inside, he inhaled deeply. "Smells good."

"Chicken bastillas."

"What?"

"A Moroccan pie." Taking his hand, she headed for the kitchen. "It should be about ready. I hope you don't mind eating in the kitchen. I haven't gotten around to furnishing parts of the house yet."

"Not at all," he said, following her through the oak-paneled den that held a burgundy leather sofa with nail-head trim and a matching chair. Over the stone fireplace was a large portrait. "Your family?"

Stephanie stopped and smiled up at the picture. "Yes. That's the Wright clan. It was taken the year I graduated from college. The portrait was a housewarming gift from my parents. They may not like it that I'm not moving back to Seattle, but they support me in everything that I do."

"Like I said, I'm glad you're staying."

"Like I said, so am I. Come on before the food burns and you think I can't cook either."

Laughing, he allowed her to pull him into the kitchen. On the ledge between the kitchen and the den was a blue betta fish swimming among the roots of a peace lily, the flower's white blooms and deep green foliage sticking out from the top of a two-foot-high clear glass bowl. "You *can* grow a plant."

Stephanie threw an amused look his way as she removed the pastries from the oven and set the insulated baking sheet on a cooling rack. "They take care of each other." With a wide spatula, she transferred the bastilles to a serving dish, then dusted them with powdered sugar.

Michael peeked over her shoulder. "The crust almost looks like a gift-wrapped package of petals."

"But I bet it tastes better." She picked up the platter. "Let's sit down and eat."

As a bachelor Michael knew good food. He'd just been served the best meal he'd had in a long time, including dinner the night before, and he told Stephanie as much. "You're a superb cook."

"Thank you." Getting up, she began clearing the table.

"Let me help." Taking his plate, he went to the sink. "When we finish we'll go over the instructions for the hibiscus and then I can do the lawn."

Stephanie stopped dumping the leftover green salad in the disposal. "I don't have a spreader. I can ask the yard man to do it."

"You could, but I'm doing it. I brought one just in case." He went to the table and returned with the empty serving platter. There had been four of the pastries filled with poached chicken, almonds, and spices. Stephanie had eaten one. "I told you, I can't stand to see a yard in need."

She wrinkled her nose. "Like Stan said, mine will make you weep."

"We'll soon fix that." Michael kissed her lightly on the mouth. "Come on, let's finish and get to work outside. I know you're going to want to come with me, and I don't want you getting too hot."

She was already hot, but didn't think it wise to say so. Taking a deep steadying breath, Stephanie finished feeding the garbage disposal.

*   *   *

Stephanie thought Michael was just going to fertilize her front yard. He did, but first he had to cut it, edge it, then trim the Japanese boxwoods bordering the front and sides of the house, all the while muttering some uncharitable comments about her yard man. He didn't like it that the limbs of her fruitless mulberry were dragging against her wood shingle roof. The next thing she knew, three men were there cutting limbs and feeding them into a mulcher. The mulch was then put in her shrubbery beds.

She would have tried to stop him, but it was work that needed doing and she did plan to pay him when he finished. Going into the house to get Michael and the men water, she heard the phone ring. It was her father with his usual Sunday after call.

With the cordless in her hand she went back outside with the water. Her dad immediately wanted to know what the noise was and, when she told him, he'd insisted on talking with Michael. She felt as if she was sixteen again, but she asked one of the men to go up on the ladder and ask Michael to come down from the tree.

He came down the ladder with the grace and agility of a large cat. He'd tied a bandana around his head. His white T-shirt was drenched with perspiration and sticking to his impressive chest.

A bead of perspiration rolled down the side of his strong, handsome face and Stephanie had to clamp her teeth together to keep from leaning over and touching it with her tongue. Instead she offered him the water.

"Thanks." He drained half the tall glass. "What is it, honey?"

Her eyes widened. His did also. It was obvious the

endearment had slipped out. Any other time she would have been overjoyed at hearing him call her honey, but not within her father's hearing. "My father would like to speak to you."

To give Michael credit, he didn't throw down the pruning shears and run to his truck. He handed her the glass and took the phone. "Good evening, Mr. Wright. Michael Dunbar here."

Courtesy would probably dictate that she allow them privacy in their conversation, but not when your date was talking to your very protective father for the first time . . . even if the father was in another state.

"Yes, sir. I know it's Sunday, but the men and the mulch machine will be a hundred miles away in the morning on another job." He nodded. "The weather forecast is for light showers Tuesday and Wednesday, which should help the fertilizer soak in so Stephanie won't have to worry about watering." He sent her a warm smile. "She says she's death on plants. My mother is the same way. Yes, sir. She lives in Houston."

There was some more nodding by Michael, who occasionally gave the men hand signals before they started to the back of the house.

"I trimmed and mowed the front and will do the same to the back," he continued, starting around the side of the house. Stephanie followed hard on his heels. She could hear the hedge trimmers in the backyard before they went through the wooden side gate.

"You need a lock on this," Michael said, then explained what he was talking about to her father. "Yes, sir. I'll see that it's done before I leave."

Stephanie rolled her eyes. "I can get my own lock." She was not helpless.

"Sorry, sir. Stephanie was just telling me something."

He had the audacity to grin at her. "No problem, sir. It's the least I could do to thank her for the meal. Chicken bastillas. Yes, sir. She's a wonderful cook. Nice talking to you, too. Good-bye, Mr. Wright." He handed the phone to Stephanie. "Your father is nice."

He walked off, his blue jeans curving over his long legs and tight butt like a shadow. How could a woman be upset with a man who made her mouth water? "I'm back, Daddy."

It wasn't her father but her mother who wanted to know all about Michael Dunbar and why hadn't she told them about him. She'd been listening on the extension, a common practice when they talked. Stephanie went for the "he's just a friend" line, which her mother didn't buy but let slide. Thankful, Stephanie listened to her mother give her an update on her sister and brothers. But all the while she watched Michael.

It was almost five when the men left. By five thirty Stephanie and Michael were back from the home improvement store with a lock for her gate. Ten minutes later the new lock was installed. Her yard looked better than it had in the five months she had lived there.

"I can't get over how much better it looks," she told him.

Hands on his hips, he surveyed the yard. "It will look even better once the yard greens up. So will the back once it's watered and fertilized. Wish I had thought to bring a couple of extra bags. The home improvement store didn't have the brand I prefer." He nodded toward the sixty-foot tree, its branches spanning thirty feet. "The mulberry is thinned out enough to allow low maintenance hostas or monkey grass to grow around the trunk."

Stephanie wasn't sure what a hosta plant was and had no intention of asking. "Maybe next summer," she said, not realizing the implication that they would still be seeing each other then. "But after seeing the improvements, it almost makes me want to get a couple of hanging baskets for my patio. Those two plastic chairs look rather pitiful all by themselves."

"Begonias and ivy would be good. They don't take a lot of watering," he said. "In fact, too much water rots begonia roots."

"Maybe after I finish the business assignment." She turned toward the front door. "Come inside where it's cool and I can get my checkbook."

Michael's eyes narrowed, but he followed her inside.

"Please have a seat and I'll get my purse."

When she came back Michael was standing, hand on his hips and he wasn't smiling.

"What's the matter?"

"Do you actually think I'm going to accept pay for helping you?"

"Yes. Garden supplies aren't cheap and neither is trimming a tree. Why do you think I've been putting it off?" She marched to the kitchen. "How much do I owe you and the men?"

"I don't want your money."

"Tough." She wrote out his name on the check, signed and dated it, leaving only the amount blank.

Michael didn't have any experience with stubborn women and could have happily lived without acquiring any. "The food I ate cost money."

She rolled her eyes. "That's different and you know it. Besides, I invited you."

"Right, and I invited myself to do your yard. The men who came over did it as a favor to me."

"I'm paying you, Michael. You can tell me how much or you can let me guess."

He was not taking hundreds of dollars from Stephanie. But who said he had to cash the check? "One fifty."

Her brows bunched. "That's way below what I was quoted or what my neighbor paid."

"Family and friend discount."

She wrote the check and handed it to him. "Thank you. You made my house look more like a home."

Her mouth twisted wryly. He reached for her instead of the check and pulled her to her feet. "You really know how to diffuse a guy's anger."

"I don't want to fight, but I also don't want to take advantage of you."

He nuzzled her neck. "What if I take advantage of you?"

"I'm not sure you would be."

He went very, very still, then slowly lifted his head and gazed into her eyes. He saw a simmering passion that mirrored his own. "Lady, do you know what you do to me?"

"I hope it's the same thing you do to me."

"Let's see."

His mouth closed hungrily over hers. She answered back with the same hunger. He couldn't seem to get enough of her sweet mouth, the heavenly weight of her in his arms. She was all that he desired.

Her unique scent tantalized him, beckoned him, lured him. He was powerless to keep from going in search of the fragrance. His mouth freely roamed the curve of her jaw, the slope of her shoulder. His tongue lapped the rounded curve of her breast as his hands absorbed the shudders he drew from her.

Need and desire racked his body. His hands didn't seem able to touch her yielding body enough. Through the thin material of her dress his palm, then a finger and thumb, found the round fullness of her breast, the pebbled hardness of her nipple.

Both moaned.

She was bent like a taut bow over his arms and, like that bow, quivering and waiting for release. He could give it to her, to both of them. All he had to do was take her.

He couldn't.

There was something intensely trusting and special about Stephanie. She trusted him and believed in fairness. Slowly she opened her eyes and stared at him. In that instant, he knew what it was.

He didn't know whether to laugh or cry. "You're a virgin, aren't you?"

Chapter 7

Stephanie told herself that she would act sophisticated, but the words that came out of her mouth were more of a challenge. "You've never kissed a virgin before, Michael?"

"Not since high school."

She pushed out of his arms and straightened on legs that refused to steady. "What happened?"

"I ran the other way," he said and damned if he didn't want to do so again.

Stephanie linked her fingers, wondering if he was going to run this time as well. And if she dared stop him if he did.

"How old are you anyway?" He tossed the question nonchalantly, but there was an edge of accusation to it.

She lifted a delicate brow. "Twenty-seven. And you?"

"Thirty-two," he flung back at her as if his age implied worldly experience.

"And how old were you the first time—"

"We are not discussing that!"

Stephanie let it go. The answer would probably depress her anyway. She went to the refrigerator and took out a plastic covered bowl. "Would you care for some pasta salad?"

"You're acting mighty calm."

And it obviously didn't put him in a very good mood. She wished she had enough experience to know if that was good or bad. Placing the container on the cabinet, she took out a box of crackers, then grabbed two plates. "The subject was bound to come up sooner or later."

His scowl deepened. He didn't like the idea of it coming up at all. It complicated everything. Virgins expected commitments, and he didn't think he was ready for that.

She ignored his bad humor and put everything on the table. "It's almost six thirty. You have to be hungry. You can wash up in the bathroom behind you."

He'd go because he needed a minute or two to take it all in. Spinning on his heels he went into the small bath that was barely large enough to fit in. Touches of Stephanie filled the room—framed seascapes, ornate toilet articles, and an intricate burgundy-and-turquoise tassel that had to be a special order hanging from the tip of the valance at the window. Elegantly embossed hand towels were neatly lined up on the chrome rack. She'd put her mark here just as she was slowly and surely putting her mark on him.

He barely kept a curse between his teeth. What the hell was he doing with a virgin? Worse, a virgin that left him aching with need, and one who tied his guts in knots.

He stared at his fierce reflection in the gold-framed mirror. He'd *known* she would be trouble. He should have kept walking. Drying his hands, he came out of the bathroom.

The door to the garage and freedom were mere inches away. All he had to do was reach out and twist the knob. He'd never see Stephanie again. The thought sent a pain straight to his heart.

He went back into the kitchen. She looked up when he entered the room, then away, but not before he'd seen the fear she'd tried to mask. She had thought he'd bail. She'd given him the opportunity to do so. She wouldn't beg him to stay if he wanted to leave. Although the possibility was still there, he didn't like the idea that she'd accept it so easily if he left.

"Please have a seat." She heaped the shrimp-loaded salad on the burgundy plate. "It's even better than the bastilla." Picking up a cracker, she dug into her own food.

If he hadn't been watching her closely, he might not have seen her hand tremble. He relaxed a bit. She wasn't as clam as she pretended. That still left them with a big problem.

How did a man who wanted a woman as badly as

he wanted Stephanie keep from taking her? Because once he did, he wasn't sure if he'd be able to walk away. An experienced woman might not have expectations, but a twenty-seven-year-old virgin sure as hell would.

He swiped his hand over his face and discovered she wasn't the only one whose hands weren't quite steady. Perhaps it would be best for both of them if he made his apologies, gave her the instructions to take care of her yard and plant, then ran for his life.

He was seriously considering that course of action when she looked up at him. If he hadn't been sitting down he would have dropped to his knees. There was passion there, but something deeper, more lasting, that wrapped around him like velvet vines, a sweet yearning she didn't even try to hide. Somehow he knew she had never looked at any man that way before. He didn't want her to. The vines closed a little tighter.

If he'd felt trapped, he might have panicked. He didn't. He wasn't sure what his feelings were except that, with this new development, it wasn't the time to tell her he owned Evergreen Landscaping.

Stephanie, thy name is complication.

Picking up a cracker in the shape of a cloverleaf, he dipped it into the salad. "When we finish, I'll tell you how to care for your hibiscus and water the yard. Do you have any lemonade?"

"I'll get it." Standing, she did something she probably shouldn't have done, but she couldn't help herself. She kissed him tenderly on the forehead. "I'm glad you didn't leave."

He caught her hand and held it tightly. His gaze drilled into her. "I still may."

Her smile was sweetly tender. "You're here now," she said, and went to get the lemonade. She wondered if he had stopped to realize that, by not pushing his advantage, he'd revealed that he cared for her. If he didn't, he would have made love to her with no thought of why she had waited so long to let a man love her.

From the ice dispenser in front of the refrigerator ice clinked into the tall glasses. She glanced over her shoulder and he was looking at her. Need and desire shone back at her.

The sudden clenching of her body caused her hand to tighten around the glass. She wouldn't have stopped him if he had wanted to go further. She wasn't being reckless or irresponsible. She'd realized this afternoon, while he was working on her yard, that she was in love with him. There had been no time to examine her newly discovered feelings, but she trusted her instincts. Despite his brooding nature she believed he cared deeply for her as well. It didn't take weeks or months to fall in love, just the right person.

Of course, just like a man, he hadn't realized it yet. But he would. She refused to consider the possibility that he wouldn't. Being around a man whose very touch left her weak and hungry for more was risky, but the rewards could be wonderful.

Setting the slender glass pitcher and the glasses on the tray, she returned to the table and sat down. "So, tell me about my hibiscus."

She wasn't sure how it happened.

They were in the backyard getting ready to water

by hand since she only had one sprinkler and it was being used in front. They both insisted on doing the job.

"Michael, I can water my yard."

"I didn't say you couldn't."

Water gushed out of the hose between them. They stared belligerently into each other's eyes.

"It will be dark soon. Let go." She jerked upward, sending a stream of water straight into Michael's astonished face.

She gasped and froze, drenching him completely. He was the one who moved the hose. She knew she was in trouble when he didn't even try to wipe the dripping water from his face.

Dropping the hose, she began backing away, trying to keep the smile off her lips. He looked so funny. "Michael, I'm sorry."

He calmly picked up the hose and matched her step for step.

"You wouldn't," she said, knowing she'd never make it to the gate or the sliding glass door of the patio.

He kept coming.

"It was an accident." Her lips twitched. His eyes narrowed. "You should have let me do it."

The brass-plated nozzle in his hand slowly rose.

"Michael!"

He grinned.

She took two running steps before water fell from the sky. She yelped, then laughed after the first shock of cold water rained on her head, soaking her sundress. "I give!" she cried, hearing his laugh as he approached her.

"That'll teach you."

"I wouldn't bet on it," she said, making a successful dive for possession of the hose. One of the favorite games of her siblings had been water fights.

Michael reacted quickly, trying to come in low and grab her. With a playful squeal, she darted away and caught him with a blast of water on the forehead. "Be glad you aren't wearing your Stetson."

Michael didn't respond. He just kept coming, grabbing her around the waist and taking her down onto the freshly cut grass, with him on the bottom. Her initial thought was that her weight was too much for him, then her mind emptied as she felt the muscled hardness of his body beneath hers. With her cotton sundress soaked and only her bra and panties beneath, she realized from the hot blaze in his eyes he could intimately feel *everywhere* they touched.

"M-Michael."

They moved at the same time. The touch of their lips was tentative, as if they remembered the firestorm of their previous kisses and were determined to take it slow. They did. For all of three seconds.

Michael's arms wrapped around Stephanie like a vise. Her hands palmed his face as if she'd never wanted to turn loose. Together they sank into the oblivion where there was only the two of them locked in shared passion and need.

The angry blast of a car horn pulled them back to reality. They moved apart just enough to stare into each other's eyes. "You touch me and I lose all reasoning," he whispered.

His words went straight to her heart. Momentarily unable to think of anything to say, she lay her head on his chest and listened to the erratic beat of his heart, a fast staccato that matched her own. In her direct line of vision was the water hose a few feet away, still aimed in their direction.

Frowning, she pressed her hand into the grass by his broad shoulders. It came back moist.

"Michael, you're lying in water," she announced, scrambling to her knees.

He was slow to rise. "I didn't notice at first, then I thought it might cool me down. Seems I was wrong."

Stephanie gulped. She recalled all too well the distinctive bulge pressed against her stomach. "I shouldn't have started the water fight."

His hand curved around her neck. "You enjoy life, you give as good as you get, and you're fiercely independent. You make life interesting."

Interesting enough to stick around? "I made us both wet."

His gaze dropped briefly to her breasts where her soaked dress was plastered against her body. Her nipples hardened. "I noticed."

With his usual easy strength and grace he came to his feet, bringing her with him. "I guess I better head home. I'll move the sprinkler to the other side of the yard. Cut the water off in an hour."

"I will. Thank you for everything."

His thumb grazed her chin. "My pleasure."

Stephanie sighed as he walked to the gate. He waved, then he was gone.

No, she thought, the pleasure was all mine.

Stephanie fully expected Michael to drop by the shop Monday. She planned to give him the check he'd forgotten when he left Sunday. When he didn't, she went home disappointed and waited for the phone to ring. It didn't. On Tuesday, not sure of what her next step should be, she had done nothing. She couldn't keep running after Michael. He had to want to come to her.

"Men can be a little dense at time," Rose offered Wednesday night when they were walking to their cars after closing the store.

"That's an understatement." The overcast skies matched Stephanie's mood. She held open the back door of the hotel for Rose, then together they followed the winding path past the convention site buildings to the back parking lot. "My mother has called every night since Sunday, trying to figure out if Michael and I are more than friends."

Rose stopped at a bright yellow Volkswagen bug. She adored the sporty little car and its ability to squeeze into the tiniest parking space. "What did you tell her?"

"The truth. That I thought we could have been." It hurt saying the words, but she had to accept them and move on.

"Men are notorious for being slow on the uptake." Rose opened the car door. "Stan was."

"I'm sure he had given you some indication that he cared." Stephanie bit her lip. Would kissing her mindless count?

"Men are different. Good night and stop worrying," she advised. "I saw him with you. He cares."

But did he care enough? "Good night, Rose. See you in the morning."

By the time Stephanie pulled into her garage the light rain the weatherman had forecasted had begun to fall. The rain made her think of Michael. Going inside, she undressed and slipped on a pair of lounging pajamas, then warmed up homemade tomato soup she didn't want to eat.

She looked around the kitchen. Michael had only been there once, but the memory of him remained strong. Wrapping her arms around herself, she went to the patio door, unlocked it, and stepped outside. She blinked then blinked again.

The area was alive with a rainbow of flowers sprouting from terra cotta bowls and Mexican pottery. Bright blooms and succulents surrounded a three-foot-tall Grecian woman statue with water pouring from an urn held high over her head. Four huge moss hanging baskets filled with begonias and ivy hung from the weathered beams of her patio cover.

It was beautiful.

And high-handed of him to do this without her permission.

Stephanie was trying to be incensed instead of touched when a thought struck. How had he gotten the things over the gate?

She didn't have to check the gate to know it remained locked and she knew exactly where the only two keys were. One was on a nail in the garage; the other was on the key ring in the kitchen.

Her hand grazed over the solid stone statue. How had he accomplished this and when? It certainly hadn't been here yesterday. But what really steamed her was that, with no phone number, she had no way of asking him.

Chapter 8

"I want to speak with you."

Michael heard the snap in Stephanie's voice Thursday morning and slowly turned from pulling a flat of pink begonias from the truck. It was barely eight and he was at the south end of the hotel. Obviously she'd asked one of his men where he was working. He'd already warned them not to tell anyone he was the owner. "Good morning, Stephanie."

"Good morning. You forgot your check and here is another one for the things you left on my patio." Her arm was rigidly extended toward him. "I checked out prices on the Internet. If I've made an error, please let me know and I'll write you another check."

She was beautiful when she was angry. Yet aware of how unpredictable an angry woman could be, he took the checks and stuffed them into his shirt pocket without looking at them. "I hope you figured in the friend and family discount."

Her eyebrow shot up. "Is that what we are, Michael? Friends?"

An uneasiness rolled though him. He got the impression that he had let himself walk into a trap. "Yes."

"Then why don't I have your phone number? Why do you disappear on me?"

He couldn't think of an answer fast enough.

She blinked rapidly. "Please do not bring any more

plants or anything else to my house. Please don't call me. Good-bye, Michael."

He caught her a couple of feet away. "Wait a minute. You can't walk out on me."

Her chin came up. "I didn't. You did. Please let go of my arm."

He didn't dare do as she said. "My home phone number is 972–555–7654. I took off because I was afraid if we saw each other again, we'd end up making love and that's a commitment I'm not sure I'm ready to make."

She'd asked. How did the old saying go? *Don't ask if you can't stand to hear the answer.* "I'd like to go inside now."

He took her other arm and talked fast although she refused to look at him. "No, you asked and you're going to hear it. You scare the hell out of me, but I can't get you out of my mind. I might have sent a woman flowers before, but I've never bothered to turn her home or apartment into a flower garden. I certainly never spent most of the day working on her yard or lifting a cement statue and flowers over a fence at the risk of getting arrested."

Slowly Stephanie's head turned and she faced Michael. He wasn't happy about his feelings for her, but he wasn't running away from them or her. "How about a water fight?"

The tension began to ease from his shoulders and he slipped his arms around her waist. "You're my first and only," he said with a small, self-conscious smile.

When he would have stepped closer, her hands splayed on his chest to stop him. "Do you plan to get moody and disappear again?"

He opened his mouth to speak, but she put her fingertips over his mouth. "Think carefully before you answer, Michael. One thing I demand in a relationship is honesty. If two people can't trust each other, there is nothing to build upon."

Her statement hit him square in the chest. There it was again . . . her honesty and her demand that others be the same way. It struck him as ironic that he had always wanted honesty from a woman, but now that he had found it, he was the one keeping secrets. If he admitted now that he owned Evergreen Landscape, that he'd finally decided to tell her, would she understand and forgive him or would she walk away? His arms tightened around her waist.

He couldn't take that chance. He wasn't going through another day without seeing Stephanie, enjoying her smile, holding her, kissing her. He'd find a way to tell her soon, but he couldn't risk it now.

Kissing her fingertips, he took her hand in his. "What nights do you have to stay home with your online courses?"

"Monday, Wednesday, and Friday."

"How about a movie tonight, dinner and dancing Saturday night, and brunch on Sunday. Then we'll go from there?"

She played with the buttons on his shirt. "We don't have to go out all the time."

He wished he could kiss her and take the frown from her brow. She was probably worried about the money he'd spend on her. "I think it's best for the time being that we keep the time alone to a minimum."

"Oh." She moistened his lips and stared at the button she'd undone on his shirt. She quickly redid the blue button. "Good thinking."

He stepped back. "Go to work. If it's all right with

you I'll pick you up around seven forty-five. We can decide then if we have time to eat or if we should go straight to the movie."

"All right. Bye."

"Bye." Hoping he had made the right decision in not telling her, Michael watched her go.

Stephanie chose a chick flick. Michael didn't bat an eye when she told him the title. He also stayed awake in the movie theater, which was more than the guy snoring two rows head of them did. Every once in a while he'd wake up and proclaim to the woman sitting beside him that he wasn't sleeping. Finally, after the third or fourth time, another man yelled, "Yes, you were, and you're in trouble, buddy." The entire theater laughed.

Afterward, they'd gone to eat, then Michael had driven her home. He kissed her a long time before he said good night. Stephanie had gone to sleep smiling.

The next morning she was barely out of the shower when he called and invited her to breakfast. A simple thing for a man dating a woman to ask, but for her it posed a problem. Unless she was very careful, and she hadn't been, eating a diet high in proteins and carbohydrates would go straight to her hips.

She could make excuses or face reality. It wasn't likely that he had missed the fact that she wasn't Miss Twiggy. "Thank you, but I have absolutely no willpower when I'm starting at a breakfast menu. All those calories will settle in one unwanted place, my hips."

"I like your hips. How about I come over and show you?"

"Michael," she said, trying to sound outraged, but she couldn't quite mask the excitement in her voice.

"Spoil sport. How about eight thirty by the tennis court. I'll be in one of the company trucks. I'll bring the coffee and a couple of muffins."

"Make it blueberry and orange juice, and you have a deal."

"See you in a bit. Bye."

A smile on her face, she went to get dressed.

Michael was waiting for her when she arrived. Inside the truck's spacious and clean cab, she was surprised to see a small bouquet of cut flowers in the cup holder, sky blue linen napkins, and a crystal glass. "Michael, this is nice, but you didn't have to go to this much trouble."

Proudly he handed her the glass of orange juice. "No trouble. I'm finally using a few of the things Mama bought for me."

Stephanie sipped her juice. "What are your plans today?"

He didn't hesitate. "Now that we've transported all the trees and shrubs, it's time to prepare the soil for the new plants. Things should start taking shape quickly." He sipped his coffee. "That should make Stevenson happy."

"He's a stickler for detail, but fair. He nearly drove us crazy with questions about the changes we wanted to make in the store." She bit into her muffin. "Now he couldn't be prouder. We're the only business in the hotel that is specifically slated for the executives to visit."

"I don't know much about retail shops, but I liked the open brightness of Texas Chic. They should be pleased," he said, polishing off his second blueberry muffin.

"We have high hopes that they will." Finishing her juice and muffin, Stephanie dabbed the napkin to her lips. "I enjoyed breakfast, but I have to go. I'm opening the shop this morning."

"These are for you. Hydrangeas and peonies." He handed her the bouquet.

A smile touched Stephanie's lips. He'd used a water glass, not a vase. His mother would faint if she knew he had casually given away cut crystal. "They're beautiful."

"So are you."

While her heart was still galloping at his compliment, he leaned over and kissed her lightly on the lips. She wanted nothing more than to deepen the kiss. From the intense look in his eyes, he wanted the same. Reluctantly, she straightened. "Coffee tastes good on your lips."

His eyes narrowed and Stephanie reached for the door. "I better go. Thanks again."

Straightening, he got out of the truck and opened the door for her. "I'll call you around seven thirty tonight."

"All right." She started down the curved walkway that would lead back to the hotel.

"Stephanie." He jogged to catch up with her. "Like I said, I like your hips."

Blushing, she started walking back to the hotel, but darn if she didn't put a little extra in the swing of her hips, then giggled like a schoolgirl when she heard Michael whistle.

*   *   *

Michael was an early riser, but Saturday morning he had no plans to work in his yard or check on a job site. He was going to Wally World, Wal-Mart to the uninitiated, to buy Stephanie a coffeemaker. He and Stephanie had been going out for over a week, and since she didn't have to be at work until eleven, she had invited him over for breakfast. He'd thought it was a good time to follow through on his promise to show her how to make coffee. His wasn't the greatest, but it was better than hers. It was a total mystery to him how a woman who cooked as well as she did could make such bad coffee.

Hands in the pockets of his jeans, he strolled into the store with a smile on his face and asked a store clerk for directions to the small appliance department, then tipped his Stetson and headed in that direction. He didn't notice that she and the two women with her were elbowing each other and grinning after him.

Turning into the aisle, his hands slipped out of his pockets. Lines of concentration crinkled his brow. He'd given his mother his credit card and asked her to stock his kitchen. She'd also purchased most of the furniture and decorated his house and office. To him, shopping was right up there with water torture. Yet here he was at seven thirty in the morning because he planned to be at Stephanie's house by eight thirty with the coffeemaker as a surprise.

Well aware that the most expensive wasn't always the best and, more important, that Stephanie would try to pay him for it, he passed over the espresso maker and chose a stainless steel thermal coffeemaker because he liked its sleekness. He'd tell her it was on sale. Smiling in triumph, he went to find the coffee and while he was there, he might as well see if they had any plants she might like. Whistling, he strolled off.

Stephanie was angrier than she had ever been in her life. She took her displeasure out on the eggs she was beating for the omelets. Men! At lest *one* man. Stephanie set the bowl aside and peeked in the oven at the banana nut bread. The way Michael liked sweets, he'd probably wolf half the loaf down before realizing it was made with whole-wheat flour with no added sugar.

Hearing the doorbell, she glanced at the oven clock: 8:17. Michael was early. She went to the front door and opened it. "Good morning."

The smile on his face faded. "What's the matter?" he asked, stepping inside and closing the door behind him.

"Nothing. Come on in the kitchen. Breakfast is almost ready."

He caught her arm before she had gone more than a couple of steps. "Stephanie. If I can help I'd like to."

"If only you could." She nodded at the package beneath his arm. "What's that?"

"A coffeemaker," he answered, wishing he could take the misery from her eyes.

She almost smiled. "I hope you brought coffee."

"I did," he said, studying her unhappy face closely.

"You unbox it and I'll start the omelet." In the kitchen, she set a skillet on the stove. "If you need anything, holler."

"Is it something I did?" he asked, unable to let the subject drop. Stephanie was always so happy and full of life.

She spun toward him. "Of course not! This has nothing to do with you."

Michael didn't want to pry, so he set the box on the kitchen table. "I can see you've gone to a lot of trouble, but why don't we do this another time?"

She closed her eyes tightly. By the time she opened them, Michael was there. "Please tell me how I can help."

She stared at him for a long moment, then went into his arms. "My sister split up with her boyfriend. She called me after I got home last night. We were on the phone for two hours and most of the time she was crying her heart out."

"And you feel even worse because we're going out."

She lifted her face. Misery stared back at him. "She's my baby sister."

Palming her face, Michael kissed Stephanie gently on the forehead. "And you love her, but do you think she'd want to see you miserable?"

"No." Her lips tightened. "I'd like to get my hands on Keith. All she'd tell me is that he'd been lying to her since day one of their relationship. Regina is as rock-steady as they come. So it had to be something pretty major."

Michael went cold inside. He wasn't sure what to say.

"If he's married he'll be lucky if my brothers don't pay him a visit and rearrange his face," Stephanie said, perking up a bit.

In spite of himself, Michael smiled. "I didn't know you were bloodthirsty."

"My family is very close. You mess with one and you mess with all of us. My brothers are all over six feet tall."

All humor left Michael at the thought of five irate brothers on his doorstep.

"Don't worry," Stephanie said, giving him a quick peck on the lips before turning back to the omelets. "You have nothing to worry about."

Michael knew he did, and the knowledge twisted his insides. But the thought of being beaten to a pulp wasn't nearly as daunting as the possibility of losing Stephanie. "Perhaps the guy had a reason for whatever he did."

"There is never a reason for lying." The wire whisk scraped against the bowl. "She trusted him and he lied to her."

Michael went to remove the coffeemaker from the box. He hadn't lied to get anything over on Stephanie or to take advantage of her. He just hoped that when he found the right time to tell her, she'd listen.

Chapter 9

Over the next three weeks Michael made sure they saw each other every day. Each time he found himself enjoying Stephanie's company more and more. The wanting was still there, but he discovered being with her was often enough. He couldn't wait to see her each morning and was irritable on the nights they couldn't get together because she was doing classwork. On those nights they'd talk on the phone and go over her lesson plans and tests after she finished her class for the night.

Every time they were together he'd search for a way to tell her the truth about his business, but fear of losing her always held him back. He'd gotten up enough nerve to ask about her sister and her ex-boyfriend and learned the guy was out of the picture for good. Michael didn't plan to end up the same way but, as time passed, the possibility that it might happen was never far from his mind.

It was becoming increasingly difficult for Stephanie to remember a time when Michael wasn't in her life. They saw each other every day and it never seemed to be enough. He helped her with her business plan and on a couple of Sunday afternoons he'd driven her around town scouting locations. His belief that she could make The Wright Solution a success meant a lot to her. He even came up with feasible problems she hadn't thought of, like insurance for customers and securing the domain name for her store before someone else grabbed it.

Weekends found Michael teaching her how to care for her yard of ever-increasing plants. Her hibiscus was thriving, as were the plants on the patio. To her surprise, she was caught up in the transformation of her yard and admired Michael even more for his ability to turn the ordinary into the extraordinary. Coming home and seeing the flowers always relaxed her.

Since Michael had discovered she loved the color purple, he used lots of it and pink in the perennial bed with bits of blue here and there. He told her he'd added lemon yellow for punch and lots of pure white to divide colors and add sparkle. All Stephanie knew was that it was beautiful.

Little oasis of plants cropped up in her front and back yards. Neighbors noticed and began coming over when they were working outside. Like Stan, whose yard Rose had told them was improving rapidly, they often wanted advice on their own particular problems.

One Saturday afternoon, after a third neighbor had stopped to ask Michael his advice, Stephanie decided to ask Michael a question that had been on her mind for a couple of weeks. "Have you ever thought of starting your own business?"

He'd stopped pinching off a dead pink geranium stem and slowly looked at her. "Why do you ask?"

The wary look she'd thought she'd never see again was back. Deciding she wasn't going to tiptoe through their relationship, she said, "Because I think you should. You're great at what you do. No wonder the owner put you in charge." She gestured around her yard. "Just look at what you've done here."

His hands settled on her waist. "You'd be there cheering me on."

She placed her hands on his chest. "Just like you're doing me."

He kissed her there in the front yard among the flowers they'd planted together and it appeared the most natural thing in the world. It was only later that she realized he hadn't answered her question.

The phone was ringing when Michael arrived home that night. He was tired of the charade with Stephanie. He wanted to introduce her to his friends, take her to fancy restaurants and not have her worry about the bill, do things for her and not have her insist that she pay him. He hadn't cashed a single check she'd given him nor did he intend to, but what would happen when she was ready to balance her checkbook?

Still thinking about Stephanie, he continued to his office on the second and main floor. The answering machine clicked on and he heard his younger brother's deep voice. Michael quickly picked up the receiver.

"Hi, Neal. How's it going?"

"Hi. I was about to ask you the same thing. You've been out of pocket a lot lately. Everything going all right with the new project?"

Michael settled into the leather chair behind his massive desk and gazed out the arched windows at the lighted flower gardens beyond. He and his brothers had always been close and they usually talked once a week. He realized he hadn't spoken to either of them recently. "The job is going great. I've been busy helping Stephanie. She's the assistant manager at a boutique at the Anatole. We met when Mama went into her store. Stephanie is beautiful, but her coffee is worse than the cod liver oil Mama used to give us. Her yard was a mess when we met, but you should see it now. She likes purple so I put in verbenas, miniature daylily, pink wastonias, phlox, and alstroemerias. I think she'll get Yard of the Month. She'll be thrilled."

"Michael, do you know that you haven't stopped talking about this Stephanie since you answered the phone?"

Michael jerked upright. "No, you're wrong," he protested.

"Should I repeat what you said?" Neal asked with a chuckle.

Michael was silent.

"Wise decision. You've never mentioned any woman before by name. You know what this means, don't you?"

Michael was afraid to ask.

"You're in love. Better you than me. I can't wait to call Brody. When he picks himself off the floor from laughing so hard, he'll probably call you back," Neal said.

"I'm not in love." Michael surged to his feet, then looked around wildly as if seeking an avenue of escape.

"Does Mama know?"

Michael went into a full panic. "You better not say a word to her!"

More laughter. "This is priceless. I can't wait to meet the woman who trapped you."

"I'm not trapped," Michael felt compelled to say. "Stephanie and I just enjoy each other's company. She's fun to be with. I'm teaching—" His voice trailed off as he realized he was talking nonstop about Stephanie again. He sat down hard in the chair. "What am I going to do?"

"My advice would be to run like hell. But since that's not your way, I guess you'll have to figure out for yourself what you want to do." Neal snorted. "Brody won't be of any help either."

That was an understatement. Brody changed women faster than the climate changed in Texas.

"How does she feel about you?"

"What?"

"She's crazy about you, too, isn't she?"

The panic Michael felt before was mild in comparison to his feelings now. He was up and pacing. He thought Stephanie cared for him, but just how deep did it go? And did he have a right to ask her until he was completely honest with her? What if she walked away after she told him? Dread swept through him.

"Michael?"

He pushed the words through his lips. "I don't know." Then, needing desperately to talk to someone, he told Neal everything. "She doesn't care about my money. What she demands is honesty and I haven't given her that."

"I'd say you better come clean and quick. The longer you put it off the worse it's going to be for you."

"That certainly helps," Michael grumbled. His brother had spoken a truth he didn't want to hear.

"She'll come around. Use some of that Dunbar charm we're noted for," Neal said. "In view of the situation, I'll tell Brody not to call you until tomorrow. Bye, Bro. Good luck."

Michael slowly hung up the phone. He was going to need all the luck he could get.

Michael tossed and turned all night. By daybreak Sunday morning he had finally accepted two irrefutable facts: he had fallen in love with Stephanie and he had to tell her the truth. She meant too much to him to do otherwise. He could only hope and pray that she'd understand and forgive him. If it took a lifetime, he'd make it up to her.

Tossing back the bedcovers, he went to shower, then got dressed. He was supposed to pick Stephanie up for brunch after church. But he'd drive himself crazy thinking about what might happen if he waited until eleven. Besides, he wanted them to be alone when he told her.

He thought about calling before getting in his truck and backing out of his driveway a little after eight, but decided to just drive to her house. She didn't leave for church until nine. Perhaps she'd be in a more forgiving mood on a Sunday. His sweaty hands flexed on the steering wheel.

Driving across the highway over the lake he tried to come up with just the right words to explain. He couldn't. The bottom line was, he hadn't been honest with her. His reasons had seemed valid at the time, but would they be enough for Stephanie?

Once on the freeway, Michael continued to try to find the right way, the right words. Which confession should come first: his admission that he loved her or his omission that he owned the company he'd led her to believe he worked for?

He still hadn't come to any decision he was comfortable with when he turned into her street and saw the ambulance in front of her house. His heart stopped, then sped as he floored the truck. It seemed to take forever for him to come to a screeching halt behind the ambulance. He tore out of the truck without bothering to shut the door and raced across the lawn to her front door.

Chapter 10

Stephanie looked through the cluster of people in her living room and saw Michael. In his eyes she saw stark fear. She held out her hand to him.

Without a word he crossed to her, taking her hand in one that trembled. "I . . . I thought . . ."

Her hand squeezed his in reassurance, then she glanced back at the paramedics kneeling on either side of her next-door neighbor. "I went out to water my hibiscus and she came over to talk. She started having chest pains and I brought her inside and called 9-1-1, then her husband. She didn't want me to."

Michael's arm curved around Stephanie as the paramedics lifted the elderly woman gently onto the gurney. "You did right."

The woman's color was back, and with the oxygen she was breathing easier. As they passed Stephanie and Michael, the woman's husband squeezed Stephanie's shoulder in thanks and followed the paramedics out of the house. Neighbors who had seen the ambulance come over walked out behind them.

"You want to go to the hospital?" Michael asked.

"Please. They have children and friends, but I don't want Mr. Johnson to be by himself until they get there."

"Let's go."

It was nearly one before Stephanie and Michael left the hospital. Mrs. Johnson was resting comfortably after having a light heart attack and all four of her children were there with her. Over and over they had thanked Stephanie for her quick intervention, for staying with their father, then helping them all get through the fearful time while the doctors ran tests and made their diagnosis. Stephanie had been almost embarrassed by their outpouring. She was just thankful Mrs. Johnson was going to be all right. She wished she could say the same for Michael.

She had caught him watching her several times at the hospital and, oddly, the fear that she had first seen in his eyes was still there. She realized he hadn't gotten over the shock of thinking the ambulance was for her.

As soon as she closed the front door behind them,

she tapped him on the shoulder. When he turned, she walked into his arms. She had meant the kiss as simple reassurance. How could she have forgotten Michael's kisses were anything but simple?

Need slammed into her and she let herself go. She loved Michael and there was no reason to hold back.

"I thought you were hurt. I can't lose you." His voice was hoarse, ragged. The strong arms locked around her were just short of desperation.

"You'll never lose me," she said, her entire body shivering as he rained kisses over her face. "I love you."

He went still.

It took Stephanie a moment to surface from her passionate haze and realize he was no longer kissing her and when she did, she realized what she had said. Her hands clenched on the bunched muscles of his arms. He wasn't ready. "Y-you must be hungry. Would . . . would you like me to fix—"

"Steph—"

"It wouldn't be any trouble," she interrupted, not wanting to hear an excuse or explanation of why he didn't love her. She tried to push out of his arms, but found it was like trying to move her house.

"Please look at me."

She didn't want to see the pity in his eyes, but she had started this, knowing full well the risk she ran. He shouldn't remember her as a coward. She lifted her head, then gasped as she saw the deep pain in his eyes. Instantly, she moved closer. "Michael, what is it?"

His forehead dropped onto hers. "I came this morning to make a confession. It's even more important now. I just hope you won't hate me when I'm finished."

"No," she said, her hands slipping between them to gently palm his cheeks. "I could never—"

"Wait until I finish," he interrupted, then stepped away from her. "Please sit down."

Stephanie's heart thudded painfully. "If you plan to tell me good-bye, just do it."

"A man doesn't voluntarily walk away from his heart. Please." Surprise and hope flickered in her eyes. Taking her arm he led her to the chair at the kitchen table, but he didn't take a seat. He was too restless.

"There is no easy way to say this except that the women I dated before you were more interested in my money than in me. I had made up my mind that the next woman I took out would see me, the real me. Then I walked into Texas Chic and you smiled at me and took my breath away." Hunkering down, he took her hands into his. "You fascinated me from the first, but I let my old fears get the better of me and I didn't tell you the truth about my job."

"You aren't the project manager?"

"Yes, but—"

Laughing she threw her arms around his neck. "You scared me. Some women are greedy." Leaning back, she smiled down at him, her eyes full of teasing banter. "How much are you worth anyway?"

"Five million." His hands tightened on hers as shock replaced the laughter. "I'm not just the project manager, I own Evergreen Landscape."

Her gaze grew colder with each passing second. She didn't move, but he sensed her withdrawing from him. He talked fast. "Stephanie, I'm sorry I didn't tell you the truth sooner."

"So am I," she said, pulling her hands back and clutching them tightly in her lap. "I want you to leave."

"No. Not until you understand," he said, desperation in every line of his body. "I'd never met a woman like you before, one who wanted me and not my money. I couldn't believe that a woman could be that honest."

"And I believed too much."

He flinched. "I never meant to hurt you."

"That's what Keith told my sister. She finally told me the other day what happened. All the time I was listening to her, I kept thinking how fortunate I was that you were so honest," Stephanie said, barely above a whisper. "He said he was only trying to impress her when he said he owned the car dealership where she bought her car from him. Seems he had used that same line several times before."

"I'm not handing you a line."

"You didn't trust me and now I don't trust you." Standing, she stepped around him and started for the front door. "What was it? Did you think I'd ask for money to open my shop? I don't need yours or any other man's money."

Horror swept across his face. "I never thought that."

She continued walking as if he hadn't spoken. Michael would have argued if he thought it would have done any good. She wouldn't even look at him. "I'll never stop trying to make you believe me."

She bit her lips. Her eyelashes blinked rapidly.

He walked through the door and turned. "I lo—"

The door closed. He put his hand on the door. "I love you, Stephanie, and this is not over."

After a miserable night Stephanie wanted nothing more than to pull the covers over her head and try to forget her break-up with Michael. She got up instead. The execs were scheduled to visit Texas Chic that day, and she owed it to herself and Rose to be there.

An hour later she walked into the store. One look at her face and Rose rushed to her. "What happened?"

Stephanie's lips quivered. "Michael, and please don't ask questions."

The older woman squeezed her hands. "Do you want to stay?"

"Yes." Crying and staying in bed certainly hadn't helped.

Relief crossed Rose's face. "Go powder your nose. Stevenson and the execs should be here any moment."

"I'll be back in a minute." She started to leave when she heard the little bell announce that someone had entered the store. She turned automatically, then stiffened.

"Hello, Stephanie," Michael said, his voice as cautious as his movements. "I missed our time together this morning, but I didn't want you to miss your flowers. Hibiscus. They're called Silver Memories." He sat the bouquet on the round table under the chandelier. "Good luck today." Tipping his hat to Rose, he left.

Stephanie's fingernails dug into the soft black leather of her purse. He had lied to her and all she had wanted to do was fling herself in his arms.

"Waterford vase. He has good taste," Rose said softly from beside her.

Stephanie stared at the lush blooms of creamy flowers with yellow borders in silence. Was it a coincidence that the flowers were called Silver Memories and why should she care?

"Here come the execs with Stevenson," Rose said as she glanced through the plate glass window. "Stow the bag behind the counter. Show time."

Stephanie did as Rose asked and tried to thrust Michael from her mind as she went forward to greet the group of men and women. She was doing fairly well until the executive vice-president of sales and marketing commented on the bouquet of hibiscus. Her mother was a member of the hibiscus garden club in San Francisco, she said, and she'd love that specimen. Stevenson had looked expectantly from Rose to Stephanie. She had to swallow several times before the words would come out.

"The owner of Evergreen Landscape dropped them off this morning."

"Michael Dunbar," supplied Stevenson. "You're scheduled to meet him at one."

The woman spoke to her assistant. "Make a note, Allen, to ask him about the plant for Mother." She turned to Stephanie. "Although I think the hibiscus is spectacular, two bouquets on the table are a bit much. Perhaps by the cash register."

Stephanie started toward the flowers, but the assistant had already picked up the vase. "Thank you."

The young man smiled and sat the vase on the counter by the cash register. "My pleasure."

Stephanie had heard the words a hundred times in the hotel business, but they still threw her back to the first time Michael had said them to her. Even then he had lied to her.

"Come, Allen," said the female executive and extended her hand to Rose, then Stephanie. "I can certainly see why your store is number one. Keep up the good work."

"We will. Thank you," Rose said and walked them to the door. When she turned and saw Stephanie she had just two words to say. "Go home."

*   *   *

Each day Stephanie thought the pain of loss would lessen and each day she discovered she was wrong. It had been a week since she had broken up with Michael and her heart still felt as if it had been wrenched from her chest. She'd told Rose and her family, of course, and had been surprised when her brothers thought she should give Michael another chance. Rose, her parents, and her sister were staying out of it.

Turning onto her back in bed, Stephanie threw her arm over her eyes. How could she explain to him the pain his distrust caused her. He'd lumped her with all the other women in his life. He hadn't seen *her*. He had seen a woman who might take advantage of him. Throwing back the covers, she got out of bed and pulled a robe over her silk pajamas.

She was halfway across the floor when the doorbell rang. Her heart thudded. It could be Mr. Johnson needing something since his wife had come home from the hospital last week, but even as she started toward the door she thought that unlikely since two of their daughters had come home with them.

"Good morning. Here are your flowers."

She had known it would be Michael. He'd brought flowers every day to the store. Today they were roses. She looked at him, loving him, knowing there was nothing she could do to stop loving him until the day she died. Tears rolled down her cheeks.

Panic swept across his face. "Don't cry, honey." He pulled on the glass storm door and discovered it was locked. Any other time he would have been pleased by her caution. "Open the door, please."

"You thought I was like all the other women you had met."

"I was a fool," he said hotly. "I was so busy trying

to play it safe I jeopardized everything we had together. Let me make it up to you."

She shook her head. "It's better to end it now. I'll ship the coffeemaker to you." She started to close the door.

"No! Wait!" he yelled. "I love you, Stephanie."

The half-closed door crept back open. "W-what did you say?"

"I'll make it up to you," he quickly told her, sticking the bouquet of flowers under one arm while he fished in his pockets, looking panicky before pulling out a ring box in the shape of a Fabergé egg. "See, I bought this for you."

"Michael," she said, her voice trembling, her eyes never leaving his. "You have one more chance to get this right."

His mouth dried, his chest felt tight. One chance. He started to swipe his hand across his face and felt the ring box. Inside was a three-carat heart-shaped diamond. He lifted his head, ready to thumb open the case and hand it to her, but something held him back, then he remembered what it was. Stephanie valued the person, not what they could buy.

"I gave you Silver Memories to remind you of the wonderful times we had together and the hope that years from now we'll still be together making more memories. I love you, Stephanie, with all my heart. If you'll forgive me, I promise never to lie to you again."

The lock clicked on the door. She stepped back.

He was inside the door in seconds. The flowers and ring box fell to the floor as he swept her into his arms and kissed her. His tilting world finally came upright as she kissed him back. He felt the lush fullness of her body against his and fought for control. Slowly, he eased back from the kiss, then looked around until he found the ring box. His hands were shaking as much as hers when he slid the ring on her finger. "You are the very heart of me. I love you."

Her eyes were misty as she glanced from the ring to him. "I love you so much. I thought you cared and that Silver Memories had some significance, but you have no reason to ask me to marry you if you don't really love me."

"I have every reason. You're all that I've ever wanted in a woman. I've finally found the right woman." He pulled her against him, enjoying the feel of her soft, warm body even as it made his hot and hard for her. "I tried to tell you last Sunday, but you closed the door in my face."

"I was so miserable," she said, her arms going around his neck. "My brothers were right about giving you another chance. Now they won't have to beat you up as they'd threatened," she said with a smile.

"I probably deserve it."

"No. You deserve this." Her lips pressed against his, her tongue darting into his mouth. Both moaned. His hands seemed to be everywhere as they swept endlessly over her flesh. Every touch left her wanting more. His mouth closed around one nipple, then the other, until her body was weak and trembling and aching with need.

"Stephanie, help me stop," he groaned. "Please."

She heard him as if from a great distance, then she nipped him on his lips. "I don't want to. I trust you."

Her words went straight through him, giving him the strength to hold her. "Honey, you waited this long for a reason."

"I was waiting for you."

"You aren't making this easy."

Still shivering with need, she curled her body against him. "Planning a wedding could take months."

He groaned. "I won't last that long."

"Neither will I." They looked at each other. Their lips touched, clung. The kiss felt right as heat built.

"I love you, Stephanie."

"Then show me."

Picking her up, he carried her into the bedroom and laid her on the unmade bed, following her down into the waiting softness. "Are you sure?"

Tenderly her hands cupped his face. She'd never known the weight of a man's body on hers could feel so erotic, so good. "More than anything I want to belong to you." She kissed him, giving him everything.

Clothes were quickly shed. He was magnificent in every detail. She thought she'd be shy when Michael stared down at her naked body, but the reverent look on his face made desire twist through her. His thumb grazed her taut nipple. She whimpered.

"You're beautiful."

Stephanie was too full of emotion to speak. As Michael fastened his warm, moist mouth over her nipple, all she could do was feel. Those feelings heightened as his hand found the very heat and core of her. She whimpered in satisfaction.

"I knew you'd be everything I ever desired in a woman," Michael breathed. Then, staring into her eyes, he made them one.

Stephanie vaguely realized it hadn't hurt. There was exquisite pleasure as Michael stroked her and took everything but the intensity of her emotions from her mind. She wrapped her legs around him, drawing him deeper into her satin heat.

Michael tried to go slow, but the lure of her body was too strong. Love overwhelmed him for this woman and thankfully he had a lifetime to show her. This was just the beginning. With the Wright woman, love was everything.

Epilogue

A month later on the Caribbean island of Vieques, Puerto Rico, Stephanie and Michael were married at the newest Wyndham's resort. Both mothers cried buckets, both sets of brothers were glad it wasn't them, and the bride's sister found the executive manager of the resort as fascinating as he found her.

"Happy?" Michael asked Stephanie when they were alone in the bridal suite.

"Very." She sighed as she laid her head on his chest and looked at the full moon suspended over the sea. "It's breathtaking here and the wedding was everything I dreamed of. Stevenson certainly came through for us in helping us coordinate our wedding."

He turned her to him. "Seems the execs were pleased with both of us and want to keep us happy." His lips grazed the line of her jaw as he undid the sash on her cream-colored silk robe and let it fall to the floor. "They want you to stay."

She kissed his bare chest. "The only wants I'm concerned about are yours."

He drew her gown over her head and stared down at her with undying love. "Show me," he whispered.

"My pleasure."

And it was.

About the Authors

Donna Hill began her writing career back in 1987 with the short story "The Long Walk." Since that time she has nineteen published novels to her credit and is included in eleven short story collections. She has been featured in *Essence, USA Today, Today's Black Woman, Black Enterprise*, and the *NY Daily News*, among many others. Her work has appeared on several bestseller lists and she is the recipient of numerous awards for her body of work. Three of her novels have been adapted for television. She is currently the host of her own internet radio show, *Literally Yours*, heard weekly on http://bookcrazy.net. She still holds a full-time job as a Public Relations Associate for the Queens Library system in New York. She lives in Brooklyn, NY, with her family. To find out more you can visit Donna on her Web site at www.donnahill.com.

Brenda Jackson lives in the city where she was born, Jacksonville, Florida. She has a Bachelor of Science degree in Business Administration from Jacksonville University. She has been married for thirty-two years to her high school sweetheart, and they have two sons, ages twenty-six and twenty-four. She is also a member of the First Coast Chapter of Romance Writers of America, and is a founding member of the national chapter of Women Writers of Color. Brenda is the recipient of numerous awards, including the prestigious Vivian Stephens Career Achievement Award for Excellence in Romance Writing; the Emma Award for Author of the Year in Romance; the Shades of Romance Multi-cultural Award of the Year, and the Romance in Color Award of Excellence.

Tempting Fate is her twenty-third story.

You can visit her Web site at www.brendajackson.net.

In addition to being in love with words, **Monica Jackson** had worked in the field of nursing for over twenty years. She is now a registered nurse with experience in coronary intensive care, community health, psychiatric and nursing administration, and management.

Descended from the "Exodusters" who migrated to Kansas from the South, her roots are deep in the Kansas soil. But her adventurous spirit has led her to live in several different places—St. Louis, Houston, greater San Francisco, and Atlanta. She has also spent extended amounts of time in South America and the Far East.

Monica is now back in Kansas, where she's a single parent happily nurturing her child and her muse and writing tales she hopes you will love.

Visit her Web site at www.monicajackson.com.

Francis Ray is a native Texan and lives with her husband and daughter in Dallas. A graduate of Texas Woman's University, she is a school nurse practitioner with the Dallas Independent School District. She was nominated in 1999 and 2000 for the Distinguished Alumni Award. Ms. Ray's titles consistently make bestseller lists in *Blackboard* and *Essence* magazines. *Incognito*, her sixth title, was the first made-for-TV movie for BET. She has written twelve single titles and for six anthologies. Awards include *Romantic Times* Career Achievement, EMMA, and the Golden Pen. At the release event for her novel *The Turning Point*, she established The Turning Point Legal Defense Fund to assist women of domestic violence in restructuring their lives. With the release of her second mainstream novel, national bestseller *I Know Who Holds Tomorrow*, Ms. Ray has pledged to continue that effort. Visit her Web site at www.francisray.com.